THE
MELROSE
EDITION

EDITH PLANTAGENET

S. A. HART

The Talisman

And

The Two Drovers
My Aunt Margaret's Mirror
The Tapestried Chamber
The Laird's Jock

By

Sir Walter Scott, Bart.

London

The Caxton Publishing Company

84, 85 & 86 Chancery Lane, W.C.

THE TALISMAN

CHAPTER I

—— They, too, retired
To the wilderness, but 'twas with arms.
—Paradise Regained.

THE burning sun of Syria had not yet attained its highest
point in the horizon, when a knight of the Red-cross, who had
left his distant northern home, and joined the host of the
Crusaders in Palestine, was pacing slowly along the sandy
deserts which lie in the vicinity of the Dead Sea, or, as it is
called, the Lake Asphaltites, where the waves of the Jordan
pour themselves into an inland sea, from which there is no discharge of waters.

The warlike pilgrim had toiled among cliffs and precipices
during the earlier part of the morning; more lately, issuing
from those rocky and dangerous defiles, he had entered upon
that great plain, where the accursed cities provoked, in ancient
days, the direct and dreadful vengeance of the Omnipotent.

The toil, the thirst, the dangers of the way, were forgotten,
as the traveller recalled the fearful catastrophe, which had converted into an arid and dismal wilderness the fair and fertile
valley of Siddim, once well watered, even as the Garden of the
Lord, now a parched and blighted waste, condemned to eternal
sterility.

Crossing himself, as he viewed the dark mass of rolling
waters, in colour as in quality unlike those of every other lake,
the traveller shuddered as he remembered, that beneath these
sluggish waves lay the once proud cities of the plain, whose
grave was dug by the thunder of the heavens, or the eruption
of subterraneous fire, and whose remains were hid, even by
that sea which holds no living fish in its bosom, bears no skiff
on its surface, and, as if its own dreadful bed were the only fit
receptacle for its sullen waters, sends not, like other lakes, a
tribute to the ocean. The whole land around, as in the days
of Moses, was "brimstone and salt; it is not sown, nor beareth,

A

nor any grass groweth thereon;" the land as well as the lake might be termed dead, as producing nothing having resemblance to vegetation, and even the very air was entirely devoid of its ordinary winged inhabitants, deterred probably by the odour of bitumen and sulphur, which the burning sun exhaled from the waters of the lake, in steaming clouds, frequently assuming the appearance of waterspouts. Masses of the slimy and sulphurous substance called naphtha, which floated idly on the sluggish and sullen waves, supplied those rolling clouds with new vapours, and afforded awful testimony to the truth of the Mosaic history.

Upon this scene of desolation the sun shone with almost intolerable splendour, and all living nature seemed to have hidden itself from the rays, excepting the solitary figure which moved through the flitting sand at a foot's pace, and appeared the sole breathing thing on the wide surface of the plain. The dress of the rider, and the accoutrements of his horse, were peculiarly unfit for the traveller in such a country. A coat of linked mail, with long sleeves, plated gauntlets, and a steel breastplate, had not been esteemed a sufficient weight of armour; there was also his triangular shield suspended round his neck, and his barred helmet of steel, over which he had a hood and collar of mail, which was drawn around the warrior's shoulders and throat, and filled up the vacancy between the hauberk and the head-piece. His lower limbs were sheathed, like his body, in flexible mail, securing the legs and thighs, while the feet rested in plated shoes, which corresponded with the gauntlets. A long, broad, straight-shaped, double-edged falchion, with a handle formed like a cross, corresponded with a stout poniard on the other side. The Knight also bore, secured to his saddle, with one end resting on his stirrup, the long steel-headed lance, his own proper weapon, which, as he rode, projected backwards and displayed its little pennoncelle, to dally with the faint breeze, or drop in the dead calm. To this cumbrous equipment must be added a surcoat of embroidered cloth, much frayed and worn, which was thus far useful, that it excluded the burning rays of the sun from the armour, which they would otherwise have rendered intolerable to the wearer. The surcoat bore, in several places, the arms of the owner, although much defaced. These seemed to be a couchant leopard, with the motto, "I sleep—wake me not." An outline of the same device might be traced on his shield, though many a blow had almost effaced the painting. The flat top of his cumbrous cylindrical helmet was unadorned with any crest. In retaining their own unwieldy defensive armour, the northern Crusaders seemed to set at defiance the nature of the climate and country to which they had come to war.

The accoutrements of the horse were scarcely less massive and unwieldy than those of the rider. The animal had a heavy saddle plated with steel, uniting in front with a species of breast-plate, and behind with defensive armour made to cover the loins. Then there was a steel axe, or hammer, called a mace-of-arms, and which hung to the saddle-bow; the reins were secured by chain-work, and the front-stall of the bridle was a steel plate, with apertures for the eyes and nostrils, having in the midst a short sharp pike, projecting from the forehead of the horse like the horn of the fabulous unicorn.

But habit had made the endurance of this load of panoply a second nature, both to the knight and his gallant charger. Numbers, indeed, of the western warriors who hurried to Palestine, died ere they became inured to the burning climate; but there were others to whom that climate became innocent and even friendly, and among this fortunate number was the solitary horseman who now traversed the border of the Dead Sea.

Nature, which cast his limbs in a mould of uncommon strength, fitted to wear his linked hauberk with as much ease as if the meshes had been formed of cobwebs, had endowed him with a constitution as strong as his limbs, and which bade defiance to almost all changes of climate, as well as to fatigue and privations of every kind. His disposition seemed, in some degree, to partake of the qualities of his bodily frame; and as the one possessed great strength and endurance, united with the power of violent exertion, the other, under a calm and undisturbed semblance, had much of the fiery and enthusiastic love of glory which constituted the principal attribute of the renowned Norman line, and had rendered them sovereigns in every corner of Europe, where they had drawn their adventurous swords.

It was not, however, to all the race that fortune proposed such tempting rewards; and those obtained by the solitary knight during two years' campaign in Palestine, had been only temporal fame, and, as he was taught to believe, spiritual privileges. Meantime, his slender stock of money had melted away, the rather that he did not pursue any of the ordinary modes by which the followers of the Crusade condescended to recruit their diminished resources, at the expense of the people of Palestine; he exacted no gifts from the wretched natives for sparing their possessions when engaged in warfare with the Saracens, and he had not availed himself of any opportunity of enriching himself by the ransom of prisoners of consequence. The small train which had followed him from his native country had been gradually diminished, as the means of maintaining them disappeared, and his only remaining squire was at present on a sick-bed, and unable to attend his master, who travelled,

as we have seen, singly and alone. This was of little consequence to the Crusader, who was accustomed to consider his
good sword as his safest escort, and devout thoughts as his best
companion.

Nature had, however, her demands for refreshment and
repose, even on the iron frame and patient disposition of the
Knight of the Sleeping Leopard; and at noon, when the Dead
Sea lay at some distance on his right, he joyfully hailed the
sight of two or three palm trees, which arose beside the well
which was assigned for his mid-day station. His good horse,
too, which had plodded forward with the steady endurance of
his master, now lifted his head, expanded his nostrils, and
quickened his pace, as if he snuffed afar off the living waters,
which marked the place of repose and refreshment. But labour
and danger were doomed to intervene ere the horse or horseman reached the desired spot.

As the Knight of the Couchant Leopard continued to fix his
eyes attentively on the yet distant cluster of palm trees, it
seemed to him as if some object was moving among them.
The distant form separated itself from the trees, which partly
hid its motions, and advanced towards the knight with a speed
which soon showed a mounted horseman, whom his turban,
long spear, and green caftan floating in the wind, on his nearer
approach, showed to be a Saracen cavalier. "In the desert,"
saith an Eastern proverb, "no man meets a friend." The
Crusader was totally indifferent whether the infidel, who now
approached on his gallant barb, as if borne on the wings of an
eagle, came as friend or foe—perhaps, as a vowed champion of
the Cross, he might rather have preferred the latter. He disengaged his lance from his saddle, seized it with the right
hand, placed it in rest with its point half elevated, gathered up
the reins in the left, waked his horse's mettle with the spur,
and prepared to encounter the stranger with the calm self-con-
fidence belonging to the victor in many contests.

The Saracen came on at the speedy gallop of an Arab horseman, managing his steed more by his limbs, and the inflection
of his body, than by any use of the reins, which hung loose in
his left hand; so that he was enabled to wield the light round
buckler of the skin of the rhinoceros, ornamented with silver
loops, which he wore on his arm, swinging it as if he meant to
oppose its slender circle to the formidable thrust of the western
lance. His own long spear was not couched or levelled like
that of his antagonist, but grasped by the middle with his
right hand, and brandished at arm's length above his head.
As the cavalier approached his enemy at full career, he seemed
to expect that the Knight of the Leopard should put his horse
to the gallop to encounter him. But the Christian knight,

well acquainted with the customs of Eastern warriors, did not mean to exhaust his good horse by any unnecessary exertion; and, on the contrary, made a dead halt, confidant that if the enemy advanced to the actual shock, his own weight, and that of his powerful charger, would give him sufficient advantage, without the additional momentum of rapid motion. Equally sensible and apprehensive of such a probable result, the Saracen cavalier, when he had approached towards the Christian within twice the length of his lance, wheeled his steed to the left with inimitable dexterity, and rode twice round his antagonist, who, turning without quitting his ground, and presenting his front constantly to his enemy, frustrated his attempts to attack him on an unguarded point; so that the Saracen, wheeling his horse, was fain to retreat to the distance of an hundred yards. A second time, like a hawk attacking a heron, the Heathen renewed the charge, and a second time was fain to retreat without coming to a close struggle. A third time he approached in the same manner, when the Christian knight, desirous to terminate this elusory warfare, in which he might at length have been worn out by the activity of his foeman, suddenly seized the mace which hung at his saddle-bow, and, with a strong hand and unerring aim, hurled it against the head of the Emir, for such and not less his enemy appeared. The Saracen was just aware of the formidable missile in time to interpose his light buckler betwixt the mace and his head; but the violence of the blow forced the buckler down on his turban, and though that defence also contributed to deaden its violence, the Saracen was beaten from his horse. Ere the Christian could avail himself of this mishap, his nimble foe-man sprung from the ground, and calling on his horse, which instantly returned to his side, he leaped into his seat without touching the stirrup, and regained all the advantage of which the Knight of the Leopard hoped to deprive him. But the latter had in the meanwhile recovered his mace, and the Eastern cavalier, who remembered the strength and dexterity with which his antagonist had aimed it, seemed to keep cautiously out of reach of that weapon, of which he had so lately felt the force, while he showed his purpose of waging a distant warfare with missile weapons of his own. Planting his long spear in the sand at a distance from the scene of combat, he strung, with great address, a short bow, which he carried at his back, and putting his horse to the gallop, once more described two or three circles of a wider extent than formerly, in the course of which he discharged six arrows at the Christian with such unerring skill, that the goodness of his harness alone saved him from being wounded in as many places. The seventh shaft apparently found a less perfect part of the armour, and the

Christian dropped heavily from his horse. But what was the surprise of the Saracen, when, dismounting to examine the condition of his prostrate enemy, he found himself suddenly within the grasp of the European, who had had recourse to this artifice to bring his enemy within his reach! Even in this deadly grapple, the Saracen was saved by his agility and presence of mind. He unloosed the sword-belt, in which the Knight of the Leopard had fixed his hold, and, thus eluding his fatal grasp, mounted his horse, which seemed to watch his motions with the intelligence of a human being, and again rode off. But in the last encounter the Saracen had lost his sword and his quiver of arrows, both of which were attached to the girdle, which he was obliged to abandon. He had also lost his turban in the struggle. These disadvantages seemed to incline the Moslem to a truce: He approached the Christian with his right hand extended, but no longer in a menacing attitude.

"There is truce betwixt our nations," he said, in the Lingua Franca commonly used for the purpose of communication with the Crusaders; "wherefore should there be war betwixt thee and me?—Let there be peace betwixt us."

"I am well contented," answered he of the Couchant Leopard; "but what security dost thou offer that thou wilt observe the truce?"

"The word of a follower of the Prophet was never broken," answered the Emir. "It is thou, brave Nazarene, from whom I should demand security, did I not know that treason seldom dwells with courage."

The Crusader felt that the confidence of the Moslem made him ashamed of his own doubts.

"By the cross of my sword," he said, laying his hand on the weapon as he spoke, "I will be true companion to thee, Saracen, while our fortune wills that we remain in company together."

"By Mahommed, Prophet of God, and by Allah, God of the Prophet," replied his late foeman, "there is not treachery in my heart towards thee. And now wend we to yonder fountain, for the hour of rest is at hand, and the stream had hardly touched my lip when I was called to battle by thy approach."

The Knight of the Couchant Leopard yielded a ready and courteous assent; and the late foes, without an angry look, or gesture of doubt, rode side by side to the little cluster of palm trees.

CHAPTER II

TIMES of danger have always, and in a peculiar degree, their seasons of goodwill and of security ; and this was particularly so in the ancient feudal ages, in which, as the manners of the period had assigned war to be the chief and most worthy occupation of mankind, the intervals of peace, or rather of truce, were highly relished by those warriors to whom they were seldom granted, and endeared by the very circumstances which rendered them transitory. It is not worth while preserving any permanent enmity against a foe, whom a champion has fought with to-day, and may again stand in bloody opposition to on the next morning. The time and situation afforded so much room for the ebullition of violent passions, that men, unless when peculiarly opposed to each other, or provoked by the recollection of private and individual wrongs, cheerfully enjoyed in each other's society the brief intervals of pacific intercourse, which a warlike life admitted.

The distinction of religions, nay, the fanatical zeal which animated the followers of the Cross and of the Crescent against each other, was much softened by a feeling so natural to generous combatants, and especially cherished by the spirit of chivalry. This last strong impulse had extended itself gradually from the Christians to their mortal enemies, the Saracens, both of Spain and of Palestine. The latter were indeed no longer the fanatical savages, who had burst from the centre of Arabian deserts, with the sabre in one hand, and the Koran in the other, to inflict death or the faith of Mahommed, or at the best, slavery and tribute, upon all who dared to oppose the belief of the prophet of Mecca. These alternatives indeed had been offered to the warlike Greeks and Syrians ; but in contending with the western Christians, animated by a zeal as fiery as their own, and possessed of as unconquerable courage, address, and success in arms, the Saracens gradually caught a part of their manners, and especially of those chivalrous observances, which were so well calculated to charm the minds of a proud and conquering people. They had their tournaments and games of chivalry ; they had even their knights, or some rank analogous ; and above all, the Saracens observed their plighted faith with an accuracy which might sometimes put to shame those who owned a better religion. Their truces, whether national or betwixt individuals, were faithfully observed ; and thus it was that war, in itself perhaps the greatest of evils, yet gave occasion for display of good faith, generosity, clemency, and even kindly affections, which less frequently occur in more tranquil periods, where the passions of men, experiencing wrongs, or entertaining quarrels which cannot be brought to instant decision, are apt to smoulder for a length of time in the bosoms of those who are so unhappy as to be their prey.

It was under the influence of these milder feelings, which soften the horrors of warfare, that the Christian and Saracen, who had so lately done their best for each other's mutual destruction, rode at a slow pace towards the fountain of palm trees, to which the Knight of the Couchant Leopard had been tending, when interrupted in mid-passage by his fleet and dangerous adversary. Each was wrapt for some time in his own reflections, and took breath after an encounter which had threatened to be fatal to one or both ; and their good horses seemed no less to enjoy the interval of repose. That of the Saracen, however, though he had been forced into much the more violent and extended sphere of motion, appeared to have suffered less from fatigue than the charger of the European knight. The sweat hung still clammy on the limbs of the last when those of the noble Arab were completely dried by the interval of tranquil exercise, all saving the foam-flakes which were still visible on his bridle and housings. The loose soil on which he trode so much augmented the distress of the Christian's horse, heavily loaded by his own armour and the weight of his rider, that the latter jumped from his saddle, and led his charger along the deep dust of the loamy soil, which was burnt in the sun into a substance more impalpable than the finest sand, and thus gave the faithful horse refreshment at the expense of his own additional toil ; for, iron-sheathed as he was, he sunk over the mailed shoes at every step which he placed on a surface so light and unresisting.

"You are right," said the Saracen ; and it was the first word that either had spoken since their truce was concluded,—"your strong horse deserves your care ; but what do you in the desert with an animal, which sinks over the fetlock at every step, as if he would plant each foot deep as the root of a date tree ? "

"Thou speakest rightly, Saracen," said the Christian knight, not delighted at the tone with which the infidel criticised his favourite horse,—"rightly, according to thy knowledge and observation. But my good horse hath ere now borne me, in mine own land, over as wide a lake as thou seest yonder spread out behind us, yet not wet one hair above his hoof."

The Saracen looked at him with as much surprise as his manners permitted him to testify, which was only expressed by a slight approach to a disdainful smile, that hardly curled perceptibly the broad thick mustache which enveloped his upper lip.

" It is justly spoken," he said, instantly composing himself to his usual serene gravity,—" list to a Frank, and hear a fable."

" Thou art not courteous, misbeliever," replied the Crusader, " to doubt the word of a dubbed knight ; and were it not that thou speakest in ignorance, and not in malice, our truce had its ending ere it is well begun. Thinkest thou I tell thee an untruth when I say, that I, one of five hundred horsemen, armed in complete mail, have ridden—ay, and ridden for miles, upon water as solid as the crystal, and ten times less brittle ! "

" What wouldst thou tell me ? " answered the Moslem ; " yonder inland sea thou dost point at is peculiar in this, that, by the special curse of God, it suffereth nothing to sink in its waves, but wafts them away, and casts them on its margin ; but neither the Dead Sea, nor any of the seven oceans which environ the earth, will endure on their surface the pressure of a horse's foot, more than the Red Sea endured to sustain the advance of Pharaoh and his host."

" You speak truth after your knowledge, Saracen," said the Christian knight ; " and yet, trust me, I fable not, according to mine. Heat, in this climate, converts the soil into something almost as unstable as water ; and in my land cold often converts the water itself into a substance as hard as rock. Let us speak of this no longer ; for the thoughts of the calm, clear, blue refulgence of a winter's lake, glimmering to stars and moonbeam, aggravate the horrors of this fiery desert, where, methinks, the very air which we breathe is like the vapour of a fiery furnace seven times heated."

The Saracen looked on him with some attention, as if to discover in what sense he was to understand words, which, to him, must have appeared either to contain something of mystery, or of imposition. At length he seemed determined in what manner to receive the language of his new companion.

" You are," he said, " of a nation that loves to laugh, and you make sport with yourselves, and with others, by telling what is impossible, and reporting what never chanced. Thou art one of the knights of France, who hold it for glee and pastime to *gab*,* as they term it, of exploits that are beyond human power. I were wrong to challenge, for the time, the privilege of thy speech, since boasting is more natural to thee than truth."

" I am not of their land, neither of their fashion," said the Knight, " which is, as thou well sayest, to *gab* of that which they dare not undertake, or undertaking cannot perfect. But

---

* *Gaber.* This French word signified a sort of sport much used among the French chivalry, which consisted in vying with each other in making the most romantic gasconades. The verb and the meaning are retained in Scottish.

in this I have imitated their folly, brave Saracen, that in talking to thee of what thou canst not comprehend, I have, even
in speaking most simple truth, fully incurred the character of
a braggart in thine eyes; so, I pray you, let my words pass."

They had now arrived at the knot of palm trees, and the
fountain which welled out from beneath their shade in sparkling profusion.

We have spoken of a moment of truce in the midst of war;
and this, a spot of beauty in the midst of a sterile desert, was
scarce less dear to the imagination. It was a scene which,
perhaps, would elsewhere have deserved little notice; but as
the single speck in a boundless horizon, which promised the
refreshment of shade and living water, these blessings, held
cheap where they are common, rendered the fountain and its
neighbourhood a little paradise. Some generous or charitable
hand, ere yet the evil days of Palestine began, had walled in
and arched over the fountain, to preserve it from being absorbed
in the earth, or choked by the flitting clouds of dust with which
the least breath of wind covered the desert. The arch was now
broken, and partly ruinous; but it still so far projected over,
and covered in the fountain, that it excluded the sun in a great
measure from its waters, which, hardly touched by a straggling
beam while all around was blazing, lay in a steady repose,
alike delightful to the eye and the imagination. Stealing from
under the arch, they were first received in a marble basin,
much defaced indeed, but still cheering the eye, by showing
that the place was anciently considered as a station, that the
hand of man had been there, and that man's accommodation
had been in some measure attended to. The thirsty and weary
traveller was reminded by these signs, that others had suffered
similar difficulties, reposed in the same spot, and, doubtless,
found their way in safety to a more fertile country. Again, the
scarce visible current which escaped from the basin, served to
nourish the few trees which surrounded the fountain, and where
it sunk into the ground and disappeared, its refreshing presence
was acknowledged by a carpet of velvet verdure.

In this delightful spot the two warriors halted, and each,
after his own fashion, proceeded to relieve his horse from saddle,
bit, and rein, and permitted the animals to drink at the basin
ere they refreshed themselves from the fountain head, which
arose under the vault. They then suffered the steeds to go
loose, confident that their interest, as well as their domesticated
habits, would prevent their straying from the pure water and
fresh grass.

Christian and Saracen next sat down together on the turf,
and produced each the small allowance of store which they
carried for their own refreshment. Yet, ere they severally pro-

ceeded to their scanty meal, they eyed each other with that
curiosity which the close and doubtful conflict in which they
had been so lately engaged was calculated to inspire. Each was
desirous to measure the strength, and form some estimate of the
character, of an adversary so formidable; and each was compelled to acknowledge, that had he fallen in the conflict, it had
been by a noble hand.

The champions formed a striking contrast to each other in
person and features, and might have formed no inaccurate representatives of their different nations. The Frank seemed a
powerful man, built after the ancient Gothic cast of form, with
light brown hair, which, on the removal of his helmet, was seen
to curl thick and profusely over his head. His features had
acquired, from the hot climate, a hue much darker than those
parts of his neck which were less frequently exposed to view, or
than was warranted by his full and well-opened blue eye, the
colour of his hair, and of the mustaches which thickly shaded
his upper lip, while his chin was carefully divested of beard,
after the Norman fashion. His nose was Grecian and well-
formed; his mouth a little large in proportion, but filled with
well-set, strong, and beautifully white teeth; his head small,
and set upon the neck with much grace. His age could not
exceed thirty, but if the effects of toil and climate were allowed
for, might be three or four years under that period. His form
was tall, powerful, and athletic, like that of a man whose
strength might, in later life, become unwieldy, but which was
hitherto united with lightness and activity. His hands, when
he withdrew the mailed gloves, were long, fair, and well-proportioned; the wrist-bones peculiarly large and strong; and
the arms themselves remarkably well shaped and brawny. A
military hardihood, and careless frankness of expression, characterised his language and his motions; and his voice had the
tone of one more accustomed to command than to obey, and
who was in the habit of expressing his sentiments aloud and
boldly, whenever he was called upon to announce them.

The Saracen Emir formed a marked and striking contrast
with the western Crusader. His stature was indeed above the
middle size, but he was at least three inches shorter than the
European, whose size approached the gigantic. His slender
limbs, and long spare hands and arms, though well proportioned
to his person, and suited to the style of his countenance, did
not at first aspect promise the display of vigour and elasticity
which the Emir had lately exhibited. But on looking more
closely, his limbs, where exposed to view, seemed divested of all
that was fleshy or cumbersome; so that nothing being left but
bone, brawn, and sinew, it was a frame fitted for exertion and
fatigue, far beyond that of a bulky champion, whose strength

and size are counterbalanced by weight, and who is exhausted by his own exertions. The countenance of the Saracen natur- ally bore a general national resemblance to the Eastern tribe from whom he descended, and was as unlike as possible to the exaggerated terms in which the minstrels of the day were wont to represent the infidel champions, and the fabulous description which a sister art still presents as the Saracen's head upon sign- posts. His features were small, well formed, and delicate, though deeply embrowned by the Eastern sun, and terminated by a flowing and curled black beard, which seemed trimmed with peculiar care. The nose was straight and regular, the eyes keen, deep-set, black, and glowing, and his teeth equalled in beauty the ivory of his deserts. The person and proportions of the Saracen, in short, stretched on the turf near to his powerful antagonist, might have been compared to his sheeny and crescent-formed sabre, with its narrow and light, but bright and keen Damascus blade, contrasted with the long and ponderous Gothic war-sword which was flung unbuckled on the same sod. The Emir was in the very flower of his age, and might perhaps have been termed eminently beautiful, but for the narrowness of his forehead, and something of too much thinness and sharpness of feature, or at least what might have seemed such in a European estimate of beauty.

The manners of the Eastern warrior were grave, graceful, and decorous ; indicating, however, in some particulars, the habitual restraint which men of warm and choleric tempers often set as a guard upon their native impetuosity of disposition, and at the same time a sense of his own dignity, which seemed to impose a certain formality of behaviour in him who entertained it.

This haughty feeling of superiority was perhaps equally entertained by his new European acquaintance, but the effect was different ; and the same feeling, which dictated to the Christian knight a bold, blunt, and somewhat careless bearing, as one too conscious of his own importance to be anxious about the opinions of others, appeared to prescribe to the Saracen a style of courtesy more studiously and formally observant of ceremony. Both were courteous ; but the courtesy of the Christian seemed to flow rather from a good-humoured sense of what was due to others ; that of the Moslem, from a high feeling of what was to be expected from himself.

The provision which each had made for his refreshment was simple, but the meal of the Saracen was abstemious. A handful of dates, and a morsel of coarse barley-bread, sufficed to relieve the hunger of the latter, whose education had habituated him to the fare of the desert, although, since their Syrian conquests, the Arabian simplicity of life frequently gave place to the most unbounded profusion of luxury. A few draughts from the lovely fountain by which they reposed completed his meal. That of the Christian, though coarse, was more genial. Dried hog's-flesh, the abomination of the Moslemah, was the chief part of his repast; and his drink, derived from a leathern bottle, contained something better than pure element. He fed with more display of appetite, and drank with more appearance of satisfaction, than the Saracen judged it becoming to show in the performance of a mere bodily function; and, doubtless, the secret contempt which each entertained for the other, as the follower of a false religion, was considerably increased by the marked difference of their diet and manners. But each had found the weight of his opponent's arm, and the mutual respect which the bold struggle had created was sufficient to subdue other and inferior considerations. Yet the Saracen could not help remarking the circumstances which displeased him in the Christian's conduct and manners; and, after he had witnessed for some time in silence the keen appetite which protracted the knight's banquet long after his own was concluded, he thus addressed him—

"Valiant Nazarene, is it fitting that one who can fight like a man, should feed like a dog or a wolf? Even a misbelieving Jew would shudder at the food which you seem to eat with as much relish as if it were fruit from the trees of Paradise."

"Valiant Saracen," answered the Christian, looking up with some surprise at the accusation thus unexpectedly brought, "know thou that I exercise my Christian freedom, in using that which is forbidden to the Jews, being, as they esteem themselves, under the bondage of the old law of Moses. We, Saracen, be it known to thee, have a better warrant for what we do—Ave Maria!—be we thankful." And, as if in defiance of his companion's scruples, he concluded a short Latin grace with a long draught from the leathern bottle.

"That, too, you call a part of your liberty," said the Saracen; "and as you feed like the brutes, so you degrade yourself to the bestial condition, by drinking a poisonous liquor which even they refuse!"

"Know, foolish Saracen," replied the Christian, without hesitation, "that thou blasphemest the gifts of God, even with the blasphemy of thy father Ishmael. The juice of the grape is given to him that will use it wisely, as that which cheers the heart of man after toil, refreshes him in sickness, and comforts him in sorrow. He who so enjoyeth it may thank God for his wine-cup as for his daily bread; and he who abuseth the gift of Heaven, is not a greater fool in his intoxication than thou in thine abstinence."

The keen eye of the Saracen kindled at this sarcasm, and his hand sought the hilt of his poniard. It was but a momentary thought, however, and died away in the recollection of the powerful champion with whom he had to deal, and the desperate grapple, the impression of which still throbbed in his limbs and veins; and he contented himself with pursuing the contest in colloquy, as more convenient for the time.

"Thy words," he said, "O Nazarene, might create anger, did not thy ignorance raise compassion. See'st thou not, O thou more blind than any who asks alms at the door of the Mosque, that the liberty thou dost boast of is restrained even in that which is dearest to man's happiness, and to his household; and that thy law, if thou dost practise it, binds thee in marriage to one single mate, be she sick or healthy, be she fruitful or barren, bring she comfort and joy, or clamour and strife, to thy table and to thy bed? This, Nazarene, I do indeed call slavery; whereas, to the faithful, hath the Prophet assigned upon earth the patriarchal privileges of Abraham our father, and of Solomon, the wisest of mankind, having given us here a succession of beauty at our pleasure, and beyond the grave the black-eyed houris of Paradise."

"Now, by His name that I most reverence in heaven," said the Christian, "and by hers whom I most worship on earth, thou art but a blinded and a bewildered infidel!—That diamond signet, which thou wearest on thy finger, thou holdest it, doubtless, as of inestimable value?"

"Balsora and Bagdad cannot show the like," replied the Saracen; "but what avails it to our purpose?"

"Much," replied the Frank, "as thou shalt thyself confess. Take my war-axe, and dash the stone into twenty shivers;—would each fragment be as valuable as the original gem, or would they, all collected, bear the tenth part of its estimation?"

"That is a child's question," answered the Saracen; "the fragments of such a stone would not equal the entire jewel in the degree of hundreds to one."

"Saracen," replied the Christian warrior, "the love which a true knight binds on one only, fair and faithful, is the gem entire; the affection thou flingest among thy enslaved wives, and half-wedded slaves, is worthless, comparatively, as the sparkling shivers of the broken diamond."

"Now, by the Holy Caaba," said the Emir, "thou art a madman, who hugs his chain of iron as if it were of gold!— Look more closely. This ring of mine would lose half its beauty were not the signet encircled and enchased with these lesser brilliants, which grace it and set it off. The central diamond is man, firm and entire, his value depending on himself alone; and this circle of lesser jewels are women, borrowing his lustre, which he deals out to them as best suits his pleasure or his convenience. Take the central stone from the signet, and the diamond itself remains as valuable as ever, while the lesser gems are comparatively of little value. And this is the true reading of thy parable; for, what sayeth the poet Mansour : ' It is the favour of man which giveth beauty and comeliness to woman, as the stream glitters no longer when the sun ceaseth to shine.' "

" Saracen," replied the Crusader, " thou speakest like one who never saw a woman worthy the affection of a soldier. Believe me, couldst thou look upon those of Europe, to whom, after Heaven, we of the order of knighthood vow fealty and devotion, thou wouldst loathe for ever the poor sensual slaves who form thy harem. The beauty of our fair ones gives point to our spears, and edge to our swords ; their words are our law ; and as soon will a lamp shed lustre when unkindled, as a knight distinguish himself by feats of arms, having no mistress of his affection."

" I have heard of this frenzy among the warriors of the west," said the Emir, " and have ever accounted it one of the accompanying symptoms of that insanity, which brings you hither to obtain possession of an empty sepulchre. But yet, methinks, so highly have the Franks whom I have met with extolled the beauty of their women, I could be well contented to behold with mine own eyes those charms, which can transform such brave warriors into the tools of their pleasure."

" Brave Saracen," said the Knight, " if I were not on a pilgrimage to the Holy Sepulchre, it should be my pride to conduct you, on assurance of safety, to the camp of Richard of England, than whom none knows better how to do honour to a noble foe ; and though I be poor and unattended, yet have I interest to secure for thee, or any such as thou seemest, not safety only, but respect and esteem. There shouldst thou see several of the fairest beauties of France and Britain form a small circle, the brilliancy of which exceeds ten-thousand-fold the lustre of mines of diamonds such as thine."

" Now, by the corner-stone of the Caaba," said the Saracen, " I will accept thy invitation as freely as it is given, if thou wilt postpone thy present intent ; and, credit me, brave Nazarene, it were better for thyself to turn back thy horse's head towards the camp of thy people, for, to travel towards Jerusalem without a passport, is but a wilful casting away of thy life."

" I have a pass," answered the Knight, producing a parchment, " under Saladin's hand and signet."

The Saracen bent his head to the dust as he recognised the seal and handwriting of the renowned Soldan of Egypt and Syria ; and having kissed the paper with profound respect, he pressed it to his forehead, then returned it to the Christian, saying, "Rash Frank, thou hast sinned against thine own blood and mine, for not showing this to me when we met."

"You came with levelled spear," said the Knight; "had a troop of Saracens so assailed me, it might have stood with my honour to have shown the Soldan's pass, but never to one man."

"And yet one man," said the Saracen haughtily, "was enough to interrupt your journey."

"True, brave Moslem," replied the Christian; "but there are few such as thou art. Such falcons fly not in flocks, or if they do, they pounce not in numbers upon one."

"Thou dost us but justice," said the Saracen, evidently gratified by the compliment, as he had been touched by the implied scorn of the European's previous boast; "from us thou shouldst have had no wrong; but well was it for me that I failed to slay thee, with the safeguard of the king of kings upon thy person. Certain it were, that the cord or the sabre had justly avenged such guilt."

"I am glad to hear that its influence shall be availing to me," said the Knight; "for I have heard that the road is infested with robber-tribes, who regard nothing in comparison of an opportunity of plunder."

"The truth has been told to thee, brave Christian," said the Saracen; "but I swear to thee, by the turban of the Prophet, that shouldst thou miscarry in any haunt of such villains, I will myself undertake thy revenge with five thousand horse; I will slay every male of them, and send their women into such distant captivity, that the name of their tribe shall never again be heard within five hundred miles of Damascus. I will sow with salt the foundations of their village, and there shall never live thing dwell there, even from that time forward."

"I had rather the trouble which you design for yourself, were in revenge of some other more important person than of me, noble Emir," replied the Knight; "but my vow is recorded in Heaven, for good or for evil, and I must be indebted to you for pointing me out the way to my resting-place for this evening."

"That," said the Saracen, "must be under the black covering of my father's tent."

"This night," answered the Christian, "I must pass in prayer and penitence with a holy man, Theodorick of Engaddi, who dwells amongst these wilds, and spends his life in the service of God."

"I will at least see you safe thither," said the Saracen.

"That would be pleasant convoy for me," said the Christian, "yet might endanger the future security of the good father;

for the cruel hand of your people has been red with the blood of the servants of the Lord, and therefore do we come hither in plate and mail, with sword and lance, to open the road to the Holy Sepulchre, and protect the chosen saints and anchorites who yet dwell in this land of promise and of miracle."

"Nazarene," said the Moslem, "in this the Greeks and Syrians have much belied us, seeing we do but after the word of Abubeker Alwakel, the successor of the Prophet, and, after him, the first commander of true believers. 'Go forth,' he said, 'Yezed Ben Sophian,' when he sent that renowned general to take Syria from the infidels, 'quit yourselves like men in battle, but slay neither the aged, the infirm, the women, nor the children. Waste not the land, neither destroy corn and fruit-trees, they are the gifts of Allah. Keep faith when you have made any covenant, even if it be to your own harm. If ye find holy men labouring with their hands, and serving God in the desert, hurt them not, neither destroy their dwellings. But when you find them with shaven crowns, they are of the synagogue of Satan! smite with the sabre, slay, cease not till they become believers or tributaries.' As the Caliph, companion of the Prophet, hath told us, so have we done, and those whom our justice has smitten are but the priests of Satan. But unto the good men who, without stirring up nation against nation, worship sincerely in the faith of Issa Ben Marian, we are a shadow and a shield; and such being he whom you seek, even though the light of the Prophet hath not reached him, from me he will only have love, favour, and regard."

"The anchorite, whom I would now visit," said the warlike pilgrim, "is, I have heard, no priest; but were he of that anointed and sacred order, I would prove with my good lance, against paynim and infidel—— "

"Let us not defy each other, brother," interrupted the Saracen; "we shall find, either of us, enough of Franks or of Moslemah on whom to exercise both sword and lance. This Theodorick is protected both by Turk and Arab; and though one of strange conditions at intervals, yet, on the whole, he bears himself so well as the follower of his own prophet, that he merits the protection of him who was sent—— "

"Now, by Our Lady, Saracen," exclaimed the Christian, "if thou darest name in the same breath, the camel-driver of Mecca with—— "

An electrical shock of passion thrilled through the form of the Emir; but it was only momentary, and the calmness of his reply had both dignity and reason in it, when he said, "Slander not him whom thou knowest not; the rather that we venerate the founder of thy religion, while we condemn the doctrine which priests have spun from it. I will myself guide thee to

B

the cavern of the hermit, which, methinks, without my help, thou wouldst find it a hard matter to reach. And on the way, let us leave to mollahs and to monks, to dispute about the divinity of our faith, and speak on themes which belong to youthful warriors,—upon battles, upon beautiful women, upon sharp swords, and upon bright armour."

CHAPTER III

THE warriors arose from their place of brief rest and simple refreshment, and courteously aided each other while they carefully replaced and adjusted the harness, from which they had relieved for the time their trusty steeds. Each seemed familiar with an employment which, at that time, was a part of necessary, and, indeed, of indispensable duty. Each also seemed to possess, as far as the difference betwixt the animal and rational species admitted, the confidence and affection of the horse, which was the constant companion of his travels and his warfare. With the Saracen, this familiar intimacy was a part of his early habits; for, in the tents of the Eastern military tribes, the horse of the soldier ranks next to, and almost equal in importance with, his wife and his family; and, with the European warrior, circumstances, and indeed necessity, rendered his warhorse scarcely less than his brother-in-arms. The steeds, therefore, suffered themselves quietly to be taken from their food and liberty, and neighed and snuffled fondly around their masters, while they were adjusting their accoutrements for farther travel and additional toil. And each warrior, as he prosecuted his own task, or assisted with courtesy his companion, looked with observant curiosity at the equipments of his fellow-traveller, and noted particularly what struck him as peculiar in the fashion in which he arranged his riding accoutrements.

Ere they remounted to resume their journey, the Christian knight again moistened his lips, and dipt his hands in the living fountain, and said to his Pagan associate of the journey —" I would I knew the name of this delicious fountain, that I might hold it in my grateful remembrance; for never did water slake more deliciously a more oppressive thirst than I have this day experienced."

"It is called in the Arabic language," answered the Saracen, "by a name which signifies the Diamond of the Desert."

"And well is it so named," replied the Christian. "My native valley hath a thousand springs, but not to one of them shall I attach hereafter such precious recollection as to this solitary fount, which bestows its liquid treasures where they are not only delightful, but nearly indispensable."

"You say truth," said the Saracen; "for the curse is still on yonder sea of death, and neither man nor beast drinks of its waves, nor of the river which feeds without filling it, until this inhospitable desert be passed."

They mounted, and pursued their journey across the sandy waste. The ardour of noon was now past, and a light breeze somewhat alleviated the terrors of the desert, though not without bearing on its wings an impalpable dust, which the Saracen little heeded, though his heavily-armed companion felt it as such an annoyance, that he hung his iron casque at his saddle-bow, and substituted the light riding-cap, termed in the language of the time a *mortier*, from its resemblance in shape to an ordinary mortar. They rode together for some time in silence, the Saracen performing the part of director and guide of the journey, which he did by observing minute marks and bearings of the distant rocks, to a ridge of which they were gradually approaching. For a little time he seemed absorbed in the task, as a pilot when navigating a vessel through a difficult channel; but they had not proceeded half a league when he seemed secure of his route, and disposed, with more frankness than was usual to his nation, to enter into conversation.

"You have asked the name," he said, "of a mute fountain, which hath the semblance, but not the reality, of a living thing. Let me be pardoned to ask the name of the companion with whom I have this day encountered, both in danger and in repose, and which I cannot fancy unknown, even here among the deserts of Palestine?"

"It is not yet worth publishing," said the Christian. "Know, however, that among the soldiers of the Cross I am called Kenneth—Kenneth of the Crouching Leopard; at home I have other titles, but they would sound harsh in an Eastern ear. Brave Saracen, let me ask which of the tribes of Arabia claims your descent, and by what name you are known?"

"Sir Kenneth," said the Moslem; "I joy that your name is such as my lips can easily utter. For me, I am no Arab, yet derive my descent from a line neither less wild nor less warlike. Know, Sir Knight of the Leopard, that I am Sheerkohf, the Lion of the Mountain, and that Kurdistan, from which I derive my descent, holds no family more noble than that of Seljook."

"I have heard," answered the Christian, "that your great Soldan claims his blood from the same source?"

"Thanks to the Prophet, that hath so far honoured our

mountains, as to send from their bosom him whose word is victory," answered the Paynim. "I am but as a worm before the King of Egypt and Syria, and yet in my own land something my name may avail.—Stranger, with how many men didst thou come on this warfare?"

"By my faith," said Sir Kenneth, "with aid of friends and kinsmen, I was hardly pinched to furnish forth ten well-appointed lances, with maybe some fifty more men archers, and varlets included. Some have deserted my unlucky pennon—some have fallen in battle—several have died of disease—and one trusty armour-bearer, for whose life I am now doing my pilgrimage, lies on the bed of sickness."

"Christian," said Sheerkohf, "here I have five arrows in my quiver, each feathered from the wing of an eagle. When I send one of them to my tents, a thousand warriors mount on horseback—when I send another, an equal force will arise—for the five I can command five thousand men; and if I send my bow, ten thousand mounted riders will shake the desert. And with thy fifty followers thou hast come to invade a land in which I am one of the meanest!"

"Now, by the rood, Saracen," retorted the western warrior, "thou shouldst know ere thou vauntest thyself, that one steel glove can crush a whole handful of hornets."

"Ay, but it must first enclose them within its grasp," said the Saracen, with a smile which might have endangered their new alliance, had he not changed the subject by adding, "And is bravery so much esteemed amongst the Christian princes, that thou, thus void of means and of men, canst offer, as thou didst of late, to be my protector and security in the camp of thy brethren?"

"Know, Saracen," said the Christian, "since such is thy style, that the name of a knight, and the blood of a gentleman, entitle him to place himself on the same rank with sovereigns even to the first degree in so far as regards all but regal authority and dominion. Were Richard of England himself to wound the honour of a knight as poor as I am, he could not, by the law of chivalry, deny him the combat."

"Methinks I should like to look upon so strange a scene," said the Emir, "in which a leathern belt and a pair of spurs put the poorest on a level with the most powerful."

"You must add free blood and a fearless heart," said the Christian; "then, perhaps, you will not have spoken untruly of the dignity of knighthood."

"And mix you as boldly amongst the females of your chiefs and leaders?" asked the Saracen.

"God forbid," said the Knight of the Leopard, "that the poorest Knight in Christendom should not be free, in all honourable service, to devote his hand and sword, the fame of his actions, and the fixed devotion of his heart, to the fairest princess who ever wore coronet on her brow!"

"But a little while since," said the Saracen, "and you described love as the highest treasure of the heart—thine hath undoubtedly been highly and nobly bestowed?"

"Stranger," answered the Christian, blushing deeply as he spoke, "we tell not rashly where it is we have bestowed our choicest treasures—it is enough for thee to know, that, as thou sayest, my love is highly and nobly bestowed—most highly— most nobly; but if thou wouldst hear of love and broken lances, venture thyself, as thou sayest, to the Camp of the Crusaders, and thou wilt find exercise for thine ears, and, if thou wilt, for thy hands too."

The Eastern warrior, raising himself in his stirrups, and shaking aloft his lance, replied, "Hardly, I fear, shall I find one with a crossed shoulder, who will exchange with me the cast of the jerrid."

"I will not promise for that," replied the Knight, "though there be in the camp certain Spaniards, who have right good skill in your Eastern game of hurling the javelin."

"Dogs, and sons of dogs!" ejaculated the Saracen; "what have these Spaniards to do to come hither to combat the true believers, who, in their own land, are their lords and taskmasters? with them I would mix in no warlike pastime."

"Let not the knights of Leon or Asturias hear you speak thus of them," said the Knight of the Leopard; "but," added he, smiling at the recollection of the morning's combat, "if instead of a reed, you were inclined to stand the cast of a battle-axe, there are enough of western warriors who would gratify your longing."

"By the beard of my father, sir," said the Saracen, with an approach to laughter, "the game is too rough for mere sport— I will never shun them in battle, but my head" (pressing his hand to his brow) "will not, for a while, permit me to seek them in sport."

"I would you saw the axe of King Richard," answered the western warrior, "to which that which hangs at my saddle-bow weighs but as a feather."

"We hear much of that island sovereign," said the Saracen, "art thou one of his subjects?"

"One of his followers I am, for this expedition," answered the Knight, "and honoured in the service; but not born his subject, although a native of the island in which he reigns."

"How mean you?" said the Eastern soldier; "have you then two kings in one poor island?"

"As thou sayest," said the Scot, for such was Sir Kenneth

by birth,—"It is even so; and yet, although the inhabitants
of the two extremities of that island are engaged in frequent
war, the country can, as thou seest, furnish forth such a body
of men-at-arms, as may go far to shake the unholy hold which
your master hath laid on the cities of Zion."

"By the beard of Saladin, Nazarene, but that it is a thoughtless and boyish folly, I could laugh at the simplicity of your
great Sultan, who comes hither to make conquests of deserts
and rocks, and dispute the possession of them with those who
have tenfold numbers at command, while he leaves a part of his
narrow islet, in which he was born a sovereign, to the dominion
of another sceptre than his. Surely, Sir Kenneth, you and the
other good men of your country should have submitted yourself
to the dominion of this King Richard, ere you left your native
land, divided against itself, to set forth on this expedition?"

Hasty and fierce was Kenneth's answer. "No, by the bright
light of Heaven! If the King of England had not set forth to
the Crusade till he was sovereign of Scotland, the crescent might,
for me, and all true-hearted Scots, glimmer for ever on the walls
of Zion."

Thus far he had proceeded, when suddenly recollecting himself, he muttered, "*Mea culpa! mea culpa!* what have I, a
soldier of the Cross, to do with recollection of war betwixt
Christian nations?"

The rapid expression of feeling corrected by the dictates of
duty, did not escape the Moslem, who, if he did not entirely
understand all which it conveyed, saw enough to convince him
with the assurance, that Christians, as well as Moslemah, had
private feelings of personal pique, and national quarrels, which
were not entirely reconcilable. But the Saracens were a race,
polished, perhaps, to the utmost extent which their religion
permitted, and particularly capable of entertaining high ideas of
courtesy and politeness; and such sentiments prevented his
taking any notice of the inconsistency of Sir Kenneth's feelings,
in the opposite characters of a Scot and a Crusader.

Meanwhile, as they advanced, the scene began to change
around them. They were now turning to the eastward, and
had reached the range of steep and barren hills which binds in
that quarter the naked plain, and varies the surface of the
country, without changing its sterile character. Sharp rocky
eminences began to arise around them, and, in a short time,
deep declivities and ascents, both formidable in height, and
difficult from the narrowness of the path, offered to the
travellers obstacles of a different kind from those with which
they had recently contended. Dark caverns and chasms amongst
the rocks, those grottos so often alluded to in Scripture, yawned
fearfully on either side as they proceeded, and the Scottish

knight was informed by the Emir, that these were often the refuge of beasts of prey, or of men still more ferocious, who, driven to desperation by the constant war, and the oppression exercised by the soldiery, as well of the Cross as of the Crescent, had become robbers, and spared neither rank nor religion, neither sex nor age, in their depredations.

The Scottish knight listened with indifference to the accounts of ravages committed by wild beasts or wicked men, secure as he felt himself in his own valour and personal strength; but he was struck with mysterious dread, when he recollected that he was now in the awful wilderness of the forty days' fast, and the scene of the actual personal temptation, wherewith the Evil Principle was permitted to assail the Son of Man. He withdrew his attention gradually from the light and worldly conversation of the infidel warrior beside him, and, however acceptable his gay and gallant bravery would have rendered him as a companion elsewhere, Sir Kenneth felt as if, in those wildernesses—the waste and dry places, in which the foul spirits were wont to wander when expelled the mortals whose forms they possessed—a bare-footed friar would have been a better associate than the gay but unbelieving Paynim.

These feelings embarrassed him; the rather that the Saracen's spirits appeared to rise with the journey, and because the farther he penetrated into the gloomy recesses of the mountains, the lighter became his conversation, and when he found that unanswered, the louder grew his song. Sir Kenneth knew enough of the Eastern languages, to be assured that he chanted sonnets of love, containing all the glowing praises of beauty, in which the Oriental poets are so fond of luxuriating, and which, therefore, were peculiarly unfitted for a serious or devotional strain of thought, the feeling best becoming the Wilderness of the Temptation. With inconsistency enough, the Saracen also sung lays in praise of wine, the liquid ruby of the Persian poets, and his gaiety at length became so unsuitable to the Christian knight's contrary train of sentiments, as, but for the promise of amity which they had exchanged, would most likely have made Sir Kenneth take measures to change his note. As it was, the Crusader felt as if he had by his side some gay licentious fiend, who endeavoured to ensnare his soul, and endanger his immortal salvation, by inspiring loose thoughts of earthly pleasure, and thus polluting his devotion at a time when his faith as a Christian, and his vow as a pilgrim, called on him for a serious and penitential state of mind. He was thus greatly perplexed, and undecided how to act; and it was in a tone of hasty displeasure, that, at length breaking silence, he interrupted the lay of the celebrated Rudpiki, in which he prefers the mole on his mistress's bosom to all the wealth of Bokhara and Samarcand.

"Saracen," said the Crusader sternly, "blinded as thou art, and plunged amidst the errors of a false law, thou shouldst yet comprehend that there are some places more holy than others, and that there are some scenes also, in which the Evil One hath more than ordinary power over sinful mortals. I will not tell thee for what awful reason this place—these rocks—these caverns with their gloomy arches, leading as it were to the central abyss—are held an especial haunt of Satan and his angels. It is enough that I have been long warned to beware of this place by wise and holy men, to whom the qualities of the unholy region are well known. Wherefore, Saracen, forbear thy foolish and ill-timed levity, and turn thy thoughts to things more suited to the spot; although, alas, for thee! thy best prayers are but as blasphemy and sin."

The Saracen listened with some surprise, and then replied, with good-humour and gaiety, only so far repressed as courtesy required, "Good Sir Kenneth, methinks you deal unequally by your companion, or else ceremony is but indifferently taught amongst your western tribes. I took no offence when I saw you gorge hog's flesh and drink wine, and permitted you to enjoy a treat which you called your Christian liberty, only pitying in my heart your foul pastimes — Wherefore, then, shouldst thou take scandal, because I cheer, to the best of my power, a gloomy road with a cheerful verse?—What saith the poet,—'Song is like the dews of Heaven on the bosom of the desert; it cools the path of the traveller.'"

"Friend Saracen," said the Christian, "I blame not the love of minstrelsy and of the *gaie science;* albeit, we yield unto it even too much room in our thoughts when they should be bent on better things. But prayers and holy psalms are better fitting than lays of love, or of wine-cups, when men walk in this Valley of the Shadow of Death, full of fiends and demons, whom the prayers of holy men have driven forth from the haunts of humanity to wander amidst scenes as accursed as themselves."

"Speak not thus of the Genii, Christian," answered the Saracen, "for know, thou speakest to one whose line and nation drew their origin from the immortal race, which your sect fear and blaspheme."

"I well thought," answered the Crusader, "that your blinded race had their descent from the foul fiend, without whose aid you would never have been able to maintain this blessed land of Palestine against so many valiant soldiers of God. I speak not thus of thee in particular, Saracen, but generally of thy people and religion. Strange is it to me, however, not that you should have the descent from the Evil One, but that you should boast of it."

"From whom should the bravest boast of descending, saving

from him that is bravest?" said the Saracen; "from whom should the proudest trace their line so well as from the Dark Spirit, which would rather fall headlong by force, than bend the knee by his will? Eblis may be hated, stranger, but he must be feared; and such as Eblis are his descendants of Kurdistan."

Tales of magic and of necromancy were the learning of the period, and Sir Kenneth heard his companion's confession of diabolical descent without any disbelief, and without much wonder; yet not without a secret shudder at finding himself in this fearful place, in the company of one who avouched himself to belong to such a lineage. Naturally unsusceptible, however, of fear, he crossed himself, and stoutly demanded of the Saracen an account of the pedigree which he had boasted. The latter readily complied.

"Know, brave stranger," he said, "that when the cruel Zohauk, one of the descendants of Giamschid, held the throne of Persia, he formed a league with the Powers of Darkness, amidst the secret vaults of Istakhar, vaults which the hands of the elementary spirits had hewn out of the living rock long before Adam himself had an existence. Here he fed, with daily oblations of human blood, two devouring serpents, which had become, according to the poets, a part of himself, and to sustain whom he levied a tax of daily human sacrifices, till the exhausted patience of his subjects caused some to raise up the scimitar of resistance like the valiant Blacksmith, and the victorious Feridoun, by whom the tyrant was at length dethroned, and imprisoned for ever in the dismal caverns of the mountain Damavend. But ere that deliverance had taken place, and whilst the power of the bloodthirsty tyrant was at its height, the band of ravening slaves, whom he had sent forth to purvey victims for his daily sacrifice, brought to the vaults of the palace of Istakhar seven sisters so beautiful, that they seemed seven houris. These seven maidens were the daughters of a sage, who had no treasures save these beauties and his own wisdom. The last was not sufficient to foresee this misfortune, the former seemed ineffectual to prevent it. The eldest exceeded not her twentieth year, the youngest had scarce attained her thirteenth; and so like were they to each other, that they could not have been distinguished but for the difference of height, in which they gradually rose in easy gradation above each other, like the ascent which leads to the gates of Paradise. So lovely were these seven sisters when they stood in the darksome vault, disrobed of all clothing saving a cymar of white silk, that their charms moved the hearts of those who were not mortal. Thunder muttered, the earth shook, the wall of the vault was rent, and at the chasm entered one dressed like a hunter, with bow and shafts, and followed by six others, his brethren. They were tall men, and, though dark, yet comely to behold, but their eyes had more the glare of those of the dead, than the light which lives under the eyelids of the living. 'Zeineb,' said the leader of the band—and as he spoke he took the eldest sister by the hand, and his voice was soft, low, and melancholy, —'I am Cothrob, king of the subterranean world, and supreme chief of Ginnistan. I and my brethren are of those, who, created out of the pure elementary fire, disdained, even at the command of Omnipotence, to do homage to a clod of earth, because it was called Man. Thou may'st have heard of us as cruel, unrelenting, and persecuting. It is false. We are by nature kind and generous; only vengeful when insulted, only cruel when affronted. We are true to those who trust us; and we have heard the invocations of thy father, the sage Mithrasp, who wisely worships not alone the Origin of Good, but that which is called the Source of Evil. You and your sisters are on the eve of death; but let each give to us one hair from your fair tresses, in token of fealty, and we will carry you many miles from hence to a place of safety, where you may bid defiance to Zohauk and his ministers.' The fear of instant death, saith the poet, is like the rod of the prophet Haroun, which devoured all other rods when transformed into snakes before the King of Pharaoh; and the daughters of the Persian sage were less apt than others to be afraid of the addresses of a spirit. They gave the tribute which Cothrob demanded, and in an instant the sisters were transported to an enchanted castle on the mountains of Tugrut, in Kurdistan, and were never again seen by mortal eye. But in process of time seven youths, distinguished in the war and in the chase, appeared in the environs of the castle of the demons. They were darker, taller, fiercer, and more resolute, than any of the scattered inhabitants of the valleys of Kurdistan; and they took to themselves wives, and became fathers of the seven tribes of the Kurdmans, whose valour is known throughout the universe."

The Christian knight heard with wonder the wild tale, of which Kurdistan still possesses the traces, and after a moment's thought, replied,—"Verily, Sir Knight, you have spoken well— your genealogy may be dreaded and hated, but it cannot be contemned. Neither do I any longer wonder at your obstinacy in a false faith; since, doubtless, it is part of the fiendish disposition which hath descended from your ancestors, those infernal huntsmen, as you have described them, to love falsehood rather than truth; and I no longer marvel that your spirits become high and exalted, and vent themselves in verse and in tunes, when you approach to the places encumbered by the haunting of evil spirits, which must excite in you that joyous feeling which others experience when approaching the land of their human ancestry."

"By my father's beard, I think thou hast the right," said the Saracen, rather amused than offended by the freedom with which the Christian had uttered his reflections; "for, though the Prophet (blessed be his name!) hath sown amongst us the seed of a better faith than our ancestors learned in the ghostly halls of Tugrut, yet we are not willing, like other Moslemah, to pass hasty doom on the lofty and powerful elementary spirits from whom we claim our origin. These Genii, according to our belief and hope, are not altogether reprobate, but are still in the way of probation, and may hereafter be punished or rewarded. Leave we this to the mollahs and the imaums. Enough that with us the reverence for these spirits is not altogether effaced by what we have learned from the Koran, and that many of us still sing, in memorial of our fathers' more ancient faith, such verses as these."

So saying, he proceeded to chant verses, very ancient in the language and structure, which some have thought derive their source from the worshippers of Arimanes, the Evil Principle.

AHRIMAN.

Dark Ahriman, whom Irak still
Holds origin of woe and ill!
　　When, bending at thy shrine,
We view the world with troubled eye,
Where see we 'neath the extended sky,
　　An empire matching thine?

If the Benigner Power can yield
A fountain in the desert field,
　　Where weary pilgrims drink;
Thine are the waves that lash the rock,
Thine the tornado's deadly shock,
　　Where countless navies sink!

Or if He bid the soil dispense
Balsams to cheer the sinking sense,
　　How few can they deliver
From lingering pains, or pang intense,
Red Fever, spotted Pestilence,
　　The arrows of thy quiver!

Chief in Man's bosom sits thy sway,
And frequent, while in words we pray
　　Before another throne,
Whate'er of specious form be there,
The secret meaning of the prayer
　　Is, Ahriman, thine own.

Say, hast thou feeling, sense, and form,
Thunder thy voice, thy garments storm,
   As Eastern Magi say;
With sentient soul of hate and wrath,
And wings to sweep thy deadly path,
   And fangs to tear thy prey?

Or art thou mix'd in Nature's source,
An ever-operating force,
   Converting good to ill;
An evil principle innate,
Contending with our better fate,
   And oh! victorious still?

Howe'er it be, dispute is vain,
On all without thou hold'st thy reign,
   Nor less on all within;
Each mortal passion's fierce career,
Love, hate, ambition, joy, and fear,
   Thou goadest into sin.

Whene'er a sunny gleam appears,
To brighten up our vale of tears,
   Thou art not distant far;
'Mid such brief solace of our lives,
Thou whett'st our very banquet-knives
   To tools of death and war.

Thus, from the moment of our birth,
Long as we linger on the earth,
   Thou rul'st the fate of men;
Thine are the pangs of life's last hour,
And—who dare answer?—is thy power,
   Dark Spirit! ended THEN? *

These verses may perhaps have been the not unnatural
effusion of some half-enlightened philosopher, who, in the
fabled deity, Arimanes, saw but the prevalence of moral and
physical evil; but in the ears of Sir Kenneth of the Leopard,

---

* The worthy and learned clergyman, by whom this species of hymn
has been translated, desires that, for fear of misconception, we should
warn the reader to recollect, that it is composed by a heathen, to whom
the real causes of moral and physical evil are unknown, and who views
their predominance in the system of the universe, as all must view that
appalling fact, who have not the benefit of the Christian Revelation. On
our own part, we beg to add, that we understand the style of the
translator is more paraphrastic than can be approved by those who are
acquainted with the singularly curious original. The translator seems to
have despaired of rendering into English verse the flights of Oriental
poetry; and, possibly, like many learned and ingenious men, finding it
impossible to discover the sense of the original, he may have tacitly
substituted his own.

they had a different effect, and, sung as they were by one who had just boasted himself a descendant of demons, sounded very like an address of worship to the Arch-fiend himself. He weighed within himself, whether, on hearing such blasphemy in the very desert where Satan had stood rebuked for demanding homage, taking an abrupt leave of the Saracen was sufficient to testify his abhorrence; or whether he was not rather constrained by his vow as a Crusader, to defy the infidel to combat on the spot, and leave him food for the beasts of the wilderness, when his attention was suddenly caught by an unexpected apparition.

The light was now verging low, yet served the knight still to discern that they two were no longer alone in the forest, but were closely watched by a figure of great height and very thin, which skipped over rocks and bushes with so much agility, as, added to the wild and hirsute appearance of the individual, reminded him of the fauns and silvans, whose images he had seen in the ancient temples of Rome. As the single-hearted Scotsman had never for a moment doubted these gods of the ancient Gentiles to be actually devils, so he now hesitated not to believe that the blasphemous hymn of the Saracen had raised up an infernal spirit.

"But what recks it!" said stout Sir Kenneth to himself; "down with the fiend and his worshippers!"

He did not, however, think it necessary to give the same warning of defiance to two enemies, as he would unquestionably have afforded to one. His hand was upon his mace, and perhaps the unwary Saracen would have been paid for his Persian poetry, by having his brains dashed out on the spot, without any reason assigned for it; but the Scottish knight was spared from committing what would have been a sore blot in his shield of arms. The apparition, on which his eyes had been fixed for some time, had at first appeared to dog their path by concealing itself behind rocks and shrubs, using those advantages of the ground with great address, and surmounting its irregularities with surprising agility. At length, just as the Saracen paused in his song, the figure, which was that of a tall man clothed in goat-skins, sprung into the midst of the path, and seized a rein of the Saracen's bridle in either hand, confronting thus and bearing back the noble horse, which, unable to endure the manner in which this sudden assailant pressed the long-armed bit, and the severe curb, which, according to the Eastern fashion, was a solid ring of iron, reared upright, and finally fell backwards on his master, who, however, avoided the peril of the fall by lightly throwing himself to one side.

The assailant then shifted his grasp from the bridle of the horse to the throat of the rider, flung himself above the struggling Saracen, and, despite of his youth and activity, kept him undermost, wreathing his long arms above those of his prisoner, who called out angrily, and yet, half-laughing at the same time —" Hamako—fool—unloose me—this passes thy privilege— unloose me, or I will use my dagger."

"Thy dagger!—infidel dog!" said the figure in the goat-skins, "hold it in thy gripe if thou canst!" and in an instant he wrenched the Saracen's weapon out of its owner's hand, and brandished it over his head.

"Help, Nazarene!" cried Sheerkohf, now seriously alarmed; "help, or the Hamako will slay me."

"Slay thee!" replied the dweller of the desert; "and well hast thou merited death, for singing thy blasphemous hymns, not only to the praise of thy false prophet, who is the foul fiend's harbinger, but to the Author of Evil himself."

The Christian Knight had hitherto looked on as one stupefied, so strangely had this rencontre contradicted, it its progress and event, all that he had previously conjectured. He felt, how-ever, at length, that it touched his honour to interfere in behalf of his discomfited companion; and therefore addressed himself to the victorious figure in the goat-skins.

"Whosoe'er thou art," he said, "and whether of good or of evil, know that I am sworn for the time to be true companion to the Saracen whom thou holdest under thee; therefore, I pray thee to let him arise, else I will do battle with thee in his behalf."

"And a proper quarrel it were," answered the Hamako, "for a Crusader to do battle in—for the sake of an unbaptized dog to combat one of his own holy faith! Art thou come forth to the wilderness to fight for the Crescent against the Cross? A goodly soldier of God art thou to listen to those who sing the praises of Satan!"

Yet while he spoke thus, he arose himself, and suffering the Saracen to arise also, returned him his cangiar, or poniard.

"Thou seest to what a point of peril thy presumption hath brought thee," continued he of the goat-skins, now addressing Sheerkohf, "and by what weak means thy practised skill and boasted agility can be foiled, when such is Heaven's pleasure. Wherefore, beware, O Ilderim! for know that, were there not a twinkle in the star of thy nativity, which promises for thee something that is good and gracious in Heaven's good time, we two had not parted till I had torn asunder the throat which so lately thrilled forth blasphemies."

"Hamako," said the Saracen, without any appearance of resenting the violent language, and yet more violent assault to which he had been subjected, "I pray thee, good Hamako, to beware how thou dost again urge thy privilege over far; for though, as a good Moslem, I respect those whom Heaven hath deprived of ordinary reason, in order to endow them with the spirit of prophecy, yet I like not other men's hands on the bridle of my horse, neither upon my own person. Speak, therefore, what thou wilt, secure of any resentment from me; but gather so much sense as to apprehend, that if thou shalt again proffer me any violence, I will strike thy shagged head from thy meagre shoulders.—And to thee, friend Kenneth," he added, as he remounted his steed, "I must needs say that, in a companion through the desert, I love friendly deeds better than fair words. Of the last thou hast given me enough; but it had been better to have aided me more speedily in my struggle with this Hamako, who had well-nigh taken my life in his frenzy."

"By my faith," said the Knight, "I did somewhat fail— was somewhat tardy in rendering thee instant help; but the strangeness of the assailant, the suddenness of the scene—it was as if thy wild and wicked lay had raised the devil among us—and such was my confusion, that two or three minutes elapsed ere I could take to my weapon."

"Thou art but a cold and considerate friend," said the Saracen; "and, had the Hamako been one grain more frantic, thy companion had been slain by thy side, to thy eternal dishonour, without thy stirring a finger in his aid, although thou satest by, mounted and in arms."

"By my word, Saracen," said the Christian, "if thou wilt have it in plain terms, I thought that strange figure was the devil; and being of thy lineage, I knew not what family secret you might be communicating to each other, as you lay lovingly rolling together on the sand."

"Thy gibe is no answer, brother Kenneth," said the Saracen; "for know, that had my assailant been in very deed the Prince of Darkness, thou wert bound not the less to enter into combat with him in thy comrade's behalf. Know, also, that whatever there may be of foul or of fiendish about the Hamako, belongs more to your lineage than to mine; this Hamako being, in truth, the anchorite whom thou art come hither to visit."

"This!" said Sir Kenneth, looking at the athletic yet wasted figure before him—"this!—thou mockest, Saracen—this cannot be the venerable Theodorick!"

"Ask himself, if thou wilt not believe me," answered Sheerkohf; and ere the words had left his mouth, the hermit gave evidence in his own behalf.

"I am Theodorick of Engaddi," he said—"I am the walker of the desert—I am friend of the cross, and flail of all infidels, heretics, and devil-worshippers. Avoid ye, avoid ye!—Down with Mahound, Termagaunt, and all their adherents!"—So saying, he pulled from under his shaggy garment a sort of flail, or jointed club, bound with iron, which he brandished round his head with singular dexterity.

"Thou see'st thy saint," said the Saracen, laughing, for the first time, at the unmitigated astonishment with which Sir Kenneth looked on the wild gestures, and heard the wayward muttering of Theodorick, who, after swinging his flail in every direction, apparently quite reckless whether it encountered the head of either of his companions, finally showed his own strength, and the soundness of the weapon, by striking into fragments a large stone which lay near him.

"This is a madman," said Sir Kenneth.

"Not the worse saint," returned the Moslem, speaking according to the well-known Eastern belief, that madmen are under the influence of immediate inspiration. "Know, Christian, that when one eye is extinguished, the other becomes more keen—when one hand is cut off, the other becomes more powerful; so, when our reason in human things is disturbed or destroyed, our view heavenward becomes more acute and perfect."

Here the voice of the Saracen was drowned in that of the hermit, who began to hollo aloud in a wild chanting tone,— "I am Theodorick of Engaddi—I am the torch-brand of the desert—I am the flail of the infidels! The lion and the leopard shall be my comrades, and draw nigh to my cell for shelter; neither shall the goat be afraid of their fangs—I am the torch and the lantern—Kyrie Eleison!"

He closed his song by a short race, and ended that again by three forward bounds, which would have done him great credit in a gymnastic academy, but became his character of hermit so indifferently, that the Scottish knight was altogether confounded and bewildered.

The Saracen seemed to understand him better. "You see," he said, "that he expects us to follow him to his cell, which, indeed, is our only place of refuge for the night. You are the leopard, from the portrait on your shield—I am the lion, as my name imports—and, by the goat, alluding to his garb of goatskins, he means himself. We must keep him in sight, however, for he is as fleet as a dromedary."

In fact, the task was a difficult one, for though the reverend guide stopped from time to time, and waved his hand, as if to encourage them to come on, yet, well acquainted with all the winding dells and passes of the desert, and gifted with uncommon activity, which, perhaps, an unsettled state of mind kept in constant exercise, he led the knights through chasms, and along footpaths, where even the light-armed Saracen, with his well-trained barb, was in considerable risk, and where the iron-sheathed European, and his over-burdened horse, found themselves in such imminent peril, as the rider would gladly have exchanged for the dangers of a general action. Glad he was when, at length, after this wild race, he beheld the holy man who had led it standing in front of a cavern, with a large torch in his hand, composed of a piece of wood dipped in bitumen, which cast a broad and flickering light, and emitted a strong sulphurous smell.

Undeterred by the stifling vapour, the knight threw himself from his horse and entered the cavern, which afforded small appearance of accommodation. The cell was divided into two parts, in the outward of which were an altar of stone, and a crucifix made of reeds : this served the anchorite for his chapel. On one side of this outward cave the Christian knight, though not without scruple, arising from religious reverence to the objects around, fastened up his horse, and arranged him for the night, in imitation of the Saracen, who gave him to understand that such was the custom of the place. The hermit, meanwhile, was busied putting his inner apartment in order to receive his guests, and there they soon joined him. At the bottom of the outer cave, a small aperture closed with a door of rough plank, led into the sleeping apartment of the hermit, which was more commodious. The floor had been brought to a rough level by the labour of the inhabitant, and then strewed with white sand, which he daily sprinkled with water from a small fountain which bubbled out of the rock in one corner, affording, in that stifling climate, refreshment alike to the ear and the taste. Mattresses, wrought of twisted flags, lay by the side of the cell ; the sides, like the floor, had been roughly brought to shape, and several herbs and flowers were hung around them. Two waxen torches, which the hermit lighted, gave a cheerful air to the place, which was rendered agreeable by its fragrance and coolness.

There were implements of labour in one corner of the apartment, in another was a niche for a rude statue of the Virgin. A table and two chairs showed that they must be the handiwork of the anchorite, being different in their form from Oriental accommodations. The former was covered, not only with reeds and pulse, but also with dried flesh, which Theodorick assiduously placed in such arrangement as should invite the appetite of his guests. This appearance of courtesy, though mute, and expressed by gesture only, seemed to Sir Kenneth something entirely irreconcilable with his former wild and violent demeanour. The movements of the hermit were now become composed, and apparently it was only a sense of religious humiliation which prevented his features, emaciated as they were by his austere mode of life, from being majestic and noble. He trod his cell, as one who seemed born to rule over men, but who had abdicated his empire to become the servant of Heaven. Still, it must be allowed that his gigantic size, the length of his unshaven locks and beard, and the fire of a deep-set and wild eye, were rather attributes of a soldier than of a recluse.

Even the Saracen seemed to regard the anchorite with some veneration, while he was thus employed, and he whispered in a low tone to Sir Kenneth, "The Hamako is now in his better mind, but he will not speak until we have eaten—such is his vow."

It was in silence, accordingly, that Theodorick motioned to the Scot to take his place on one of the low chairs, while Sheerkohf placed himself, after the custom of his nation, upon a cushion of mats. The hermit then held up both hands, as if blessing the refreshment which he had placed before his guests, and they proceeded to eat in silence as profound as his own. To the Saracen this gravity was natural, and the Christian imitated his taciturnity, while he employed his thoughts on the singularity of his own situation, and the contrast betwixt the wild, furious gesticulations, loud cries, and fierce actions of Theodorick, when they first met him, and the demure, solemn, decorous assiduity with which he now performed the duties of hospitality.

When their meal was ended, the hermit, who had not himself eaten a morsel, removed the fragments from the table, and placing before the Saracen a pitcher of sherbet, assigned to the Scot a flask of wine.

"Drink," he said, "my children,"—they were the first words he had spoken,—"the gifts of God are to be enjoyed, when the Giver is remembered."

Having said this he retired to the outward cell, probably for performance of his devotions, and left his guests together in the inner apartment; when Sir Kenneth endeavoured by various questions, to draw from Sheerkohf what that Emir knew concerning his host. He was interested by more than mere curiosity in these inquiries. Difficult as it was to reconcile the outrageous demeanour of the recluse at his first appearance, to his present humble and placid behaviour, it seemed yet more impossible to think it consistent with the high consideration in which, according to what Sir Kenneth had learned, this hermit was held by the most enlightened divines of the Christian world. Theodorick, the Hermit of Engaddi, had, in that character, been the correspondent of popes and councils; to whom his letters, full of eloquent fervour, had described the miseries imposed by the unbelievers upon the Latin Christians in the Holy Land, in colours scarce inferior to those employed at the Council of Clermont by the Hermit Peter, when he preached the first Crusade. To find, in a person so reverend, and so much revered, the frantic gestures of a mad fakir, induced the Christian knight to pause ere he could resolve to communicate to him certain important matters, which he had in charge from some of the leaders of the Crusade.

It had been a main object of Sir Kenneth's pilgrimage, attempted by a route so unusual, to make such communications; but what he had that night seen, induced him to pause and reflect ere he proceeded to the execution of his commission. From the Emir he could not extract much information, but the general tenor was as follows :—That, as he had heard, the hermit had been once a brave and valiant soldier, wise in council, and fortunate in battle, which last he could easily believe from the great strength and agility which he had often seen him display; —that he had appeared at Jerusalem in the character not of a pilgrim, but in that of one who had devoted himself to dwell for the remainder of his life in the Holy Land. Shortly afterwards he fixed his residence amid the scenes of desolation where they now found him, respected by the Latins for his austere devotion, and by the Turks and Arabs on account of the symptoms of insanity which he displayed, and which they ascribed to inspiration. It was from them he had the name of Hamako, which expresses such a character in the Turkish language. Sheerkohf himself seemed at a loss how to rank their host. He had been, he said, a wise man, and could often for many hours together speak lessons of virtue or wisdom, without the slightest appearance of inaccuracy. At other times he was wild and violent, but never before had he seen him so mischievously disposed as he had that day appeared to be. His rage was chiefly provoked by any affront to his religion; and there was a story of some wandering Arabs, who had insulted his worship and defaced his altar, and whom he had on that account attacked and slain with the short flail which he carried with him in lieu of all other weapons. This incident had made a great noise, and it was as much the fear of the hermit's iron flail, as regard for his character as a Hamako, which caused the roving tribes to respect his dwelling and his chapel. His fame had spread so far, that Saladin had issued particular orders that he should be spared and protected. He himself, and other Moslem lords of rank, had visited the cell more than once, partly from curiosity, partly that they expected from a man so learned as the Christian Hamako, some insight into the secrets of futurity. "He had," continued the Saracen, "a rashid, or observatory, of great height, contrived to view the heavenly bodies, and particularly the planetary system; by whose movements and influences, as both Christian and Moslem believed, the course of human events was regulated, and might be predicted."

This was the substance of the Emir Sheerkohf's information, and it left Sir Kenneth in doubt whether the character of insanity arose from the occasional excessive fervour of the hermit's zeal, or whether it was not altogether fictitious, and assumed for the sake of the immunities which it afforded. Yet it seemed that the infidels had carried their complaisance towards him to an uncommon length, considering the fanaticism of the followers of Mohammed, in the midst of whom he was living, though the professed enemy of their faith. He thought also there was more intimacy of acquaintance betwixt the hermit and the Saracen, than the words of the latter had induced him to anticipate ; and it had not escaped him, that the former had called the latter by a name different from that which he himself had assumed. All these considerations authorised caution, if not suspicion. He determined to observe his host closely, and not to be over hasty in communicating with him on the important charge entrusted to him.

"Beware, Saracen," he said ; "methinks our host's imagination wanders as well on the subject of names as upon other matters. Thy name is Sheerkohf, and he called thee but now by another."

"My name, when in the tent of my father," replied the Kurdman, "was Ilderim, and by this I am still distinguished by many. In the field, and to soldiers, I am known as the Lion of the Mountain, being the name my good sword hath won for me.—But hush, the Hamako comes—it is to warn us to rest—I know his custom—none must watch him at his vigils."

The anchorite accordingly entered, and folding his arms on his bosom as he stood before them, said with a solemn voice— "Blessed be His name, who hath appointed the quiet night to follow the busy day, and the calm sleep to refresh the wearied limbs, and to compose the troubled spirit !"

Both warriors replied "Amen !" and, arising from the table, prepared to betake themselves to the couches, which their host indicated by waving his hand, as, making a reference to each, he again withdrew from the apartment.

The Knight of the Leopard then disarmed himself of his heavy panoply, his Saracen companion kindly assisting him to undo his buckler and clasps, until he remained in the close dress of chamois leather, which knights and men-at-arms used to wear under their harness. The Saracen, if he had admired the strength of his adversary when sheathed in steel, was now no less struck with the accuracy of proportion displayed in his nervous and well-compacted figure. The knight, on the other hand, as, in exchange of courtesy, he assisted the Saracen to disrobe himself of his upper garments, that he might sleep with more convenience, was, on his side, at a loss to conceive how

such slender proportions, and slimness of figure, could be reconciled with the vigour he had displayed in personal contest.

Each warrior prayed, ere he addressed himself to his place
of rest. The Moslem turned towards his *kebla*, the point to
which the prayer of each follower of the Prophet was to be
addressed, and murmured his heathen orisons, while the Christian, withdrawing from the contamination of the infidel's
neighbourhood, placed his huge cross-handled sword upright,
and kneeling before it as the sign of salvation, told his rosary
with a devotion, which was enhanced by the recollection of the
scenes through which he had passed, and the dangers from
which he had been rescued in the course of the day. Both
warriors, worn by toil and travel, were soon fast asleep, each
on his separate pallet.

CHAPTER IV

KENNETH the Scot was uncertain how long his senses had been
lost in profound repose, when he was roused to recollection by
a sense of oppression on his chest, which at first suggested a
flitting dream of struggling with a powerful opponent, and at
length recalled him fully to his senses. He was about to
demand who was there, when, opening his eyes, he beheld
the figure of the anchorite, wild and savage-looking as we have
described him, standing by his bedside, and pressing his right
hand upon his breast, while he held a small silver lamp in the
other.

"Be silent," said the hermit, as the prostrate knight looked
up in surprise; "I have that to say to you which yonder infidel
must not hear."

These words he spoke in the French language, and not in the
Lingua Franca, or compound of Eastern and European dialects,
which had hitherto been used amongst them.

"Arise," he continued, "put on thy mantle—speak not, but
tread lightly, and follow me."

Sir Kenneth arose, and took his sword.

"It needs not," answered the anchorite, in a whisper; "we
are going where spiritual arms avail much, and fleshly weapons
are but as the reed and the decayed gourd."

The knight deposited his sword by the bedside as before,
and, armed only with his dagger, from which, in this perilous
country, he never parted, prepared to attend his mysterious
host.

The hermit then moved slowly forwards, and was followed

by the knight, still under some uncertainty whether the dark form which glided on before to show him the path, was not, in fact, the creation of a disturbed dream. They passed, like shadows, into the outer apartment, without disturbing the paynim Emir, who lay still buried in repose. Before the cross and altar, in the outward room, a lamp was still burning, a missal was displayed, and on the floor lay a discipline, or penitential scourge of small cord and wire, the lashes of which were stained with recent blood, a token, no doubt, of the severe penance of the recluse. Here Theodorick kneeled down, and pointed to the knight to take his place beside him upon the sharp flints, which seemed placed for the purpose of rendering the posture of reverential devotion as uneasy as possible; he read many prayers of the Catholic Church, and chanted, in a low but earnest voice, three of the penitential psalms. These last he intermixed with sighs and tears, and convulsive throbs, which bore witness how deeply he felt the divine poetry which he recited. The Scottish knight assisted with profound sincerity at these acts of devotion, his opinions of his host beginning, in the meantime, to be so much changed, that he doubted whether from the severity of his penance, and the ardour of his prayers, he ought not to regard him as a saint; and when they arose from the ground, he stood with reverence before him, as a pupil before an honoured master. The hermit was on his side silent and abstracted for the space of a few minutes.

"Look into yonder recess, my son," he said, pointing to the farther corner of the cell; "there thou wilt find a veil—bring it hither."

The knight obeyed; and, in a small aperture cut out of the wall, and secured with a door of wicker, he found the veil inquired for. When he brought it to the light, he discovered that it was torn, and soiled in some places with some dark substance. The anchorite looked at it with a deep but smothered emotion, and ere he could speak to the Scottish knight, was compelled to vent his feelings in a convulsive groan.

"Thou art now about to look upon the richest treasure that the earth possesses," he at length said; "woe is me, that my eyes are unworthy to be lifted towards it! Alas! I am but the vile and despised sign, which points out to the wearied traveller a harbour of rest and security, but must itself remain for ever without doors. In vain have I fled to the very depths of the rocks, and the very bosom of the thirsty desert. Mine enemy hath found me—even he whom I have denied has pursued me to my fortresses."

He paused again for a moment, and turning to the Scottish knight, said, in a firmer tone of voice, " You bring me a greeting from Richard of England ? "

"I come from the Council of Christian Princes," said the knight; "but the King of England being indisposed, I am not honoured with his Majesty's commands."

"Your token?" demanded the recluse.

Sir Kenneth hesitated—former suspicions, and the marks of insanity which the hermit had formerly exhibited, rushed suddenly on his thoughts; but how suspect a man whose manners were so saintly?—"My password," he said at length, "is this —Kings begged of a beggar."

"It is right," said the hermit, while he paused; "I know you well; but the sentinel upon his post—and mine is an important one—challenges friend as well as foe."

He then moved forward with the lamp, leading the way into the room which they had left. The Saracen lay on his couch, still fast asleep. The hermit paused by his side, and looked down on him.

"He sleeps," he said, "in darkness, and must not be awakened."

The attitude of the Emir did indeed convey the idea of profound repose. One arm, flung across his body, as he lay with his face half turned to the wall, concealed, with its loose and long sleeve, the greater part of his face; but the high forehead was yet visible. Its nerves, which during his waking hours were so uncommonly active, were now motionless, as if the face had been composed of dark marble, and his long silken eyelashes closed over his piercing and hawk-like eyes. The open and relaxed hand, and the deep, regular, and soft breathing, gave all tokens of the most profound repose. The slumberer formed a singular group along with the tall forms of the hermit in his shaggy dress of goat-skins, bearing the lamp, and the knight in his close leathern coat; the former with an austere expression of ascetic gloom, the latter with anxious curiosity deeply impressed on his manly features.

"He sleeps soundly," said the hermit, in the same low tone as before, and repeating the words, though he had changed the meaning from that which is literal to a metaphorical sense,— "He sleeps in darkness, but there shall be for him a dayspring. —O Ilderim, thy waking thoughts are yet as vain and wild as those which are wheeling their giddy dance through thy sleeping brain; but the trumpet shall be heard, and the dream shall be dissolved."

So saying, and making the knight a sign to follow him, the hermit went towards the altar, and passing behind it, pressed a spring, which, opening without noise, showed a small iron door wrought on the side of the cavern, so as to be almost imperceptible, unless upon the most severe scrutiny. The hermit, ere he ventured fully to open the door, dropt some oil on the hinges, which the lamp supplied. A small staircase, hewn in the rock, was discovered, when the iron door was at length completely opened.

"Take the veil which I hold," said the hermit, in a melancholy tone, "and blind mine eyes; for I may not look on the treasure which thou art presently to behold, without sin and presumption."

Without reply, the knight hastily muffled the recluse's head in the veil, and the latter began to ascend the staircase as one too much accustomed to the way to require the use of light, while at the same time he held the lamp to the Scot, who followed him for many steps up the narrow ascent. At length they rested in a small vault of irregular form, in one nook of which the staircase terminated, while in another corner a corresponding stair was seen to continue the ascent. In a third angle was a Gothic door, very rudely ornamented with the usual attributes of clustered columns and carving, and defended by a wicket, strongly guarded with iron, and studded with large nails. To this last point the hermit directed his steps, which seemed to falter as he approached it.

"Put off thy shoes," he said to his attendant; "the ground on which thou standest is holy. Banish from thy innermost heart each profane and carnal thought, for to harbour such while in this place were a deadly impiety."

The knight laid aside his shoes as he was commanded, and the hermit stood in the meanwhile as if communing with his soul in secret prayer, and when he again moved, commanded the knight to knock at the wicket three times. He did so. The door opened spontaneously, at least Sir Kenneth beheld no one, and his senses were at once assailed by a stream of the purest light, and by a strong and almost oppressive sense of the richest perfumes. He stepped two or three paces back, and it was the space of a minute ere he recovered the dazzling and overpowering effects of the sudden change from darkness to light.

When he entered the apartment in which this brilliant lustre was displayed, he perceived that the light proceeded from a combination of silver lamps, fed with purest oil, and sending forth the richest odours, hanging by silver chains from the roof of a small Gothic chapel, hewn, like most part of the hermit's singular mansion, out of the sound and solid rock. But, whereas, in every other place which Sir Kenneth had seen, the labour employed upon the rock had been of the simplest and coarsest description, it had in this chapel employed the invention and the chisels of the most able architects. The groined roofs rose from six columns on each side, carved with the rarest skill; and the manner in which the crossings of the concave

arches were bound together, as it were, with appropriate ornaments, were all in the finest tone of the architecture, and of the
age. Corresponding to the line of pillars, there were on each
side six richly wrought niches, each of which contained the image
of one of the twelve apostles.

At the upper and eastern end of the chapel stood the altar,
behind which a very rich curtain of Persian silk, embroidered
deeply with gold, covered a recess, containing, unquestionably,
some image or relic of no ordinary sanctity, in honour of whom
this singular place of worship had been erected. Under the
persuasion that this must be the case, the knight advanced to
the shrine, and kneeling down before it, repeated his devotions
with fervency, during which his attention was disturbed by the
curtain being suddenly raised, or rather pulled aside, how or by
whom he saw not; but in the niche which was thus disclosed,
he beheld a cabinet of silver and ebony, with a double folding-
door, the whole formed into the miniature resemblance of a
Gothic church.

As he gazed with anxious curiosity on the shrine, the two
folding doors also flew open, discovering a large piece of wood,
on which were blazoned the words, VERA CRUX, at the same
time a choir of female voices sung GLORIA PATRI. The instant
the strain had ceased, the shrine was closed, and the curtain
again drawn, and the knight who knelt at the altar might now
continue his devotions undisturbed, in honour of the holy relic
which had been just disclosed to his view. He did this under
the profound impression of one who had witnessed, with his
own eyes, an awful evidence of the truth of his religion, and it
was some time ere, concluding his orisons, he arose, and ventured to look around him for the hermit, who had guided him
to this sacred and mysterious spot. He beheld him, his head
still muffled in the veil, which he had himself wrapped around
it, couching, like a rated hound, upon the threshold of the
chapel; but apparently, without venturing to cross it; the
holiest reverence, the most penitential remorse, was expressed
by his posture, which seemed that of a man borne down and
crushed to the earth by the burden of his inward feelings. It
seemed to the Scot, that only the sense of the deepest penitence, remorse, and humiliation, could have thus prostrated a
frame so strong, and a spirit so fiery.

He approached him as if to speak, but the recluse anticipated his purpose, murmuring in stifled tones, from beneath the
fold in which his head was muffled, and which sounded like a
voice proceeding from the cerements of a corpse,—"Abide,
abide—happy thou that may'st—the vision is not yet ended."
—So saying, he reared himself from the ground, drew back
from the threshold on which he had hitherto lain prostrate,

and closed the door of the chapel, which, secured by a spring bolt within, the snap of which resounded through the place, appeared so much like a part of the living rock from which the cavern was hewn, that Kenneth could hardly discern where the aperture had been. He was now alone in the lighted chapel, which contained the relic to which he had lately rendered his homage, without other arms than his dagger, or other companion than his pious thoughts and dauntless courage.

Uncertain what was next to happen, but resolved to abide the course of events, Sir Kenneth paced the solitary chapel till about the time of the earliest cock crowing. At this dead season, when night and morning met together, he heard, but from what quarter he could not discover, the sound of such a small silver bell as is rung at the elevation of the host, in the ceremony, or sacrifice, as it has been called, of the mass. The hour and the place rendered the sound fearfully solemn, and, bold as he was, the knight withdrew himself into the farther nook of the chapel, at the end opposite to the altar, in order to observe, without interruption, the consequences of this unexpected signal.

He did not wait long ere the silken curtain was again withdrawn, and the relic again presented to his view. As he sunk reverentially on his knee, he heard the sound of the lauds, or earliest office of the Catholic Church, sung by female voices, which united together in the performance as they had done in the former service. The knight was soon aware that the voices were no longer stationary in the distance, but approached the chapel and became louder, when a door, imperceptible when closed, like that by which he had himself entered, opened on the other side of the vault, and gave the tones of the choir more room to swell along the ribbed arches of the roof.

The knight fixed his eyes on the opening with breathless anxiety, and, continuing to kneel in the attitude of devotion which the place and scene required, expected the consequence of these preparations. A procession appeared about to issue from the door. First, four beautiful boys, whose arms, neck, and legs were bare, showing the bronze complexion of the East, and contrasting with the snow-white tunics which they wore, entered the chapel by two and two. The first pair bore censers, which they swung from side to side, adding double fragrance to the odours with which the chapel already was impregnated. The second pair scattered flowers.

After these followed, in due and majestic order, the females who composed the choir; six, who, from their black scapularies, and black veils over their white garments, appeared to be professed nuns of the order of Mount Carmel; and as many whose veils, being white, argued them to be novices, or occa-

sional inhabitants in the cloister, who were not as yet bound to
it by vows. The former held in their hands large rosaries,
while the younger and lighter figures who followed, carried
each a chaplet of red and white roses. They moved in procession around the chapel, without appearing to take the slightest
notice of Kenneth, although passing so near him that their
robes almost touched him; while they continued to sing, the
knight doubted not that he was in one of those cloisters where
the noble Christian maidens had formerly openly devoted themselves to the services of the Church. Most of them had been
suppressed since the Mahometans had reconquered Palestine,
but many, purchasing connivance by presents, or receiving it
from the clemency or contempt of the victors, still continued
to observe in private the ritual to which their vows had consecrated them. Yet, though Kenneth knew this to be the case,
the solemnity of the place and hour, the surprise at the sudden
appearance of these votresses, and the visionary manner in
which they moved past him, had such influence on his imagination, that he could scarce conceive that the fair procession
which he beheld was formed of creatures of this world, so much
did they resemble a choir of supernatural beings, rendering
homage to the universal object of adoration.

Such was the knight's first idea, as the procession passed him,
scarce moving, save just sufficiently to continue their progress;
so that, seen by the shadowy and religious light, which the
lamps shed through the clouds of incense which darkened the
apartment, they appeared rather to glide than to walk.

But as a second time, in surrounding the chapel, they passed
the spot on which he kneeled, one of the white-stoled maidens,
as she glided by him, detached from the chaplet which she
carried a rosebud, which dropped from her fingers, perhaps unconsciously, on the foot of Sir Kenneth. The knight started
as if a dart had suddenly struck his person; for, when the mind
is wound up to a high pitch of feeling and expectation, the
slightest incident, if unexpected, gives fire to the train which
imagination has already laid. But he suppressed his emotion,
recollecting how easily an incident so indifferent might have
happened, and that it was only the uniform monotony of the
movement of the choristers, which made the incident in the
slightest degree remarkable.

Still, while the procession, for the third time, surrounded the
chapel, the thoughts and the eyes of Kenneth followed ex-
clusively the one among the novices who had dropped the
rosebud. Her step, her face, her form, were so completely
assimilated to the rest of the choristers, that it was impossible
to perceive the least marks of individuality, and yet Kenneth's
heart throbbed like a bird that would burst from its cage, as if

to assure him, by its sympathetic suggestions, that the female who held the right file on the second rank of the novices, was dearer to him, not only than all the rest that were present, but than the whole sex besides. The romantic passion of love, as it was cherished, and indeed enjoined, by the rules of chivalry, associated well with the no less romantic feelings of devotion; and they might be said much more to enhance than to counteract each other. It was, therefore, with a glow of expectation, that had something even of a religious character, that Sir Kenneth, his sensations thrilling from his heart to the ends of his fingers, expected some second sign of the presence of one, who, he strongly fancied, had already bestowed on him the first. Short as the space was during which the procession again completed a third perambulation of the chapel, it seemed an eternity to Kenneth. At length the form, which he had watched with such devoted attention, drew nigh—there was no difference betwixt that shrouded figure and the others, with whom it moved in concert and in unison, until, just as she passed for the third time the kneeling Crusader, a part of a little and well-proportioned hand, so beautifully formed as to give the highest idea of the perfect proportions of the form to which it belonged, stole through the folds of the gauze, like a moonbeam through the fleecy cloud of a summer night, and again a rose-bud lay at the feet of the Knight of the Leopard.

This second intimation could not be accidental—it could not be fortuitous the resemblance of that half-seen, but beautiful female hand, with one which his lips had once touched, and while they touched it, had internally sworn allegiance to the lovely owner. Had farther proof been wanting, there was the glimmer of that matchless ruby ring on that snow-white finger, whose invaluable worth Kenneth would yet have prized less than the slightest sign which that finger could have made—and, veiled too, as she was, he might see, by chance, or by favour, a stray curl of the dark tresses, each hair of which was dearer to him a hundred times than a chain of massive gold. It was the lady of his love! But that she should be here—in the savage and sequestered desert, among vestals, who rendered themselves habitants of wilds and of caverns, that they might perform in secret those Christian rites which they dared not assist in openly—that this should be so—in truth and in reality—seemed too incredible—it must be a dream—a delusive trance of the imagination. While these thoughts passed through the mind of Kenneth, the same passage, by which the procession had entered the chapel, received them on their return. The young sacristans, the sable nuns, vanished successively through the open door—at length she from whom he had received this double intimation, passed also—yet, in passing, turned her head, slightly indeed, but perceptibly, towards the place where he remained fixed as an image. He marked the last wave of her veil—it was gone—and a darkness sunk upon his soul, scarce less palpable than that which almost immediately enveloped his external sense; for the last chorister had no sooner crossed the threshold of the door, than it shut with a loud sound, and at the same instant the voices of the choir were silent, the lights of the chapel were at once extinguished, and Sir Kenneth remained solitary, and in total darkness. But to Kenneth, solitude, and darkness, and the uncertainty of his mysterious situation, were as nothing—he thought not of them —cared not for them—cared for nought in the world save the flitting vision which had just glided past him, and the tokens of her favour which she had bestowed. To grope on the floor for the buds which she had dropped—to press them to his lips —to his bosom—now alternately, now together—to rivet his lips to the cold stones on which, as near as he could judge, she had so lately stepped—to play all the extravagances which strong affection suggests and vindicates to those who yield themselves up to it, were but the tokens of passionate love, proper to all ages. But it was peculiar to the times of chivalry, that in his wildest rapture the knight imagined of no attempt to follow or to trace the object of such romantic attachment; that he thought of her as of a deity, who, having deigned to show herself for an instant to her devoted worshipper, had again returned to the darkness of her sanctuary—or as an influential planet, which, having darted in some auspicious minute one favourable ray, wrapped itself again in its veil of mist. The motions of the lady of his love were to him those of a superior being, who was to move without watch or control, rejoice him by her appearance, or depress him by her absence, animate him by her kindness, or drive him to despair by her cruelty—all at her own free will, and without other importunity or remonstrance than that expressed by the most devoted services of the heart and sword of the champion, whose sole object in life was to fulfil her commands, and, by the splendour of his own achievements, to exalt her fame.

Such were the rules of chivalry, and of the love which was its ruling principle. But Sir Kenneth's attachment was rendered romantic by other and still more peculiar circumstances. He had never even heard the sound of his lady's voice, though he had often beheld her beauty with rapture. She moved in a circle, which his rank of knighthood permitted him indeed to approach, but not to mingle with ; and highly as he stood distinguished for warlike skill and enterprise, still the poor Scottish soldier was compelled to worship his divinity at a distance, almost as great as divides the Persian from the sun which he adores. But when was the pride of woman too lofty to overlook the passionate devotion of a lover, however inferior in degree? Her eye had been on him in the tournament, her ear had heard his praises in the report of the battles which were daily fought; and while count, duke, and lord, contended for her grace, it flowed, unwillingly perhaps at first, or even unconsciously, towards the poor Knight of the Leopard, who, to support his rank, had little besides his sword. When she looked, and when she listened, the lady saw and heard enough to encourage her in her partiality, which had at first crept on her unawares. If a knight's personal beauty was praised, even the most prudish dames of the military court of England would make an exception in favour of the Scottish Kenneth; and it oftentimes happened, that notwithstanding the very considerable largesses which princes and peers bestowed on the minstrels, an impartial spirit of independence would seize the poet, and the harp was swept to the heroism of one, who had neither palfreys nor garments to bestow in guerdon of his applause.

The moments when she listened to the praises of her lover became gradually more and more dear to the high-born Edith, relieving the flattery with which her ear was weary, and presenting to her a subject of secret contemplation, more worthy, as he seemed by general report, than those who surpassed him in rank and in the gifts of fortune. As her attention became constantly, though cautiously, fixed on Sir Kenneth, she grew more and more convinced of his personal devotion to herself, and more and more certain in her mind, that in Kenneth of Scotland she beheld the fated knight doomed to share with her through weal and woe—and the prospect looked gloomy and dangerous—the passionate attachment to which the poets of the age ascribed such universal dominion, and which its manners and morals placed nearly on the same rank with devotion itself.

Let us not disguise the truth from our readers. When Edith became aware of the state of her own sentiments, chivalrous as were her sentiments, becoming a maiden not distant from the throne of England—gratified as her pride must have been with the mute though unceasing homage rendered to her by the knight whom she had distinguished, there were moments when the feelings of the woman, loving and beloved, murmured against the restraints of state and form by which she was surrounded, and when she almost blamed the timidity of her lover, who seemed resolved not to infringe them. The etiquette, to use a modern phrase, of birth and rank, had drawn around her a magical circle, beyond which Sir Kenneth might indeed bow and gaze, but within which he could no more pass, than an evoked spirit can transgress the boundaries prescribed by the rod of a powerful enchanter. The thought involuntarily pressed on her that she herself must venture, were it but the point of her fairy foot, beyond the prescribed boundary, if she ever hoped to give a lover, so reserved and bashful, an opportunity of so slight a favour, as but to salute her shoe-tie. There was an example, the noted precedent of the "King's daughter of Hungary," who thus generously encouraged the "Squire of low degree;" and Edith, though of kingly blood, was no King's daughter, any more than her lover was of low degree—fortune had put no such extreme barrier in obstacle to their affections. Something, however, within the maiden's bosom—that modest pride, which throws fetters even on love itself—forbade her, notwithstanding the superiority of her condition, to make those advances, which, in every case, delicacy assigns to the other sex ; above all, Sir Kenneth was a knight so gentle and honourable, so highly accomplished—as her imagination at least suggested, together with the strictest feelings of what was due to himself and to her—that however constrained her attitude might be while receiving his adorations, like the image of some deity, who is neither supposed to feel nor to reply to the homage of its votaries, still the idol feared that to step prematurely from her pedestal, would be to degrade herself in the eyes of her devoted worshipper.

Yet the devout adorer of an actual idol can even discover signs of approbation in the rigid and immovable features of a marble image, and it is no wonder that something, which could be as favourably interpreted, glanced from the bright eye of the lovely Edith, whose beauty, indeed, consisted rather more in that very power of expression, than on absolute regularity of contour, or brilliancy of complexion. Some light marks of distinction had escaped from her, notwithstanding her own jealous vigilance, else how could Sir Kenneth have so readily, and so undoubtingly, recognised the lovely hand, of which scarce two fingers were visible from under the veil, or how could he have rested so thoroughly assured that two flowers, successively dropt on the spot, were intended as a recognition on the part of his lady-love ? By what train of observation —by what secret signs, looks, or gestures—by what instinc- tive freemasonry of love, this degree of intelligence came to subsist between Edith and her lover, we cannot attempt to trace ; for we are old, and such slight vestiges of affection, quickly discovered by younger eyes, defy the power of ours. Enough, that such affection did subsist between parties who had never even spoken to one another, though, on the side of Edith, it was checked by a deep sense of the difficulties and dangers which must necessarily attend the farther progress of their attachment, and upon that of the knight by a thousand doubts and fears, lest he had over-estimated the slight tokens of the lady's notice, varied, as they necessarily were, by long intervals of apparent coldness, during which, either the fear of exciting the observation of others, and thus drawing danger upon her lover, or that of sinking in his esteem by seeming too willing to be won, made her behave with indifference, as if unobservant of his presence.

This narrative, tedious perhaps, but which the story renders necessary, may serve to explain the state of intelligence, if it deserves so strong a name, betwixt the lovers, when Edith's unexpected appearance in the chapel produced so powerful an effect on the feelings of her knight.

CHAPTER V

Their necromantic forms in vain
Haunt us on the tented plain;
We bid these spectre shapes avaunt,
Ashtaroth and Termagaunt.
—WARTON.

THE most profound silence, the deepest darkness, continued to brood for more than an hour over the chapel in which we left the Knight of the Leopard still kneeling, alternately expressing thanks to Heaven, and gratitude to his lady, for the boon which had been vouchsafed to him. His own safety, his own destiny, for which he was at all times little anxious, had not now the weight of a grain of dust in his reflections. He was in the neighbourhood of Lady Edith, he had received tokens of her grace, he was in a place hallowed by relics of the most awful sanctity. A Christian soldier, a devoted lover, could fear nothing, think of nothing, but his duty to Heaven, and his devoir to his lady.

At the lapse of the space of time which we have noticed, a shrill whistle, like that with which a falconer calls his hawk, was heard to ring sharply through the vaulted chapel. It was a sound ill suited to the place, and reminded Sir Kenneth how necessary it was he should be upon his guard. He started from his knee, and laid his hand upon his poniard. A creaking sound, as of a screw or pulleys, succeeded, and a light streaming upwards, as from an opening in the floor, showed that a trap-door had been raised or depressed. In less than a minute, a long skinny arm, partly naked, partly clothed in a sleeve of red samite, arose out of the aperture, holding a lamp as high as it could stretch upwards, and the figure to which the arm belonged,

SIR KENNETH AND THE DWARFS IN THE CHAPEL

ETCHING BY CRUIKSHANK

ascended step by step to the level of the chapel floor. The form and face of the being who thus presented himself were those of a frightful dwarf, with a large head, a cap fantastically adorned with three peacock-feathers, a dress of red samite, the richness of which rendered his ugliness more conspicuous, distinguished by gold bracelets and armlets, and a white silk sash, in which he wore a gold-hilted dagger. This singular figure had in his left hand a kind of broom. So soon as he had stepped from the aperture through which he arose, he stood still, and, as if to show himself more distinctly, moved the lamp which he held slowly over his face and person, successively illuminating his wild and fantastic features, and his misshapen, but nervous limbs. Though disproportioned in person, the dwarf was not so distorted as to argue any want of strength or activity. While Sir Kenneth gazed on this disagreeable object, the popular creed occurred to his remembrance, concerning gnomes, or earthly spirits, which make their abode in the caverns of the earth; and so much did this figure correspond with ideas he had formed of their appearance, that he looked on it with disgust, mingled not indeed with fear, but that sort of awe which the presence of a supernatural creature may infuse into the most steady bosom.

The dwarf again whistled, and summoned from beneath a companion. This second figure ascended in the same manner as the first; but it was a female arm, in this second instance, which upheld the lamp from the subterranean vault out of which these presentments arose, and it was a female form, much resembling the first in shape and proportions, which slowly emerged from the floor. Her dress was also of red samite, fantastically cut and flounced, as if she had been dressed for some exhibition of mimes or jugglers; and with the same minuteness which her predecessor had exhibited, she passed the lamp over her face and person, which seemed to rival the male in ugliness. But with all this most unfavourable exterior, there was one trait in the features of both which argued alertness and intelligence in the most uncommon degree. This arose from the brilliancy of their eyes, which, deep set beneath black and shaggy brows, gleamed with a lustre which, like that in the eye of the toad, seemed to make some amends for the extreme ugliness of countenance and person.

Sir Kenneth remained as if spell-bound, while this unlovely pair, moving round the chapel close to each other, appeared to perform the duty of sweeping it, like menials; but, as they used only one hand, the floor was not much benefited by the exercise, which they plied with such oddity of gestures and manner, as befitted their bizarre and fantastic appearance. When they approached near to the knight, in the course of

D

their occupation, they ceased to use their brooms, and placing themselves side by side, directly opposite to Sir Kenneth, they again slowly shifted the lights which they held, so as to allow him distinctly to survey features which were not rendered more agreeable by being brought nearer, and to observe the extreme quickness and keenness with which their black and glittering eyes flashed back the light of the lamps. They then turned the gleam of both lights upon the knight, and having accurately surveyed him, turned their faces to each other, and set up a loud yelling laugh, which resounded in his ears. The sound was so ghastly, that Sir Kenneth started at hearing it, and hastily demanded, in the name of God, who they were who profaned that holy place with such antic gestures and elritch exclamations.

"I am the dwarf Nectabanus," said the abortion-seeming male, in a voice corresponding to his figure, and resembling that of the night-crow more than any sound which is heard by daylight.

"And I am Guenevra, his lady and his love," replied the female, in tones which, being shriller, were yet wilder than those of her companion.

"Wherefore are you here?" again demanded the knight, scarcely yet assured that it was human beings which he saw before him.

"I am," replied the male dwarf, with much assumed gravity and dignity, "the twelfth Imaum—I am Mahommed Mohadi, the guide and the conductor of the faithful. An hundred horses stand ready saddled for me and my train at the Holy City, and as many at the City of Refuge. I am he who shall bear witness, and this is one of my houris."

"Thou liest!" answered the female, interrupting her companion, in tones yet shriller than his own; "I am none of thy houris, and thou art no such infidel trash as the Mahommed of whom thou speakest. May my curse rest upon his coffin!—I tell thee, thou ass of Issachar, thou art King Arthur of Britain, whom the fairies stole away from the field of Avalon; and I am Dame Guenevra, famed for her beauty."

"But in truth, noble sir," said the male, "we are distressed princes, dwelling under the wing of King Guy of Jerusalem, until he was driven out from his own nest by the foul infidels—Heaven's bolts consume them!"

"Hush," said a voice from the side upon which the knight had entered—"Hush, fools, and begone; your ministry is ended."

The dwarfs had no sooner heard the command, than gibbering in discordant whispers to each other, they blew out their lights at once, and left the knight in utter darkness, which, when the pattering of their retiring feet had died away, was soon accompanied by its fittest companion, total silence.

The knight felt the departure of these unfortunate creatures a relief. He could not, from their language, manners, and appearance, doubt that they belonged to the degraded class of beings, whom deformity of person, and weakness of intellect, recommended to the painful situation of appendages to great families, where their personal appearance and imbecility were food for merriment to the household. Superior in no respect to the ideas and manners of his time, the Scottish knight might, at another period, have been much amused by the mummery of these poor effigies of humanity; but now, their appearance, gesticulations, and language, broke the train of deep and solemn feeling with which he was impressed, and he rejoiced in the disappearance of the unhappy objects.

A few minutes after they had retired, the door at which he had entered opened slowly, and, remaining ajar, discovered a faint light arising from a lantern placed upon the threshold. Its doubtful and wavering gleam showed a dark form reclined beside the entrance, but without its precincts, which, on approaching it more nearly, he recognised to be the hermit, couching in the same humble posture in which he had at first laid himself down, and which doubtless he had retained during the whole time of his guest's continuing in the chapel.

"All is over," said the hermit, as he heard the knight approaching—"and the most wretched of earthly sinners, with him, who should think himself most honoured and most happy among the race of humanity, must retire from this place. Take the light, and guide me down the descent, for I may not uncover my eyes until I am far from this hallowed spot."

The Scottish knight obeyed in silence, for a solemn and yet ecstatic sense of what he had seen had silenced even the eager workings of curiosity. He led the way, with considerable accuracy, through the various secret passages and stairs by which they had ascended, until at length they found themselves in the outward cell of the hermit's cavern.

"The condemned criminal is restored to his dungeon, reprieved from one miserable day to another, until his awful judge shall at length appoint the well-deserved sentence to be carried into execution."

As the hermit spoke these words, he laid aside the veil with which his eyes had been bound, and looked at it with a suppressed and hollow sigh. No sooner had he restored it to the crypt from which he had caused the Scot to bring it, than he said hastily and sternly to his companion—"Begone, begone, —to rest, to rest. You may sleep—you can sleep—I neither can nor may."

Respecting the profound agitation with which this was spoken, the knight retired into the inner cell; but casting back his eye as he left the exterior grotto, he beheld the anchorite stripping his shoulders with frantic haste of their shaggy mantle, and ere he could shut the frail door which separated the two compartments of the cavern, he heard the clang of the scourge, and the groans of the penitent under his self-inflicted penance. A cold shudder came over the knight as he reflected what could be the foulness of the sin, what the depth of the remorse, which, apparently, such severe penance could neither cleanse nor assuage. He told his beads devoutly, and flung himself on his rude couch, after a glance at the still sleeping Moslem, and, wearied by the various scenes of the day and the night, soon slept as sound as infancy. Upon his awaking in the morning, he held certain conferences with the hermit upon matters of importance, and the result of their intercourse induced him to remain for two days longer in the grotto. He was regular, as became a pilgrim, in his devotional exercises, but was not again admitted to the chapel in which he had seen such wonders.

CHAPTER VI

Now change the scene—and let the trumpets sound,
For we must rouse the lion from his lair.
—OLD PLAY.

THE scene must change, as our programme has announced, from the mountain wilderness of Jordan to the camp of King Richard cf England, then stationed betwixt Jean d'Acre and Ascalon; and containing that army with which he of the Lion Heart had promised himself a triumphant march to Jerusalem, and in which he would probably have succeeded, if not hindered by the jealousies of the Christian princes engaged in the same enterprise, and the offence taken by them at the uncurbed haughtiness of the English monarch, and Richard's unveiled contempt for his brother sovereigns, who, his equals in rank, were yet far his inferiors in courage, hardihood, and military talents. Such discords, and particularly those betwixt Richard and Philip of France, created disputes and obstacles which impeded every active measure proposed by the heroic though impetuous Richard, while the ranks of the Crusaders were daily thinned, not only by the desertion of individuals, but of entire bands, headed by their respective feudal leaders, who withdrew from a contest in which they had ceased to hope for success.

The effects of the climate became, as usual, fatal to soldiers from the north, and the more so that the dissolute licence of the Crusaders, forming a singular contrast to the principles and purpose of their taking up arms, rendered them more easy victims to the insalubrious influence of burning heat and chilling dews. To these discouraging causes of loss was to be added the sword of the enemy. Saladin, than whom no greater name is recorded in Eastern history, had learnt, to his fatal experience, that his light-armed followers were little able to meet in close encounter with the iron-clad Franks, and had been taught, at the same time, to apprehend and dread the adventurous character of his antagonist Richard. But if his armies were more than once routed with great slaughter, his numbers gave the Saracen the advantage in those lighter skirmishes, of which many were inevitable.

As the army of his assailants decreased, the enterprises of the Sultan became more numerous and more bold in this species of petty warfare. The camp of the Crusaders was surrounded, and almost besieged, by clouds of light cavalry, resembling swarms of wasps, easily crushed when they are once grasped, but furnished with wings to elude superior strength, and stings to inflict harm and mischief. There was perpetual warfare of posts and foragers, in which many valuable lives were lost, without any corresponding object being gained ; convoys were intercepted, and communications were cut off. The Crusaders had to purchase the means of sustaining life, by life itself; and water, like that of the well of Bethlehem, longed for by King David, one of its ancient monarchs, was then, as before, only obtained by the expenditure of blood.

These evils were, in a great measure, counterbalanced by the stern resolution and restless activity of King Richard, who, with some of his best knights, was ever on horseback, ready to repair to any point where danger occurred, and often, not only bringing unexpected succour to the Christians, but discomfiting the infidels when they seemed most secure of victory. But even the iron frame of Cœur de Lion could not support, without injury, the alternations of the unwholesome climate, joined to ceaseless exertions of body and mind. He became afflicted with one of those slow and wasting fevers peculiar to Asia, and in despite of his great strength, and still greater courage, grew first unfit to mount on horseback, and then unable to attend the councils of war, which were, from time to time, held by the Crusaders. It was difficult to say whether this state of personal inactivity was rendered more galling or more endurable to the English monarch, by the resolution of the council to engage in a truce of thirty days with the Sultan Saladin ; for, on the one hand, if he was incensed at the delay which this interposed to the progress of the great enterprise, he was, on the other, somewhat consoled by knowing that others were not acquiring laurels, while he remained inactive upon a sick-bed.

That, however, which Cœur de Lion could least excuse, was the general inactivity which prevailed in the camp of the Crusaders, so soon as his illness assumed a serious aspect; and the reports which he extracted from his unwilling attendants gave him to understand, that the hopes of the host had abated in proportion to his illness, and that the interval of truce was employed, not in recruiting their numbers, reanimating their courage, fostering their spirit of conquest, and preparing for a speedy and determined advance upon the Holy City, which was the object of their expedition, but in securing the camp occupied by their diminished followers, with trenches, palisades, and other fortifications, as if preparing rather to repel an attack from a powerful enemy so soon as hostilities should recommence, than to assume the proud character of conquerors and assailants.

The English king chafed under these reports, like the imprisoned lion viewing his prey from the iron barriers of his cage. Naturally rash and impetuous, the irritability of his temper preyed on itself. He was dreaded by his attendants, and even the medical assistants feared to assume the necessary authority, which a physician, to do justice to his patient, must needs exercise over him. One faithful baron, who, perhaps, from the congenial nature of his disposition, was devoutly attached to the King's person, dared alone to come between the dragon and his wrath, and quietly, but firmly, maintained a control which no other dared assume over the dangerous invalid, and which Thomas de Multon only exercised, because he esteemed his sovereign's life and honour more than he did the degree of favour which he might lose, or even the risk which he might incur, in nursing a patient so intractable, and whose displeasure was so perilous.

Sir Thomas was the Lord of Gilsland, in Cumberland, and in an age when surnames and titles were not distinctly attached, as now, to the individuals who bore them, he was called by the Normans the Lord de Vaux, and in English, by the Saxons, who clung to their native language, and were proud of the share of Saxon blood in this renowned warrior's veins, he was termed Thomas, or more familiarly, Thom of the Gills, or Narrow Valleys, from which his extensive domains derived their well-known appellation.

This chief had been exercised in almost all the wars, whether waged betwixt England and Scotland, or amongst the various domestic factions which then tore the former country asunder, and in all had been distinguished, as well from his military conduct as his personal prowess. He was, in other respects, a rude soldier, blunt and careless in his bearing, and taciturn, nay, almost sullen in his habits of society, and seeming, at least, to disclaim all knowledge of policy and of courtly art. There were men, however, who pretended to look deeply into character, who asserted that the Lord de Vaux was not less shrewd and aspiring, than he was blunt and bold, and who thought that, while he assimilated himself to the king's own character of blunt hardihood, it was in some degree at least, with an eye to establish his favour, and to gratify his own hopes of deep-laid ambition. But no one cared to thwart his schemes, if such he had, by rivalling him in the dangerous occupation of daily attendance on the sick-bed of a patient, whose disease was pronounced infectious, and more especially when it was remembered that the patient was Cœur de Lion, suffering under all the furious impatience of a soldier withheld from battle, and a sovereign sequestered from authority; and the common soldiers, at least in the English army, were generally of opinion that De Vaux attended on the King like comrade upon comrade, in the honest and disinterested frankness of military friendship, contracted between the partakers of daily dangers.

It was on the decline of a Syrian day that Richard lay on his couch of sickness, loathing it as much in his mind as his illness made it irksome to his body. His bright blue eye, which at all times shone with uncommon keenness and splendour, had its vivacity augmented by fever and mental impatience, and glanced from among his curled and unshorn locks of yellow hair, as fitfully and as vividly as the last gleams of the sun shoot through the clouds of an approaching thunderstorm, which still, however, are gilded by its beams. His manly features showed the progress of wasting illness, and his beard, neglected and untrimmed, had overgrown both lips and chin. Casting himself from side to side, now clutching towards him the coverings, which at the next moment he flung as impatiently from him, his tossed couch and impatient gestures showed at once the energy and the reckless impatience of a disposition, whose natural sphere was that of the most active exertion.

Beside his couch stood Thomas de Vaux, in face, attitude, and manner, the strongest possible contrast to the suffering monarch. His stature approached the gigantic, and his hair in thickness might have resembled that of Samson, though only after the Israelitish champion's locks had passed under the shears of the Philistines, for those of De Vaux were cut short, that they might be enclosed under his helmet. The light of his broad, large hazel eye, resembled that of the autumn morn, and it was only perturbed for a moment, when from time to time it was attracted by Richard's vehement marks of agitation and restlessness. His features, though massive like his person, might have been handsome before they were defaced with scars ; his upper lip, after the fashion of the Normans, was covered with thick mustaches, which grew so long and luxuriantly as to mingle with his hair, and, like his hair, were dark brown, slightly brindled with grey. His frame seemed of that kind which most readily defies both toil and climate, for he was thin flanked, broad chested, long armed, deep breathed, and strong limbed. He had not laid aside his buff-coat, which displayed ·the cross-cut on the shoulder, for more than three nights, enjoying but such momentary repose as the warder of a sick monarch's couch might by snatches indulge. This Baron rarely changed his posture, except to administer to Richard the medicine or refreshments, which none of his less favoured attendants could persuade the impatient monarch to take ; and there was something affecting in the kindly, yet awkward manner in which he discharged offices so strangely contrasted with his blunt and soldierly habits and manners.

The pavilion in which these personages were, had, as became the time, as well as the personal character of Richard, more of a warlike than a sumptuous or royal character. Weapons offensive and defensive, several of them of strange and newly-invented construction, were scattered about the tented apartment, or disposed upon the pillars which supported it. Skins of animals slain in the chase were stretched on the ground, or extended along the sides of the pavilion, and upon a heap of these silvan spoils, lay three *alans,* as they were then called (wolf-greyhounds, that is), of the largest size, and as white as snow. Their faces, marked with many a scar from clutch and fang, showed their share in collecting the trophies upon which they reposed, and their eyes, fixed from time to time with an expressive stretch and yawn upon the bed of Richard, evinced how much they marvelled at and regretted the unwonted inactivity which they were compelled to share. These were but the accompaniments of the soldier and huntsman ; but, on a small table close by the bed, was placed a shield of wrought steel, of triangular form, bearing the three lions passant, first assumed by the chivalrous monarch, and before it the golden circlet, resembling much a ducal coronet, only that it was higher in front than behind, which, with the purple velvet and embroidered tiara that lined it, formed then the emblem of England's sovereignty. Beside it, as if prompt for defending the regal symbol, lay a mighty curtal axe, which would have wearied the arm of any other than Cœur de Lion.

In an outer partition of the pavilion waited two or three officers of the royal household, depressed, anxious for their master's health, and not less so for their own safety, in case of his decease. Their gloomy apprehensions spread themselves to the warders without, who paced about in downcast and silent contemplation, or, resting on their halberds, stood motionless on their post, rather like armed trophies than living warriors.

"So thou hast no better news to bring me from without, Sir Thomas?" said the King, after a long and perturbed silence, spent in the feverish agitation which we have endeavoured to describe. "All our knights turned women, and our ladies become devotees, and neither a spark of valour nor of gallantry to enlighten a camp which contains the choicest of Europe's chivalry—Ha!"

"The truce, my lord," said De Vaux, with the same patience with which he had twenty times repeated the explanation— "the truce prevents us bearing ourselves as men of action; and, for the ladies, I am no great reveller, as is well known to your Majesty, and seldom exchange steel and buff for velvet and gold —but thus far I know, that our choicest beauties are waiting upon the Queen's Majesty and the Princess, to a pilgrimage to the convent of Engaddi, to accomplish their vows for your Highness's deliverance from this trouble."

"And is it thus," said Richard, with the impatience of indisposition, "that royal matrons and maidens should risk themselves, where the dogs who defile the land have as little truth to man, as they have faith towards God?"

"Nay, my lord," said De Vaux, "they have Saladin's word for their safety."

"True, true!" replied Richard, "and I did the heathen Soldan injustice—I owe him reparation for it.—Would God I were but fit to offer it him upon my body between the two hosts—Christendom and Heathenesse both looking on!"

As Richard spoke, he thrust his right arm out of bed, naked to the shoulder, and painfully raising himself in his couch, shook his clenched hand, as if it grasped sword or battle-axe, and was then brandished over the jewelled turban of the Soldan. It was not without a gentle degree of violence, which the king would scarce have endured from another, that De Vaux, in his character of sick-nurse, compelled his royal master to replace himself in the couch, and covered his sinewy arm, neck, and shoulders, with the care which a mother bestows upon an impatient child.

"Thou art a rough nurse, though a willing one, De Vaux," said the King, laughing with a bitter expression, while he submitted to the strength which he was unable to resist; "methinks a coif would become thy lowering features as well as a child's biggin would beseem mine. We should be a babe and nurse to frighten girls with."

"We have frightened men in our time, my liege," said De Vaux; "and, I trust, may live to frighten them again. What is a fever-fit, that we should not endure it patiently, in order to get rid of it easily?"

"Fever-fit!" exclaimed Richard impetuously; "thou mayest think, and justly, that it is a fever-fit with me; but what is it with all the other Christian princes—with Philip of France—with that dull Austrian—with him of Montserrat—with the Hospitallers—with the Templars—what is it with all them?—I will tell thee—it is a cold palsy—a dead lethargy—a disease that deprives them of speech and action—a canker that has eaten into the heart of all that is noble, and chivalrous, and virtuous among them—that has made them false to the noblest vow ever knights were sworn to—has made them indifferent to their fame, and forgetful of their God!"

"For the love of Heaven, my liege," said De Vaux, "take it less violently—you will be heard without doors, where such speeches are but too current already among the common soldiery, and engender discord and contention in the Christian host. Bethink you that your illness mars the mainspring of their enterprise: a mangonel will work without screw and lever better than the Christian host without King Richard."

"Thou flatterest me, De Vaux," said Richard; and, not insensible to the power of praise, he reclined his head on the pillow, with a more deliberate attempt to repose than he had yet exhibited. But Thomas de Vaux was no courtier; the phrase which had offered had risen spontaneously to his lips; and he knew not how to pursue the pleasing theme, so as to soothe and prolong the vein which he had excited. He was silent, therefore, until, relapsing into his moody contemplations, the King demanded of him sharply, "Despardieux! This is smoothly said to soothe a sick man; but does a league of monarchs, an assemblage of nobles, a convocation of all the chivalry of Europe, droop with the sickness of one man, though he chances to be King of England? Why should Richard's illness, or Richard's death, check the march of thirty thousand men, as brave as himself? When the master stag is struck down, the herd do not disperse upon his fall—when the falcon strikes the leading crane, another takes the guidance of the phalanx.—Why do not the powers assemble and choose some one, to whom they may entrust the guidance of the host?"

"Forsooth, and if it please your Majesty," said De Vaux, "I hear consultations have been held among the Royal leaders for some such purpose."

"Ha!" exclaimed Richard, his jealousy awakened, giving his mental irritation another direction—"Am I forgot by my allies ere I have taken the last sacrament?—do they hold me dead already?—But no, no—they are right—And whom do they select as leader of the Christian host?"

"Rank and dignity," said De Vaux, "point to the King of France."

"Oh ay," answered the English monarch, "Philip of France and Navarre—Dennis Mountjoie—his Most Christian Majesty! mouth-filling words these! There is but one risk—that he might mistake the words *En arrière* for *En avant*, and lead us back to Paris instead of marching to Jerusalem. His politic head has learned by this time, that there is more to be gotten by oppressing his feudatories, and pillaging his allies, than fighting with the Turks for the Holy Sepulchre."

"They might choose the Archduke of Austria," said De Vaux.

"What! because he is big and burly like thyself, Thomas— nearly as thick-headed, but without thy indifference to danger, and carelessness of offence? I tell thee that Austria has in all that mass of flesh no bolder animation than is afforded by the peevishness of a wasp, and the courage of a wren. Out upon him!—*he* a leader of chivalry to deeds of glory!—Give him a flagon of Rhenish to drink with his besmirched baaren-hauters and lanceknechts."

"There is the Grand Master of the Templars," continued the baron, not sorry to keep his master's attention engaged on other topics than his own illness, though at the expense of the characters of prince and potentate—"There is the Grand Master of the Templars," he continued, "undaunted, skilful, brave in battle, and sage in council, having no separate kingdoms of his own to divert his exertions from the recovery of the Holy Land —what thinks your Majesty of the Master as a general leader of the Christian host?"

"Ha, Beau-Seant!" answered the King. "Oh, no exception can be taken to Brother Giles Amaury—he understands the ordering of a battle, and the fighting in front when it begins. But, Sir Thomas, were it fair to take the Holy Land from the heathen Saladin, so full of all the virtues which may distinguish unchristened man, and give it to Giles Amaury, a worse Pagan than himself—an idolater—a devil-worshipper—a necromancer —who practises crimes the most dark and unnatural, in the vaults and secret places of abomination and darkness?"

"The Grand Master of the Hospitallers of St. John of Jerusalem is not tainted by fame, either with heresy or magic," said Thomas de Vaux.

"But is he not a sordid miser?" said Richard hastily; "has he not been suspected—ay, more than suspected—of selling to the infidels those advantages which they would never have won by fair force? Tush, man, better give the army to be made merchandise of by Venetian skippers and Lombardy pedlars, than trust it to the Grand Master of St. John."

"Well, then, I will venture but another guess, said the

Baron de Vaux—"What say you to the gallant Marquis of
Montserrat, so wise, so elegant, such a good man-at-arms?"

"Wise? cunning, you would say," replied Richard; "elegant
in a lady's chamber, if you will.   Oh ay, Conrade of Montserrat,
—who knows not the popinjay?   Politic and versatile, he will
change you his purposes as often as the trimmings of his doublet,
and you shall never be able to guess the hue of his inmost
vestments from their outward colours.   A man-at-arms? ay, a
fine figure on horseback, and can bear him well in the tilt-yard,
and at the barriers, when swords are blunted at point and edge,
and spears are tipped with trenchers of wood, instead of steel-
pikes.   Wert thou not with me, when I said to that same gay
Marquis, 'Here we be, three good Christians, and on yonder
plain there pricks a band of some threescore Saracens, what say
you to charge them briskly?   There are but twenty unbelieving
miscreants to each true knight.'"

"I recollect the Marquis replied," said De Vaux, "that his
limbs were of flesh, not of iron, and that he would rather bear
the heart of a man than of a beast, though that beast were the
lion.   But I see how it is—we shall end where we began, without hope of praying at the Sepulchre, until Heaven shall restore
King Richard to health."

At this grave remark, Richard burst out into a hearty fit of
laughter, the first which he had for some time indulged in.
"Why, what a thing is conscience," he said, "that through its
means even such a thick-witted northern lord as thou canst
bring thy sovereign to confess his folly!   It is true, that, did
they not propose themselves as fit to hold my leading-staff,
little should I care for plucking the silken trappings off the
puppets thou hast shown me in succession—What concerns it
me what fine tinsel robes they swagger in, unless when they
are named as rivals in the glorious enterprise to which I have
vowed myself?   Yes, De Vaux, I confess my weakness, and
the wilfulness of my ambition.   The Christian camp contains,
doubtless, many a better knight than Richard of England, and
it would be wise and worthy to assign to the best of them the
leading of the host—but," continued the warlike monarch,
raising himself in his bed, and shaking the cover from his
head, while his eyes sparkled as they were wont to do on the
eve of battle, "were such a knight to plant the banner of the
Cross on the Temple of Jerusalem, while I was unable to bear
my share in the noble task, he should, so soon as I was fit to lay
lance in rest, undergo my challenge to mortal combat, for having
diminished my fame, and pressed in before to the object of my
enterprise.—But hark, what trumpets are those at a distance?"

"Those of King Philip, as I guess, my liege," said the stout
Englishman.

"Thou art dull of ear, Thomas," said the King, endeavouring to start up—"hearest thou not that clash and clang? By Heaven, the Turks are in the camp—I hear their lelies."*

He again endeavoured to get out of bed, and De Vaux was obliged to exercise his own great strength, and also to summon the assistance of the chamberlains from the inner tent, to restrain him.

"Thou art a false traitor, De Vaux," said the incensed monarch, when, breathless and exhausted with struggling, he was compelled to submit to superior strength, and to repose in quiet on his couch. "I would I were—I would I were but strong enough to dash thy brains out with my battle-axe!"

"I would you had the strength, my liege," said De Vaux, "and would even take the risk of its being so employed. The odds would be great in favour of Christendom, were Thomas Multon dead, and Cœur de Lion himself again."

"Mine honest faithful servant," said Richard, extending his hand, which the baron reverentially saluted, "forgive thy master's impatience of mood. It is this burning fever which chides thee, and not thy kind master, Richard of England. But go, I prithee, and bring me word what strangers are in the camp, for these sounds are not of Christendom."

De Vaux left the pavilion on the errand assigned, and in his absence, which he had resolved should be brief, he charged the chamberlains, pages, and attendants to redouble their attention on their sovereign, with threats of holding them to responsibility, which rather added to than diminished their timid anxiety in the discharge of their duty; for next perhaps to the ire of the monarch himself, they dreaded that of the stern and inexorable Lord of Gilsland.

CHAPTER VII

There never was a time on the March parts yet,
    When Scottish with English met,
But it was marvel if the red blood ran not
    As the rain does in the street.
                    —BATTLE OF OTTERBOURN.

A CONSIDERABLE band of Scottish warriors had joined the Crusaders, and had naturally placed themselves under the command of the English monarch, being, like his native troops, most of them of Saxon and Norman descent, speaking the same languages, possessed, some of them, of English as well as

* The war-cries of the Moslemah.

Scottish demesnes, and allied, in some cases, by blood and intermarriage. The period also preceded that when the grasping ambition of Edward I. gave a deadly and envenomed character to the wars betwixt the two nations; the English fighting for the subjugation of Scotland, and the Scottish, with all the stern determination and obstinacy which has ever characterised their nation, for the defence of their independence, by the most violent means, under the most disadvantageous circumstances, and at the most extreme hazard. As yet, wars betwixt the two nations, though fierce and frequent, had been conducted on principles of fair hostility, and admitted of those softening shades by which courtesy, and the respect for open and generous foemen, qualify and mitigate the horrors of war. In time of peace, therefore, and especially when both, as at present, were engaged in war, waged in behalf of a common cause, and rendered dear to them by their ideas of religion, the adventurers of both countries frequently fought side by side, their national emulation serving only to stimulate them to excel each other in their efforts against the common enemy.

The frank and martial character of Richard, who made no distinction betwixt his own subjects and those of William of Scotland, excepting as they bore themselves in the field of battle, tended much to conciliate the troops of both nations. But upon his illness, and the disadvantageous circumstances in which the Crusaders were placed, the national disunion between the various bands united in the Crusade began to display itself, just as old wounds break out afresh in the human body, when under the influence of disease or debility.

The Scottish and English, equally jealous and high-spirited, and apt to take offence,—the former the more so, because the poorer and the weaker nation,—began to fill up, by internal dissension, the period when the truce forbade them to wreak their united vengeance on the Saracens. Like the contending Roman chiefs of old, the Scottish would admit no superiority, and their southern neighbours would brook no equality. There were charges and recriminations, and both the common soldiery, and their leaders and commanders, who had been good comrades in time of victory, lowered on each other in the period of adversity, as if their union had not been then more essential than ever, not only to the success of their common cause, but to their joint safety. The same disunion had began to show itself betwixt the French and English, the Italians and the Germans, and even between the Danes and Swedes; but it is only that which divided the two nations whom one island bred, and who seemed more animated against each other for the very reason, that our narrative is principally concerned with.

Of all the English nobles who had followed their King to

Palestine, De Vaux was most prejudiced against the Scottish; they were his near neighbours, with whom he had been engaged during his whole life in private or public warfare, and on whom he had inflicted many calamities, while he had sustained at their hands not a few. His love and devotion to the King was like the vivid affection of the old English mastiff to his master, leaving him churlish and inaccessible to all others, even towards those to whom he was indifferent, and rough and dangerous to any against whom he entertained a prejudice. De Vaux had never observed, without jealousy and displeasure, his King exhibit any mark of courtesy or favour to the wicked, deceitful, and ferocious race born on the other side of a river, or an imaginary line drawn through waste and wilderness, and he even doubted the success of a Crusade in which they were suffered to bear arms, holding them in his secret soul little better than the Saracens whom he came to combat. It may be added, that, as being himself a blunt and downright Englishman, unaccustomed to conceal the slightest movement either of love or of dislike, he accounted the fair-spoken courtesy, which the Scots had learned, either from imitation of their frequent allies, the French, or which might have arisen from their own proud and reserved character, as a false and astucious mark of the most dangerous designs against their neighbours, over whom he believed, with genuine English confidence, they could, by fair manhood, never obtain any advantage.

Yet, though De Vaux entertained these sentiments concerning his northern neighbours, and extended them, with little mitigation, even to such as had assumed the Cross, his respect for the King, and a sense of the duty imposed by his vow as a Crusader, prevented him from displaying them otherwise than by regularly shunning all intercourse with his Scottish brethren-at-arms, as far as possible,—by observing a sullen taciturnity, when compelled to meet them occasionally,—and by looking scornfully upon them when they encountered on the march and in camp. The Scottish barons and knights were not men to bear his scorn unobserved or unreplied to; and it came to that pass, that he was regarded as the determined and active enemy of a nation whom, after all, he only disliked, and in some sort despised. Nay, it was remarked by close observers, that if he had not towards them the charity of Scripture, which suffereth long, and judges kindly, he was by no means deficient in the subordinate and limited virtue, which alleviates and relieves the wants of others. The wealth of Thomas of Gilsland procured supplies of provisions and medicines, and some of these usually flowed by secret channels into the quarters of the Scottish; his surly benevolence proceeding on the principle, that, next to a man's friend, his foe was of most importance to him, passing over all the intermediate relations, as too indifferent to merit even a thought. This explanation is necessary, in order that the reader may fully understand what we are now to detail.

Thomas de Vaux had not made many steps beyond the entrance of the royal pavilion, when he was aware of what the far more acute ear of the English monarch, no mean proficient in the art of minstrelsy, had instantly discovered, that the musical strains, namely, which had reached their ears, were produced by the pipes, shalms, and kettle-drums of the Saracens; and at the bottom of an avenue of tents, which formed a broad access to the pavilion of Richard, he could see a crowd of idle soldiers assembled around the spot from which the music was heard, almost in the centre of the camp; and he saw, with great surprise, mingled amid the helmets of various forms worn by the Crusaders of different nations, white turbans and long pikes, announcing the presence of armed Saracens, and the huge deformed heads of several camels or dromedaries, overlooking the multitude by aid of their long disproportioned necks.

Wondering and displeased at a sight so unexpected and singular,—for it was customary to leave all flags of truce and other communications from the enemy at an appointed place without the barriers, — the baron looked eagerly round for some one of whom he might inquire the cause of this alarming novelty.

The first person whom he met advancing to him, he set down at once, by his grave and haughty step, as a Spaniard or a Scot; and presently after muttered to himself—"And a Scot it is—he of the Leopard.—I have seen him fight indifferently well, for one of his country."

Loath to ask even a passing question, he was about to pass Sir Kenneth, with that sullen and lowering port which seems to say, "I know thee, but I will hold no communication with thee;" but his purpose was defeated by the Northern Knight, who moved forward directly to him, and accosting him with formal courtesy, said, "My Lord de Vaux of Gilsland, I have in charge to speak with you."

"Ha!" returned the English baron, "with me? But say your pleasure, so it be shortly spoken—I am on the King's errand."

"Mine touches King Richard yet more nearly," answered Sir Kenneth; "I bring him, I trust, health."

The Lord of Gilsland measured the Scot with incredulous eyes, and replied, "Thou art no leech, I think, Sir Scot—I had as soon thought of your bringing the King of England wealth."

Sir Kenneth, though displeased with the manner of the

baron's reply, answered calmly, " Health to Richard is glory and wealth to Christendom.—But my time presses ; I pray you, may I see the King ? "

" Surely not, fair sir," said the baron, " until your errand be told more distinctly. The sick chambers of princes open not to all who inquire, like a northern hostelry."

" My lord," said Kenneth, " the cross which I wear in common with yourself, and the importance of what I have to tell, must, for the present, cause me to pass over a bearing, which else I were unapt to endure. In plain language, then, I bring with me a Moorish physician, who undertakes to work a cure on King Richard."

" A Moorish physician ! " said De Vaux ; " and who will warrant that he brings not poisons instead of remedies ? "

" His own life, my lord—his head, which he offers as a guarantee."

" I have known many a resolute ruffian," said De Vaux, " who valued his own life as little as it deserved, and would troop to the gallows as merrily as if the hangman were his partner in a dance."

" But thus it is, my lord," replied the Scot ; " Saladin, to whom none will deny the credit of a generous and valiant enemy, hath sent this leech hither with an honourable retinue and guard, befitting the high estimation in which El Hakim * is held by the Soldan, and with fruits and refreshments for the King's private chamber, and such message as may pass betwixt honourable enemies, praying him to be recovered of his fever, that he may be the fitter to receive a visit from the Soldan, with his naked scimitar in his hand, and an hundred thousand cavaliers at his back. Will it please you, who are of the King's secret council, to cause these camels to be discharged of their burdens, and some order taken as to the reception of the learned physician ? "

" Wonderful ! " said De Vaux, as speaking to himself.—" And who will vouch for the honour of Saladin, in a case when bad faith would rid him at once of his most powerful adversary ? "

" I myself," replied Sir Kenneth, " will be his guarantee, with honour, life, and fortune."

" Strange ! " again ejaculated De Vaux ; " the North vouches for the South—the Scot for the Turk !—May I crave of you, Sir Knight, how you became concerned in this affair ? "

" I have been absent on a pilgrimage, in the course of which," replied Sir Kenneth, " I had a message to discharge towards the holy hermit of Engaddi."

" May I not be entrusted with it, Sir Kenneth, and with the answer of the holy man ? "

* The physician.

E

"It may not be, my lord," answered the Scot.

"I am of the secret council of England," said the Englishman haughtily.

"To which land I know no allegiance," said Kenneth. "Though I have voluntarily followed in this war the personal fortunes of England's sovereign, I was despatched by the General Council of the kings, princes, and supreme leaders of the army of the Blessed Cross, and to them only I render my errand."

"Ha! say'st thou?" said the proud Baron de Vaux. "But know, messenger of the kings and princes as thou may'st be, no leech shall approach the sick bed of Richard of England, without the consent of him of Gilsland; and they will come on evil errand who dare to intrude themselves against it."

He was turning loftily away, when the Scot, placing himself closer, and more opposite to him, asked, in a calm voice, yet not without expressing his share of pride, whether the Lord of Gilsland esteemed him a gentleman and a good knight.

"All Scots are ennobled by their birthright," answered Thomas de Vaux, something ironically; but sensible of his own injustice, and perceiving that Kenneth's colour rose, he added, "For a good knight it were sin to doubt you, in one at least who has seen you well and bravely discharge your devoir."

"Well, then," said the Scottish knight, satisfied with the frankness of the last admission, "and let me swear to you, Thomas of Gilsland, that as I am true Scottish man, which I hold a privilege equal to my ancient gentry, and as sure as I am a belted knight, and come hither to acquire *los* * and fame in this mortal life, and forgiveness of my sins in that which is to come—so truly, and by the blessed Cross which I wear, do I protest unto you, that I desire but the safety of Richard Cœur de Lion, in recommending the ministry of this Moslem physician."

The Englishman was struck with the solemnity of the obtestation, and answered with more cordiality than he had yet exhibited, "Tell me, Sir Knight of the Leopard, granting (which I do not doubt) that thou art thyself satisfied in this matter, shall I do well, in a land where the art of poisoning is as general as that of cooking, to bring this unknown physician to practise with his drugs on a health so valuable to Chistendom?"

"My lord," replied the Scot, "thus only can I reply; that my squire, the only one of my retinue whom war and disease had left in attendance on me, has been of late suffering danger-

* *Los—laus*, praise, or renown.

ously under this same fever, which, in valiant King Richard, has disabled the principal limb of our holy enterprise. This leech, this El Hakim, hath ministered remedies to him not two hours since, and already he hath fallen into a refreshing sleep. That he *can* cure the disorder, which has proved so fatal, I nothing doubt; that he hath the purpose to do it, is, I think, warranted by his mission from the royal Soldan, who is true-hearted and loyal, so far as a blinded infidel may be called so ; and, for his eventual success, the certainty of reward in case of succeeding, and punishment in case of voluntary failure, may be a sufficient guarantee."

The Englishman listened with downcast looks, as one who doubted, yet was not unwilling to receive conviction. At length he looked up and said, " May I see your sick squire, fair sir ? "

The Scottish knight hesitated and coloured, yet answered at last, " Willingly, my Lord of Gilsland ; but you must remember, when you see my poor quarter, that the nobles and knights of Scotland feed not so high, sleep not so soft, and care not for the magnificence of lodgment, which is proper to their southern neighbours. I am poorly lodged, my Lord of Gilsland," he added, with a haughty emphasis on the word, while, with some unwillingness, he led the way to his temporary place of abode.

Whatever were the prejudices of De Vaux against the nation of his new acquaintance, and though we undertake not to deny that some of these were excited by its proverbial poverty, he had too much nobleness of disposition to enjoy the mortification of a brave individual, thus compelled to make known wants which his pride would gladly have concealed.

"Shame to the soldier of the Cross," he said, "who thinks of worldly splendour, or of luxurious accommodation, when pressing forward to the conquest of the Holy City. Fare as hard as we may, we shall yet be better than the host of martyrs and of saints, who, having trod these scenes before us, now hold golden lamps and evergreen palms."

This was the most metaphorical speech which Thomas of Gilsland was ever known to utter, the rather, perhaps (as will sometimes happen), that it did not entirely express his own sentiments, being somewhat a lover of good cheer and splendid accommodation. By this time they reached the place of the camp, where the Knight of the Leopard had assumed his abode.

Appearances here did indeed promise no breach of the laws of mortification, to which the Crusaders, according to the opinion expressed by him of Gilsland, ought to subject themselves. A space of ground large enough to accommodate perhaps thirty tents according to the Crusaders' rules of castramentation, was partly vacant—because, in ostentation, the knight had demanded ground to the extent of his original retinue—partly occupied by a few miserable huts, hastily constructed of boughs, and covered with palm-leaves. These habitations seemed entirely deserted, and several of them were ruinous. The central hut, which represented the pavilion of the leader, was distinguished by the swallow-tailed pennon, placed on the point of a spear; from which its long folds dropt motionless to the ground, as if sickening under the scorching rays of the Asiatic sun. But no pages or squires, not even a solitary warder, was placed by the emblem of feudal power and knightly degrees. If its reputation defended it not from insult, it had no other guard.

Sir Kenneth cast a melancholy look around him, but, suppressing his feelings, entered the hut, making a sign to the Baron of Gilsland to follow. He also cast around a glance of examination, which implied pity not altogether unmingled with contempt, to which, perhaps, it is as nearly akin as it is said to be to love. He then stooped his lofty crest, and entered a lowly hut, which his bulky form seemed almost entirely to fill.

The interior of the hut was chiefly occupied by two beds. One was empty, but composed of collected leaves, and spread with an antelope's hide. It seemed, from the articles of armour laid beside it, and from a crucifix of silver, carefully and reverentially disposed at the head, to be the couch of the knight himself. The other contained the invalid of whom Sir Kenneth had spoken, a strong-built and harsh-featured man, past, as his looks betokened, the middle age of life. His couch was trimmed more softly than his master's, and it was plain, that the more courtly garments of the latter, the loose robe, in which the knights showed themselves on pacific occasions, and the other little spare articles of dress and adornment, had been applied by Sir Kenneth to the accommodation of his sick domestic. In an outward part of the hut, which yet was within the range of the English baron's eye, a boy rudely attired with buskins of deer's hide, a blue cap or bonnet, and a doublet, whose original finery was much tarnished, sat on his knees by a chafing-dish filled with charcoal, cooking upon a plate of iron the cakes of barley-bread, which were then, and still are, a favourite food with the Scottish people. Part of an antelope was suspended against one of the main props of the hut, nor was it difficult to know how it had been procured; for a large stag greyhound, nobler in size and appearance than those even which guarded King Richard's sick-bed, lay eyeing the process of baking the cake. The sagacious animal, on their first entrance, uttered a stifled growl, which sounded from his deep chest like distant thunder. But he saw his master, and ac-

knowledged his presence by wagging his tail and couching his
head, abstaining from more tumultuous or noisy greeting, as if
his noble instinct had taught him the propriety of silence in a
sick man's chamber.

Beside the couch, sat on a cushion, also composed of skins,
the Moorish physician of whom Sir Kenneth had spoken, cross-
legged after the Eastern fashion. The imperfect light showed
little of him, save that the lower part of his face was covered
with a long black beard, which descended over his breast—that
he wore a high *tolpach*, a Tartar cap of the lamb's wool manu-
factured at Astracan, bearing the same dusky colour, and that
his ample caftan, or Turkish robe, was also of a dark hue.
Two piercing eyes, which gleamed with unusual lustre, were
the only lineaments of his visage that could be discerned
amid the darkness in which he was enveloped. The English
lord stood silent with a sort of reverential awe; for, notwithstanding the roughness of his general bearing, a scene of distress
and poverty, firmly endured without complaint or murmur,
would at any time have claimed more reverence from Thomas
de Vaux, than would all the splendid formalities of a royal
presence-chamber, unless that presence-chamber were King
Richard's own. Nothing was, for a time, heard, but the heavy
and regular breathings of the invalid, who seemed in profound
repose.

"He hath not slept for six nights before," said Sir Kenneth,
"as I am assured by the youth his attendant."

"Noble Scot," said Thomas de Vaux, grasping the Scottish
knight's hand, with a pressure which had more of cordiality
than he permitted his words to utter, "this gear must be
amended—Your esquire is but too evil fed and looked to."

In the latter part of this speech he naturally raised his
voice to its usual decided tone. The sick man was disturbed
in his slumbers.

"My master," he said, murmuring as in a dream, "noble
Sir Kenneth—taste not, to you as to me, the waters of the
Clyde cold and refreshing, after the brackish springs of
Palestine?"

"He dreams of his native land, and is happy in his slumbers," whispered Sir Kenneth to De Vaux; but had scarce
uttered the words, when the physician, arising from the place
which he had taken near the couch of the sick, and laying the
hand of the patient, whose pulse he had been carefully watching, quietly upon the couch, came to the two knights, and
taking them each by the arm, while he intimated to them to
remain silent, led them to the front of the hut.

"In the name of Issa Ben Mariam," he said, "whom we
honour as you, though not with the same blinded superstition,

disturb not the effect of the blessed medicine of which he hath partaken. To awaken him now is death or deprivation of reason; but return at the hour when the Muezzin calls from the minaret to evening prayer in the mosque, and, if left undisturbed until then, I promise you, this same Frankish soldier shall be able, without prejudice to his health, to hold some brief converse with you, on any matters on which either, and especially his master, may have to question him."

The knights retreated before the authoritative commands of the leech, who seemed fully to comprehend the importance of the Eastern proverb, that the sick chamber of the patient is the kingdom of the physician.

They paused, and remained standing together at the door of the hut, Sir Kenneth, with the air of one who expected his visitor to say farewell—and De Vaux, as if he had something on his mind which prevented him from doing so. The hound, however, had pressed out of the tent after them, and now thrust his long rough countenance into the hand of his master, as if modestly soliciting some mark of his kindness. He had no sooner received the notice which he desired, in the shape of a kind word and slight caress, than eager to acknowledge his gratitude and joy for his master's return, he flew off at full speed, galloping in full career, and with outstretched tail, here and there, about and around, crossways and endlong, through the decayed huts, and the esplanade we have described, but never transgressing those precincts which his sagacity knew were protected by his master's pennon. After a few gambols of this kind, the dog, coming close up to his master, laid at once aside his frolicsome mood, relapsed into his usual gravity and slowness of gesture and deportment, and looked as if he were ashamed that anything should have moved him to depart so far out of his sober self-control.

Both knights looked on with pleasure; for Sir Kenneth was justly proud of his noble hound, and the northern English baron was of course an admirer of the chase, and a judge of the animal's merits.

"A right able dog," he said; "I think, fair sir, King Richard hath not an *alan* which may match him, if he be as stanch as he is swift. But let me pray you—speaking in all honour and kindness—have you not heard the proclamation, that no one, under the rank of earl, shall keep hunting dogs within King Richard's camp, without the royal licence, which, I think, Sir Kenneth, hath not been issued to you?—I speak as Master of the Horse."

"And I answer as a free Scottish knight," said Kenneth sternly. "For the present I follow the banner of England, but I cannot remember that I have ever subjected myself to the forest-laws of that kingdom, nor have I such respect for them as would incline me to do so. When the trumpet sounds to arms, my foot is in the stirrup as soon as any—when it clangs for the charge, my lance has not yet been the last laid in the rest. But for my hours of liberty or of idleness, King Richard has no title to bar my recreation."

"Nevertheless," said De Vaux, "it is a folly to disobey the King's ordinance—so, with your good leave, I, as having authority in that matter, will send you a protection for my friend here."

"I thank you," said the Scot coldly; "but he knows my allotted quarters, and within these I can protect him myself.—And yet," he said, suddenly changing his manner, "this is but a cold return for a well-meant kindness. I thank you, my lord, most heartily. The King's equerries, or prickers, might find Roswal at disadvantage, and do him some injury, which I should not, perhaps, be slow in returning, and so ill might come of it. You have seen so much of my housekeeping, my lord," he added, with a smile, "that I need not shame to say that Roswal is our principal purveyor; and well I hope our Lion Richard will not be like the lion in the minstrel fable, that went a-hunting, and kept the whole booty to himself. I cannot think he would grudge a poor gentleman, who follows him faithfully, his hour of sport, and his morsel of game, more especially when other food is hard enough to come by."

"By my faith, you do the King no more than justice—and yet," said the baron, "there is something in these words, vert and venison, that turns the very brains of our Norman princes."

"We have heard of late," said the Scot, "by minstrels and pilgrims, that your outlawed yeomen have formed great bands in the shires of York and Nottingham, having at their head a most stout archer, called Robin Hood, with his lieutenant, Little John. Methinks it were better that Richard relaxed his forest-code in England, than endeavoured to enforce it in the Holy Land."

"Wild work, Sir Kenneth," replied De Vaux, shrugging his shoulders, as one who would avoid a perilous or unpleasing topic—"a mad world, sir.—I must now bid you adieu, having presently to return to the King's pavilion. At vespers, I will again, with your leave, visit your quarters, and speak with this same infidel physician. I would, in the meantime, were it no offence, willingly send you what would somewhat mend your cheer."

"I thank you, sir," said Sir Kenneth, "but it needs not; Roswal hath already stocked my larder for two weeks, since the sun of Palestine, if it brings diseases, serves also to dry venison."

The two warriors parted much better friends than they had met; but ere they separated, Thomas de Vaux informed himself at more length of the circumstances attending the mission of the Eastern physician, and received from the Scottish knight the credentials which he had brought to King Richard on the part of Saladin.

CHAPTER VIII

A wise physician, skill'd our wounds to heal,
Is more than armies to the common weal.
—Pope's Iliad.

"This is a strange tale, Sir Thomas," said the sick monarch, when he had heard the report of the trusty Baron of Gilsland; "art thou sure this Scottish man is a tall man and true?"

"I cannot say, my lord," replied the jealous Borderer; "I live a little too near the Scots to gather much truth among them, having found them ever fair and false. But this man's bearing is that of a true man, were he a devil as well as a Scot —that I must needs say for him in conscience."

"And for his carriage as a knight, how say'st thou, De Vaux?" demanded the King.

"It is your Majesty's business more than mine to note men's bearings; and I warrant you have noted the manner in which this man of the Leopard hath borne himself. He hath been well spoken of."

"And justly, Thomas," said the King. "We have ourselves witnessed him. It is indeed our purpose, in placing ourselves ever in the front of battle, to see how our liegemen and followers acquit themselves, and not from a desire to accumulate vainglory to ourselves, as some have supposed. We know the vanity of the praise of man, which is but a vapour, and buckle on our armour for other purposes than to win it."

De Vaux was alarmed when he heard the King make a declaration so inconsistent with his nature, and believed at first that nothing short of the approach of death could have brought him to speak in depreciating terms of military renown, which was the very breath of his nostrils. But recollecting he had met the royal confessor in the outer pavilion, he was shrewd enough to place this temporary self-abasement to the effect of the reverend man's lesson, and suffered the King to proceed without reply.

"Yes," continued Richard, "I have indeed marked the manner in which this knight does his devoir. My leading-staff

SIR KENNETH AND THE BARON OF GILSLAND

Painted and Engraved by F. W. Topham

were not worth a fool's bauble, had he escaped my notice—and he had ere now tasted of our bounty, but that I have also marked his overweening and audacious presumption."

"My liege," said the Baron of Gilsland, observing the King's countenance change, "I fear I have transgressed your pleasure in lending some countenance to his transgression."

"How, De Multon, thou?" said the King, contracting his brows, and speaking in a tone of angry surprise,—"Thou countenance his insolence?—It cannot be."

"Nay, your Majesty will pardon me to remind you, that I have by mine office right to grant liberty to men of gentle blood, to keep them a hound or two within the camp, just to cherish the noble art of venerie; and besides, it were a sin to have maimed or harmed a thing so noble as this gentleman's dog."

"Has he then a dog so handsome?" said the King.

"A most perfect creature of heaven," said the baron, who was an enthusiast in field-sports—"of the noblest Northern breed—deep in the chest, strong in the stern, black colour, and brindled on the breast and legs, not spotted with white, but just shaded into grey—strength to pull down a bull—swiftness to cote an antelope."

The King laughed at his enthusiasm. "Well, thou hast given him leave to keep the hound, so there is an end of it. Be not, however, liberal of your licences among those knights adventurers, who have no prince or leader to depend upon—they are ungovernable, and leave no game in Palestine.—But to this piece of learned heathenesse—say'st thou the Scot met him in the desert?"

"No, my liege, the Scot's tale runs thus:—He was despatched to the old hermit of Engaddi, of whom men talk so much———"

"'Sdeath and hell!" said Richard, starting up, "By whom despatched, and for what? Who dared send any one thither, when our Queen was in the Convent of Engaddi, upon her pilgrimage for our recovery?"

"The Council of the Crusade sent him, my lord," answered the Baron de Vaux; "for what purpose he declined to account to me. I think it is scarce known in the camp that your royal consort is on a pilgrimage—and even the princes may not have been aware, as the Queen has been sequestered from company since your love prohibited her attendance in case of infection."

"Well, it shall be looked into," said Richard.—"So this Scottish man, this envoy, met with a wandering physician at the grotto of Engaddi—ha?"

"Not so, my liege," replied De Vaux; "but he met, I think, near that place, with a Saracen Emir, with whom he had some mêlée in the way of proof of valour, and finding him worthy to bear brave men company, they went together, as errant knights are wont, to the grotto of Engaddi."

Here De Vaux stopped, for he was not one of those who can tell a long story in a sentence.

"And did they there meet the physician?" demanded the King impatiently.

"No, my liege," replied De Vaux; "but the Saracen, learning your Majesty's grievous illness, undertook that Saladin should send his own physician to you, and with many assurances of his eminent skill; and he came to the grotto accordingly, after the Scottish Knight had tarried a day for him and more. He is attended as if he were a prince, with drums and atabals, and servants on horse and foot, and brings with him letters of credence from Saladin."

"Have they been examined by Giacomo Loredani?"

"I showed them to the interpreter ere bringing them hither, and behold their contents in English."

Richard took a scroll, in which were inscribed these words: —"The blessing of Allah and his Prophet Mahommed ['Out upon the hound!' said Richard, spitting in contempt, by way of interjection]; Saladin, king of kings, Soldan of Egypt and of Syria, the light and refuge of the earth, to the great Melech Ric, Richard of England, greeting. Whereas, we have been informed that the hand of sickness hath been heavy upon thee, our royal brother, and that thou hast with thee only such Nazarene and Jewish mediciners, as work without the blessing of Allah and our holy Prophet ['Confusion on his head!' again muttered the English monarch], we have therefore sent, to tend and wait upon thee at this time, the physician to our own person, Adonbec el Hakim, before whose face the angel Azrael * spreads his wings and departs from the sick chamber; who knows the virtues of herbs and stones, the path of the sun, moon, and stars, and can save man from all that is not written on his forehead. And this we do, praying you heartily to honour and make use of his skill; not only that we may do service to thy worth and valour, which is the glory of all the nations of Frangistan, but that we may bring the controversy which is at present between us to an end, either by honourable agreement, or by open trial thereof with our weapons, in a fair field; seeing that it neither becomes thy place and courage, to die the death of a slave who hath been overwrought by his taskmaster, nor befits it our fame that a brave adversary be snatched from our weapon by such a disease. And, therefore, may the holy——"

"Hold, hold," said Richard, "I will have no more of his dog of a Prophet! It makes me sick to think the valiant and

* The Angel of Death.

orthy Soldan should believe in a dead dog.—Yes, I will see
is physician. I will put myself into the charge of this Hakim
—I will repay the noble Soldan his generosity—I will meet
aladin in the field, as he so worthily proposes, and he shall
ave no cause to term Richard of England ungrateful. I will
trike him to the earth with my battle-axe—I will convert him
o Holy Church with such blows as he has rarely endured—He
hall recant his errors before my good cross-handled sword, and
will have him baptized in the battlefield, from my own helmet,
hough the cleansing waters were mixed with the blood of us
oth.—Haste, De Vaux, why dost thou delay a conclusion so
leasing? Fetch the Hakim hither."

"My lord," said the baron, who perhaps saw some accession
f fever in this overflow of confidence,—"bethink you, the
oldan is a pagan, and that you are his most formidable
nemy——"

"For which reason he is the more bound to do me service in
his matter, lest a paltry fever end the quarrel betwixt two
uch kings. I tell thee, he loves me as I love him—as noble
dversaries ever love each other—by my honour, it were sin to
oubt his good faith!"

"Nevertheless, my lord, it were well to wait the issue of
hose medicines upon the Scottish squire," said the Lord of
Gilsland; "my own life depends upon it, for worthy were I to
ie like a dog, did I proceed rashly in this matter, and make
hipwreck of the weal of Christendom."

"I never knew thee before hesitate for fear of life," said
Richard upbraidingly.

"Nor would I now, my liege," replied the stout-hearted baron,
"save that yours lie at pledge as well as my own."

"Well, thou suspicious mortal," answered Richard, "begone
hen, and watch the progress of this remedy. I could almost
ish it might either cure or kill me, for I am weary of lying here
ke an ox dying of the murrain, when tambours are beating,
orses stamping, and trumpets sounding without."

The Baron hastily departed, resolved, however, to communi-
ate his errand to some churchman, as he felt something
urdened in conscience at the idea of his master being attended
y an unbeliever.

The Archbishop of Tyre was the first to whom he confided
is doubts, knowing his interest with his master, Richard, who
oth loved and honoured that sagacious prelate. The bishop
eard the doubts which De Vaux stated, with that acuteness
f intelligence which distinguishes the Roman Catholic clergy.
he religious scruples of De Vaux he treated with as much
ghtness as propriety permitted him to exhibit on such a subject
o a layman.

"Mediciners," he said, "like the medicines which they em
ployed, were often useful, though the one were by birth o
manners the vilest of humanity, as the others are, in man
cases, extracted from the basest materials. Men may use th
assistance of pagans and infidels," he continued, "in the
need, and there is reason to think, that one cause of the
being permitted to remain on earth, is that they might minist
to the convenience of true Christians—Thus, we lawfully mak
slaves of heathen captives.—Again," proceeded the prelat
"there is no doubt that the primitive Christians used the servic
of the unconverted heathen—thus, in the ship of Alexandria, i
which the blessed Apostle Paul sailed to Italy, the sailors wer
doubtless pagans; yet what said the holy saint when the
ministry was needful—' *Nisi hi in navi manserint, vos salvi fie
non potestis*—Unless these men abide in the ship, ye cannot b
saved.' Again, Jews are infidels to Christianity, as well a
Mahommedans. But there are few physicians in the cam
excepting Jews, and such are employed without scandal o
scruple. Therefore, Mahommedans may be used for their servic
in that capacity—*quod erat demonstrandum.*"

This reasoning entirely removed the scruples of Thomas d
Vaux, who was particularly moved by the Latin quotation, a
he did not understand a word of it.

But the bishop proceeded with far less fluency, when he cor
sidered the possibility of the Saracen's acting with bad faith
and here he came not to a speedy decision. The baron showe
him the letters of credence. He read and re-read them, an
compared the original with the translation.

"It is a dish choicely cooked," he said, "to the palate o
King Richard, and I cannot but have my suspicions of th
wily Saracen. They are curious in the art of poisons, and ca
so temper them that they shall be weeks in acting upon th
party, during which time the perpetrator has leisure to escap
They can impregnate cloth and leather, nay, even paper an
parchment, with the most subtle venom—Our Lady forgiv
me!—And wherefore, knowing this, hold I these letters o
credence so close to my face?—Take them, Sir Thomas, tak
them speedily."

Here he gave them at arm's-length, and with some appearanc
of haste, to the baron. "But come, my Lord de Vaux," he con
tinued, "wend we to the tent of this sick squire, where we sha
learn whether this Hakim hath really the art of curing which h
professeth, ere we consider whether there be safety in permittin
him to exercise his art upon King Richard.—Yet hold! let m
first take my pouncet-box, for these fevers spread like an in
fection. I would advise you to use dried rosemary steeped
vinegar, my lord. I, too, know something of the healing art."

"I thank your reverend lordship," replied Thomas of Gilsland; "but had I been accessible to the fever, I had caught it long since by the bed of my master."

The Bishop of Tyre blushed, for he had rather avoided the presence of the sick monarch ; and he bid the baron lead on.

As they paused before the wretched hut in which Kenneth of the Leopard and his follower abode, the bishop said to De Vaux, "Now, of a surety, my lord, these Scottish knights have worse care of their followers than we of our dogs. Here is a knight, valiant they say in battle, and thought fitting to be graced with charges of weight in time of truce, whose esquire of the body is lodged worse than in the worst dog-kennel in England. What say you of your neighbours ?"

"That a master doth well enough for his servant, when he lodgeth him in no worse dwelling than his own," said De Vaux, and entered the hut.

The bishop followed, not without evident reluctance ; for though he lacked not courage in some respects, yet it was tempered with a strong and lively regard for his own safety. He recollected, however, the necessity there was for judging personally of the skill of the Arabian physician, and entered the hut with a stateliness of manner, calculated, as he thought, to impose respect on the stranger.

The prelate was, indeed, a striking and commanding figure. In his youth he had been eminently handsome, and, even in age, was unwilling to appear less so. His episcopal dress was of the richest fashion, trimmed with costly fur, and surrounded by a cope of curious needlework. The rings on his fingers were worth a goodly barony, and the hood which he wore, though now unclasped and thrown back for heat, had studs of pure gold to fasten it around his throat and under his chin when he so inclined. His long beard, now silvered with age, descended over his breast. One of two youthful acolytes who attended him, created an artificial shade, peculiar then to the East, by bearing over his head an umbrella of palmetto leaves, while the other refreshed his reverend master by agitating a fan of peacock feathers.

When the Bishop of Tyre entered the hut of the Scottish knight, the master was absent; and the Moorish physician, whom he had come to see, sat in the very posture in which De Vaux had left him several hours before, cross-legged upon a mat made of twisted leaves, by the side of the patient, who appeared in deep slumber, and whose pulse he felt from time to time. The bishop remained standing before him in silence for two or three minutes, as if expecting some honourable salutation, or at least that the Saracen would seem struck with the dignity of his appearance. But Adonbec el Hakim took no notice of him beyond a passing glance, and when the prelate at length saluted him in the Lingua Franca current in the country, he only replied by the ordinary Oriental greeting, " *Salam alicum* —peace be with you."

" Art thou a physician, infidel ? " said the bishop, somewhat mortified at this cold reception. " I would speak with thee on that art."

" If thou knewest aught of medicine," answered El Hakim, " thou wouldst be aware, that physicians hold no counsel or debate in the sick chamber of their patient. Hear," he added, as the low growling of the staghound was heard from the inner hut, " even the dog might teach thee reason, Ulemat. His instinct teaches him to suppress his barking in the sick man's hearing.—Come without the tent," said he, rising and leading the way, " if thou hast aught to say with me."

Notwithstanding the plainness of the Saracen leech's dress, and his inferiority of size, when contrasted with the tall prelate and gigantic English baron, there was something striking in his manner and countenance, which prevented the Bishop of Tyre from expressing strongly the displeasure he felt at this unceremonious rebuke. When without the hut, he gazed upon Adonbec in silence, for several minutes, before he could fix on the best manner to renew the conversation. No locks were seen under the high bonnet of the Arabian, which hid also part of a brow that seemed lofty and expanded, smooth, and free from wrinkles, as were his cheeks, where they were seen under the shade of his long beard. We have elsewhere noticed the piercing quality of his dark eyes.

The prelate, struck with his apparent youth, at length broke a pause, which the other seemed in no haste to interrupt, by demanding of the Arabian how old he was ?

" The years of ordinary men," said the Saracen, " are counted by their wrinkles ; those of sages by their studies. I dare not call myself older than an hundred revolutions of the Hegira." *

The Baron of Gilsland, who took this for a literal assertion, that he was a century old, looked doubtfully upon the prelate, who though he better understood the meaning of El Hakim, answered his glance by mysteriously shaking his head. He resumed an air of importance, when he again authoritatively demanded, what evidence Adonbec could produce of his medical proficiency.

" Ye have the word of the mighty Saladin," said the sage touching his cap in sign of reverence ; " a word which was never broken towards friend or foe—what, Nazarene, wouldst thou demand more ? "

* Meaning, that his attainments were those which might have been made in a hundred years.

"I would have ocular proof of thy skill," said the baron, "and without it thou approachest not to the couch of King Richard."

"The praise of the physician," said the Arabian, "is in the recovery of his patient. Behold this sergeant, whose blood has been dried up by the fever which has whitened your camp with skeletons, and against which the art of your Nazarene leeches hath been like a silken doublet against a lance of steel. Look at his fingers and arms, wasted like the claws and shanks of the crane. Death had this morning his clutch on him; but had Azrael been on one side of the couch, I being on the other, his soul should not have been reft from his body. Disturb me not with further questions, but await the critical minute, and behold in silent wonder the marvellous event."

The physician had then recourse to his astrolabe, the oracle of Eastern science, and, watching with grave precision until the precise time of the evening prayer had arrived, he sunk on his knees, with his face turned to Mecca, and recited the petitions which close the Moslemah's day of toil. The bishop and the English baron looked on each other, meanwhile, with symptoms of contempt and indignation, but neither judged it fit to interrupt El Hakim in his devotions, unholy as they considered them to be.

The Arab arose from the earth, on which he had prostrated himself, and, walking into the hut where the patient lay extended, he drew a sponge from a small silver box, dipt perhaps in some aromatic distillation; for when he put it to the sleeper's nose, he sneezed, awoke, and looked wildly around. He was a ghastly spectacle, as he sat up almost naked on his couch, the bones and cartilages as visible through the surface of his skin, as if they had never been clothed with flesh; his face was long, and furrowed with wrinkles, but his eye, though it wandered at first, became gradually more settled. He seemed to be aware of the presence of his dignified visitors, for he attempted feebly to pull the covering from his head, in token of reverence, as he inquired, in a subdued and submissive voice, for his master.

"Do you know us, vassal?" said the Lord of Gilsland.

"Not perfectly, my lord," replied the Squire faintly. "My sleep has been long and full of dreams. Yet I know that you are a great English lord, as seemeth by the red cross, and this holy prelate, whose blessing I crave on me a poor sinner."

"Thou hast it—*Benedictio Domini sit vobiscum*," said the prelate, making the sign of the cross, but without approaching nearer to the patient's bed.

"Your eyes witness," said the Arabian, "the fever hath been subdued—he speaks with calmness and recollection—his pulse beats composedly as yours—try its pulsations yourself."

The prelate declined the experiment; but Thomas of Gilsland, more determined on making the trial, did so, and satisfied himself that the fever was indeed gone.

"This is most wonderful," said the knight, looking to the bishop; "the man is assuredly cured. I must conduct this mediciner presently to King Richard's tent—What thinks your reverence?"

"Stay, let me finish one cure ere I commence another," said the Arab; "I will pass with you when I have given my patient the second cup of this most holy elixir."

So saying he pulled out a silver cup, and filling it with water from a gourd which stood by the bedside, he next drew forth a small silken bag made of network, twisted with silver, the contents of which the bystanders could not discover, and immersing it in the cup, continued to watch it in silence during the space of five minutes. It seemed to the spectators as if some effervescence took place during the operation, but if so, it instantly subsided.

"Drink," said the physician to the sick man—"sleep, and awaken free from malady."

"And with this simple-seeming draught, thou wilt undertake to cure a monarch?" said the Bishop of Tyre.

"I have cured a beggar, as you may behold," replied the sage. "Are the kings of Frangistan made of other clay than the meanest of their subjects?"

"Let us have him presently to the King," said the Baron of Gilsland. "He hath shown that he possesses the secret which may restore his health. If he fails to exercise it, I will put himself past the power of medicine."

As they were about to leave the hut, the sick man, raising his voice as much as his weakness permitted, exclaimed, "Reverend father, noble knight, and you, kind leech, if you would have me sleep and recover, tell me in charity what has become of my dear master?"

"He is upon a distant expedition, friend," replied the prelate; "on an honourable embassy, which may detain him for some days."

"Nay," said the Baron of Gilsland, "why deceive the poor fellow?—Friend, thy master has returned to the camp, and you will presently see him."

The invalid held up, as if in thankfulness, his wasted hand to Heaven, and resisting no longer the soporiferous operation of the elixir, sunk down in a gentle sleep.

"You are a better physician than I, Sir Thomas," said the prelate; "a soothing falsehood is fitter for a sick room than an unpleasing truth."

"How mean you, my reverend lord?" said De Vaux hastily,

"Think you I would tell a falsehood to save the lives of a dozen such as he?"

"You said," replied the bishop, with manifest symptoms of alarm—"you said, the esquire's master was returned—he, I mean, of the Couchant Leopard."

"And he *is* returned," said De Vaux. "I spoke with him but a few hours since. This learned leech came in his company."

"Holy Virgin! why told you not of his return to me?" said the bishop, in evident perturbation.

"Did I not say that this same Knight of the Leopard had returned in company with the physician?—I thought I had," replied De Vaux carelessly; "but what signified his return, to the skill of the physician, or the cure of his Majesty?"

"Much, Sir Thomas—it signified much," said the bishop, clenching his hands, pressing his foot against the earth, and giving signs of impatience, as if in an involuntary manner. "But where can he be gone now, this same knight?—God be with us—here may be some fatal errors!"

"Yonder serf in the outer space," said De Vaux, not without wonder at the bishop's emotion, "can probably tell us whither his master has gone."

The lad was summoned, and, in a language nearly incomprehensible to them, gave them at length to understand, that an officer had summoned his master to the royal tent, some time before their arrival at that of his master. The anxiety of the bishop appeared to rise to the highest, and became evident to De Vaux, though neither an acute observer, nor of a suspicious temper. But with his anxiety seemed to increase his wish to keep it subdued and unobserved. He took a hasty leave of De Vaux, who looked after him with astonishment; and, after shrugging up his shoulders in silent wonder, proceeded to conduct the Arabian physician to the tent of King Richard.

CHAPTER IX

This is the prince of leeches; fever, plague,
Cold rheum, and hot podagra, do but look on him,
And quit their grasp upon the tortured sinews.
—ANONYMOUS.

THE Baron of Gilsland walked with slow step and an anxious countenance towards the royal pavilion. He had much diffidence of his own capacity, except in a field of battle, and conscious of no very acute intellect, was usually contented to

wonder at circumstances, which a man of livelier imagination
would have endeavoured to investigate and understand, or at
least would have made the subject of speculation. But it
seemed very extraordinary, even to him, that the attention of
the bishop should have been at once abstracted from all reflection on the marvellous cure which they had witnessed, and
upon the probability it afforded of Richard being restored to
health, by what seemed a very trivial piece of information,
announcing the motions of a beggarly Scottish knight, than
whom Thomas of Gilsland knew nothing within the circle of
gentle blood more unimportant or contemptible; and, despite
his usual habit of passively beholding passing events, the baron's
spirit toiled with unwonted attempts to form conjectures on
the cause.

At length the idea occurred at once to him, that the whole
might be a conspiracy against King Richard, formed within
the camp of the allies, and to which the bishop, who was by
some represented as a politic and unscrupulous person, was not
unlikely to have been accessory. It was true, that, in his own
opinion, there existed no character so perfect as that of his
master; for Richard being the flower of chivalry, and the chief
of Christian leaders, and obeying in all points the commands
of Holy Church, De Vaux's ideas of perfection went no farther.
Still he knew that, however unworthily, it had been always his
master's fate to draw as much reproach and dislike, as honour
and attachment, from the display of his great qualities; and
that in the very camp, and amongst those princes bound by
oath to the Crusade, were many who would have sacrificed all
hope of victory over the Saracens, to the pleasure of ruining
or at least of humbling, Richard of England.

"Wherefore," said the baron to himself, "it is in no sense
impossible that this El Hakim, with this his cure, or seeming
cure, wrought on the body of the Scottish squire, may mean
nothing but a trick, to which he of the Leopard may be accessory, and wherein the Bishop of Tyre, prelate as he is, may
have some share."

This hypothesis, indeed, could not be so easily reconciled
with the a arm manifested by the bishop, on learning that
contrary to his expectation, the Scottish knight had suddenl
returned to the Crusaders' camp. But De Vaux was influ-
enced only by his general prejudices, which dictated to him
the assured belief, that a wily Italian priest, a false-hearted
Scot, and an infidel physician, formed a set of ingredients from
which all evil, and no good, was likely to be extracted. H
resolved, however, to lay his scruples bluntly before the King
of whose judgment he had nearly as high an opinion as of hi
valour.

Meantime, events had taken place very contrary to the suppositions which Thomas de Vaux had entertained. Scarce had he left the royal pavilion, when, betwixt the impatience of the fever, and that which was natural to his disposition, Richard began to murmur at his delay, and express an earnest desire for his return. He had seen enough to try to reason himself out of this irritation, which greatly increased his bodily malady. He wearied his attendants by demanding from them amusements, and the breviary of the priest, the romance of the clerk, even the harp of his favourite minstrel, were had recourse to in vain. At length, some two hours before sundown, and long, therefore, ere he could expect a satisfactory account of the process of the cure which the Moor or Arabian had undertaken, he sent, as we have already heard, a messenger, commanding the attendance of the Knight of the Leopard, determined to soothe his impatience by obtaining from Sir Kenneth a more particular account of the cause of his absence from the camp, and the circumstances of his meeting with this celebrated physician.

The Scottish knight, thus summoned, entered the Royal presence, as one who was no stranger to such scenes. He was scarcely known to the King of England, even by sight, although, tenacious of his rank, as devout in the adoration of the lady of his secret heart, he had never been absent on those occasions when the munificence and hospitality of England opened the Court of its monarch to all who held a certain rank in chivalry. The King gazed fixedly on Sir Kenneth approaching his bedside, while the knight bent his knee for a moment, then arose, and stood before him in a posture of deference, but not of subservience or humility, as became an officer in the presence of his sovereign.

"Thy name," said the King, "is Kenneth of the Leopard —From whom hadst thou degree of knighthood?"

"I took it from the sword of William the Lion, King of Scotland," replied the Scot.

"A weapon," said the King, "well worthy to confer honour, nor has it been laid on an undeserving shoulder. We have seen thee bear thyself knightly and valiantly in press of battle, when most need there was; and thou hadst not been yet to learn that thy deserts were known to us, but that thy presumption in other points has been such, that thy services can challenge no better reward than that of pardon for thy transgression. What sayest thou—ha?"

Kenneth attempted to speak, but was unable to express himself distinctly; the consciousness of his too ambitious love, and the keen falcon glance with which Cœur de Lion seemed to penetrate his inmost soul, combining to disconcert him.

"And yet," said the King, "although soldiers should obey command, and vassals be respectful towards their superiors, we might forgive a brave knight greater offence than the keeping a simple hound, though it were contrary to our express public ordinance."

Richard kept his eye fixed on the Scot's face, beheld, and beholding, smiled inwardly at the relief produced by the turn he had given to his general accusation.

"So please you, my lord," said the Scot, "your Majesty must be good to us poor gentlemen of Scotland in this matter. We are far from home, scant of revenues, and cannot support ourselves as your wealthy nobles, who have credit of the Lombards. The Saracens shall feel our blows the harder that we eat a piece of dried venison from time to time, with our herbs and barley-cakes."

"It skills not asking my leave," said Richard, "since Thomas de Vaux, who doth, like all around me, that which is fittest in his own eyes, hath already given thee permission for hunting and hawking."

"For hunting only, and please you," said the Scot; "but if it please your Majesty to indulge me with the privilege of hawking also, and you list to trust me with a falcon on fist, I trust I could supply your royal mess with some choice water-fowl."

"I dread me, if thou hadst but the falcon," said the King, "thou wouldst scarce wait for the permission. I wot well it is said abroad that we of the line of Anjou resent offence against our forest laws, as highly as we would do treason against our crown. To brave and worthy men, however, we could pardon either misdemeanour.—But enough of this—I desire to know of you, Sir Knight, wherefore, and by whose authority, you took this recent journey to the wilderness of the Dead Sea, and Engaddi?"

"By order," replied the knight, "of the Council of Princes of the Holy Crusade."

"And how dared any one to give such an order, when I—not the least, surely, in the league—was unacquainted with it?"

"It was not my part, please your highness," said the Scot, "to inquire into such particulars. I am a soldier of the Cross —serving, doubtless, for the present, under your highness's banner, and proud of the permission to do so—but still, one who hath taken on him the holy symbol for the rights of Christianity, and the recovery of the Holy Sepulchre, and bound, therefore, to obey, without question, the orders of the princes and chiefs by whom the blessed enterprise is directed. That indisposition should seclude, I trust for but a short time, your highness from their councils, in which you hold so potential a voice, I must lament with all Christendom ; but, as a soldier, I must obey those on whom the lawful right of command devolves, or set but an evil example in the Christian camp."

"Thou say'st well," said King Richard ; "and the blame rests not with thee, but with those with whom, when it shall please Heaven to raise me from this accursed bed of pain and inactivity, I hope to reckon roundly. What was the purport of thy message ? "

"Methinks, and please your highness," replied Sir Kenneth, "that were best asked of those who sent me, and who can render the reasons of mine errand ; whereas I can only tell its outward form and purport."

"Palter not with me, Sir Scot—it were ill for thy safety," said the irritable monarch.

"My safety, my lord," replied the knight firmly, "I cast behind me as a regardless thing when I avowed myself to this enterprise, looking rather to my immortal welfare, than to that which concerns my earthly body."

"By the mass," said King Richard, "thou art a brave fellow ! Hark thee, Sir Knight, I love the Scottish people ; they are hardy, though dogged and stubborn, and, I think, true men in the main, though the necessity of state has sometimes constrained them to be dissemblers. I deserve some love at their hand, for I have voluntarily done what they could not by arms have extorted from me, any more than from my predecessors— I have re-established the fortresses of Roxburgh and Berwick, which lay in pledge to England—I have restored your ancient boundaries—and, finally, I have renounced a claim to homage upon the crown of England, which I thought unjustly forced on you. I have endeavoured to make honourable and independent friends, where former kings of England attempted only to compel unwilling and rebellious vassals."

"All this you have done, my Lord King," said Sir Kenneth, bowing—"All this you have done, by your royal treaty with our sovereign at Canterbury. Therefore have you me, and many better Scottish men, making war against the infidels, under your banners, who would else have been ravaging your frontiers in England. If their numbers are now few, it is because their lives have been freely waged and wasted."

"I grant it true," said the King ; "and for the good offices I have done your land, I require you to remember, that, as a principal member of the Christian league, I have a right to know the negotiations of my confederates. Do me, therefore, the justice to tell me what I have a title to be acquainted with, and which I am certain to know more truly from you than from others."

"My lord," said the Scot, "thus conjured, I will speak the

truth; for I well believe that your purposes towards the principal object of our expedition are single-hearted and honest; and it is more than I dare warrant for others of the Holy League. Be pleased, therefore, to know, my charge was to propose, through the medium of the hermit of Engaddi—a holy man, respected and protected by Saladin himself——"

"A continuation of the truce, I doubt not," said Richard, hastily interrupting him.

"No, by Saint Andrew, my liege," said the Scottish knight, "but the establishment of a lasting peace, and the withdrawing our armies from Palestine."

"Saint George!" said Richard in astonishment—"Ill as I have justly thought of them, I could not have dreamed they would have humbled themselves to such dishonour. Speak, Sir Kenneth, with what will did you carry such a message?"

"With right goodwill, my lord," said Kenneth; "because, when we had lost our noble leader, under whose guidance alone I hoped for victory, I saw none who could succeed him likely to lead us to conquest, and I accounted it well in such circumstances to avoid defeat."

"And on what conditions was this hopeful peace to be contracted?" said King Richard, painfully suppressing the passion with which his heart was almost bursting.

"These were not entrusted to me, my lord," answered the Knight of the Couchant Leopard. "I delivered them sealed to the hermit."

"And for what hold you this reverend hermit?—for fool, madman, traitor, or saint?" said Richard.

"His folly, sire," replied the shrewd Scottishman, "I hold to be assumed to win favour and reverence from the Paynimrie, who regard madmen as the inspired of Heaven; at least it seemed to me as exhibited only occasionally, and not as mixing, like natural folly, with the general tenor of his mind."

"Shrewdly replied," said the monarch, throwing himself back on his couch, from which he had half-raised himself.—"Now of his penitence?"

"His penitence," continued Kenneth, "appears to me sincere, and the fruits of remorse for some dreadful crime, for which he seems, in his own opinion, condemned to reprobation."

"And for his policy?" said King Richard.

"Methinks, my lord," said the Scottish knight, "he despairs of the security of Palestine, as of his own salvation, by any means short of a miracle—at least since the arm of Richard of England hath ceased to strike for it."

"And, therefore, the coward policy of this hermit is like that of these miserable princes, who, forgetful of their knighthood and their faith, are only resolved and determined when the

question is retreat, and, rather than go forward against an armed
Saracen, would trample in their flight over a dying ally!"

"Might I so far presume, my Lord King," said the Scottish
knight, "this discourse but heats your disease, the enemy from
which Christendom dreads more evil, than from armed hosts of
infidels."

The countenance of King Richard was, indeed, more flushed,
and his action became more feverishly vehement, as, with
clenched hand, expanded arm, and flashing eyes, he seemed at
once to suffer under bodily pain, and at the same time under
vexation of mind, while his high spirit led him to speak on, as if
in contempt of both,

"You can flatter, Sir Knight," he said, "but you escape me
not. I must know more from you than you have yet told me.
Saw you my royal consort when at Engaddi?"

"To my knowledge—no, my lord," replied Sir Kenneth, with
considerable perturbation; for he remembered the midnight
procession in the chapel of the rocks.

"I ask you," said the King, in a sterner voice, "whether you
were not in the chapel of the Carmelite nuns at Engaddi, and
there saw Berengaria, Queen of England, and the ladies of her
Court, who went thither on pilgrimage?"

"My lord," said Sir Kenneth, "I will speak the truth as in
the confessional. In a subterranean chapel, to which the
anchorite conducted me, I beheld a choir of ladies do homage
to a relic of the highest sanctity; but as I saw not their faces,
nor heard their voices, unless in the hymns which they chanted,
I cannot tell whether the Queen of England was of the bevy."

"And was there no one of these ladies known to you?"

Sir Kenneth stood silent.

"I ask you," said Richard, raising himself on his elbow, "as
a knight and a gentleman, and I shall know by your answer
how you value either character—did you, or did you not, know
any lady amongst that band of worshippers?"

"My lord," said Kenneth, not without much hesitation, "I
might guess."

"And I also may guess," said the King, frowning sternly;
"but it is enough. Leopard as you are, Sir Knight, beware
tempting the lion's paw. Hark ye—to become enamoured of
the moon would be but an act of folly; but to leap from the
battlements of a lofty tower, in the wild hope of coming within
her sphere, were self-destructive madness."

At this moment some bustling was heard in the outer apartment, and the King, hastily changing to his more natural
manner, said, "Enough—begone—speed to De Vaux, and send
him hither with the Arabian physician. My life for the faith
of the Soldan! Would he but abjure his false law, I would aid

him with my sword to drive this scum of French and Austrians from his dominions, and think Palestine as well ruled by him as when her kings were anointed by the decree of Heaven itself."

The Knight of the Leopard retired, and presently afterwards the chamberlain announced a deputation from the Council, who had come to wait on the Majesty of England.

"It is well they allow that I am living yet," was his reply. "Who are the reverend ambassadors?"

"The Grand Master of the Templars and the Marquis of Montserrat."

"Our brother of France loves not sick-beds," said Richard; "yet, had Philip been ill, I had stood by his couch long since. —Jocelyn, lay me the couch more fairly, it is tumbled like a stormy sea—reach me yonder steel mirror—pass a comb through my hair and beard. They look, indeed, liker a lion's mane than a Christian man's locks—bring water."

"My lord," said the trembling chamberlain, "the leeches say that cold water may be fatal."

"To the foul fiend with the leeches!" replied the monarch; "if they cannot cure me, think you I will allow them to torment me?—There, then"—he said, after having made his ablutions, "admit the worshipful envoys; they will now, I think, scarcely see that disease has made Richard negligent of his person."

The celebrated Master of the Templars was a tall, thin, war-worn man, with a slow yet penetrating eye, and a brow on which a thousand dark intrigues had stamped a portion of their obscurity. At the head of that singular body, to whom their order was everything, and their individuality nothing—seeking the advancement of its power, even at the hazard of that very religion which the fraternity were originally associated to protect—accused of heresy and witchcraft, although by their character Christian priests—suspected of secret league with the Soldan, though by oath devoted to the protection of the Holy Temple, or its recovery—the whole order, and the whole personal character of its commander, or Grand Master, was a riddle, at the exposition of which most men shuddered. The Grand Master was dressed in his white robes of solemnity, and he bare the *abacus*, a mystic staff of office, the peculiar form of which has given rise to such singular conjectures and commentaries, leading to suspicions that this celebrated fraternity of Christian knights were embodied under the foulest symbols of Paganism.

Conrade of Montserrat had a much more pleasing exterior than the dark and mysterious priest-soldier by whom he was accompanied. He was a handsome man, of middle age, or something past that term, bold in the field, sagacious in council, gay and gallant in times of festivity; but, on the other hand, he was generally accused of versatility, of a narrow and selfish ambition, of a desire to extend his own principality, without regard to the weal of the Latin kingdom of Palestine, and of seeking his own interest, by private negotiations with Saladin, to the prejudice of the Christian leaguers.

When the usual salutations had been made by these dignitaries, and courteously returned by King Richard, the Marquis of Montserrat commenced an explanation of the motives of their visit, sent, as he said they were, by the anxious Kings and Princes who composed the Council of the Crusaders, to "inquire into the health of their magnanimous ally, the valiant King of England."

"We know the importance in which the Princes of the Council hold our health," replied the English King; "and are well aware how much they must have suffered by suppressing all curiosity concerning it for fourteen days, for fear, doubtless, of aggravating our disorder, by showing their anxiety regarding the event."

The flow of the Marquis's eloquence being checked, and he himself thrown into some confusion by this reply, his more austere companion took up the thread of the conversation, and, with as much dry and brief gravity as was consistent with the presence which he addressed, informed the King that they came from the Council to pray, in the name of Christendom, "that he would not suffer his health to be tampered with by an infidel physician, said to be despatched by Saladin, until the Council had taken measures to remove or confirm the suspicion which they at present conceived did attach itself to the mission of such a person."

"Grand Master of the Holy and Valiant Order of Knights Templars, and you, Most Noble Marquis of Montserrat," replied Richard, "if it please you to retire into the adjoining pavilion, you shall presently see what account we make of the tender remonstrances of our royal and princely colleagues in this most religious warfare."

The Marquis and Grand Master retired accordingly; nor had they been many minutes in the outward pavilion when the Eastern physician arrived, accompanied by the Baron of Gilsland and Kenneth of Scotland. The baron, however, was a little later of entering the tent than the other two, stopping, perchance, to issue some orders to the warders without.

As the Arabian physician entered, he made his obeisance, after the Oriental fashion, to the Marquis and Grand Master, whose dignity was apparent, both from their appearance and their bearing. The Grand Master returned the salutation with an expression of disdainful coldness, the Marquis, with the popular courtesy which he habitually practised to men of every rank and nation. There was a pause; for the Scottish knight, waiting for the arrival of De Vaux, presumed not, of his own authority, to enter the tent of the King of England, and, during this interval, the Grand Master sternly demanded of the Moslem, —" Infidel, hast thou the courage to practise thine art upon the person of an anointed sovereign of the Christian host?"

"The sun of Allah," answered the sage, "shines on the Nazarene as well as on the true believer, and his servant dare make no distinction betwixt them, when called on to exercise his art of healing."

"Misbelieving Hakim," said the Grand Master, "or what-soever they call thee for an unbaptized slave of darkness, dost thou well know, that thou shalt be torn asunder by wild horses should King Richard die under thy charge?"

"That were hard justice," answered the physician; "seeing that I can but use human means, and that the issue is written in the book of light."

"Nay, reverend and valiant Grand Master," said the Marquis of Montserrat, "consider that this learned man is not acquainted with our Christian order, adopted in the fear of God, and for the safety of His anointed. Be it known unto thee, grave physician, whose skill we doubt not, that your wisest course is to repair to the presence of the illustrious Council of our Holy League, and there to give account and reckoning to such wise and learned leeches as they shall nominate, concerning your means of process and cure of this illustrious patient; so shall you escape all the danger, which, rashly taking such a high matter upon your sole answer, you may else most likely incur."

"My lords," said El Hakim, "I understand you well. But knowledge hath its champions as well as your military art, nay, hath sometimes had its martyrs as well as religion. I have the command of my sovereign, the Soldan Saladin, to heal this Nazarene King, and, with the blessing of the Prophet, I will obey his commands. If I fail ye wear swords thirsting for the blood of the faithful, and I proffer my body to your weapons. But I will not reason with one uncircumcised upon the virtue of the medicines of which I have obtained knowledge, through the grace of the Prophet, and I pray you interpose no delay between me and my office."

"Who talks of delay?" said the Baron de Vaux, hastily entering the tent; "we have had but too much already.—I salute you, my Lord of Montserrat, and you, valiant Grand Master. But I must presently pass with this learned physician to the bedside of my master."

"My lord," said the Marquis, in Norman French, or the language of Ouie, as it was then called, "are you well advised that we came to expostulate on the part of the Council of the Monarchs and Princes of the Crusade, against the risk of permitting an infidel and Eastern physician to tamper with a health so valuable as that of your master King Richard?"

"Noble Lord Marquis," replied the Englishman bluntly, "I can neither use many words, nor do I delight in listening to them—moreover, I am much more ready to believe what my eyes have seen, than what my ears have heard. I am satisfied that this heathen can cure the sickness of King Richard, and I believe and trust he will labour to do so. Time is precious. If Mahommed—may God's curse be on him!—stood at the door of the tent, with such fair purpose as this Adonbec el Hakim entertains, I would hold it sin to delay him for a minute.—So, give ye God'en, my lords."

"Nay, but," said Conrade of Montserrat, "the King himself said we should be present when this same physician dealt upon him."

The baron whispered the chamberlain, probably to know whether the Marquis spoke truly, and then replied, "My lords, if you will hold your patience, you are welcome to enter with us; but if you interrupt, by action or threat, this accomplished physician in his duty, be it known, that, without respect to your high quality, I will enforce your absence from Richard's tent; for know, I am so well satisfied with the virtue of this man's medicines, that were Richard himself to refuse them, by Our Lady of Lanercost, I think I could find in my heart to force him to take the means of his cure whether he would or no.—Move onward, El Hakim."

The last word was spoken in the Lingua Franca, and instantly obeyed by the physician. The Grand Master looked grimly on the unceremonious old soldier, but, on exchanging a glance with the Marquis, smoothed his frowning brow as well as he could, and both followed de Vaux and the Arabian into the inner tent, where Richard lay expecting them, with that impatience with which the sick patient watches the step of his physician. Sir Kenneth, whose attendance seemed neither asked nor prohibited, felt himself, by the circumstances in which he stood, entitled to follow these high dignitaries, but, conscious of his inferior power and rank, remained aloof during the scene which took place.

Richard, when they entered his apartment, immediately exclaimed, "So ho! a goodly fellowship come to see Richard take his leap in the dark.—My noble allies, I greet you as the representatives of our assembled league; Richard will again be amongst you in his former fashion, or ye shall bear to the grave what is left of him.—De Vaux, lives he or dies he, thou hast the thanks of thy prince.—There is yet another—but this fever hath wasted my eyesight—what, the bold Scot, who would climb heaven without a ladder?—he is welcome too.—Come, Sir Hakim, to the work, to the work."

The physician, who had already informed himself of the various symptoms of the King's illness, now felt his pulse for a long time, and with deep attention, while all around stood silent, and in breathless expectation. The sage next filled a cup with spring water, and dipt into it the small red purse, which, as formerly, he took from his bosom. When he seemed to think it sufficiently medicated, he was about to offer it to the sovereign, who prevented him, by saying, "Hold an instant.—Thou hast felt my pulse—let me lay my finger on thine—I too, as becomes a good knight, know something of thine art."

The Arabian yielded his hand without hesitation, and his long slender dark fingers were, for an instant, enclosed, and almost buried, in the large enfoldment of King Richard's hand.

"His blood beats calm as an infant's," said the King; "so throb not theirs who poison princes. De Vaux, whether we live or die, dismiss this Hakim with honour and safety—Commend us, friend, to the noble Saladin. Should I die, it is without doubt of his faith—should I live, it will be to thank him as a warrior would desire to be thanked."

He then raised himself in bed, took the cup in his hand, and, turning to the Marquis and the Grand Master,—"Mark what I say, and let my royal brethren pledge me in Cyprus wine,—'To the immortal honour of the first Crusader, who shall strike lance or sword on the gate of Jerusalem; and to the shame and eternal infamy of whomsoever shall turn back from the plough on which he hath laid his hand!'"

He drained the cup to the bottom, resigned it to the Arabian, and sunk back, as if exhausted, upon the cushions which were arranged to receive him. The physician, then, with silent but expressive signs, directed that all should leave the tent excepting himself and De Vaux, whom no remonstrance could induce to withdraw. The apartment was cleared accordingly.

CHAPTER X

And now I will unclasp a secret book,
And, to your quick-conceiving discontent,
I'll read you matter deep and dangerous.
—HENRY IV. *Part I.*

THE Marquis of Montserrat, and the Grand Master of the Knights Templars, stood together in the front of the royal pavilion, within which this singular scene had passed, and beheld a strong guard of bills and bows drawn out to form a circle around it, and keep at distance all which might disturb the sleeping monarch. The soldiers wore the downcast, silent, and sullen looks, with which they trail their arms at a funeral, and stepped with such caution that you could not hear a buckler ring, or a sword clatter, though so many men in armour were moving around the tent. They lowered their weapons in deep reverence, as the dignitaries passed through their files, but with the same profound silence.

"There is a change of cheer among these island dogs," said the Grand Master to Conrade, when they had passed Richard's guards. "What hoarse tumult and revel used to be before this pavilion! nought but pitching the bar, hurling the ball, wrestling, roaring of songs, clattering of wine-pots, and quaffing of flagons, among these burly yeomen, as if they were holding some country wake with a Maypole in the midst of them, instead of a royal standard."

"Mastiffs are a faithful race," said Conrade; "and the King their master has won their love by being ready to wrestle, brawl, or revel amongst the foremost of them whenever the humour seized him."

"He is totally compounded of humours," said the Grand Master. "Marked you the pledge he gave us, instead of a prayer, over his grace-cup yonder?"

"He would have felt it a grace-cup, and a well-spiced one too," said the Marquis, "were Saladin like any other Turk that ever wore turban, or turned him to Mecca at call of the Muezzin. But he affects faith, and honour, and generosity,—as if it were for an unbaptized dog like him to practise the virtuous bearing of a Christian knight! It is said he hath applied to Richard to be admitted within the pale of chivalry."

"By Saint Bernard!" exclaimed the Grand Master, "it were time then to throw off our belts and spurs, Sir Conrade, deface our armorial bearings, and renounce our burgonets, if the highest honour of Christianity were conferred on an unchristened Turk of tenpence."

"You rate the Soldan cheap," replied the Marquis; "yet though he be a likely man, I have seen a better heathen sold for forty pence at the bagnio."

They were now near their horses, which stood at some distance from the royal tent, prancing among the gallant train of esquires and pages by whom they were attended, when Conrade, after a moment's pause, proposed that they should enjoy the coolness of the evening breeze which had arisen, and, dismissing their steeds and attendants, walk homewards to their own quarters, through the lines of the extended Christian camp. The Grand Master assented, and they proceeded to walk together accordingly, avoiding, as if by mutual consent, the more inhabited parts of the canvas city, and tracing the broad esplanade which lay between the tents and the external defences, where they could converse in private, and unmarked, save by the sentinels as they passed them.

They spoke for a time upon the military points and preparations for defence; but this sort of discourse, in which neither seemed to take interest, at length died away, and there was a long pause, which terminated by the Marquis of Montserrat stopping short, like a man who has formed a sudden resolution, and gazing for some moments on the dark inflexible countenance of the Grand Master, he at length addressed him thus:— "Might it consist with your valour and sanctity, reverend Sir Giles Amaury, I would pray you for once to lay aside the dark visor which you wear, and to converse with a friend barefaced."

The Templar half smiled.

"There are light-coloured masks," he said, "as well as dark visors, and the one conceals the natural features as completely as the other."

"Be it so," said the Marquis, putting his hand to his chin, and withdrawing it with the action of one who unmasks himself; "there lies my disguise. And now, what think you, as touching the interests of your own Order, of the prospects of this Crusade?"

"This is tearing the veil from *my* thoughts rather than exposing your own," said the Grand Master; "yet I will reply with a parable told to me by a santon of the desert.—'A certain farmer prayed to Heaven for rain, and murmured when it fell not at his need. To punish his impatience, Allah,' said the santon, 'sent the Euphrates upon his farm, and he was destroyed with all his possessions, even by the granting of his own wishes.'"

"Most truly spoken," said the Marquis Conrade; "would that the ocean had swallowed up nineteen parts of the armaments of these western princes! what remained would better have served the purpose of the Christian nobles of Palestine, the wretched remnant of the Latin kingdom of Jerusalem. Left to ourselves, we might have bent to the storm, or, moderately supported with money and troops, we might have compelled Saladin to respect our valour, and grant us peace and protection on easy terms. But from the extremity of danger with which this powerful Crusade threatens the Soldan, we cannot suppose, should it pass over, that the Saracen will suffer any one of us to hold possessions or principalities in Syria, far less permit the existence of the Christian military fraternities, from whom they have experienced so much mischief."

" Ay, but," said the Templar, "these adventurous Crusaders may succeed, and again plant the Cross on the bulwarks of Zion."

"And what will that advantage either the Order of the Templars, or Conrade of Montserrat ?" said the Marquis.

"You it may advantage," replied the Grand Master. "Conrade of Montserrat might become Conrade King of Jerusalem."

"That sounds like something," said the Marquis, "and yet it rings but hollow.—Godfrey of Bouillon might well choose the crown of thorns for his emblem. Grand Master, I will confess to you I have caught some attachment to the Eastern form of government: A pure and simple monarchy should consist but of king and subjects. Such is the simple and primitive structure—a shepherd and his flock. All this internal chain of feudal dependence is artificial and sophisticated, and I would rather hold the baton of my poor marquisate with a firm gripe, and wield it after my pleasure, than the sceptre of a monarch, to be in effect restrained and curbed by the will of as many proud feudal barons as hold land under the Assize of Jerusalem.* A King should tread freely, Grand Master, and should not be controlled by here a ditch, and there a fence— here a feudal privilege, and there a mail-clad baron, with his sword in his hand to maintain it. To sum the whole, I am aware that Guy de Lusignan's claims to the throne would be preferred to mine, if Richard recovers, and has aught to say in the choice."

"Enough," said the Grand Master; "thou hast indeed convinced me of thy sincerity. Others may hold the same opinions, but few, save Conrade of Montserrat, dared frankly avow that he desires not the restitution of the kingdom of Jerusalem, but rather prefers being master of a portion of its fragments; like the barbarous islanders who labour not for the deliverance of a goodly vessel from the billows, expecting rather to enrich themselves at the expense of the wreck."

"Thou wilt not betray my counsel ?" said Conrade, looking sharply and suspiciously. "Know, for certain, that my tongue shall never wrong my head, nor my hand forsake the defence of either. Impeach me if thou wilt—I am prepared to defend myself in the lists against the best Templar who ever laid lance in rest."

"Yet thou start'st somewhat suddenly for so bold a steed," said the Grand Master. "However, I swear to thee by the

---

* The Assises de Jerusalem were the digest of feudal law, composed by Godfrey of Boulogne, for the government of the Latin kingdom of Palestine, when reconquered from the Saracens. "It was composed with advice of the patriarch and barons, the clergy and laity, and is," says the historian Gibbon, "a precious monument of feudatory jurisprudence, founded upon those principles of freedom which were essential to the system."

Holy Temple, which our Order is sworn to defend, that I will keep counsel with thee as a true comrade."

"By which Temple?" said the Marquis of Montserrat, whose love of sarcasm often outran his policy and discretion;— "swearest thou by that on the hill of Zion, which was built by King Solomon, or by that symbolical emblematical edifice, which is said to be spoken of in the councils held in the vaults of your Preceptories, as something which infers the aggrandisement of thy valiant and venerable Order?"

The Templar scowled upon him with an eye of death, but answered calmly, "By whatever Temple I swear, be assured, Lord Marquis, my oath is sacred—I would I knew how to bind *thee* by one of equal obligation."

"I will swear truth to thee," said the Marquis, laughing, "by the Earl's coronet, which I hope to convert, ere these wars are over, into something better. It feels cold on my brow, that same slight coronal; a duke's cap of maintenance were a better protection against such a night-breeze as now blows, and a king's crown more preferable still, being lined with comfortable ermine and velvet. In a word, our interests bind us together; for think not, Lord Grand Master, that, were these allied Princes to regain Jerusalem, and place a king of their own choosing there, they would suffer your Order, any more than my poor Marquisate, to retain the independence which we now hold. No, by Our Lady! In such case the proud knights of Saint John must again spread plasters, and dress plague-sores in the hospitals; and you, most puissant and venerable Knights of the Temple, must return to your condition of simple men-at-arms, sleep three on a pallet, and mount two upon one horse, as your present seal still expresses to have been your ancient most simple custom."

"The rank, privileges, and opulence of our Order prevent so much degradation as you threaten," said the Templar haughtily.

"These are your bane," said Conrade of Montserrat; "and you, as well as I, reverend Grand Master, know, that, were the allied Princes to be successful in Palestine, it would be their first point of policy to abate the independence of your Order, which, but for the protection of our holy father the Pope, and the necessity of employing your valour in the conquest of Palestine, you would long since have experienced. Give them complete success, and you will be flung aside, as the splinters of a broken lance are tossed out of the tilt-yard."

"There may be truth in what you say," said the Templar, darkly smiling; "but what were our hopes should the allies withdraw their forces, and leave Palestine in the grasp of Saladin?"

"Great and assured," replied Conrade; "the Soldan would give large provinces to maintain at his behest a body of well-appointed Frankish lances. In Egypt, in Persia, an hundred such auxiliaries, joined to his own light cavalry, would turn the battle against the most fearful odds. This dependence would be but for a time—perhaps during the life of this enterprising Soldan—but in the East, empires arise like mushrooms. Suppose him dead, and us strengthened with a constant succession of fiery and adventurous spirits from Europe, what might we not hope to achieve, uncontrolled by these monarchs, whose dignity throws us at present into the shade—and, were they to remain here, and succeed in this expedition, would willingly consign us for ever to degradation and dependence?"

"You say well, my Lord Marquis," said the Grand Master; "and your words find an echo in my bosom. Yet must we be cautious; Philip of France is wise as well as valiant."

"True, and will be therefore the more easily diverted from an expedition, to which, in a moment of enthusiasm, or urged by his nobles, he rashly bound himself. He is jealous of King Richard, his natural enemy, and longs to return to prosecute plans of ambition nearer to Paris than Palestine. Any fair pretence will serve him for withdrawing from a scene, in which he is aware he is wasting the force of his kingdom."

"And the Duke of Austria?" said the Templar.

"Oh, touching the Duke," returned Conrade, "his self-conceit and folly lead him to the same conclusions as do Philip's policy and wisdom. He conceives himself, God help the while, ungratefully treated, because men's mouths,—even those of his own *minne-singers*,*—are filled with the praises of King Richard, whom he fears and hates, and in whose harm he would rejoice, like those unbred dastardly curs, who, if the foremost of the pack is hurt by the gripe of the wolf, are much more likely to assail the sufferer from behind, than to come to his assistance.—But wherefore tell I this to thee, save to show that I am in sincerity in desiring that this league be broken up, and the country freed of these great monarchs with their hosts? and thou well knowest, and hast thyself seen, how all the princes of influence and power, one alone excepted, are eager to enter into treaty with the Soldan."

"I acknowledge it," said the Templar; "he were blind that had not seen this in their last deliberations. But lift yet thy mask an inch higher, and tell me thy real reason for pressing upon the Council that Northern Englishman, or Scot, or whatever you call yonder Knight of the Leopard, to carry their proposals for a treaty?"

"There was a policy in it," replied the Italian; "his char-

---

* The German minstrels were so termed.

G

acter of native of Britain was sufficient to meet what Saladin required, who knew him to belong to the band of Richard, while his character of Scot, and certain other personal grudges which I wot of, rendered it most unlikely that our envoy should, on his return, hold any communication with the sick-bed of Richard, to whom his presence was ever unacceptable."

"Oh, too fine-spun policy," said the Grand Master; "trust me, that Italian spiders' webs will never bind this unshorn Samson of the Isle—well if you can do it with new cords, and those of the toughest. See you not that the envoy whom you have selected so carefully, hath brought us, in this physician, the means of restoring the lion-hearted, bull-necked English-man, to prosecute his Crusading enterprise; and so soon as he is able once more to rush on, which of the princes dare hold back?—They must follow him for very shame, although they would march under the banner of Satan as soon."

"Be content," said Conrade of Montserrat; "ere this phy-sician, if he work by anything short of miraculous agency, can accomplish Richard's cure, it may be possible to put some open rupture betwixt the Frenchman, at least the Austrian, and his allies of England, so that the breach shall be irreconcilable; and Richard may arise from his bed, perhaps to command his own native troops, but never again, by his sole energy, to wield the force of the whole Crusade."

"Thou art a willing archer," said the Templar; "but, Conrade of Montserrat, thy bow is over slack to carry an arrow to the mark."

He then stopt short, cast a suspicious glance to see that no one overheard him, and taking Conrade by the hand, pressed it eagerly as he looked the Italian in the face, and repeated slowly,—"Richard arise from his bed, say'st thou?—Conrade, he must never arise!"

The Marquis of Montserrat started—"What!—spoke you of Richard of England—of Cœur de Lion—the champion of Christendom?"

His cheek turned pale, and his knees trembled as he spoke. The Templar looked at him, with his iron visage contorted into a smile of contempt.

"Know'st thou what thou look'st like, Sir Conrade, at this moment? Not like the politic and valiant Marquis of Mont-serrat—not like him who would direct the Council of Princes and determine the fate of empires—but like a novice, who stumbling upon a conjuration in his master's book of gramarye has raised the devil when he least thought of it, and now stands terrified at the spirit which appears before him."

"I grant you," said Conrade, recovering himself, "that—unless some other sure road could be discovered—thou has hinted at that which leads most direct to our purpose. But, blessed Mary! we shall become the curse of all Europe, the malediction of every one, from the Pope on his throne to the very beggar at the church-gate, who, ragged and leprous, in the last extremity of human wretchedness, shall bless himself that he is neither Giles Amaury, nor Conrade of Montserrat."

"If thou takest it thus," said the Grand Master, with the same composure which characterised him all through this re-markable dialogue, "let us hold there has nothing passed be-tween us—that we have spoken in our sleep—have awakened, and the vision is gone."

"It never can depart," answered Conrade.

"Visions of ducal crowns and kingly diadems are, indeed, somewhat tenacious of their place in the imagination," replied the Grand Master.

"Well," answered Conrade, "let me but first try to break peace between Austria and England."

They parted.—Conrade remained standing still upon the spot, and watching the flowing white cloak of the Templar, as he stalked slowly away, and gradually disappeared amid the fast-sinking darkness of the Oriental night. Proud, ambitious, un-scrupulous, and politic, the Marquis of Montserrat was yet not cruel by nature. He was a voluptuary and an epicurean, and, like many who profess this character, was averse, even upon selfish motives, from inflicting pain, or witnessing acts of cruelty; and he retained also a general sense of respect for his own reputation, which sometimes supplies the want of the better principles by which reputation is to be maintained.

"I have," he said, as his eyes still watched the point at which he had seen the last slight wave of the Templar's mantle,—"I have, in truth, raised the devil with a vengeance! Who would have thought this stern ascetic Grand Master, whose whole fortune and misfortune are merged in that of his Order, would be willing to do more for its advancement, than I who labour for my own interest? To check this wild Crusade was my motive, indeed, but I durst not think on the ready mode which this determined priest has dared to suggest—yet it is the surest—perhaps even the safest."

Such were the Marquis's meditations, when his muttered soliloquy was broken by a voice from a little distance, which proclaimed with the emphatic tone of a herald,—"Remember the Holy Sepulchre!"

The exhortation was echoed from post to post, for it was the duty of the sentinels to raise this cry from time to time upon their periodical watch, that the host of the Crusaders might always have in their remembrance the purpose of their being in arms. But though Conrade was familiar with the custom, and had heard the warning voice on all former occasions as a matter of habit ; yet it came at the present moment so strongly in contact with his own train of thought, that it seemed a voice from heaven warning him against the iniquity which his heart meditated. He looked around anxiously, as if, like the patriarch of old, though from very different circumstances, he was expecting some ram caught in a thicket—some substitution for the sacrifice, which his comrade proposed to offer, not to the Supreme Being, but to the Moloch of their own ambition. As he looked, the broad folds of the ensign of England, heavily distending itself to the failing night-breeze, caught his eye. It was displayed upon an artificial mound, nearly in the midst of the camp, which perhaps of old some Hebrew chief or champion had chosen as a memorial of his place of rest. If so, the name was now forgotten, and the Crusaders had christened it Saint George's Mount, because from that commanding height the banner of England was supereminently displayed, as if an emblem of sovereignty over the many distinguished, noble, and even royal ensigns which floated in lower situations.

A quick intellect like that of Conrade catches ideas from the glance of a moment. A single look on the standard seemed to dispel the uncertainty of mind which had affected him. He walked to his pavilion with the hasty and determined step of one who has adopted a plan which he is resolved to achieve, dismissed the almost princely train who waited to attend him, and, as he committed himself to his couch, muttered his amended resolution, that the milder means are to be tried before the more desperate are resorted to.

"To-morrow," he said, "I sit at the board of the Archduke of Austria—we will see what can be done to advance our purpose, before prosecuting the dark suggestions of this Templar."

CHAPTER XI

One thing is certain in our Northern land,
Allow that birth, or valour, wealth, or wit,
Give each precedence to their possessor.
Envy, that follows on such eminence,
As comes the lyme-hound on the roebuck's trace,
Shall pull them down each one.
—Sir David Lindsay.

LEOPOLD, Grand Duke of Austria, was the first possessor of that noble country to whom the princely rank belonged. He had been raised to the ducal sway in the German empire, on account of his near relationship to the Emperor, Henry the

Stern, and held under his government the finest provinces which are watered by the Danube. His character has been stained in history, on account of one action of violence and perfidy, which arose out of these very transactions in the Holy Land ; and yet the shame of having made Richard a prisoner, when he returned through his dominions, unattended and in disguise, was not one which flowed from Leopold's natural disposition. He was rather a weak and a vain, than an ambitious or tyrannical prince. His mental powers resembled the qualities of his person. He was tall, strong, and handsome, with a complexion in which red and white were strongly contrasted, and had long flowing locks of fair hair. But there was an awkwardness in his gait, which seemed as if his size was not animated by energy sufficient to put in motion such a mass; and in the same manner, wearing the richest dresses, it always seemed as if they became him not. As a prince, he appeared too little familiar with his own dignity, and being often at a loss how to assert his authority when the occasion demanded it, he frequently thought himself obliged to recover, by acts and expressions of ill-timed violence, the ground which might have been easily and gracefully maintained by a little more presence of mind in the beginning of the controversy.

Not only were these deficiencies visible to others, but the Archduke himself could not but sometimes entertain a painful consciousness that he was not altogether fit to maintain and assert the high rank which he had acquired ; and to this was joined the strong, and sometimes the just suspicion, that others esteemed him lightly accordingly.

When he first joined the Crusade, with a most princely attendance, Leopold had desired much to enjoy the friendship and intimacy of Richard, and had made such advances towards cultivating his regard, as the King of England ought, in policy, to have received and answered. But the Archduke, though not deficient in bravery, was so infinitely inferior to Cœur de Lion in that ardour of mind which wooed danger as a bride, that the King very soon held him in a certain degree of contempt. Richard, also, as a Norman Prince, a people with whom temperance was habitual, despised the inclination of the German for the pleasures of the table, and particularly his liberal indulgence in the use of wine. For these and other personal reasons, the King of England very soon looked upon the Austrian Prince with feelings of contempt, which he was at no pains to conceal or modify, and which, therefore, were speedily remarked, and returned with deep hatred, by the suspicious Leopold. The discord between them was fanned by the secret and politic arts of Philip of France, one of the most sagacious monarchs of the time, who, dreading the fiery and overbearing character of Richard, considering him as his natural rival, and feeling offended, moreover, at the dictatorial manner in which he, a vassal of France for his continental domains, conducted himself towards his liege lord, endeavoured to strengthen his own party, and weaken that of Richard, by uniting the Crusading princes of inferior degree, in resistance to what he termed the usurping authority of the King of England. Such was the state of politics and opinions entertained by the Archduke of Austria, when Conrade of Montserrat resolved upon employing his jealousy of England as the means of dissolving, or loosening at least, the league of the Crusaders.

The time which he chose for his visit was noon, and the pretence, to present the Archduke with some choice Cyprus wine which had lately fallen into his hands, and discuss its comparative merits with those of Hungary and of the Rhine. An intimation of his purpose was of course answered by a courteous invitation to partake of the Archducal meal, and every effort was used to render it fitting the splendour of a sovereign prince. Yet, the refined taste of the Italian saw more cumbrous profusion, than elegance or splendour, in the display of provisions under which the board groaned.

The Germans, though still possessing the martial and frank character of their ancestors, who subdued the Roman empire, had retained withal no slight tinge of their barbarism. The practices and principles of chivalry were not carried to such a nice pitch amongst them, as amongst the French and English knights, nor were they strict observers of the prescribed rules of society, which among those nations were supposed to express the height of civilisation. Sitting at the table of the Archduke, Conrade was at once stunned and amused, with the clang of Teutonic sounds assaulting his ears on all sides, notwithstanding the solemnity of a princely banquet. Their dress seemed equally fantastic to him, many of the Austrian nobles retaining their long beards, and almost all of them wearing short jerkins of various colours, cut, and flourished, and fringed, in a manner not common in Western Europe.

Numbers of dependents, old and young, attended in the pavilion, mingled at times in the conversation, received from their masters the relics of the entertainment, and devoured them as they stood behind the backs of the company. Jesters, dwarfs, and minstrels, were there in unusual numbers, and more noisy and intrusive than they were permitted to be in better regulated society. As they were allowed to share freely in the wine, which flowed round in large quantities, their licensed tumult was the more excessive.

All this while, and in the midst of a clamour and confusion,

which would better have become a German tavern during a
fair, than the tent of a sovereign prince, the Archduke was
waited upon with a minuteness of form and observance, which
showed how anxious he was to maintain rigidly the state and
character to which his elevation had entitled him. He was
served on the knee, and only by pages of noble blood, fed upon
plate of silver, and drank his Tokay and Rhenish wines from
a cup of gold. His ducal mantle was splendidly adorned with
ermine, his coronet might have equalled in value a royal crown,
and his feet, cased in velvet shoes (the length of which, peaks
included, might be two feet), rested upon a footstool of solid
silver. But it served partly to intimate the character of the
man, that although desirous to show attention to the Marquis
of Montserrat, whom he had courteously placed at his right
hand, he gave much more of his attention to his *spruch-sprecher*,
that is, his man of conversation, or *sayer of sayings*, who stood
behind the Duke's right shoulder.

This personage was well attired, in a coat and doublet of
black velvet, the last of which was decorated with various silver
and gold coins, stitched upon it, in memory of the munificent
princes who had conferred them, and bearing a short staff, to
which also bunches of silver coins were attached by rings, which
he jingled by way of attracting attention, when he was about
to say anything which he judged worthy of it. This person's
capacity in the household of the Archduke, was somewhat
betwixt that of a minstrel and a counsellor; he was by turns a
flatterer, a poet, and an orator; and those who desired to be
well with the Duke, generally studied to gain the goodwill of
the *spruch-sprecher*.

Lest too much of this officer's wisdom should become tiresome, the Duke's other shoulder was occupied by his *hoff-narr*,
or court jester, called Jonas Schwanker, who made almost as
much noise with his fool's-cap, bells, and bauble, as did the
orator, or man of talk, with his jingling baton.

These two personages threw out grave and comic nonsense
alternately, while their master, laughing or applauding them
himself, yet carefully watched the countenance of his noble
guest, to discern what impressions so accomplished a cavalier
received from this display of Austrian eloquence and wit. It
is hard to say whether the man of wisdom or the man of folly
contributed most to the amusement of the party, or stood
highest in the estimation of their princely master; but the
sallies of both seemed excellently well received. Sometimes
they became rivals for the conversation, and clanged their
flappers in emulation of each other, with a most alarming contention; but, in general, they seemed on such good terms, and
so accustomed to support each other's play, that the *spruch-*

sprecher often condescended to follow up the jester's witticisms with an explanation, to render them more obvious to the capacity of the audience; so that his wisdom became a sort of commentary on the buffoon's folly. And sometimes, in requital, the *hoff-narr*, with a pithy jest, wound up the conclusion of the orator's tedious harangue.

Whatever his real sentiments might be, Conrade took especial care that his countenance should express nothing but satisfaction with what he heard, and smiled or applauded as zealously, to all appearance, as the Archduke himself, at the solemn folly of the *spruch-sprecher*, and the gibbering wit of the fool. In fact, he watched carefully until the one or other should introduce some topic, favourable to the purpose which was uppermost in his mind.

It was not long ere the King of England was brought on the carpet by the jester, who had been accustomed to consider Dickon of the Broom (which irreverent epithet he substituted for Richard Plantagenet) as a subject of mirth, acceptable and inexhaustible. The orator, indeed, was silent, and it was only when applied to by Conrade, that he observed, "The *genista*, or broom-plant, was an emblem of humility; and it would be well when those who wore it would remember the warning."

The allusion to the illustrious badge of Plantagenet was thus rendered sufficiently manifest, and Jonas Schwanker observed, that they who humbled themselves had been exalted with a vengeance.

"Honour unto whom honour is due," answered the Marquis of Montserrat; "we have all had some part in these marches and battles, and methinks other princes might share a little in the renown which Richard of England engrosses amongst minstrels and *minne-singers*. Has no one of the Joyeuse science here present a song in praise of the royal Archduke of Austria, our princely entertainer?"

Three minstrels emulously stepped forward with voice and harp. Two were silenced with difficulty by the *spruch-sprecher*, who seemed to act as master of the revels, and a hearing was at length procured for the poet preferred, who sung, in high German, stanzas which may be thus translated:—

> What brave chief shall head the forces,
> Where the red-cross legions gather?
> Best of horsemen, best of horses,
> Highest head and fairest feather.

Here the orator, jingling his staff, interrupted the bard to intimate to the party, what they might not have inferred from the description, that their royal host was the party indicated, and a full crowned goblet went round to the acclamation—*Hoch lebe der Herzog Leopold!* Another stanza followed.

> Ask not Austria why, midst princes,
>   Still her banner rises highest;
> Ask as well the strong-wing'd eagle,
>   Why to Heaven he soars the nighest.

"The eagle," said the expounder of dark sayings, "is the cognisance of our noble lord the Archduke—of his royal Grace, I would say—and the eagle flies the highest and nearest to the sun of all the feathered creation."

"The lion hath taken a spring above the eagle," said Conrade carelessly.

The Archduke reddened, and fixed his eyes on the speaker, while the *spruch-sprecher* answered, after a minute's consideration, "The Lord Marquis will pardon me—a lion cannot fly above an eagle, because no lion hath got wings."

"Except the Lion of Saint Mark," responded the jester.

"That is the Venetian's banner," said the Duke; "but assuredly, that amphibious race, half nobles, half merchants, will not dare to place their rank in comparison with ours?"

"Nay, it was not of the Venetian lion that I spoke," said the Marquis of Montserrat; "but of the three lions passant of England—formerly, it is said, they were leopards, but now they are become lions at all points, and must take precedence of beast, fish, or fowl, or woe worth the gainstander."

"Mean you seriously, my lord?" said the Austrian, now considerably flushed with wine; "think you that Richard of England asserts any pre-eminence over the free sovereigns who have been his voluntary allies in this Crusade?"

"I know not but from circumstances," answered Conrade; "yonder hangs his banner alone in the midst of our camp, as if he were king and generalissimo of our whole Christian army."

"And do you endure this so patiently, and speak of it so coldly?" said the Archduke.

"Nay, my lord," answered Conrade, "it cannot concern the poor Marquis of Montserrat to contend against an injury, patiently submitted to by such potent princes as Philip of France and Leopold of Austria. What dishonour you are pleased to submit to, cannot be a disgrace to me."

Leopold closed his fist, and struck on the table with violence.

"I have told Philip of this," he said; "I have often told him that it was our duty to protect the inferior princes against the usurpation of this islander—but he answers me ever with cold respects of their relations together as suzerain and vassal, and that it were impolitic in him to make an open breach at this time and period."

"The world knows that Philip is wise," said Conrade, "and will judge his submission to be policy.—Yours, my lord, you can yourself alone account for; but I doubt not you have deep reasons for submitting to English domination."

"*I* submit!" said Leopold indignantly—"*I*, the Archduke of Austria, so important and vital a limb of the Holy Roman empire—*I* submit myself to this King of half an island—this grandson of a Norman bastard!—No, by Heaven! The camp, and all Christendom, shall see that I know how to right myself, and whether I yield ground one inch to the English bandog.— Up, my lieges and merry men, up and follow me! We will— and that without losing one instant—place the eagle of Austria, where she shall float as high as ever floated the cognisance of king or kaisar."

With that he started from his seat, and, amidst the tumultuous cheering of his guests and followers, made for the door of the pavilion, and seized his own banner, which stood pitched before it.

"Nay, my lord," said Conrade, affecting to interfere, "it will blemish your wisdom to make an affray in the camp at this hour, and perhaps it is better to submit to the usurpation of England a little longer than to—— "

"Not an hour—not a moment longer," vociferated the Duke; and, with the banner in his hand, and followed by his shouting guests and attendants, marched hastily to the central mount, from which the banner of England floated, and laid his hand on the standard-spear, as if to pluck it from the ground.

"My master, my dear master!" said Jonas Schwanker, throwing his arms about the Duke—"take heed—lions have teeth—— "

"And eagles have claws," said the Duke, not relinquishing his hold on the banner-staff, yet hesitating to pull it from the ground.

The speaker of sentences, notwithstanding such was his occupation, had nevertheless some intervals of sound sense. He clashed his staff loudly, and Leopold, as if by habit, turned his head towards his man of counsel.

"The eagle is king among the fowls of the air," said the *spruch-sprecher*, "as is the lion among the beasts of the field —each has his dominion, separated as wide as England and Germany—do thou, noble eagle, no dishonour to the princely lion, but let your banners remain floating in peace side by side."

Leopold withdrew his hand from the banner-spear, and looked round for Conrade of Montserrat, but he saw him not; for the Marquis, so soon as he saw the mischief afoot, had withdrawn himself from the crowd, taking care, in the first place, to express before several neutral persons his regret, that the Archduke should have chosen the hours after dinner to avenge any wrong of which he might think he had a right to complain. Not seeing his guest, to whom he wished more particularly to have addressed himself, the Archduke said aloud, that having no wish to breed dissension in the army of the Cross, he did but vindicate his own privileges and right to stand upon an equality with the King of England, without desiring, as he might have done, to advance his banner, which he derived from Emperors, his progenitors, above that of a mere descendant of the Counts of Anjou; and, in the meantime, he commanded a cask of wine to be brought hither and pierced, for regaling the bystanders, who, with tuck of drum and sound of music, quaffed many a carouse round the Austrian standard.

This disorderly scene was not acted without a degree of noise, which alarmed the whole camp.

The critical hour had arrived, at which the physician, according to the rules of his art, had predicted that his royal patient might be awakened with safety, and the sponge had been applied for that purpose; and the leech had not made many observations ere he assured the Baron of Gilsland that the fever had entirely left his sovereign, and that such was the happy strength of his constitution, it would not be even necessary, as in most cases, to give a second dose of the powerful medicine. Richard himself seemed to be of the same opinion, for, sitting up and rubbing his eyes, he demanded of De Vaux what present sum of money was in the royal coffers.

The baron could not exactly inform him of the amount.

"It matters not," said Richard; "be it greater or smaller, bestow it all on this learned leech, who hath, I trust, given me back again to the service of the Crusade. If it be less than a thousand byzants, let him have jewels to make it up."

"I sell not the wisdom with which Allah has endowed me," answered the Arabian physician; "and be it known to you, great Prince, that the divine medicine, of which you have partaken, would lose its effects in my unworthy hands, did I exchange its virtues either for gold or diamonds."

"The physician refuseth a gratuity!" said De Vaux to himself. "This is more extraordinary than his being an hundred years old."

"Thomas de Vaux," said Richard, "thou knowest no courage but what belongs to the sword, no bounty and virtue but what are used in chivalry—I tell thee that this Moor in his independence, might set an example to them who account themselves the flower of knighthood."

"It is reward enough for me," said the Moor, folding his

arms on his bosom, and maintaining an attitude at once respectful and dignified, "that so great a King as the Melech Ric* should thus speak of his servant.—But now, let me pray you again to compose yourself on your couch; for though I think there needs no farther repetition of the divine draught, yet injury might ensue from any too early exertion, ere your strength be entirely restored."

"I must obey thee, Hakim," said the King; "yet, believe me, my bosom feels so free from the wasting fire, which for so many days hath scorched it, that I care not how soon I expose it to a brave man's lance.—But hark! what mean these shouts, and that distant music in the camp? Go, Thomas de Vaux, and make inquiry."

"It is the Archduke Leopold," said De Vaux, returning after a minute's absence, "who makes with his pot companions some procession through the camp."

"The drunken fool!" exclaimed King Richard, "can he not keep his brutal inebriety within the veil of his pavilion, that he must needs show his shame to all Christendom?—What say you, Sir Marquis?" he added, addressing himself to Conrade of Montserrat, who at that moment entered the tent.

"Thus much, honoured Prince," answered the Marquis, "that I delight to see your Majesty so well, and so far recovered; and that is a long speech for any one to make who has partaken of the Duke of Austria's hospitality."

"What! you have been dining with the Teutonic wine-skin," said the monarch; "and what frolic has he found out to cause all this disturbance? Truly, Sir Conrade, I have still held you so good a reveller, that I wonder at your quitting the game."

De Vaux, who had got a little behind the King, now exerted himself, by look and sign, to make the Marquis understand that he should say nothing to Richard of what was passing without. But Conrade understood not, or heeded not, the prohibition.

"What the Archduke does," he said, "is of little consequence to any one, least of all to himself, since he probably knows not what he is acting—yet, to say truth, it is a gambol I should not like to share in, since he is pulling down the banner of England from Saint George's Mount in the centre of the camp yonder, and displaying his own in its stead."

"WHAT say'st thou?" said the King, in a tone which might have waked the dead.

"Nay," said the Marquis, "let it not chafe your Highness, that a fool should act according to his folly——"

"Speak not to me," said Richard, springing from his couch, and casting on his clothes with a despatch which seemed marvellous—"speak not to me, Lord Marquis!—De Multon, I

---

* Richard was thus called by the Eastern nations.

command thee speak not a word to me—he that breathes but a syllable, is no friend to Richard Plantagenet.—Hakim, be silent, I charge thee!"

All this while the King was hastily clothing himself, and, with the last word, snatched his sword from the pillar of the tent, and without any other weapon, or calling any attendance, he rushed out of the tent. Conrade holding up his hands, as if in astonishment, seemed willing to enter into conversation with De Vaux, but Sir Thomas pushed rudely past him, and calling to one of the royal equerries, said hastily, "Fly to Lord Salisbury's quarters, and let him get his men together, and follow me instantly to Saint George's Mount. Tell him the King's fever has left his blood, and settled in his brain."

Imperfectly heard, and still more imperfectly comprehended, by the startled attendant whom De Vaux addressed thus hastily, the equerry and his fellow-servants of the royal chamber rushed hastily into the tents of the neighbouring nobility, and quickly spread an alarm, as general as the cause seemed vague, through the whole British forces. The English soldiers, waked in alarm from that noonday rest which the heat of the climate had taught them to enjoy as a luxury, hastily asked each other the cause of the tumult, and, without waiting an answer, supplied, by the force of their own fancy, the want of information. Some said the Saracens were in the camp, some that the King's life was attempted, some that he had died of the fever the preceding night, many that he was assassinated by the Duke of Austria. The nobles and officers, at an equal loss with the common men to ascertain the real cause of the disorder, laboured only to get their followers under arms and under authority, lest their rashness should occasion some great misfortune to the Crusading army. The English trumpets sounded loud, shrill, and continuously. The alarm-cry of "Bows and bills—bows and bills!" was heard from quarter to quarter, again and again shouted, and again and again answered by the presence of the ready warriors, and their national invocation, "Saint George for Merry England!"

The alarm went through the nearest quarter of the camp, and men of all the various nations assembled, where, perhaps, every people in Christendom had their representatives, flew to arms, and drew together under circumstances of general confusion, of which they knew neither the cause nor the object. It was, however, lucky, amid a scene so threatening, that the Earl of Salisbury, while he hurried after De Vaux's summons, with a few only of the readiest English men-at-arms, directed the rest of the English host to be drawn up and kept under arms, to advance to Richard's succour if necessity should require, but in fit array, and under due command, and not

with the tumultuary haste which their own alarm, and zeal for
the King's safety, might have dictated.

In the meanwhile, without regarding for one instant the
shouts, the cries, the tumult, which began to thicken around
him, Richard, with his dress in the last disorder, and his
sheathed blade under his arm, pursued his way with the utmost
speed, followed only by De Vaux, and one or two household
servants, to Saint George's Mount.

He outsped even the alarm which his impetuosity only had
excited, and passed the quarter of his own gallant troops of Normandy, Poitou, Gascony, and Anjou, before the disturbance had
reached them, although the noise accompanying the German revel
had induced many of the soldiery to get on foot to listen. The
handful of Scots were also quartered in the vicinity, nor had they
been disturbed by the uproar. But the King's person, and his
haste, were both remarked by the Knight of the Leopard, who,
aware that danger must be afoot, and hastening to share in it,
snatched his shield and sword, and united himself to De Vaux,
who with some difficulty kept with his impatient and fiery master.
De Vaux answered a look of curiosity, which the Scottish knight
directed towards him, with a shrug of his broad shoulders, and
they continued, side by side, to pursue Richard's steps.

The King was soon at the foot of Saint George's Mount, the
sides as well as platform of which were now surrounded and
crowded, partly by those belonging to the Duke of Austria's
retinue, who were celebrating, with shouts of jubilee, the act
which they considered as an assertion of national honour;
partly by bystanders of different nations, whom dislike to the
English, or mere curiosity, had assembled together, to witness
the end of these extraordinary proceedings. Through this disorderly troop Richard burst his way, like a goodly ship under
full sail, which cleaves her forcible passage through the rolling
billows, and heeds not that they unite after her passage, and
roar upon her stern.

The summit of the eminence was a small level space, on
which were pitched the rival banners, surrounded still by the
Archduke's friends and retinue. In the midst of the circle
was Leopold himself, still contemplating with self-satisfaction
the deed he had done, and still listening to the shouts of
applause which his partisans bestowed with no sparing breath.
While he was in this state of self-gratulation, Richard burst
into the circle, attended, indeed, only by two men, but in his
own headlong energies an irresistible host.

"Who has dared," he said, laying his hands upon the
Austrian standard, and speaking in a voice like the sound
which precedes an earthquake; "who has dared to place this
paltry rag beside the banner of England?"

The Archduke wanted not personal courage, and it was impossible he could hear this question without reply. Yet, so much was he troubled and surprised by the unexpected arrival of Richard, and affected by the general awe inspired by his ardent and unyielding character, that the demand was twice repeated, in a tone which seemed to challenge heaven and earth, ere the Archduke replied with such firmness as he could command, " It was I, Leopold of Austria."

"Then shall Leopold of Austria," replied Richard, "presently see the rate at which his banner and his pretensions are held by Richard of England."

So saying, he pulled up the standard-spear, splintered it to pieces, threw the banner itself on the ground, and placed his foot upon it.

"Thus," said he, "I trample on the banner of Austria—Is there a knight among your Teutonic chivalry dare impeach my deed?"

There was a momentary silence; but there are no braver men than the Germans.

"I," and "I," and "I," was heard from several knights of the Duke's followers; and he himself added his voice to those which accepted the King of England's defiance.

"Why do we dally thus?" said the Earl Wallenrode, a gigantic warrior from the frontiers of Hungary. "Brethren, and noble gentlemen, this man's foot is on the honour of your country—Let us rescue it from violation, and down with the pride of England!"

So saying, he drew his sword, and struck at the King a blow which might have proved fatal, had not the Scot intercepted and caught it upon his shield.

"I have sworn," said King Richard—and his voice was heard above all the tumult, which now waxed wild and loud—"never to strike one whose shoulder bears the cross; therefore live, Wallenrode—but live to remember Richard of England."

As he spoke, he grasped the tall Hungarian round the waist, and, unmatched in wrestling, as in other military exercises, hurled him backwards with such violence that the mass flew as if discharged from a military engine, not only through the ring of spectators who witnessed the extraordinary scene, but over the edge of the mount itself, down the steep side of which Wallenrode rolled headlong, until, pitching at length upon his shoulder, he dislocated the bone, and lay like one dead. This almost supernatural display of strength did not encourage either the Duke or any of his followers, to renew a personal contest so inauspiciously commenced. Those who stood farthest back did, indeed, clash their swords, and cry out, "Cut the island mastiff to pieces!" but those who were nearer, veiled, perhaps, their personal fears under an affected regard for order, and cried, for the most part, "Peace! peace! the peace of the Cross—the peace of Holy Church, and our Father the Pope!"

These various cries of the assailants, contradicting each other, showed their irresolution; while Richard, his foot still on the archducal banner, glared round him, with an eye that seemed to seek an enemy, and from which the angry nobles shrunk appalled, as from the threatened grasp of a lion. De Vaux and the Knight of the Leopard kept their places beside him; and though the swords which they held were still sheathed, it was plain that they were prompt to protect Richard's person to the very last, and their size and remarkable strength plainly showed the defence would be a desperate one.

Salisbury and his attendants were also now drawing near, with bills and partisans brandished, and bows already bended.

At this moment, King Philip of France, attended by one or two of his nobles, came on the platform to inquire the cause of the disturbance, and made gestures of surprise at finding the King of England raised from his sick-bed, and confronting their common ally the Duke of Austria, in such a menacing and insulting posture. Richard himself blushed at being discovered by Philip, whose sagacity he respected as much as he disliked his person, in an attitude neither becoming his character as a monarch, nor as a Crusader; and it was observed that he withdrew his foot, as if accidentally, from the dishonoured banner, and exchanged his look of violent emotion for one of affected composure and indifference. Leopold also struggled to attain some degree of calmness, mortified as he was by having been seen by Philip in the act of passively submitting to the insults of the fiery King of England.

Possessed of many of those royal qualities for which he was termed by his subjects the August, Philip might be termed the Ulysses, as Richard was indisputably the Achilles, of the Crusade. The King of France was sagacious, wise, deliberate in council, steady and calm in action, seeing clearly, and steadily pursuing the measures most for the interest of his kingdom—dignified and royal in his deportment, brave in person, but a politician rather than a warrior. The Crusade would have been no choice of his own, but the spirit was contagious, and the expedition was enforced upon him by the Church, and by the unanimous wish of his nobility. In any other situation, or in a milder age, his character might have stood higher than that of the adventurous Cœur de Lion. But in the Crusade, itself an undertaking wholly irrational, sound reason was the quality, of all others, least estimated, and the chivalric valour which both the age and the enterprise demanded, was considered as debased, if mingled with the least touch of discretion. So that the merit of Philip,

RICHARD, CŒUR DE LION

T. A. PRIOR

compared with that of his haughty rival, showed like the clear but minute flame of a lamp, placed near the glare of a huge blazing torch, which, not possessing half the utility, makes ten times more impression on the eye. Philip felt his inferiority in public opinion, with the pain natural to a high-spirited prince; and it cannot be wondered at if he took such opportunities as offered, for placing his own character in more advantageous contrast with that of his rival. The present seemed one of those occasions, in which prudence and calmness might reasonably expect to triumph over obstinacy and impetuous violence.

"What means this unseemly broil betwixt the sworn brethren of the Cross—the royal Majesty of England and the princely Duke Leopold? How is it possible that those who are the chiefs and pillars of this holy expedition——"

"A truce with thy remonstrance, France," said Richard, enraged inwardly at finding himself placed on a sort of equality with Leopold, yet not knowing how to resent it,—"this duke, or prince, or pillar, if you will, hath been insolent, and I have chastised him—that is all. Here is a coil, forsooth, because of spurning a hound!"

"Majesty of France," said the Duke, "I appeal to you and every sovereign prince against the foul indignity which I have sustained. This King of England hath pulled down my banner —torn and trampled on it."

"Because he had the audacity to plant it beside mine," said Richard.

"My rank as thine equal entitled me," replied the Duke, emboldened by the presence of Philip.

"Assert such equality for thy person," said King Richard, "and, by Saint George, I will treat thy person as I did thy broidered kerchief there, fit but for the meanest use to which kerchief may be put."

"Nay, but patience, brother of England," said Philip, "and I will presently show Austria that he is wrong in this matter.— Do not think, noble Duke," he continued, "that, in permitting the standard of England to occupy the highest point in our camp, we, the independent sovereigns of the Crusade, acknowledge any inferiority to the royal Richard. It were inconsistent to think so; since even the oriflamme itself—the great banner of France, to which the royal Richard himself, in respect of his French possessions, is but a vassal—holds for the present an inferior place to the Lions of England. But as sworn brethren of the Cross, military pilgrims, who, laying aside the pomp and pride of this world, are hewing with our swords the way to the Holy Sepulchre, I myself, and the other princes, have renounced to King Richard, from respect to his high renown and great feats of arms, that precedence, which elsewhere, and upon other motives, would not have been yielded. I am satisfied, that when your royal grace of Austria shall have considered this, you will express sorrow for having placed your banner on this spot, and that the royal Majesty of England will then give satisfaction for the insult he has offered."

The *spruch-sprecher* and the jester had both retired to a safe distance when matters seemed coming to blows, but returned when words, their own commodity, seemed again about to become the order of the day.

The man of proverbs was so delighted with Philip's politic speech, that he clashed his baton at the conclusion by way of emphasis, and forgot the presence in which he was, so far as to say aloud, that he himself had never said a wiser thing in his life.

"It may be so," whispered Jonas Schwanker, "but we shall be whipt if you speak so loud."

The Duke answered sullenly, that he would refer his quarrel to the General Council of the Crusade—a motion which Philip highly applauded, as qualified to take away a scandal most harmful to Christendom.

Richard, retaining the same careless attitude, listened to Philip until his oratory seemed exhausted, and then said aloud, "I am drowsy—this fever hangs about me still. Brother of France, thou art acquainted with my humour, and that I have at all times but few words to spare—know, therefore, at once, I will submit a matter touching the honour of England neither to Prince, Pope, nor Council. Here stands my banner—whatsoever pennon shall be reared within three butts' length of it —ay, were it the oriflamme, of which you were, I think, but now speaking, shall be treated as that dishonoured rag; nor will I yield other satisfaction than that which these poor limbs can render in the lists to any bold challenge—ay, were it against five champions instead of one."

"Now," said the jester, whispering his companion, "that is as complete a piece of folly, as if I myself had said it—but yet, I think, there may be in this matter a greater fool than Richard yet."

"And who may that be?" asked the man of wisdom.

"Philip," said the jester, "or our own Royal Duke, should either accept the challenge—But oh, most sage *spruch-sprecher*, what excellent kings would thou and I have made, since those on whose heads these crowns have fallen, can play the proverb-monger and the fool as completely as ourselves!"

While these worthies plied their offices apart, Philip answered calmly to the almost injurious defiance of Richard,—"I came not hither to awaken fresh quarrels, contrary to the oath we have sworn, and the holy cause in which we have engaged.

part from my brother of England as brothers should part, and the only strife between the Lions of England and the Lilies of France shall be, which shall be carried deepest into the ranks of the infidels."

"It is a bargain, my royal brother," said Richard, stretching out his hand with all the frankness which belonged to his rash but generous disposition; "and soon may we have the opportunity to try this gallant and fraternal wager!"

"Let this noble Duke also partake in the friendship of this happy moment," said Philip; and the Duke approached half-sullenly, half-willing to enter into some accommodation.

"I think not of fools, nor of their folly," said Richard carelessly; and the Archduke, turning his back on him, withdrew from the ground.

Richard looked after him as he retired.

"There is a sort of glow-worm courage," he said, "that shows only by night. I must not leave this banner unguarded in darkness—by daylight the look of the Lions will alone defend it. Here, Thomas of Gilsland, I give thee the charge of the standard—watch over the honour of England."

"Her safety is yet more dear to me," said De Vaux, "and the life of Richard is the safety of England—I must have your Highness back to your tent, and that without further tarriance."

"Thou art a rough and peremptory nurse, De Vaux," said the King, smiling; and then added, addressing Sir Kenneth, "Valiant Scot, I owe thee a boon, and I will pay it richly. There stands the banner of England! Watch it as a novice does his armour on the night before he is dubbed—Stir not from it three spears' length, and defend it with thy body against injury or insult—Sound thy bugle, if thou art assailed by more than three at once. Dost thou undertake the charge?"

"Willingly," said Kenneth; "and will discharge it upon penalty of my head. I will but arm me, and return hither instantly."

The Kings of France and England then took formal leave of each other, hiding, under an appearance of courtesy, the grounds of complaint which either had against the other,—Richard against Philip, for what he deemed an officious interference betwixt him and Austria, and Philip against Cœur de Lion, for the disrespectful manner in which his mediation had been received. Those whom this disturbance had assembled, now drew off in different directions, leaving the contested mount in the same solitude which had subsisted till interrupted by the Austrian bravado. Men judged of the events of the day according to their partialities; and while the English charged the Austrian with having afforded the first ground of quarrel, those of other nations concurred in casting the greater blame upon the insular haughtiness and assuming character of Richard.

"Thou seest," said the Marquis of Montserrat to the Grand Master of the Templars, "that subtle courses are more effective than violence. I have unloosed the bonds which held together this bunch of sceptres and lances—thou wilt see them shortly fall asunder."

"I would have called thy plan a good one," said the Templar, "had there been but one man of courage among yonder cold-blooded Austrians, to sever the bonds of which you speak, with his sword. A knot that is unloosed may again be fastened, but not so the cord which has been cut to pieces."

CHAPTER XII

'Tis woman that seduces all mankind.

—GAY.

IN the days of chivalry, a dangerous post, or a perilous adventure, was a reward frequently assigned to military bravery as a compensation for its former trials—just as, in ascending a precipice, the surmounting one crag only lifts the climber to points yet more dangerous.

It was midnight, and the moon rode clear and high in heaven, when Kenneth of Scotland stood upon his watch on Saint George's Mount, beside the banner of England, a solitary sentinel, to protect the emblem of that nation against the insults which might be meditated among the thousands whom Richard's pride had made his enemies. High thoughts rolled, one after another, upon the mind of the warrior. It seemed to him as if he had gained some favour in the eyes of the chivalrous monarch, who till now had not seemed to distinguish him among the crowds of brave men whom his renown had assembled under his banner, and Sir Kenneth little recked that the display of royal regard consisted in placing him upon a post so perilous. The devotion of his ambitious and high-placed affection inflamed his military enthusiasm.

Hopeless as that attachment was, in almost any conceivable circumstances, those which had lately occurred had, in some degree, diminished the distance between Edith and himself. He upon whom Richard had conferred the distinction of guarding his banner was no longer an adventurer of slight note, but placed within the regard of a princess, although he was as far as ever from her level. An unknown and obscure fate could not now be his. If he was surprised and slain on the post which had been assigned him, his death—and he resolved it should be glorious—must deserve the praises, as well as call down the vengeance, of Cœur de Lion, and be followed by the regrets, and even the tears, of the high-born beauties of the English Court. He had now no longer reason to fear that he should die as a fool dieth.

Sir Kenneth had full leisure to enjoy these and similar high-souled thoughts, fostered by that wild spirit of chivalry, which, amid its most extravagant and fantastic flights, was still pure from all selfish alloy—generous, devoted, and perhaps only thus far censurable, that it proposed objects and courses of action inconsistent with the frailties and imperfections of man. All nature around him slept in calm moonshine, or in deep shadow. The long rows of tents and pavilions, glimmering or darkening as they lay in the moonlight or in the shade, were still and silent as the streets of a deserted city. Beside the banner-staff lay the large staghound already mentioned, the sole companion of Kenneth's watch, on whose vigilance he trusted for early warning of the approach of any hostile footstep. The noble animal seemed to understand the purpose of their watch, for he looked from time to time at the rich folds of the heavy pennon, and, when the cry of the sentinels came from the distant lines and defences of the camp, he answered them with one deep and reiterated bark, as if to affirm that he too was vigilant in his duty. From time to time, also, he lowered his lofty head, and wagged his tail, as his master passed and re-passed him in the short turns which he took upon his post; or, when the knight stood silent and abstracted, leaning on his lance, and looking up towards Heaven, his faithful attendant ventured sometimes, in the phrase of romance, "to disturb his thoughts," and awaken him from his reverie, by thrusting his large rough snout into the knight's gauntleted hand, to solicit a transitory caress.

Thus passed two hours of the knight's watch without anything remarkable occurring. At length, and upon a sudden, the gallant staghound bayed furiously, and seemed about to dash forward where the shadow lay the darkest, yet waited, as if in the slips, till he should know the pleasure of his master.

"Who goes there?" said Sir Kenneth, aware that there was something creeping forward on the shadowy side of the mount.

"In the name of Merlin and Maugis," answered a hoarse, disagreeable voice, "tie up your four-footed demon there, or I come not at you."

"And who art thou, that would approach my post?" said Sir Kenneth, bending his eyes as keenly as he could on some object which he could just observe at the bottom of the ascent, without being able to distinguish its form. "Beware—I am here for death and life."

"Take up thy long-fanged Sathanas," said the voice, "or I will conjure him with a bolt from my arblast."

At the same time was heard the sound of a spring or check, as when a crossbow is bent.

"Unbend thy arblast, and come into the moonlight," said the Scot, "or, by Saint Andrew, I will pin thee to the earth, be what or whom thou wilt!"

As he spoke, he poised his long lance by the middle, and, fixing his eye upon the object which seemed to move, he brandished the weapon, as if meditating to cast it from his hand—a use of the weapon, sometimes, though rarely, resorted to, when a missile was necessary. But Sir Kenneth was ashamed of his purpose, and grounded his weapon, when there stepped from the shadow into the moonlight, like an actor entering upon the stage, a stunted decrepit creature, whom, by his fantastic dress and deformity, he recognised, even at some distance, for the male of the two dwarfs whom he had seen at the chapel of Engaddi. Recollecting, at the same moment, the other, and far different, visions of that extraordinary night, he gave his dog a signal, which he instantly understood, and, returning to the standard, laid himself down beside it with a stifled growl.

The little distorted miniature of humanity, assured of his safety from an enemy so formidable, came panting up the ascent, which the shortness of his legs rendered laborious, and when he arrived on the platform on the top, shifted to his left hand the little crossbow, which was just such a toy as children at that period were permitted to shoot small birds with, and, assuming an attitude of great dignity, gracefully extended his right hand to Sir Kenneth, in an attitude as if he expected he would salute it. But such a result not following, he demanded in a sharp and angry tone of voice, "Soldier, wherefore renderest thou not to Nectabanus the homage due to his dignity? —Or, is it possible that thou canst have forgotten him?"

"Great Nectabanus," answered the knight, willing to soothe the creature's humour, "that were difficult for any one who has ever looked upon thee. Pardon me, however, that being a soldier upon my post, with my lance in my hand, I may not give to one of thy puissance the advantage of coming within my guard, or of mastering my weapon. Suffice it, that I reverence thy dignity, and submit myself to thee as humbly as a man-at-arms in my place may."

"It shall suffice," said Nectabanus, "so that you presently attend me to the presence of those who have sent me hither to summon you."

"Great sir," replied the knight, "neither in this can I gratify thee, for my orders are to abide by this banner till daybreak —so I pray you to hold me excused in that matter also."

So saying, he resumed his walk upon the platform; but the dwarf did not suffer him so easily to escape from his importunity.

"Look you," he said, placing himself before Sir Kenneth, so as to interrupt his way, "either obey me, Sir Knight, as in duty bound, or I will lay the command upon thee, in the name of one whose beauty could call down the genii from their sphere, and whose grandeur could command the immortal race when they had descended."

A wild and improbable conjecture arose in the knight's mind, but he repelled it. It was impossible, he thought, that the lady of his love should have sent him such a message by such a messenger—yet his voice trembled as he said, "Go to, Necta-banus. Tell me at once, and as a true man, whether this sublime lady of whom thou speakest, be other than the houri with whose assistance I beheld thee sweeping the chapel at Engaddi?"

"How! presumptuous knight," replied the dwarf, "think'st thou the mistress of our own royal affections, the sharer of our greatness, and the partner of our comeliness, would demean herself by laying charge on such a vassal as thou? No, highly as thou art honoured, thou has not yet deserved the notice of Queen Guenevra, the lovely bride of Arthur, from whose high seat even princes seem but pigmies. But look thou here, and as thou knowest or disownest this token, so obey or refuse her commands, who hath deigned to impose them on thee."

So saying, he placed in the knight's hands a ruby ring, which, even in the moonlight, he had no difficulty to recognise as that which usually graced the finger of the high-born lady to whose service he had devoted himself. Could he have doubted the truth of the token, he would have been convinced by the small knot of carnation-coloured ribbon, which was fastened to the ring. This was his lady's favourite colour, and more than once had he himself, assuming it for that of his own liveries, caused the carnation to triumph over all other hues in the lists and in the battle.

Sir Kenneth was struck nearly mute, by seeing such a token in such hands.

"In the name of all that is sacred, from whom didst thou receive this witness?" said the knight; "bring, if thou canst, thy wavering understanding to a right settlement for a minute or two, and tell me the person by whom thou art sent, and the real purpose of thy message—and take heed what thou say'st, for this is no subject for buffoonery."

"Fond and foolish knight," said the dwarf, "wouldst thou know more of this matter, than that thou art honoured with commands from a princess, delivered to thee by a king?—We list not to parley with thee farther than to command thee, in the name, and by the power of that ring, to follow us to her who is the owner of the ring. Every minute that thou tarriest is a crime against thy allegiance."

"Good Nectabanus—bethink thyself," said the knight,— "Can my lady know where and upon what duty I am this night engaged?—Is she aware that my life—Pshaw, why should I speak of life—but that my honour depends on my guarding this banner till daybreak—and can it be her wish that I should leave it even to pay homage to her?—It is impossible—the princess is pleased to be merry with her servant, in sending him such a message; and I must think so the rather that she hath chosen such a messenger."

"Oh, keep your belief," said Nectabanus, turning round as if to leave the platform; "it is little to me whether you be traitor or true man to this royal lady—so fare thee well."

"Stay, stay—I entreat you stay," said Sir Kenneth; "answer me but one question—Is the lady who sent thee near to this place?"

"What signifies it?" said the dwarf; "ought fidelity to reckon furlongs, or miles, or leagues—like the poor courier, who is paid for his labour by the distance which he traverses? Nevertheless, thou soul of suspicion, I tell thee, the fair owner of the ring, now sent to so unworthy a vassal, in whom there is neither truth nor courage, is not more distant from this place than this arblast can send a bolt."

The knight gazed again on the ring, as if to ascertain that there was no possible falsehood in the token.—"Tell me," he said to the dwarf, "is my presence required for any length of time?"

"Time!" answered Nectabanus, in his flighty manner; "what call you time? I see it not—I feel it not—it is but a shadowy name—a succession of breathings measured forth by night by the clank of a bell, by day by a shadow crossing along a dial-stone. Know'st thou not a true knight's time should only be reckoned by the deeds that he performs in behalf of God and his lady?"

"The words of truth, though in the mouth of folly," said the knight. "And doth my lady really summon me to some deed of action, in her name and for her sake?—and may it not be postponed for even the few hours till daybreak?"

"She requires thy presence instantly," said the dwarf, "and without the loss of so much time as would be told by ten grains of the sand-glass—Hearken, thou cold-blooded and suspicious knight, these are her very words—'Tell him, that the hand which dropped roses can bestow laurels.'"

This allusion to their meeting in the chapel of Engaddi sent a thousand recollections through Sir Kenneth's brain, and convinced him that the message delivered by the dwarf was genuine. The rosebuds, withered as they were, were still treasured under his cuirass, and nearest to his heart. He paused, and could not resolve to forego an opportunity—the only one which might ever offer, to gain grace in her eyes, whom he had installed as sovereign of his affections. The dwarf, in the meantime, augmented his confusion by insisting either that he must return the ring, or instantly attend him.

"Hold, hold, yet a moment hold," said the knight, and proceeded to mutter to himself—"Am I either the subject or slave of King Richard, more than as a free knight sworn to the service of the Crusade? And whom have I come hither to honour with lance and sword? Our holy cause and my transcendent lady!"

"The ring, the ring!" exclaimed the dwarf impatiently; "false and slothful knight, return the ring, which thou art unworthy to touch or to look upon."

"A moment, a moment, good Nectabanus," said Sir Kenneth; "disturb not my thoughts.—What if the Saracens were just now to attack our lines? Should I stay here like a sworn vassal of England, watching that her king's pride suffered no humiliation; or should I speed to the breach, and fight for the Cross?—To the breach, assuredly; and next to the cause of God, come the commands of my liege lady.—And yet, Cœur de Lion's behest—my own promise!—Nectabanus, I conjure thee once more to say, are you to conduct me far from hence?"

"But to yonder pavilion; and since you must needs know," replied Nectabanus, "the moon is glimmering on the gilded ball which crowns its roof, and which is worth a king's ransom."

"I can return in an instant," said the knight, shutting his eyes desperately to all farther consequences. "I can hear from thence the bay of my dog, if any one approaches the standard—I will throw myself at my lady's feet, and pray her leave to return to conclude my watch.—Here, Roswal" (calling his hound, and throwing down his mantle by the side of the standard-spear), "watch thou here, and let no one approach."

The majestic dog looked in his master's face, as if to be sure that he understood his charge, then sat down beside the mantle, with ears erect, and head raised, like a sentinel, understanding perfectly the purpose for which he was stationed there.

"Come now, good Nectabanus," said the knight, "let us hasten to obey the commands thou hast brought."

"Haste he that will," said the dwarf sullenly; "thou hast not been in haste to obey my summons, nor can I walk fast enough to follow your long strides—you do not walk like a man, but bound like an ostrich in the desert."

There were but two ways of conquering the obstinacy of Nectabanus, who, as he spoke, diminished his walk into a snail pace. For bribes Sir Kenneth had no means—for soothing no time; so in his impatience he snatched the dwarf up from the ground, and bearing him along, notwithstanding his entreaties and his fear, reached nearly to the pavilion pointed out as that of the Queen. In approaching it, however, the Scot observed there was a small guard of soldiers sitting on the ground, who had been concealed from him by the intervening tents. Wondering that the clash of his own armour had not yet attracted their attention, and supposing that his motions might, on the present occasion, require to be conducted with secrecy, he placed the little panting guide upon the ground to recover his breath, and point out what was next to be done. Nectabanus was both frightened and angry; but he had felt himself as completely in the power of the robust knight, as an owl in the claws of an eagle, and therefore cared not to provoke him to any farther display of his strength.

He made no complaints, therefore, of the usage he had received, but turning amongst the labyrinth of tents, he led the knight in silence to the opposite side of the pavilion, which thus screened them from the observation of the warders, who seemed either too negligent or too sleepy to discharge their duty with much accuracy. Arrived there the dwarf raised the under part of the canvas from the ground, and made signs to Sir Kenneth that he should introduce himself to the inside of the tent, by creeping under it. The knight hesitated—there seemed an indecorum in thus privately introducing himself into a pavilion, pitched, doubtless, for the accommodation of noble ladies, but he recalled to remembrance the assured token, which the dwarf had exhibited, and concluded that it was not for him to dispute his lady's pleasure.

He stooped accordingly, crept beneath the canvas enclosure of the tent, and heard the dwarf whisper from without,— "Remain there until I call thee."

CHAPTER XIII

> You talk of Gaiety and Innocence!
> The moment when the fatal fruit was eaten,
> They parted ne'er to meet again: and Malice
> Has ever since been playmate to light Gaiety,
> From the first moment when the smiling infant
> Destroys the flower or butterfly he toys with,
> To the last chuckle of the dying miser,
> Who on his deathbed laughs his last to hear
> His wealthy neighbour has become a bankrupt.
>   —OLD PLAY.

SIR KENNETH was left for some minutes alone, and in darkness. Here was another interruption, which must prolong his absence from his post, and he began almost to repent the facility with which he had been induced to quit it. But to return without seeing the Lady Edith, was now not to be thought of. He had committed a breach of military discipline, and was determined at least to prove the reality of the seductive expectations which had tempted him to do so. Meanwhile, his situation was unpleasant. There was no light to show him into what sort of apartment he had been led—the Lady Edith was in immediate attendance on the Queen of England—and the discovery of his having introduced himself thus furtively into the royal pavilion, might, were it discovered, lead to much and dangerous suspicion. While he gave way to these unpleasant reflections, and began almost to wish that he could achieve his retreat unobserved, he heard a noise of female voices, laughing, whispering, and speaking, in an adjoining apartment, from which, as the sounds gave him reason to judge, he could only be separated by a canvas partition. Lamps were burning, as he might perceive by the shadowy light which extended itself even to his side of the veil which divided the tent, and he could see shades of several figures sitting and moving in the adjoining apartment. It cannot be termed discourtesy in Sir Kenneth, that, situated as he was, he overheard a conversation, in which he found himself deeply interested.

"Call her—call her, for Our Lady's sake," said the voice of one of these laughing invisibles. "Nectabanus, thou shalt be made ambassador to Prester John's court, to show them how wisely thou canst discharge thee of a mission."

The shrill tone of the dwarf was heard, yet so much subdued, that Sir Kenneth could not understand what he said, except that he spoke something of the means of merriment given to the guard.

"But how shall we rid us of the spirit which Nectabanus hath raised, my maidens?"

"Hear me, royal madam," said another voice; "if the sage and princely Nectabanus be not over jealous of his most transcendent bride and empress, let us send her to get us rid of this insolent knight-errant, who can be so easily persuaded that high-born dames may need the use of his insolent and overweening valour."

"It were but justice, methinks," replied another, "that the Princess Guenevra should dismiss, by her courtesy, him, whom her husband's wisdom has been able to entice hither."

Struck to the heart with shame and resentment at what he had heard, Sir Kenneth was about to attempt his escape from the tent at all hazards, when what followed arrested his purpose.

"Nay, truly," said the first speaker, "our cousin Edith must first learn how this vaunted wight hath conducted himself, and we must reserve the power of giving her ocular proof that he hath failed in his duty. It may be a lesson will do good upon her; for, credit me, Calista, I have sometimes thought she has let this northern adventurer sit nearer her heart than prudence would sanction."

One of the other voices was then heard to mutter something of the Lady Edith's prudence and wisdom.

"Prudence, wench!" was the reply—"It is mere pride, and the desire to be thought more rigid than any of us. Nay, I will not quit my advantage. You know well, that when she has us at fault, no one can, in a civil way, lay your error before you more precisely than can my Lady Edith. But here she comes."

A figure, as if entering the apartment, cast upon the partition a shade, which glided along slowly until it mixed with those which already clouded it. Despite of the bitter disappointment which he had experienced—despite the insult and injury with which it seemed he had been visited by the malice, or, at best, by the idle humour of Queen Berengaria (for he already concluded that she who spoke loudest, and in a commanding tone, was the wife of Richard), the knight felt something so soothing to his feelings in learning that Edith had been no partner to the fraud practised on him, and so interesting to his curiosity in the scene which was about to take place, that, instead of prosecuting his more prudent purpose of an instant retreat, he looked anxiously, on the contrary, for some rent or crevice, by means of which he might be made eye as well as ear-witness to what was to go forward.

"Surely," said he to himself, "the Queen, who hath been pleased for an idle frolic to endanger my reputation, and perhaps my life, cannot complain if I avail myself of the chance which fortune seems willing to afford me, to obtain knowledge of her farther intentions."

It seemed, in the meanwhile, as it Edith were waiting for the commands of the Queen, and as if the other were reluctant to speak, for fear of being unable to command her laughter, and that of her companions; for Sir Kenneth could only distinguish a sound as of suppressed tittering and merriment.

"Your Majesty," said Edith, at last, "seems in a merry mood, though, methinks, the hour of night prompts a sleepy one. I was well disposed bedward, when I had your Majesty's commands to attend you."

"I will not long delay you, cousin, from your repose," said the Queen; "though I fear you will sleep less soundly when I tell you your wager is lost."

"Nay, royal madam," said Edith, "this surely is dwelling on a jest which has rather been worn out. I laid no wager, however it was your Majesty's pleasure to suppose, or to insist, that I did so."

"Nay, now, despite our pilgrimage, Satan is strong with you, my gentle cousin, and prompts thee to leasing. Can you deny that you gaged your ruby ring against my golden bracelet, that yonder Knight of the Libbard, or how call you him, could not be seduced from his post?"

"Your Majesty is too great for me to gainsay you," replied Edith; "but these ladies can, if they will, bear me witness, that it was your Highness who proposed such a wager, and took the ring from my finger, even while I was declaring that I did not think it maidenly to gage anything on such a subject."

"Nay, but, my Lady Edith," said another voice, "you must needs grant, under your favour, that you expressed yourself very confident of the valour of that same Knight of the Leopard."

"And if I did, minion," said Edith angrily, "is that a good reason why thou shouldst put in thy word to flatter her Majesty's humour? I spoke of that knight but as all men speak who have seen him in the field, and had no more interest in defending than thou in detracting from him. In a camp, what can women speak of save soldiers and deeds of arms?"

"The noble Lady Edith," said a third voice, "hath never forgiven Calista and me, since we told your Majesty that she dropped two rosebuds in the chapel."

"If your Majesty," said Edith, in a tone which Sir Kenneth could judge to be that of respectful remonstrance, "have no other commands for me than to hear the gibes of your waiting-women, I must crave your permission to withdraw."

"Silence, Florise," said the Queen, "and let not our indulgence lead you to forget the difference betwixt yourself and the kinswoman of England.—But you, my dear cousin," she continued, resuming her tone of raillery, "how can you, who are so good-natured, begrudge us poor wretches a few minutes' laughing, when we have had so many days devoted to weeping and gnashing of teeth?"

"Great be your mirth, royal lady," said Edith; "yet would I be content not to smile for the rest of my life, rather than——"

She stopped, apparently out of respect; but Sir Kenneth could hear that she was in much agitation.

"Forgive me," said Berengaria, a thoughtless but good-humoured princess of the House of Navarre,—"but what is the great offence after all? A young knight has been wiled hither—has stolen—or has *been* stolen—from his post, which no one will disturb in his absence, for the sake of a fair lady; for, to do your champion justice, sweet one, the wisdom of Nectabanus could conjure him hither in no name but yours."

"Gracious Heaven! your Majesty does not say so?" said Edith, in a voice of alarm quite different from the agitation she had previously evinced,—"you cannot say so, consistently with respect for your own honour and for mine, your husband's kinswoman!—Say you were jesting with me, my royal mistress, and forgive me that I could, even for a moment, think it possible you could be in earnest!"

"The Lady Edith," said the Queen, in a displeased tone of voice, "regrets the ring we have won of her.—We will restore the pledge to you, gentle cousin, only you must not grudge us in turn a little triumph over the wisdom which has been so often spread over us as a banner over a host."

"A triumph!" exclaimed Edith indignantly; "a triumph! —the triumph will be with the infidel, when he hears that the Queen of England can make the reputation of her husband's kinswoman the subject of a light frolic."

"You are angry, fair cousin, at losing your favourite ring," said the Queen—"Come, since you grudge to pay your wager, we will renounce our right; it was your name and that pledge brought him hither, and we care not for the bait after the fish is caught."

"Madam," replied Edith impatiently, "you know well that your Grace could not wish for anything of mine but it becomes instantly yours. But I would give a bushel of rubies ere ring or name of mine had been used to bring a brave man into a fault, and perhaps to disgrace and punishment."

"Oh, it is for the safety of our true knight that we fear!" said the Queen. "You rate our power too low, fair cousin, when you speak of a life being lost for a frolic of ours. Oh, Lady Edith, others have influence on the iron breasts of warriors as well as you—the heart even of a lion is made of flesh, not of stone; and, believe me, I have interest enough with Richard to save this knight, in whose faith Lady Edith is so deeply concerned, from the penalty of disobeying his royal commands."

"For the love of the blessed Cross, most royal lady," said Edith—and Sir Kenneth, with feelings which it were hard to unravel, heard her prostrate herself at the Queen's feet,—"for the love of our blessed Lady, and of every holy saint in the calendar, beware what you do! You know not King Richard—you have been but shortly wedded to him—your breath might as well combat the west wind when it is wildest, as your words persuade my royal kinsman to pardon a military offence. Oh! for God's sake, dismiss this gentleman, if indeed you have lured him hither! I could almost be content to rest with the shame of having invited him, did I know that he was returned again where his duty calls him!"

"Arise, cousin, arise," said Queen Berengaria, "and be assured all will be better than you think. Rise, dear Edith; I am sorry I have played my foolery with a knight in whom you take such deep interest—Nay, wring not thy hands—I will believe thou carest not for him—believe anything rather than see thee look so wretchedly miserable—I tell thee I will take the blame on myself with King Richard in behalf of thy fair northern friend—thine acquaintance, I would say, since thou own'st him not as a friend.—Nay, look not so reproachfully—We will send Nectabanus to dismiss this Knight of the Standard to his post; and we ourselves will grace him on some future day, to make amends for his wild-goose chase. He is, I warrant, but lying perdue in some neighbouring tent."

"By my crown of lilies, and my sceptre of a specially good water-reed," said Nectabanus, "your Majesty is mistaken—he is nearer at hand than you wot—he lieth ensconced there behind that canvas partition."

"And within hearing of each word we have said!" exclaimed the Queen, in her turn violently surprised and agitated—"Out, monster of folly and malignity!"

As she uttered these words Nectabanus fled from the pavilion with a yell of such a nature, as leaves it still doubtful whether Berengaria had confined her rebuke to words, or added some more emphatic expression of her displeasure.

"What can now be done?" said the Queen to Edith, in a whisper of undisguised uneasiness.

"That which must," said Edith firmly. "We must see this gentleman, and place ourselves in his mercy."

So saying, she began hastily to undo a curtain, which at one place covered an entrance or communication.

"For Heaven's sake, forbear—consider," said the Queen, "my apartment—our dress—the hour—my honour!"

But ere she could detail her remonstrances, the curtain fell, and there was no division any longer betwixt the armed knight and the party of ladies The warmth of an Eastern night occasioned the undress of Queen Berengaria and her household to be rather more simple and unstudied than their station, and the presence of a male spectator of rank, required. This the Queen remembered, and with a loud shriek fled from the apartment where Sir Kenneth was disclosed to view in a copartment of the ample pavilion, now no longer separated from that in which they stood. The grief and agitation of the Lady Edith, as well as the deep interest she felt in a hasty explanation with the Scottish knight, perhaps occasioned her forgetting that her locks were more dishevelled, and her person less heedfully covered, than was the wont of high-born damsels, in an age which was not, after all, the most prudish or scrupulous period of the ancient time. A thin loose garment of pink-coloured silk made the principal part of her vestments, with Oriental slippers, into which she had hastily thrust her bare feet, and a scarf hurriedly and loosely thrown about her shoulders. Her head had no other covering than the veil of rich and dishevelled locks falling round it on every side, that half hid a countenance, which a mingled sense of modesty, and of resentment, and other deep and agitating feelings, had covered with crimson.

But although Edith felt her situation with all that delicacy which is her sex's greatest charm, it did not seem that for a moment she placed her own bashfulness in comparison with the duty, which, as she thought, she owed to him, who had been led into error and danger on her account. She drew, indeed, her scarf more closely over her neck and bosom, and she hastily laid from her hand a lamp, which shed too much lustre over her figure; but, while Sir Kenneth stood motionless on the same spot in which he was first discovered, she rather stepped towards than retired from him, as she exclaimed, "Hasten to your post, valiant knight!—you are deceived in being trained hither—ask no questions."

"I need ask none," said the knight, sinking upon one knee, with the reverential devotion of a saint at the altar, and bending his eyes on the ground, lest his looks should increase the lady's embarrassment.

"Have you heard all?" said Edith impatiently—"Gracious saints! then wherefore wait you here, when each minute that passes is loaded with dishonour!"

"I have heard that I am dishonoured, lady, and I have heard it from you," answered Kenneth. "What reck I how soon punishment follows? I have but one petition to you, and then I seek, among the sabres of the infidels, whether dishonour may not be washed out with blood."

"Do not so, neither," said the lady. "Be wise—dally not here—all may yet be well, if you will but use despatch."

"I wait but for your forgiveness," said the knight, still

kneeling, " for my presumption in believing my poor services could have been required or valued by you."

" I do forgive you—Oh, I have nothing to forgive!—I have been the means of injuring you—But oh, begone!—I will forgive—I will value you—that is, as I value every brave Crusader—if you will but begone!"

" Receive first, this precious yet fatal pledge," said the knight, tendering the ring to Edith, who now showed gestures of impatience.

" Oh no, no," she said, declining to receive it. " Keep it—keep it as a mark of my regard—my regret, I would say. Oh, begone, if not for your own sake, for mine!"

Almost recompensed for the loss even of honour, which her voice had denounced to him, by the interest which she seemed to testify in his safety, Sir Kenneth rose from his knee, and, casting a momentary glance on Edith, bowed low and seemed about to withdraw. At the same instant that maidenly bashfulness, which the energy of Edith's feelings had till then triumphed over, became conqueror in its turn, and she hastened from the apartment, extinguishing her lamp as she went, and leaving, in Sir Kenneth's thoughts, both mental and natural gloom behind her.

She must be obeyed, was the first distinct idea which waked him from his reverie, and he hastened to the place by which he had entered the pavilion. To pass under the canvas in the manner he had entered required time and attention, and he made a readier aperture by slitting the canvas wall with his poniard. When in the free air, he felt rather stupefied and overpowered by a conflict of sensations, than able to ascertain what was the real import of the whole. He was obliged to spur himself to action, by recollecting that the commands of the Lady Edith had required haste. Even then, engaged as he was amongst tent ropes and tents, he was compelled to move with caution until he should regain the path or avenue, aside from which the dwarf had led him, in order to escape the observation of the guards before the Queen's pavilion; and he was obliged also to move slowly, and with precaution, to avoid giving an alarm, either by falling, or by the clashing of his armour. A thin cloud had obscured the moon, too, at the very instant of his leaving the tent, and Sir Kenneth had to struggle with this inconvenience at a moment when the dizziness of his head, and the fulness of his heart, scarce left him powers of intelligence sufficient to direct his motions.

But at once sounds came upon his ear, which instantly recalled him to the full energy of his faculties. These proceeded from the Mount of Saint George. He heard first a single fierce, angry, and savage bark, which was immediately followed by a

I

yell of agony. No deer ever bounded with a wilder start at the voice of Roswal, than did Sir Kenneth at what he feared was the death-cry of that noble hound, from whom no ordinary injury could have extracted even the slightest acknowledgment of pain. He surmounted the space which divided him from the avenue, and, having attained it, began to run towards the mount, although loaded with his mail, faster than most men could have accompanied him even if unarmed, relaxed not his pace for the steep sides of the artificial mound, and in a few minutes stood on the platform upon its summit.

The moon broke through the cloud at this moment, and showed him that the standard of England was vanished, that the spear on which it floated lay broken on the ground, and beside it was his faithful hound, apparently in the agonies of death.

CHAPTER XIV

——All my long arrear of honour lost,
Heap'd up in youth, and hoarded up for age,
Hath Honour's fountain then suck'd up the stream?
He hath—and hooting boys may barefoot pass,
And gather pebbles from the naked ford?
—Don Sebastian.

AFTER a torrent of afflicting sensations, by which he was at first almost stunned and confounded, Sir Kenneth's first thought was to look for the authors of this violation of the English banner; but in no direction could he see traces of them. His next, which to some persons, but scarce to any who have made intimate acquaintances among the canine race, may appear strange, was to examine the condition of his faithful Roswal, mortally wounded, as it seemed, in discharging the duty which his master had been seduced to abandon. He caressed the dying animal, who, faithful to the last, seemed to forget his own pain in the satisfaction he received from his master's presence, and continued wagging his tail and licking his hand, even while by low moanings he expressed that his agony was increased by the attempts which Sir Kenneth made to withdraw from the wound the fragment of the lance, or javelin, with which it had been inflicted; then redoubled his feeble endearments, as if fearing he had offended his master by showing a sense of the pain to which his interference had subjected him. There was something in the display of the dying creature's attachment, which mixed as a bitter ingredient with the sense of disgrace and desolation by which Sir Kenneth was oppressed. His only friend seemed removed from him, just when he had incurred the contempt and hatred of all besides. The knight's strength of mind gave way to a burst of agonised distress, and he groaned and wept aloud.

While he thus indulged his grief, a clear and solemn voice, close beside him, pronounced these words in the sonorous tone of the readers of the mosque, and in the Lingua Franca, mutually understood by Christians and Saracens :—

"Adversity is like the period of the former and of the latter rain—cold, comfortless, unfriendly to man and to animal; yet from that season have their birth the flower and the fruit, the date, the rose, and the pomegranate."

Sir Kenneth of the Leopard turned towards the speaker, and beheld the Arabian physician, who, approaching unheard, had seated himself a little behind him cross-legged, and uttered with gravity, yet not without a tone of sympathy, the moral sentences of consolation with which the Koran and its commentators supplied him; for, in the East, wisdom is held to consist, less in a display of the sage's own inventive talents, than in his ready memory, and happy application of, and reference to, "that which is written."

Ashamed at being surprised in a woman-like expression of sorrow, Sir Kenneth dashed his tears indignantly aside, and again busied himself with his dying favourite.

"The poet hath said," continued the Arab, without noticing the knight's averted looks and sullen deportment—"'the ox for the field, and the camel for the desert.' Were not the hand of the leech fitter than that of the soldier to cure wounds, though less able to inflict them?"

"This patient, Hakim, is beyond thy help," said Sir Kenneth; "and, besides, he is, by thy law, an unclean animal."

"Where Allah hath deigned to bestow life, and a sense of pain and pleasure," said the physician, "it were sinful pride should the sage, whom he has enlightened, refuse to prolong existence, or assuage agony. To the sage, the cure of a miserable groom, of a poor dog, and of a conquering monarch, are events of little distinction. Let me examine this wounded animal."

Sir Kenneth acceded in silence, and the physician inspected and handled Roswal's wound with as much care and attention as if he had been a human being. He then took forth a case of instruments, and, by the judicious and skilful application of pincers, withdrew from the wounded shoulder the fragment of the weapon, and stopped with styptics and bandages the effusion of blood which followed; the creature all the while suffering him patiently to perform these kind offices, as if he had been aware of his kind intentions.

"The animal may be cured," said El Hakim, addressing himself to Sir Kenneth, "if you will permit me to carry him to my tent, and treat him with the care which the nobleness of his nature deserves. For know, that thy servant Adonbec is no less skilful in the race and pedigree, and distinctions of good dogs and of noble steeds, than in the diseases which affect the human race."

"Take him with you," said the knight. "I bestow him on you freely if he recovers. I owe thee a reward for attendance on my squire, and have nothing else to pay it with. For myself —I will never again wind bugle, or halloo to hound!"

The Arabian made no reply, but gave a signal with a clapping of his hands, which was instantly answered by the appearance of two black slaves. He gave them his orders in Arabic received the answer, that "to hear was to obey," when, taking the animal in their arms, they removed him, without much resistance on his part; for though his eyes turned to his master he was too weak to struggle.

"Fare thee well, Roswal, then," said Sir Kenneth,—"fare thee well, my last and only friend—thou art too noble a possession to be retained by one such as I must in future call myself —I would," he said, as the slaves retired, "that, dying as he is I could exchange conditions with that noble animal."

"It is written," answered the Arabian, although the exclamation had not been addressed to him, "that all creatures are fashioned for the service of man; and the master of the earth speaketh folly when he would exchange, in his impatience his hopes here and to come, for the servile condition of an inferior being."

"A dog who dies in discharging his duty," said the knight sternly, "is better than a man who survives the desertion of it Leave me, Hakim; thou hast, on this side of miracle, the most wonderful science which man ever possessed, but the wounds of the spirit are beyond thy power."

"Not if the patient will explain his calamity, and be guided by the physician," said Adonbec el Hakim.

"Know, then," said Sir Kenneth, "since thou art so importunate, that last night the banner of England was displayed from this mound—I was its appointed guardian—morning is now breaking—there lies the broken banner-spear, the standard itself is lost—and here sit I a living man!"

"How!" said El Hakim, examining him; "thy armour is whole—there is no blood on thy weapons, and report speaks thee one unlikely to return thus from fight.—Thou hast been trained from thy post—ay, trained by the rosy cheek and black eye of one of those houris, to whom you Nazarenes vow rather such service as is due to Allah, than such love as may lawfully be rendered to forms of clay like our own. It has been thus assuredly; for so hath man ever fallen, even since the days of Sultan Adam."

"And if it were so, physician," said Sir Kenneth sullenly, "what remedy?"

"Knowledge is the parent of power," said El Hakim, "as valour supplies strength.—Listen to me. Man is not as a tree, bound to one spot of earth—nor is he framed to cling to one bare rock, like the scarce animated shell-fish. Thine own Christian writings command thee, when persecuted in one city to flee to another; and we Moslem also know that Mohammed, the Prophet of Allah, driven forth from the holy city of Mecca, found his refuge and his helpmates at Medina."

"And what does this concern me?" said the Scot.

"Much," answered the physician. "Even the sage flies the tempest which he cannot control. Use thy speed, therefore, and fly from the vengeance of Richard to the shadow of Saladin's victorious banner."

"I might indeed hide my dishonour," said Sir Kenneth ironically, "in a camp of infidel heathens, where the very phrase is unknown. But had I not better partake more fully in their reproach? Does not thy advice stretch so far as to recommend me to take the turban?—Methinks I want but apostasy to consummate my infamy."

"Blaspheme not, Nazarene," said the physician sternly; "Saladin makes no converts to the law of the Prophet, save those on whom its precepts shall work conviction. Open thine eyes to the light, and the great Soldan, whose liberality is as boundless as his power, may bestow on thee a kingdom; remain blinded if thou wilt, and, being one whose second life is doomed to misery, Saladin will yet, for this span of present time, make thee rich and happy. But fear not that thy brows shall be bound with the turban, save at thine own free choice."

"My choice were rather," said the knight, "that my writhen features should blacken, as they are like to do, in this evening's setting sun."

"Yet thou art not wise, Nazarene," said El Hakim, "to reject this fair offer; for I have power with Saladin, and can raise thee high in his grace. Look you, my son—this Crusade, as you call your wild enterprise, is like a large dromond * parting asunder in the waves. Thou thyself hast borne terms of truce from the Kings and Princes, whose force is here assembled, to the mighty Soldan, and knew'st not, perchance, the full tenor of thine own errand."

"I knew not, and I care not," said the knight impatiently;

* The largest sort of vessels then known were termed *dromonds*, or dromedaries.

"what avails it to me that I have been of late the envoy of princes, when, ere night, I shall be a gibbeted and dishonoured corse!"

"Nay, I speak that it may not be so with thee," said the physician. "Saladin is courted on all sides; the combined Princes of this league formed against him, have made such proposals of composition and peace, as, in other circumstances, it might have become his honour to have granted to them. Others have made private offers, on their own separate account, to disjoin their forces from the camp of the Kings of Frangistan, and even to lend their arms to the defence of the standard of the Prophet. But Saladin will not be served by such treacherous and interested defection. The King of kings will treat only with the Lion King. Saladin will hold treaty with none but the Melech Ric, and with him he will treat like a prince, or fight like a champion. To Richard he will yield such conditions of his free liberality, as the swords of all Europe could never compel from him by force or terror. He will permit a free pilgrimage to Jerusalem, and all the places where the Nazarenes list to worship; nay, he will so far share even his empire with his brother Richard, that he will allow Christian garrisons in the six strongest cities of Palestine, and one in Jerusalem itself, and suffer them to be under the immediate command of the officers of Richard, who, he consents, shall bear the name of King Guardian of Jerusalem. Yet farther, strange and incredible as you may think it, know, Sir Knight—for to your honour I can commit even that almost incredible secret—know that Saladin will put a sacred seal on this happy union betwixt the bravest and noblest of Frangistan and Asia, by raising to the rank of his royal spouse a Christian damsel, allied in blood to King Richard, and known by the name of the Lady Edith of Plantagenet." *

"Ha!—say'st thou!" exclaimed Sir Kenneth, who, listening with indifference and apathy to the preceding part of El Hakim's speech, was touched by this last communication, as the thrill of a nerve, unexpectedly jarred, will awaken the sensation of agony, even in the torpor of palsy. Then, moderating his tone, by dint of much effort, he restrained his indignation, and, veiling it under the appearance of contemptuous doubt, he prosecuted the conversation in order to get as much knowledge as possible of the plot, as he deemed it, against the honour and happiness of her, whom he loved not the less that his passion had ruined, apparently, his fortunes, at once, and his

* This may appear so extraordinary and improbable a proposition, that it is necessary to say such a one was actually made. The historians, however, substitute the widowed Queen of Naples, sister of Richard, for the bride, and Saladin's brother for the bridegroom. They appear to have been ignorant of the existence of Edith of Plantagenet.—See MILL'S "History of the Crusade," vol. ii. p. 61.

honour.—"And what Christian," he said, with tolerable calmness, "would sanction a union so unnatural, as that of a Christian maiden with an unbelieving Saracen?"

"Thou art but an ignorant, bigoted Nazarene," said the Hakim. "See'st thou not how the Mohammedan princes daily intermarry with the noble Nazarene maidens in Spain, without scandal either to Moor or Christian? And the noble Soldan will, in his full confidence in the blood of Richard, permit the English maid the freedom which your Frankish manners have assigned to women. He will allow her the free exercise of her religion,—seeing that, in very truth, it signifies but little to which faith females are addicted,—and he will assign her such place and rank over all the women of his zenana, that she shall be in every respect his sole and absolute Queen."

"What!" said Sir Kenneth, "darest thou think, Moslem, that Richard would give his kinswoman—a high-born and virtuous princess, to be, at best, the foremost concubine in the haram of a misbeliever? Know, Hakim, the meanest free Christian noble would scorn, on his child's behalf, such splendid ignominy."

"Thou errest," said the Hakim; "Philip of France, and Henry of Champagne, and others of Richard's principal allies, have heard the proposal without starting, and have promised, as far as they may, to forward an alliance that may end these wasteful wars; and the wise arch-priest of Tyre hath undertaken to break the proposal to Richard, not doubting that he shall be able to bring the plan to good issue. The Soldan's wisdom hath as yet kept his proposition secret from others, such as he of Montserrat, and the Master of the Templars, because he knows they seek to thrive by Richard's death or disgrace, not by his life or honour.—Up, therefore, Sir Knight, and to horse. I will give thee a scroll which shall advance thee highly with the Soldan; and deem not that you are leaving your country, or her cause, or her religion, since the interest of the two monarchs will speedily be the same. To Saladin thy counsel will be most acceptable, since thou canst make him aware of much concerning the marriages of the Christians, the treatment of their wives, and other points of their laws and usages, which, in the course of such treaty, it much concerns him that he should know. The right hand of the Soldan grasps the treasures of the East, and is the fountain of generosity. Or, if thou desirest it, Saladin, when allied with England, can have but little difficulty to obtain from Richard not only thy pardon and restoration to favour, but an honourable command in the troops which may be left of the King of England's host, to maintain their joint government in Palestine. Up, then, and mount, there lies a plain path before thee."

"Hakim," said the Scottish knight, "thou art a man of peace—also, thou hast saved the life of Richard of England—and, moreover, of my own poor esquire, Strauchan. I have, therefore, heard to an end a matter, which, being propounded by another Moslem than thyself, I would have cut short with a blow of my dagger! Hakim, in return for thy kindness, I advise thee to see that the Saracen, who shall propose to Richard a union betwixt the blood of Plantagenet and that of his accursed race, do put on a helmet, which is capable to endure such a blow of a battle-axe as that which struck down the gate of Acre. Certes, he will be otherwise placed beyond the reach even of thy skill."

"Thou art, then, wilfully determined not to fly to the Saracen host?" said the physician—"Yet, remember, thou stayest to certain destruction; and the writings of thy law, as well as ours, prohibit man from breaking into the tabernacle of his own life."

"God forbid!" replied the Scot, crossing himself; "but we are also forbidden to avoid the punishment which our crimes have deserved. And, since so poor are thy thoughts of fidelity, Hakim, it grudges me that I have bestowed my good hound on thee, for, should he live, he will have a master ignorant of his value."

"A gift that is begrudged is already recalled," said El Hakim, "only we physicians are sworn not to send away a patient uncured. If the dog recover, he is once more yours."

"Go to, Hakim," answered Sir Kenneth; "men speak not of hawk and hound when there is but an hour of day-breaking betwixt them and death. Leave me to recollect my sins, and reconcile myself to Heaven."

"I leave thee in thine obstinacy," said the physician; "the mist hides the precipice from those who are doomed to fall over it."

He withdrew slowly, turning from time to time his head, as if to observe whether the devoted knight might not recall him either by word or signal. At last his turbaned figure was lost among the labyrinth of tents which lay extended beneath, whitening in the pale light of the dawning, before which the moonbeam had now faded away.

But although the physician Adonbec's words had not made that impression upon Kenneth which the sage desired, they had inspired the Scot with a motive for desiring life, which, dishonoured as he conceived himself to be, he was before willing to part from as from a sullied vestment no longer becoming his wear. Much that had passed betwixt himself and the hermit, besides what he had observed between the anchorite and Sheer-kohf (or Ilderim), he now recalled to recollection, and tended

to confirm what the Hakim had told him of the secret article
of the treaty.

"The reverend impostor!" he exclaimed to himself; "the
hoary hypocrite! He spoke of the unbelieving husband converted by the believing wife—and what do I know but that the
traitor exhibited to the Saracen, accursed of God, the beauties
of Edith Plantagenet, that the hound might judge if the
princely Christian lady were fit to be admitted into the haram
of a misbeliever? If I had yonder infidel Ilderim, or whatsoever he is called, again in the gripe with which I once held
him fast as ever hound held hare, never again should *he* at least
come on errand disgraceful to the honour of Christian king, or
noble and virtuous maiden. But I—my hours are fast dwind-
ling into minutes—yet, while I have life and breath, something
must be done, and speedily."

He paused for a few minutes, threw from him his helmet,
then strode down the hill, and took the road to King Richard's
pavilion.

CHAPTER XV

The feather'd songster, chanticleer,
    Had wound his bugle-horn,
And told the early villager
    The coming of the morn.
King Edward saw the ruddy streaks
    Of light eclipse the grey,
And heard the Raven's croaking throat
    Proclaim the fated day.
"Thou'rt right," he said, "for, by the God
    That sits enthroned on high,
Charles Bawdwin, and his fellows twain,
    This day shall surely die."

—CHATTERTON.

ON the evening on which Sir Kenneth assumed his post,
Richard, after the stormy event which disturbed its tranquillity, had retired to rest in the plenitude of confidence inspired
by his unbounded courage, and the superiority which he had displayed in carrying the point he aimed at in presence of the whole
Christian host, and its leaders, many of whom, he was aware,
regarded in their secret souls the disgrace of the Austrian Duke
as a triumph over themselves; so that his pride felt gratified,
that in prostrating one enemy he had mortified a hundred.

Another monarch would have doubled his guards on the
evening after such a scene, and kept at least a part of his
troops under arms. But Cœur de Lion dismissed, upon the
occasion, even his ordinary watch, and assigned to his soldiers

a donative of wine to celebrate his recovery, and to drink to the Banner of Saint George; and his quarter of the camp would have assumed a character totally devoid of vigilance and military preparation, but that Sir Thomas de Vaux, the Earl of Salisbury, and other nobles, took precautions to preserve order and discipline among the revellers.

The physician attended the King from his retiring to bed till midnight was past, and twice administered medicine to him during that period, always previously observing the quarter of heaven occupied by the full moon, whose influences he declared to be most sovereign, or most baleful, to the effect of his drugs. It was three hours after midnight ere El Hakim withdrew from the royal tent, to one which had been pitched for himself and his retinue. In his way thither he visited the tent of Sir Kenneth of the Leopard, in order to see the condition of his first patient in the Christian camp, old Strauchan, as the knight's esquire was named. Inquiring there for Sir Kenneth himself, El Hakim learned on what duty he was employed, and probably this information led him to Saint George's Mount, where he found him whom he sought in the disastrous circumstances alluded to in the last chapter.

It was about the hour of sunrise, when a slow, armed tread was heard approaching the King's pavilion; and ere De Vaux, who slumbered beside his master's bed as lightly as ever sleep sat upon the eyes of a watch-dog, had time to do more than arise and say, "Who comes?" the Knight of the Leopard entered the tent, with a deep and devoted gloom seated upon his manly features.

"Whence this bold intrusion, Sir Knight?" said De Vaux sternly, yet in a tone which respected his master's slumbers.

"Hold! De Vaux," said Richard, awakening on the instant; "Sir Kenneth cometh like a good soldier to render an account of his guard—to such the General's tent is ever accessible."— Then rising from his slumbering posture, and leaning on his elbow, he fixed his large bright eye upon the warrior—"Speak, Sir Scot; thou comest to tell me of a vigilant, safe, and honourable watch, dost thou not? The rustling of the folds of the Banner of England were enough to guard it, even without the body of such a knight as men hold thee."

"As men will hold me no more," said Sir Kenneth—"my watch hath neither been vigilant, safe, nor honourable. The Banner of England has been carried off."

"And thou alive to tell it?" said Richard, in a tone of derisive incredulity.—"Away, it cannot be. There is not even a scratch on thy face.—Why dost thou stand thus mute? Speak the truth—it is ill jesting with a King—yet I will forgive thee if thou hast lied."

"Lied! Sir King!" returned the unfortunate knight, with fierce emphasis, and one glance of fire from his eye, bright and transient as the flash from the cold and stony flint. "But this also must be endured—I have spoken the truth."

"By God, and by Saint George!" said the King, bursting into fury, which, however, he instantly checked—"De Vaux, go view the spot—This fever has disturbed his brain—This cannot be—The man's courage is proof—It *cannot* be! Go speedily—or send, if thou wilt not go."

The King was interrupted by Sir Henry Neville, who came, breathless, to say that the banner was gone, and the knight who guarded it overpowered, and most probably murdered, as there was a pool of blood where the banner-spear lay shivered.

"But whom do I see here?" said Neville, his eyes suddenly resting upon Sir Kenneth.

"A traitor," said the King, starting to his feet, and seizing the curtal-axe, which was ever near his bed—"a traitor! whom thou shalt see die a traitor's death."—And he drew back the weapon as in act to strike.

Colourless, but firm as a marble statue, the Scot stood before him, with his bare head uncovered by any protection, his eyes cast down to the earth, his lips scarcely moving, yet muttering probably in prayer. Opposite to him, and within the due reach for a blow, stood King Richard, his large person wrapt in the folds of his camiscia, or ample gown of linen, except where the violence of his action had flung the covering from his right arm, shoulder, and a part of his breast, leaving to view a specimen of a frame which might have merited his Saxon predecessor's epithet of Ironside. He stood for an instant, prompt to strike—then sinking the head of the weapon towards the ground, he exclaimed, "But there was blood, Neville—there was blood upon the place. Hark thee, Sir Scot —brave thou wert once, for I have seen thee fight—Say thou hast slain two of the thieves in defence of the Standard—say but one—say thou hast struck but a good blow in our behalf, and get thee out of the camp with thy life and thy infamy!"

"You have called me liar, my Lord King," replied Kenneth firmly; "and therein, at least, you have done me wrong— Know, that there was no blood shed in defence of the Standard save that of a poor hound, which, more faithful than his master, defended the charge which he deserted."

"Now, by Saint George!" said Richard, again heaving up his arm—But De Vaux threw himself between the King and the object of his vengeance, and spoke with the blunt truth of his character, "My liege, this must not be—here, nor by your own hand. It is enough of folly for one night and day, to have entrusted your banner to a Scot—said I not they were ever fair and false?"*

"Thou didst, De Vaux; thou wast right, and I confess it," said Richard. "I should have known him better—I should have remembered how the fox William deceived me touching this Crusade."

"My lord," said Sir Kenneth, "William of Scotland never deceived; but circumstances prevented his bringing his forces."

"Peace, shameless!" said the King; "thou sulliest the name of a prince, even by speaking it.—And yet, De Vaux, it is strange," he added, "to see the bearing of the man. Coward or traitor he must be, yet he abode the blow of Richard Plantagenet, as our arm had been raised to lay knighthood on his shoulder. Had he shown the slightest sign of fear—had but a joint trembled, or an eyelid quivered, I had shattered his head like a crystal goblet. But I cannot strike where there is neither fear nor resistance."

There was a pause.

"My lord," said Kenneth——

"Ha!" replied Richard, interrupting him, "hast thou found thy speech? Ask grace from Heaven, but none from me, for England is dishonoured through thy fault; and wert thou mine own and only brother, there is no pardon for thy fault."

"I speak not to demand grace of mortal man," said the Scot; "it is in your Grace's pleasure to give or refuse me time for Christian thrift—if man denies it, may God grant me the absolution which I would otherwise ask of His Church! But whether I die on the instant, or half-an-hour hence, I equally beseech your Grace for one moment's opportunity to speak that to your royal person, which highly concerns your fame as a Christian King."

"Say on," said the King, making no doubt that he was about to hear some confession concerning the loss of the Banner.

"What I have to speak," said Sir Kenneth, "touches the royalty of England, and must be said to no ears but thine own."

"Begone with yourselves, sirs," said the King to Neville and De Vaux.

The first obeyed, but the latter would not stir from the King's presence.

"If you said I was in the right," replied De Vaux to his

* Such were the terms in which the English used to speak of their poor northern neighbours, forgetting that their own encroachments upon the independence of Scotland obliged the weaker nation to defend themselves by policy as well as force. The disgrace must be divided between Edward I. and III., who enforced their domination over a free country, and the Scots who were compelled to take compulsory oaths, without any purpose of keeping them.

sovereign, "I will be treated as one should be who hath been found to be right—that is, I will have my own will. I leave you not with this false Scot."

"How! De Vaux," said Richard angrily, and stamping slightly, "darest thou not venture our person with one traitor?"

"It is in vain you frown and stamp, my lord," said De Vaux; "I venture not a sick man with a sound one, a naked man with one armed in proof."

"It matters not," said the Scottish knight, "I seek no excuse to put off time—I will speak in presence of the Lord of Gilsland. He is good lord and true."

"But half-an-hour since," said De Vaux, with a groan, implying a mixture of sorrow and vexation, "and I had said as much for thee!"

"There is treason around you, King of England," continued Sir Kenneth.

"It may well be as thou say'st," replied Richard, "I have a pregnant example."

"Treason that will injure thee more deeply than the lost of an hundred banners in a pitched field. The—the"—Sir Kenneth hesitated, and at length continued, in a lower tone, "The Lady Edith——"

"Ha!" said the King, drawing himself suddenly into a state of haughty attention, and fixing his eye firmly on the supposed criminal; "What of her?—what of her?—what has she to do with this matter?"

"My lord," said the Scot, "there is a scheme on foot to disgrace your royal lineage by bestowing the hand of the Lady Edith on the Saracen Soldan, and thereby to purchase a peace most dishonourable to Christendom, by an alliance most shameful to England."

This communication had precisely the contrary effect from that which Sir Kenneth expected. Richard Plantagenet was one of those, who, in Iago's words, would not serve God because it was the devil who bade him; advice or information often affected him less, according to its real import, than through the tinge which it took from the supposed character and views of those by whom it was communicated. Unfortunately, the mention of his relative's name renewed his recollection of what he considered as extreme presumption in the Knight of the Leopard, even when he stood high in the rolls of chivalry, but which, in his present condition, appeared an insult sufficient to drive the fiery monarch into a frenzy of passion.

"Silence," he said, "infamous and audacious! By Heaven, I will have thy tongue torn out with hot pincers, for mentioning the very name of a noble Christian damsel! Know, degenerate traitor, that I was already aware to what height thou hadst dared to raise thine eyes, and endured it, though it were insolence, even when thou hadst cheated us—for thou art all a deceit—into holding thee as of some name and fame. But now, with lips blistered with the confession of thine own dishonour—that thou shouldst *now* dare to name our noble kinswoman as one in whose fate thou hast part or interest! What is it to thee if she marry Saracen or Christian?—what is it to thee, if in a camp where princes turn cowards by day, and robbers by night—where brave knights turn to paltry deserters and traitors—what is it, I say, to thee, or any one, if I should please to ally myself to truth, and to valour, in the person of Saladin?"

"Little to me, indeed, to whom all the world will soon be as nothing," answered Sir Kenneth boldly; "but were I now stretched on the rack, I would tell thee, that what I have said is much to thine own conscience and thine own fame. I tell thee, Sir King, that if thou dost but in thought entertain the purpose of wedding thy kinswoman, the Lady Edith ——"

"Name her not—and for an instant think not of her," said the King, again straining the curtal-axe in his gripe, until the muscles started above his brawny arm, like cordage formed by the ivy around the limb of an oak.

"Not name—not think of her!" answered Sir Kenneth, his spirits, stunned as they were by self-depression, beginning to recover their elasticity from this species of controversy,—"Now, by the Cross, on which I place my hope, her name shall be the last word in my mouth, her image the last thought in my mind. Try thy boasted strength on this bare brow, and see if thou canst prevent my purpose."

"He will drive me mad!" said Richard, who, in his despite, was once more staggered in his purpose by the dauntless determination of the criminal.

Ere Thomas of Gilsland could reply, some bustle was heard without, and the arrival of the Queen was announced from the outer part of the pavilion.

"Detain her—detain her, Neville," said the King; "this is no sight for women—Fie, that I have suffered such a paltry traitor to chafe me thus!—Away with him, De Vaux," he whispered, "through the back-entrance of our tent—coop him up close, and answer for his safe custody with your life.—And hark ye—he is presently to die—let him have a ghostly father —we would not kill soul and body.—And stay—hark thee—we will not have him dishonoured—he shall die knight-like, in his belt and spurs; for if his treachery be as black as hell, his boldness may match that of the devil himself."

De Vaux, right glad, if the truth may be guessed, that the

scene ended without Richard's descending to the unkingly act of himself slaying an unresisting prisoner, made haste to remove Sir Kenneth by a private issue to a separate tent, where he was disarmed and put in fetters for security. De Vaux looked on with a steady and melancholy attention, while the provost's officers, to whom Sir Kenneth was now committed, took these severe precautions.

When they were ended, he said solemnly to the unhappy criminal—"It is King Richard's pleasure that you die unde-graded—without mutilation of your body, or shame to your arms—and that your head be severed from the trunk by the sword of the executioner."

"It is kind," said the knight, in a low and rather submissive tone of voice, as one who received an unexpected favour ; "my family will not then hear the worst of the tale—Oh, my father —my father !"

This muttered invocation did not escape the blunt but kindly-natured Englishman, and he brushed the back of his large hand over his rough features, ere he could proceed.

"It is Richard of England's farther pleasure," he said, at length, "that you have speech with a holy man, and I have met on the passage hither with a Carmelite friar, who may fit you for your passage.—He waits without, until you are in a habit of mind to receive him."

"Let it be instantly," said the knight. "In this also Richard is kind. I cannot be more fit to see the good father at any time than now; for life and I have taken farewell, as two travellers who have arrived at the crossway, where their roads separate."

"It is well," said De Vaux, slowly and solemnly ; "for it irks me somewhat to say that which sums my message. It is King Richard's pleasure that you prepare for instant death."

"God's pleasure and the king's be done," replied the knight patiently. "I neither contest the justice of the sentence, nor desire delay of the execution."

De Vaux began to leave the tent, but very slowly—paused at the door, and looked back at the Scot, from whose aspect thoughts of the world seemed banished, as if he was composing himself into deep devotion. The feelings of the stout English Baron were in general none of the most acute, and yet, on the present occasion, his sympathy overpowered him in an unusual manner. He came hastily back to the bundle of reeds on which the captive lay, took one of his fettered hands, and said, with as much softness as his rough voice was capable of ex-pressing, "Sir Kenneth, thou art young—yet thou hast a father. My Ralph, whom I left training his little galloway nag on the banks of the Irthing, may one day attain thy years—and, but for last night, I would to God I saw his youth bear such promise as thine !—Can nothing be said or done in thy behalf?"

"Nothing," was the melancholy answer. "I have deserted my charge—the banner entrusted to me is lost—when the headsman and block are prepared, the head and trunk are ready to part company."

"Nay, then, God have mercy!" said De Vaux; "yet would I rather than my best horse I had taken that watch myself. There is mystery in it, young man, as a plain man may descry, though he cannot see through it. Cowardice? pshaw! No coward ever fought as I have seen thee do.—Treachery? I cannot think traitors die in their treason so calmly. Thou hast been trained from thy post by some deep guile—some well-devised stratagem—the cry of some distressed maiden has caught thine ear, or the laughful look of some merry one has taken thine eye. Never blush for it, we have all been led aside by such gear. Come, I pray thee, make a clean conscience of it to me, instead of the priest. Richard is merciful when his mood is abated. Hast thou nothing to entrust to me?"

The unfortunate knight turned his face from the kind warrior, and answered—"NOTHING."

And De Vaux, who had exhausted his topics of persuasion, arose and left the tent, with folded arms, and in melancholy deeper than he thought the occasion merited—even angry with himself to find that so simple a matter as the death of a Scottish man could affect him so nearly.

"Yet," as he said to himself, "though the rough-footed knaves be our enemies in Cumberland, in Palestine one almost considers them as brethren."

CHAPTER XVI

'Tis not her sense—for sure, in that
Theer's nothing more than common ;
And all her wit is only chat,
Like any other woman.
—SONG.

THE high-born Berengaria, daughter of Sanchez, King of Navarre, and the Queen-Consort of the heroic Richard, was accounted one of the most beautiful women of the period. Her form was slight, though exquisitely moulded. She was graced with a complexion not common in her country, a profusion of fair hair, and features so extremely juvenile, as to make her look several years younger than she really was, though in reality she was not above one-and-twenty. Perhaps it was under the consciousness of this extremely juvenile appearance, that she affected, or at least practised, a little childish petulance, and wilfulness of manner, not unbefitting, she might suppose, a youthful bride, whose rank and age gave her a right to have her fantasies indulged and attended to. She was by nature perfectly good-humoured, and if her due share of admiration and homage (in her opinion a very large one) was duly resigned to her, no one could possess better temper, or a more friendly disposition; but then, like all despots, the more power that was voluntarily yielded to her, the more she desired to extend her sway. Sometimes, even when all her ambition was gratified, she chose to be a little out of health, and a little out of spirits; and physicians had to toil their wits to invent names for imaginary maladies, while her ladies racked their imagination for new games, new headgear, and new court-scandal, to pass away those unpleasant hours, during which their own situation was scarce to be greatly envied. Their most frequent resource for diverting this malady was some trick or piece of mischief practised upon each other; and the good Queen, in the buoyancy of her reviving spirits, was, to speak truth, rather too indifferent whether the frolics thus practised were entirely befitting her own dignity, or whether the pain which those suffered upon whom they were inflicted, was not beyond the proportion of pleasure which she herself derived from them. She was confident in her husband's favour, in her high rank, and in her supposed power to make good whatever such pranks might cost others. In a word, she gamboled with the freedom of a young lioness, who is unconscious of the weight of her own paws when laid on those whom she sports with.

The Queen Berengaria loved her husband passionately, but she feared the loftiness and roughness of his character, and as she felt herself not to be his match in intellect, was not much pleased to see that he would often talk with Edith Plantagenet in preference to herself, simply because he found more amusement in her conversation, a more comprehensive understanding, and a more noble cast of thoughts and sentiments, than his beautiful consort exhibited. Berengaria did not hate Edith on this account, far less meditate her any harm: for, allowing for some selfishness, her character was, on the whole, innocent and generous. But the ladies of her train, sharp-sighted in such matters, had for some time discovered, that a poignant jest at the expense of the Lady Edith was a specific for relieving her Grace of England's low spirits, and the discovery saved their imagination much toil.

There was something ungenerous in this, because the Lady Edith was understood to be an orphan; and though she was

K

called Plantagenet, and the Fair Maid of Anjou, and admitted by Richard to certain privileges only granted to the royal family, and held her place in the circle accordingly, yet few knew, and none acquainted with the Court of England ventured to ask, in what exact degree of relationship she stood to Cœur de Lion. She had come with Eleanor, the celebrated Queen Mother of England, and joined Richard at Messina, as one of the ladies destined to attend on Berengaria, whose nuptials then approached. Richard treated his kinswoman with much respectful observance, and the Queen made her her most constant attendant, and, even in despite of the petty jealousy which we have observed, treated her, generally, with suitable respect.

The ladies of the household had, for a long time, no farther advantage over Edith, than might be afforded by an opportunity of censuring a less artfully disposed head attire, or an unbecoming robe; for the lady was judged to be inferior in these mysteries. The silent devotion of the Scottish knight did not, indeed, pass unnoticed; his liveries, his cognisance, his feats of arms, his mottoes and devices, were nearly watched, and occasionally made the subject of a passing jest. But then came the pilgrimage of the Queen and her ladies to Engaddi, a journey which the Queen had undertaken under a vow for the recovery of her husband's health, and which she had been encouraged to carry into effect by the Archbishop of Tyre for a political purpose. It was then, and in the chapel at that holy place, connected from above with a Carmelite nunnery, from beneath with the cell of the anchorite, that one of the Queen's attendants remarked that secret sign of intelligence which Edith had made to her lover, and failed not instantly to communicate it to her Majesty. The Queen returned from her pilgrimage enriched with this admirable recipe against dulness or ennui, and her train was at the same time augmented by a present of two wretched dwarfs from the dethroned Queen of Jerusalem, as deformed and as crazy (the excellence of that unhappy species) as any Queen could have desired. One of Berengaria's idle amusements had been to try the effect of the sudden appearance of such ghastly and fantastic forms on the nerves of the knight when left alone in the chapel; but the jest had been lost by the composure of the Scot, and the interference of the anchorite. She had now tried another, of which the consequences promised to be more serious.

The ladies again met after Sir Kenneth had retired from the tent; and the Queen, at first little moved by Edith's angry expostulations, only replied to her by upbraiding her prudery, and by indulging her wit at the expense of the garb, nation and above all, the poverty of the Knight of the Leopard, in which she displayed a good deal of playful malice, mingled with some humour, until Edith was compelled to carry her anxiety to her separate apartment. But when, in the morning, a female, whom Edith had entrusted to make inquiry, brought word that the standard was missing, and its champion vanished, she burst into the Queen's apartment, and implored her to rise and proceed to the King's tent without delay, and use her powerful mediation to prevent the evil consequences of her jest.

The Queen, frightened in her turn, cast, as is usual, the blame of her own folly on those around her, and endeavoured to comfort Edith's grief, and appease her displeasure, by a thousand inconsistent arguments. She was sure no harm had chanced—the knight was sleeping, she fancied, after his night-watch. What though, for fear of the King's displeasure, he had deserted with the standard—it was but a piece of silk, and he but a needy adventurer—or if he was put under warding for a time, she would soon get the King to pardon him—it was but waiting to let Richard's mood pass away.

Thus she continued talking thick and fast, and heaping together all sorts of inconsistencies, with the vain expectation of persuading both Edith and herself that no harm could come of a frolic, which in her heart she now bitterly repented. But while Edith in vain strove to intercept this torrent of idle talk, she caught the eye of one of the ladies who entered the Queen's apartment. There was death in her look of affright and horror, and Edith, at the first glance of her countenance, had sunk at once on the earth had not strong necessity, and her own elevation of character, enabled her to maintain at least external composure.

"Madam," she said to the Queen, "lose not another word in speaking, but save life—if, indeed," she added, her voice choking as she said it, "life may yet be saved."

"It may—it may," answered the Lady Calista. "I have just heard that he has been brought before the King—it is not yet over—but," she added, bursting into a vehement flood of weeping, in which personal apprehensions had some share—"it will soon—unless some course be taken."

"I will vow a golden candlestick to the Holy Sepulchre—a shrine of silver to our Lady of Engaddi—a pall, worth one hundred bezants, to Saint Thomas of Orthez," said the Queen in extremity.

"Up, up, madam!" said Edith; "call on the saints if you list, but be your own best saint."

"Indeed, madam," said the terrified attendant, "the Lady Edith speaks truth. Up, madam, and let us to King Richard's tent, and beg the poor gentleman's life."

"I will go—I will go instantly," said the Queen, rising and trembling excessively; while her women, in as great confusion as herself, were unable to render her those duties which were indispensable to her levee. Calm, composed, only pale as death, Edith ministered to the Queen with her own hand, and alone supplied the deficiencies of her numerous attendants.

"How you wait, wenches!" said the Queen, not able even then to forget frivolous distinctions. "Suffer ye the Lady Edith to do the duties of your attendance?—See'st thou, Edith, they can do nothing—I shall never be attired in time. We will send for the Archbishop of Tyre, and employ him as a mediator."

"Oh no, no!" exclaimed Edith—"Go yourself, madam—you have done the evil, do you confer the remedy."

"I will go—I will go," said the Queen; "but if Richard be in his mood, I dare not speak to him—he will kill me!"

"Yet go, gracious madam," said the Lady Calista, who best knew her mistress's temper; "not a lion, in his fury, could look upon such a face and form, and retain so much as an angry thought—far less a love-true knight like the royal Richard, to whom your slightest word would be a command."

"Dost thou think so, Calista?" said the Queen. "Ah, thou little knowest—yet I will go—But see you here—what means this? You have bedizened me in green, a colour he detests. Lo you! let me have a blue robe, and—search for the ruby carcanet, which was part of the King of Cyprus's ransom —it is either in the steel-casket, or somewhere else."

"This, and a man's life at stake!" said Edith indignantly; "it passes human patience. Remain at your ease, madam, I will go to King Richard—I am a party interested—I will know if the honour of a poor maiden of his blood is to be so far tampered with, that her name shall be abused to train a brave gentleman from his duty, bring him within the compass of death and infamy, and make, at the same time, the glory of England a laughing-stock to the whole Christian army."

At this unexpected burst of passion, Berengaria listened with an almost stupefied look of fear and wonder. But as Edith was about to leave the tent, she exclaimed, though faintly, "Stop her—stop her."

"You must, indeed, stop, noble Lady Edith," said Calista, taking her arm gently; "and you, royal madam, I am sure, will go, and without farther dallying. If the Lady Edith goes alone to the King, he will be dreadfully incensed, nor will it be one life that will stay his fury."

"I will go—I will go," said the Queen, yielding to necessity; and Edith reluctantly halted to wait her movements.

They were now as speedy as she could have desired. The Queen hastily wrapped herself in a large loose mantle, which covered all inaccuracies of the toilet. In this guise, attended by Edith and her women, and preceded and followed by a few officers and men-at-arms, she hastened to the tent of her lion-like husband.

CHAPTER XVII

Were every hair upon his head a life,
And every life were to be supplicated
By numbers equal to those hairs quadrupled,
Life after life should out like waning stars
Before the daybreak—or as festive lamps,
Which have lent lustre to the midnight revel,
Each after each are quench'd when guests depart !
—OLD PLAY.

THE entrance of Queen Berengaria into the interior of Richard's pavilion was withstood—in the most respectful and reverential manner indeed—but still withstood, by the chamberlains who watched in the outer tent. She could hear the stern command of the King from within, prohibiting their entrance.

" You see," said the Queen, appealing to Edith, as if she had exhausted all means of intercession in her power—" I knew it —the King will not receive us."

At the same time they heard Richard speak to some one within—" Go, speed thine office quickly, sirrah—for in that consists thy mercy—ten bezants if thou deal'st on him at one blow. —And, hark thee, villain, observe if his cheek loses colour, or his eye falters—mark me the smallest twitch of the features, or wink of the eyelid—I love to know how brave souls meet death."

" If he sees my blade waved aloft without shrinking, he is the first ever did so," answered a harsh deep voice, which a sense of unusual awe had softened into a sound much lower than its usual coarse tones.

Edith could remain silent no longer. " If your Grace," she said to the Queen, " make not your own way, I make it for you ; or if not for your Majesty, for myself, at least.—Chamberlains, the Queen demands to see King Richard—the wife to speak with her husband."

" Noble lady," said the officer, lowering his wand of office, " it grieves me to gainsay you ; but his Majesty is busied on matters of life and death."

" And we seek also to speak with him on matters of life and death," said Edith.—" I will make entrance for your Grace."— And putting aside the chamberlain with one hand, she laid hold on the curtain with the other.

"I dare not gainsay her Majesty's pleasure," said the chamberlain, yielding to the vehemence of the fair petitioner; and as he gave way, the Queen found herself obliged to enter the apartment of Richard.

The Monarch was lying on his couch, and at some distance, as awaiting his farther commands, stood a man whose profession it was not difficult to conjecture. He was clothed in a jerkin of red cloth, which reached scantly below the shoulders, leaving the arms bare from about half-way above the elbow, and, as an upper garment, he wore, when about as at present to betake himself to his dreadful office, a coat or tabard without sleeves, something like that of a herald, made of dressed bull's hide, and stained in the front with many a broad spot and speckle of dull crimson. The jerkin, and the tabard over it, reached the knee, and the nether stocks, or covering of the legs, were of the same leather which composed the tabard. A cap of rough shag served to hide the upper part of a visage, which, like that of a screech-owl, seemed desirous to conceal itself from light—the lower part of the face being obscured by a huge red beard, mingling with shaggy locks of the same colour. What features were seen were stern and misanthropical. The man's figure was short, strongly made, with a neck like a bull, very broad shoulders, arms of great and disproportioned length, a huge square trunk, and thick bandy legs. This truculent official leant on a sword, the blade of which was nearly four feet and a half in length, while the handle of twenty inches, surrounded by a ring of lead plummets to counterpoise the weight of such a blade, rose considerably above the man's head, as he rested his arm upon its hilt, waiting for King Richard's farther directions.

On the sudden entrance of the ladies, Richard, who was then lying on his couch, with his face towards the entrance, and resting on his elbow as he spoke to his grisly attendant, flung himself hastily, as if displeased and surprised, to the other side, turning his back to the Queen and the females of her train, and drawing around him the covering of his couch, which, by his own choice, or more probably the flattering selection of his chamberlains, consisted of two large lions' skins, dressed in Venice with such admirable skill that they seemed softer than the hide of the deer.

Berengaria, such as we have described her, knew well—what woman knows not?—her own road to victory. After a hurried glance of undisguised and unaffected terror at the ghastly companion of her husband's secret counsels, she rushed at once to the side of Richard's couch, dropped on her knees, flung her mantle from her shoulders, showing, as they hung down at their full length, her beautiful golden tresses, and while her

countenance seemed like a sun bursting through a cloud, yet
bearing on its pallid front traces that its splendours have been
obscured, she seized upon the right hand of the King, which,
as he assumed his wonted posture, had been employed in
dragging the covering of his couch, and gradually pulling it to
her with a force which was resisted, though but faintly, she
possessed herself of that arm, the prop of Christendom, and the
dread of Heathenesse, and imprisoning its strength in both her
little fairy hands, she bent upon it her brow, and united it to
her lips.

"What needs this, Berengaria?" said Richard, his head still
averted, but his hand remaining under her control.

"Send away that man—his look kills me!" muttered Berengaria.

"Begone, sirrah," said Richard, still without looking round.
"What wait'st thou for? art thou fit to look on these ladies?"

"Your Highness's pleasure touching the head," said the man.

"Out with thee, dog!" answered Richard—"a Christian
burial!"

The man disappeared, after casting a look upon the beautiful
Queen, in her deranged dress and natural loveliness, with a
smile of admiration more hideous in its expression than even his
usual scowl of cynical hatred against humanity.

"And now, foolish wench, what wishest thou?" said Richard,
turning slowly and half reluctantly round to his royal suppliant.

But it was not in nature for any one, far less an admirer of
beauty like Richard, to whom it stood only in the second rank
to glory, to look without emotion on the countenance and the
tremor of a creature so beautiful as Berengaria, or to feel, without any sympathy, that her lips, her brow, were on his hand,
and that it was wetted by her tears. By degrees he turned on
her his manly countenance, with the softest expression of which
his large blue eye, which so often gleamed with insufferable
light, was capable. Caressing her fair head, and mingling his
large fingers in her beautiful and dishevelled locks, he raised
and tenderly kissed the cherub countenance which seemed
desirous to hide itself in his hand. The robust form, the broad,
noble brow, and majestic looks, the naked arm and shoulder,
the lions' skins among which he lay, and the fair fragile feminine
creature that kneeled by his side, might have served for a model
of Hercules reconciling himself, after a quarrel, to his wife
Dejanira.

"And, once more, what seeks the lady of my heart in her
knight's pavilion, at this early and unwonted hour?"

"Pardon, my most gracious liege, pardon," said the Queen,
whose fears began again to unfit her for the duty of intercessor.

"Pardon! for what?" said the King.

"First, for entering your royal presence too boldly and unadvisedly——"

She stopped.

"*Thou* too boldly!—the sun might as well ask pardon, because his rays entered the windows of some wretch's dungeon. But I was busied with work unfit for thee to witness, my gentle one, and I was unwilling, besides, that thou shouldst risk thy precious health where sickness has been so lately rife."

"But thou art now well?" said the Queen, still delaying the communication which she feared to make.

"Well enough to break a lance on the bold crest of that champion who shall refuse to acknowledge thee the fairest dame in Christendom."

"Thou wilt not then refuse me one boon—only one—only a poor life?"

"Ha!—proceed," said King Richard, bending his brows.

"This unhappy Scottish knight"—said the Queen.

"Speak not of him, madam," said Richard sternly; "he dies —his doom is fixed."

"Nay, my royal liege and love, 'tis but a silken banner neglected—Berengaria will give thee another broidered with her own hand, and rich as ever dallied with the wind. Every pearl I have shall go to bedeck it, and with every pearl I will drop a tear of thankfulness to my generous knight."

"Thou knowest not what thou say'st," said the King, interrupting her in anger.—"Pearls! can all the pearls of the East atone for a speck upon England's honour—all the tears that ever woman's eye wept wash away a stain on Richard's fame?— Go to, madam, know your place, and your time, and your sphere. At present we have duties in which you cannot be our partner."

"Thou hear'st, Edith," whispered the Queen, "we shall but incense him."

"Be it so," said Edith, stepping forward.—"My lord—I, your poor kinswoman, crave you for justice rather than mercy; and, to the cry of justice, the ears of a monarch should be open at every time, place, and circumstance."

"Ha! our cousin Edith?" said Richard, rising and sitting upright on the side of his couch, covered with his long camiscia —"She speaks ever king-like, and king-like will I answer her, so she bring no request unworthy of herself or me."

The beauty of Edith was of a more intellectual and less voluptuous cast than that of the Queen; but impatience and anxiety had given her countenance a glow, which it sometimes wanted, and her mien had a character of energetic dignity that imposed silence for a moment even on Richard himself, who, to judge by his looks, would willingly have interrupted her.

QUEEN BERENGARIA AND KING RICHARD

BY F. R. PICKERSGILL, A.R.A.

"My lord," she said, "this good knight, whose blood you are about to spill, hath done, in his time, service to Christendom. He hath fallen from his duty, through a snare set for him in mere folly and idleness of spirit. A message sent to him in the name of one who—why should I not speak it?—it was in my own—induced him for an instant to leave his post—and what knight in the Christian camp might not have thus far transgressed at the command of a maiden, who, poor howsoever in other qualities, hath yet the blood of Plantagenet in her veins?"

"And you saw him, then, cousin?" replied the King, biting his lips, to keep down his passion.

"I did, my liege," said Edith. "It is no time to explain wherefore—I am here neither to exculpate myself nor to blame others."

"And where did you do him such a grace?"

"In the tent of her Majesty the Queen."

"Of our royal consort!" said Richard. "Now by Heaven, by Saint George of England, and every other saint that treads its crystal floor, this is too audacious! I have noticed and over-looked this warrior's insolent admiration of one so far above him, and I grudged him not that one of my blood should shed from her high-born sphere such influence as the sun bestows on the world beneath—But, heaven and earth! that you should have admitted him to an audience by night, in the very tent of our royal consort!—and dare to offer this as an excuse for his disobedience and desertion! By my father's soul, Edith, thou shalt rue this thy life-long in a monastery!"

"My liege," said Edith, "your greatness licenses tyranny. My honour, Lord King, is as little touched as yours, and my Lady the Queen can prove it if she think fit.—But I have already said, I am not here to excuse myself or inculpate others—I ask you but to extend to one, whose fault was committed under strong temptation, that mercy which even you yourself, Lord King, must one day supplicate at a higher tribunal, and for faults, perhaps, less venial."

"Can this be Edith Plantagenet?" said the King bitterly. —"Edith Plantagenet, the wise and the noble?—Or is it some love-sick woman, who cares not for her own fame in comparison of the life of her paramour? Now, by King Henry's soul! little hinders but I order thy minion's skull to be brought from the gibbet, and fixed as a perpetual ornament by the crucifix in thy cell!"

"And if thou dost send it from the gibbet to be placed for ever in my sight," said Edith, "I will say it is a relic of a good knight, cruelly and unworthily done to death by "—(she checked herself)—"by one, of whom I shall only say, he should have known better how to reward chivalry. Minion call'st thou him?" she continued with increasing vehemence.—"He was indeed my lover, and a most true one—but never sought he grace from me by look or word—contented with such humble observance as men pay to the saints—And the good—the valiant—the faithful, must die for this!"

"Oh, peace, peace, for pity's sake," whispered the Queen, "you do but offend him more!"

"I care not," said Edith; "the spotless virgin fears not the raging lion. Let him work his will on this worthy knight. Edith, for whom he dies, will know how to weep his memory—to me no one shall speak more of politic alliances, to be sanctioned with this poor hand. I could not—I would not—have been his bride living—our degrees were too distant. But death unites the high and the low—I am henceforth the spouse of the grave."

The King was about to answer with much anger, when a Carmelite monk entered the apartment hastily, his head and person muffled in a long mantle and hood of striped cloth of the coarsest texture, which distinguished his order, and, flinging himself on his knees before the King, conjured him, by every holy word and sign, to stop the execution.

"Now, by both sword and sceptre!" said Richard, "the world are leagued to drive me mad!—fools, women, and monks cross me at every step. How comes he to live still?"

"My gracious liege," said the monk, "I entreated of the Lord of Gilsland to stay the execution until I had thrown myself at your royal——"

"And he was wilful enough to grant thy request," said the King; "but it is of a piece with his wonted obstinacy—And what is it thou hast to say? Speak in the fiend's name!"

"My lord, there is a weighty secret—but it rests under the seal of confession—I dare not tell or even whisper it—but I swear to thee by my holy order—by the habit which I wear—by the blessed Elias, our founder, even him who was translated without suffering the ordinary pangs of mortality—that this youth hath divulged to me a secret, which, if I might confide it to thee, would utterly turn thee from thy bloody purpose in regard to him."

"Good father," said Richard, "that I reverence the Church, let the arms which I now wear for her sake bear witness. Give me to know this secret, and I will do what shall seem fitting in the matter. But I am no blind Bayard, to take a leap in the dark under the stroke of a pair of priestly spurs."

"My lord," said the holy man, throwing back his cowl and upper vesture, and discovering under the latter a garment of goatskin, and from beneath the former a visage so wildly

wasted by climate, fast, and penance, as to resemble rather
the apparition of an animated skeleton than a human face,
"for twenty years have I macerated this miserable body in the
caverns of Engaddi, doing penance for a great crime. Think
you I, who am dead to the world, would contrive a falsehood to
endanger my own soul, or that one, bound by the most sacred
oaths to the contrary—one such as I, who have but one longing
wish connected with earth, to wit, the rebuilding of our Christian Zion,—would betray the secrets of the confessional? Both
are alike abhorrent to my very soul."

"So," answered the King, "thou art that hermit of whom
men speak so much? Thou art, I confess, like enough to those
spirits which walk in dry places, but Richard fears no hob-
goblins—and thou art he, too, as I bethink me, to whom the
Christian princes sent this very criminal to open a communication with the Soldan, even while I, who ought to have been
first consulted, lay on my sick-bed? Thou and they may
content themselves—I will not put my neck into the loop of a
Carmelite's girdle—And, for your envoy, he shall die, the rather
and the sooner that thou dost entreat for him."

"Now God be gracious to thee, Lord King!" said the
hermit with much emotion; "thou art setting that mischief
on foot which thou wilt hereafter wish hadst stopt though
it had cost thee a limb. Rash, blinded man, yet forbear!"

"Away, away," said the King, stamping; "the sun has risen
on the dishonour of England, and it is not yet avenged.—
Ladies and priest, withdraw, if ye would not hear orders which
would displease you; for, by St. George, I swear——"

"Swear NOT!" said the voice of one who had just then
entered the pavilion.

"Ha! my learned Hakim," said the King; "come, I hope,
to tax our generosity."

"I come to request instant speech with you—instant—and
touching matters of deep interest."

"First look on my wife, Hakim, and let her know in you the
preserver of her husband."

"It is not for me," said the physician, folding his arms with
an air of Oriental modesty and reverence, and bending his eyes
on the ground,—"It is not for me to look upon beauty unveiled,
and armed in its splendours."

"Retire, then, Berengaria," said the Monarch; "and Edith,
do you retire also;—nay, renew not your importunities! This
I give to them, that the execution shall not be till high noon.
—Go, and be pacified—dearest Berengaria, begone.—Edith,"
he added, with a glance which struck terror even into the
courageous soul of his kinswoman, "go, if you are wise."

The females withdrew, or rather hurried from the tent, rank

and ceremony forgotten, much like a flock of wild-fowl huddled together, against whom the falcon has made a recent swoop.

They returned from thence to the Queen's pavilion, to indulge in regrets and recriminations, equally unavailing. Edith was the only one who seemed to disdain these ordinary channels of sorrow. Without a sigh, without a tear, without a word of upbraiding, she attended upon the Queen, whose weak temperament showed her sorrow in violent hysterical ecstasies, and passionate hypochondriacal effusions, in the course of which Edith sedulously, and even affectionately, attended her.

" It is impossible she can have loved this knight," said Florise to Calista, her senior in attendance upon the Queen's person. " We have been mistaken ; she is but sorry for his fate, as for a stranger who has come to trouble on her account."

" Hush, hush," answered her more experienced and more observant comrade ; " she is of that proud house of Plantagenet, who never own that a hurt grieves them. While they have themselves been bleeding to death, under a mortal wound, they have been known to bind up the scratches sustained by their more faint-hearted comrades.—Florise, we have done frightfully wrong ; and, for my own part, I would buy with every jewel I have, that our fatal jest had remained unacted."

CHAPTER XVIII

> This work desires a planetary intelligence
> Of Jupiter and Sol ; and those great spirits
> Are proud, fantastical. It asks great charges
> To entice them from the guiding of their spheres
> To wait on mortals.
> —ALBUMAZAR.

THE hermit followed the ladies from the pavilion of Richard, as shadow follows a beam of sunshine when the clouds are driving over the face of the sun. But he turned on the threshold, and held up his hand towards the King in a warning, or almost a menacing posture, as he said,—" Woe to him who rejects the counsel of the Church, and betaketh himself to the foul divan of the infidel ! King Richard, I do not yet shake the dust from my feet and depart from thy encampment—the sword falls not—but it hangs but by a hair.—Haughty monarch, we shall meet again."

" Be it so, haughty priest," returned Richard, " prouder in thy goatskins than princes in purple and fine linen."

The hermit vanished from the tent, and the King continued, addressing the Arabian,—" Do the dervises of the East, wise Hakim, use such familiarity with their princes ? "

"The dervise," replied Adonbec, "should be either a sage or a madman; there is no middle course for him who wears the khirkhah,* who watches by night, and fasts by day. Hence, hath he either wisdom enough to bear himself discreetly in the presence of princes, or else, having no reason bestowed on him, he is not responsible for his own actions."

"Methinks our monks have adopted chiefly the latter character," said Richard—"But to the matter.—In what can I pleasure you, my learned physician?"

"Great King," said El Hakim, making his profound Oriental obeisance, "let thy servant speak one word, and yet live. I would remind thee that thou owest—not to me, their humble instrument—but to the Intelligences, whose benefits I dispense to mortals, a life——"

"And I warrant me thou wouldst have another in requital, ha?" interrupted the King.

"Such is my humble prayer," said the Hakim, "to the great Melech Ric—even the life of this good knight, who is doomed to die, and but for such fault as was committed by the Sultan Adam, surnamed Aboulbeschar, or the father of all men."

"And thy wisdom might remind thee, Hakim, that Adam died for it," said the King somewhat sternly, and then began to pace the narrow space of his tent with some emotion, and to talk to himself. "Why, God-a-mercy—I knew what he desired as soon as ever he entered the pavilion!—Here is one poor life justly condemned to extinction, and I, a king and a soldier, who have slain thousands by my command, and scores with my own hand, am to have no power over it, although the honour of my arms, of my house, of my very Queen, hath been attainted by the culprit—By Saint George, it makes me laugh!—By Saint Louis, it reminds me of Blondel's tale of an enchanted castle, where the destined knight was withstood successively in his purpose of entrance by forms and figures the most dissimilar, but all hostile to his undertaking! No sooner one sunk than another appeared!—Wife—Kinswoman—Hermit—Hakim—each appears in the lists as soon as the other is defeated!—Why, this is a single knight fighting against the whole mêlée of the tournament—ha! ha! ha!"—And Richard laughed aloud; for he had, in fact, begun to change his mood, his resentment being usually too violent to be of long endurance.

The physician meanwhile looked on him with a countenance of surprise, not unmingled with contempt; for the Eastern people make no allowance for those mercurial changes in the temper, and consider open laughter, upon almost any account, as derogatory to the dignity of man, and becoming only to

* Literally, the torn robe. The habit of the dervises is so called.

women and children. At length the sage addressed the King, when he saw him more composed.

"A doom of death should not issue from laughing lips.—Let thy servant hope that thou hast granted him this man's life."

"Take the freedom of a thousand captives instead," said Richard; "restore so many of thy countrymen to their tents and families, and I will give the warrant instantly. This man's life can avail thee nothing, and it is forfeited."

"All our lives are forfeited," said the Hakim, putting his hand to his cap. "But the great Creditor is merciful, and enacts not the pledge rigorously nor untimely."

"Thou canst show me," said Richard, "no special interest thou hast to become intercessor betwixt me and the execution of justice, to which I am sworn as a crowned king."

"Thou art sworn to the dealing forth mercy as well as justice," said El Hakim; "but what thou seekest, great King, is the execution of thine own will. And, for the concern I have in this request, know that many a man's life depends upon thy granting this boon."

"Explain thy words," said Richard; "but think not to impose upon me by false pretexts."

"Be it far from thy servant!" said Adonbec. "Know, then, that the medicine to which thou, Sir King, and many one beside, owe their recovery, is a talisman, composed under certain aspects of the heavens, when the Divine Intelligences are most propitious. I am but the poor adminstrator of its virtues. I dip it in a cup of water, observe the fitting hour to administer it to the patient, and the potency of the draught works the cure."

"A most rare medicine," said the King, "and a commodious! and, as it may be carried in the leech's purse, would save the whole caravan of camels which they require to convey drugs and physic-stuff—I marvel there is any other in use."

"It is written," answered the Hakim, with imperturbable gravity, "'abuse not the steed which hath borne thee from the battle.' Know, that such talismans might indeed be framed, but rare has been the number of adepts who have dared to undertake the applications of their virtue. Severe restrictions, painful observances, fasts, and penance, are necessary on the part of the sage who uses this mode of cure; and if, through neglect of these preparations, by his love of ease, or his indulgence of sensual appetite, he omits to cure at least twelve persons within the course of each moon, the virtue of the divine gift departs from the amulet, and both the last patient and the physician will be exposed to speedy misfortune, neither will they survive the year. I require yet one life to make up the appointed number."

"Go out into the camp, good Hakim, where thou wilt find a-many," said the King, "and do not seek to rob my headsman of *his* patients; it is unbecoming a mediciner of thine eminence to interfere with the practice of another.—Besides, I cannot see how delivering a criminal from the death he deserves, should go to make up thy tale of miraculous cures."

"When thou canst show why a draught of cold water should have cured thee, when the most precious drugs failed," said the Hakim, "thou may'st reason on the other mysteries attendant on this matter. For myself, I am inefficient to the great work, having this morning touched an unclean animal. Ask, therefore, no farther questions; it is enough that, by sparing this man's life at my request, you will deliver yourself, great King, and thy servant, from a great danger."

"Hark thee, Adonbec," replied the King, "I have no objection that leeches should wrap their words in mist, and pretend to derive knowledge from the stars; but when you bid Richard Plantagenet fear that a danger will fall upon *him* from some idle omen, or omitted ceremonial, you speak to no ignorant Saxon, or doting old woman, who foregoes her purpose because a hare crosses the path, a raven croaks, or a cat sneezes."

"I cannot hinder your doubt of my words," said Adonbec; "but yet, let my Lord the King grant that truth is on the tongue of his servant—will he think it just to deprive the world, and every wretch who may suffer by the pains which so lately reduced him to that couch, of the benefit of this most virtuous talisman, rather than extend his forgiveness to one poor criminal? Bethink you, Lord King, that though thou canst slay thousands, thou canst not restore one man to health. Kings have the power of Satan to torment, sages that of Allah to heal—beware how thou hinderest the good to humanity, which thou canst not thyself render. Thou canst cut off the head, but not cure the aching tooth."

"This is over insolent," said the King, hardening himself, as the Hakim assumed a more lofty, and almost a commanding tone. "We took thee for our leech, not for our counsellor, or conscience-keeper."

"And is it thus the most renowned Prince of Frangistan repays benefit done to his royal person?" said El Hakim, exchanging the humble and stooping posture, in which he had hitherto solicited the King, for an attitude lofty and commanding. "Know, then," he said, "that through every court of Europe and Asia—to Moslem and Nazarene—to knight and lady—wherever harp is heard and sword worn—wherever honour is loved and infamy detested—to every quarter of the world will I denounce thee, Melech Ric, as thankless and ungenerous;

and even the lands—if there be any such—that never heard of thy renown, shall yet be acquainted with thy shame !"

"Are these terms to me, vile infidel !" said Richard, striding up to him in fury.—"Art weary of thy life ?"

"Strike !" said El Hakim; "thine own deed shall then paint thee more worthless than could my words, though each had an hornet's sting."

Richard turned fiercely from him, folded his arms, traversed the tent as before, and then exclaimed, "Thankless and ungenerous !—as well be termed coward and infidel !—Hakim, thou hast chosen thy boon; and though I had rather thou hadst asked my crown-jewels, yet I may not, king-like, refuse thee. Take this Scot, therefore, to thy keeping—the provost will deliver him to thee on this warrant."

He hastily traced one or two lines, and gave them to the physician. "Use him as thy bond-slave, to be disposed of as thou wilt—only, let him beware how he comes before the eyes of Richard. Hark thee—thou art wise—he hath been over bold among those in whose fair looks and weak judgments we trust our honour, as you of the East lodge your treasures in caskets of silver wire, as fine and as frail as the web of a gossamer."

"Thy servant understands the word of the King," said the sage, at once resuming the reverent style of address in which he had commenced. "When the rich carpet is soiled, the fool pointeth to the stain—the wise man covers it with his mantle. I have heard my lord's pleasure, and to hear is to obey."

"It is well," said the King; "let him consult his own safety, and never appear in my presence more.—Is there aught else in which I may do thee pleasure ?"

"The bounty of the King hath filled my cup to the brim," said the sage; "yea, it hath been abundant as the fountain which sprung up amid the camp of the descendants of Israel, when the rock was stricken by the rod of Moussa Ben Amran."

"Ay, but," said the King, smiling, "it required, as in the desert, a hard blow on the rock ere it yielded its treasures. I would that I knew something to pleasure thee, which I might yield as freely as the natural fountain sends forth its waters."

"Let me touch that victorious hand," said the sage, "in token, that if Adonbec el Hakim should hereafter demand a boon of Richard of England, he may do so, yet plead his command."

"Thou hast hand and glove upon it, man," replied Richard; "only, if thou couldst consistently make up thy tale of patients without craving me to deliver from punishment those who have deserved it, I would more willingly discharge my debt in some other form."

"May thy days be multiplied !"—answered the Hakim, and withdrew from the apartment after the usual deep obeisance.

King Richard gazed after him as he departed, like one but half-satisfied with what had passed.

"Strange pertinacity," he said, "in this Hakim, and a wonderful chance to interfere between that audacious Scot and the chastisement he has merited so richly. Yet, let him live! there is one brave man the more in the world.—And now for the Austrian.—Ho, is the Baron of Gilsland there without?"

Sir Thomas de Vaux thus summoned, his bulky form speedily darkened the opening of the pavilion, while behind him glided as a spectre unannounced, yet unopposed, the savage form of the hermit of Engaddi, wrapped in his goatskin mantle.

Richard, without noticing his presence, called in a loud tone to the Baron, "Sir Thomas de Vaux, of Lanercost and Gilsland, take trumpet and herald, and go instantly to the tent of him whom they call Archduke of Austria, and see that it be when the press of his knights and vassals is greatest around him— as is likely at this hour, for the German boar breakfasts ere he hears mass—enter his presence with as little reverence as thou may'st, and impeach him, on the part of Richard of England, that he hath this night, by his own hand, or that of others, stolen from its staff the Banner of England.—Wherefore, say to him our pleasure, that, within an hour from the time of my speaking, he restore the said banner with all reverence—he himself and his principal barons waiting the whilst with heads uncovered, and without their robes of honour. And that, moreover, he pitch beside it, on the one hand, his own Banner of Austria reversed, as that which hath been dishonoured by theft and felony—and on the other, a lance, bearing the bloody head of him who was his nearest counsellor, or assistant, in this case injury—And say, that such our behests being punctually discharged, we will, for the sake of our vow, and the weal of the Holy Land, forgive his other forfeits."

"And how if the Duke of Austria deny all accession to this act of wrong and of felony?" said Thomas de Vaux.

"Tell him," replied the King, "we will prove it upon his body—ay, were he backed with his two bravest champions. Knight-like will we prove it, on foot or on horse, in the desert or in the field, time, place, and arms, all at his own choice."

"Bethink you of the peace of God and the Church, my liege lord," said the Baron of Gilsland, "among those princes engaged in this holy Crusade."

"Bethink you how to execute my commands, my liege vassal," answered Richard impatiently. "Methinks men expect to turn our purpose by their breath, as boys blow feathers to and fro—Peace of the Church!—who, I prithee, minds it? The peace of the Church, among Crusaders, implies war with the Saracens, with whom the princes have made truce, and the

one ends with the other. And, besides, see you not how every
prince of them is seeking his own several ends?—I will seek
mine also—and that is honour. For honour I came hither, and
if I may not win it upon the Saracens, at least I will not lose
a jot from any respect to this paltry Duke, though he were bul-
warked and buttressed by every prince in the Crusade."

De Vaux turned to obey the King's mandate, shrugging his
shoulders at the same time, the bluntness of his nature being
unable to conceal that its tenor went against his judgment.
But the hermit of Engaddi stepped forward, and assumed the
air of one charged with higher commands than those of a mere
earthly potentate. Indeed, his dress of shaggy skins, his un-
combed and untrimmed hair and beard, his lean, wild, and contorted features, and the almost insane fire which gleamed from
under his bushy eyebrows, made him approach nearly to our
idea of some seer of Scripture, who, charged with high mission
to the sinful Kings of Judah or Israel, descended from the
rocks and caverns in which he dwelt in abstracted solitude, to
abash earthly tyrants in the midst of their pride, by discharging on them the blighting denunciations of Divine Majesty,
even as the cloud discharges the lightning with which it is
fraught on the pinnacles and towers of castles and palaces. In
the midst of his most wayward mood, Richard respected the
Church, and its ministers, and though offended at the intrusion
of the hermit into his tent, he greeted him with respect; at
the same time, however, making a sign to Sir Thomas de Vaux
to hasten on his message.

But the hermit prohibited the baron, by gesture, look, and
word, to stir a yard on such an errand; and, holding up his
bare arm, from which the goatskin mantle fell back in the
violence of his action, he waved it aloft, meagre with famine
and wealed with the blows of the discipline.

"In the name of God, and of the most holy Father, the
vicegerent of the Christian Church upon earth, I prohibit this
most profane, bloodthirsty, and brutal defiance betwixt two
Christian princes, whose shoulders are signed with the blessed
mark under which they swore brotherhood. Woe to him by
whom it is broken!—Richard of England, recall the most unhallowed message thou hast given to that baron—Danger and
Death are nigh thee!—the dagger is glancing at thy very
throat!——"

"Danger and Death are playmates to Richard," answered the
monarch proudly; "and he hath braved too many swords to
fear a dagger."

"Danger and Death are near," replied the seer; and sinking his voice to a hollow, unearthly tone, he added, "And after
death the judgment!"

"Good and holy father," said Richard, "I reverence thy person and thy sanctity——"

"Reverence not me!" interrupted the hermit; "reverence sooner the vilest insect that crawls by the shores of the Dead Sea, and feeds upon its accursed slime. But reverence Him whose commands I speak—Reverence Him whose sepulchre you have vowed to rescue—Revere the oath of concord which you have sworn, and break not the silver cord of union and fidelity with which you have bound yourself to your princely confederates."

"Good father," said the King, "you of the Church seem to me to presume somewhat, if a layman may say so much, upon the dignity of your holy character. Without challenging your right to take charge of our conscience, methinks you might leave us the charge of our own honour."

"Presume!" repeated the hermit—"is it for me to presume, royal Richard, who am but the bell obeying the hand of the sexton—but the senseless and worthless trumpet, carrying the command of him who sounds it?—See, on my knees I throw myself before thee, imploring thee to have mercy on Christendom, on England, and on thyself!"

"Rise, rise," said Richard, compelling him to stand up; "it beseems not that knees, which are so frequently bended to the Deity, should press the ground in honour of man. What danger awaits us, reverend father! and when stood the power of England so low, that the noisy bluster of this new-made Duke's displeasure should alarm her, or her monarch?"

"I have looked forth from my mountain turret upon the starry host of heaven, as each in his midnight circuit uttered wisdom to another, and knowledge to the few who can understand their voice. There sits an enemy in thy House of Life, Lord King, malign at once to thy fame, and thy prosperity—an emanation of Saturn, menacing thee with instant and bloody peril, and which, but thou yield thy proud will to the rule of thy duty, will presently crush thee, even in thy pride."

"Away, away—this is heathen science," said the King. "Christians practise it not—wise men believe it not.—Old man, thou dotest."

"I dote not, Richard," answered the hermit—"I am not so happy. I know my condition, and that some portion of reason is yet permitted me, not for my own use, but that of the Church, and the advancement of the Cross. I am the blind man who holds a torch to others, though it yields no light to himself. Ask me touching what concerns the weal of Christendom, and of this Crusade, and I will speak with thee as the wisest counsellor on whose tongue persuasion ever sat. Speak to me of my own wretched being, and my words shall be those of the maniac outcast which I am."

"I would not break the bands of unity asunder among the Princes of the Crusade," said Richard, with a mitigated tone and manner; "but what atonement can they render me for the injustice and insult which I have sustained?"

"Even of that I am prepared and commissioned to speak by the Council, which, meeting hastily at the summons of Philip of France, have taken measures for that effect."

"Strange," replied Richard, "that others should treat of what is due to the wounded Majesty of England!"

"They are willing to anticipate your demands, if it be possible," answered the hermit. "In a body, they consent that the Banner of England be replaced on Saint George's Mount, and they lay under ban and condemnation the audacious criminal, or criminals, by whom it was outraged, and will announce a princely reward to any who shall denounce the delinquent's guilt, and give his flesh to the wolves and ravens."

"And Austria," said Richard—"upon whom rest such strong presumptions that he was the author of the deed?"

"To prevent discord in the host," replied the hermit, "Austria will clear himself of the suspicion, by submitting to whatsoever ordeal the Patriarch of Jerusalem shall impose."

"Will he clear himself by the trial by combat?" said King Richard.

"His oath prohibits it," said the hermit; "and, moreover, the Council of the Princes——"

"Will neither authorise battle against the Saracens," interrupted Richard, "nor against any one else. But it is enough, father—thou hast shown me the folly of proceeding as I designed in this matter. You shall sooner light your torch in a puddle of rain, than bring a spark out of a cold-blooded coward. There is no honour to be gained on Austria, and so let him pass.—I will have him perjure himself, however; I will insist on the ordeal.—How I shall laugh to hear his clumsy fingers hiss, as he grasps the red-hot globe of iron!—Ay, or his huge mouth riven, and his gullet swelling to suffocation, as he endeavours to swallow the consecrated bread!"

"Peace, Richard," said the hermit—"Oh, peace, for shame if not for charity! Who shall praise or honour princes, who insult and calumniate each other?—Alas! that a creature so noble as thou art—so accomplished in princely thoughts and princely daring—so fitted to honour Christendom by thy actions and, in thy calmer mood, to rule her by thy wisdom, should yet have the brute and wild fury of the lion, mingled with the dignity and courage of that king of the forest!"

He remained an instant musing with his eyes fixed on the ground, and then proceeded—"But Heaven, that knows our imperfect nature, accepts of our imperfect obedience, and hath delayed, though not averted, the bloody end of thy daring life. The destroying angel hath stood still, as of old, by the threshing floor of Araunah the Jebusite, and the blade is drawn in his hand, by which, at no distant date, Richard, the lion-hearted, shall be as low as the meanest peasant."

"Must it then be so soon?" said Richard. "Yet, even so be it. May my course be bright, if it be but brief!"

"Alas! noble King," said the solitary, and it seemed as if a tear (unwonted guest) were gathering in his dry and glazened eye—"short and melancholy, marked with mortification, and calamity, and captivity, is the span that divides thee from the grave which yawns for thee—a grave in which thou shalt be laid without lineage to succeed thee—without the tears of a people, exhausted by thy ceaseless wars, to lament thee—without having extended the knowledge of thy subjects—without having done aught to enlarge their happiness."

"But not without renown, monk—not without the tears of the lady of my love! These consolations, which thou canst neither know nor estimate, await upon Richard to his grave."

"*Do* I not know—*can* I not estimate, the value of minstrel's praise, and of lady's love!" retorted the hermit, in a tone which for a moment seemed to emulate the enthusiasm of Richard himself. "King of England," he continued, extending his emaciated arm, "the blood which boils in thy blue veins is not more noble than that which stagnates in mine. Few and cold as the drops are, they still are of the blood of the royal Lusignan —of the heroic and sainted Godfrey. I am—that is, I was when in the world—Alberick Mortemar——"

"Whose deeds," said Richard, "have so often filled Fame's trumpet! Is it so—can it be so?—Could such a light as thine fall from the horizon of chivalry, and yet men be uncertain where its embers had alighted?"

"Seek a fallen star," said the hermit, "and thou shalt only light on some foul jelly, which, in shooting through the horizon, has assumed for a moment an appearance of splendour. Richard, if I thought that rending the bloody veil from my horrible fate could make thy proud heart stoop to the discipline of the Church, I could find in my heart to tell thee a tale, which I have hitherto kept gnawing at my vitals in concealment, like the self-devoted youth of Heathenesse.—Listen then, Richard, and may the grief and despair, which cannot avail this wretched remnant of what was once a man, be powerful as an example to so noble, yet so wild a being as thou art! Yes—I will—I *will* tear open the long-hidden wounds, although in thy very presence they should bleed to death!"

King Richard, upon whom the history of Alberick of Mortemar had made a deep impression in his early years, when minstrels were regaling his father's halls with legends of the Holy Land, listened with respect to the outlines of a tale which, darkly and imperfectly sketched, indicated sufficiently the cause of the partial insanity of this singular and most unhappy being.

"I need not," he said, "tell thee that I was noble in birth, high in fortune, strong in arms, wise in council. All these I was; but while the noblest ladies in Palestine strove which should wind garlands for my helmet, my love was fixed—unalterably and devotedly fixed—on a maiden of low degree. Her father, an ancient soldier of the Cross, saw our passion, and knowing the difference betwixt us, saw no other refuge for his daughter's honour than to place her within the shadow of the cloister. I returned from a distant expedition, loaded with spoils and honour, to find my happiness was destroyed for ever! I, too, sought the cloister, and Satan, who had marked me for his own, breathed into my heart a vapour of spiritual pride, which could only have had its source in his own infernal regions. I had risen as high in the Church as before in the State—I was, forsooth, the wise, the self-sufficient, the impeccable!—I was the counsellor of councils—I was the director of prelates—how should I stumble?—wherefore should I fear temptation?—Alas! I became confessor to a sisterhood, and amongst that sisterhood I found the long loved—the long lost. Spare me farther confession!—A fallen nun, whose guilt was avenged by self-murder, sleeps soundly in the vaults of Engaddi, while, above her very grave, gibbers, moans, and roars a creature, to whom but so much reason is left as may suffice to render him completely sensible to his fate!"

"Unhappy man!" said Richard, "I wonder no longer at thy misery. How didst thou escape the doom, which the canons denounce against thy offence?"

"Ask one who is yet in the gall of worldly bitterness," said the hermit, "and he will speak of a life spared for personal respects, and from consideration to high birth. But, Richard, I tell thee that Providence hath preserved me, to lift me on high as a light and beacon, whose ashes, when this earthly fuel is burnt out, must yet be flung into Tophet. Withered and shrunk as this poor form is, it is yet animated with two spirits —one active, shrewd, and piercing, to advocate the cause of the Church of Jerusalem—one mean, abject, and despairing, fluctuating between madness and misery, to mourn over my own wretchedness, and to guard holy relics, on which it would be most sinful for me even to cast my eye. Pity me not!— it is but sin to pity the loss of such an abject—pity me not, but profit by my example. Thou standest on the highest, and, therefore, on the most dangerous pinnacle, occupied by any Christian prince. Thou art proud of heart, loose of life, bloody of hand. Put from thee the sins which are to thee as daughters—though they be dear to the sinful Adam, expel these adopted furies from thy breast—thy pride, thy luxury, thy blood-thirstiness."

"He raves," said Richard, turning from the solitary to De Vaux, as one who felt some pain from a sarcasm which yet he could not resent—then turned him calmly, and somewhat scornfully to the anchoret, as he replied—"Thou hast found a fair bevy of daughters, reverend father, to one who hath been but few months married; but since I must put them from my roof, it were but like a father to provide them with suitable matches. Wherefore, I will part with my pride to the noble Canons of the Church—my luxury, as thou call'st it, to the Monks of the rule—and my blood-thirstiness to the Knights of the Temple."

"Oh, heart of steel, and hand of iron," said the anchoret, "upon whom example, as well as advice, is alike thrown away! —Yet shalt thou be spared for a season, in case it so be thou shouldst turn and do that which is acceptable in the sight of Heaven.—For me, I must return to my place—Kyrie Eleison! —I am he through whom the rays of heavenly grace dart like those of the sun through a burning glass, concentrating them on other objects, until they kindle and blaze, while the glass itself remains cold and uninfluenced.—Kyrie Eleison!—the poor must be called, for the rich have refused the banquet— Kyrie Eleison!"

So saying, he burst from the tent uttering loud cries.

"A mad priest!"—said Richard, from whose mind the frantic exclamations of the hermit had partly obliterated the impression produced by the detail of his personal history and misfortunes. "After him, De Vaux, and see he comes to no harm; for, Crusaders as we are, a juggler hath more reverence amongst our varlets than a priest or a saint, and they may, perchance, put some scorn upon him."

The knight obeyed, and Richard presently gave way to the thoughts which the wild prophecy of the monk had inspired.— "To die early—without lineage—without lamentation?—a heavy sentence, and well that it is not passed by a more competent judge. Yet the Saracens, who are accomplished in mystical knowledge, will often maintain, that He, in whose eyes the wisdom of the sage is but as folly, inspires wisdom and prophecy into the seeming folly of the madman. Yonder hermit is said to read the stars too, an art generally practised in these lands, where the heavenly host was of yore the object of idolatry. I would I had asked him touching the loss of my banner; for not the blessed Tishbite, the founder of his order, could seem more wildly rapt out of himself, or speak with a tongue more resembling that of a prophet.—How now, De Vaux, what news of the mad priest?"

"Mad priest, call you him, my lord?" answered De Vaux. "Methinks he resembles more the blessed Baptist himself, just issued from the wilderness. He has placed himself on one of the military engines, and from thence he preaches to the soldiers, as never man preached since the time of Peter the Hermit. The camp, alarmed by his cries, crowd around him in thousands; and breaking off every now and then from the main thread of his discourse, he addresses the several nations, each in their own language, and presses upon each the arguments best qualified to urge them to perseverance in the delivery of Palestine."

"By this light, a noble hermit!" said King Richard. "But what else could come from the blood of Godfrey? *He* despair of safety, because he hath in former days lived *par amours?* I will have the Pope send him an ample remission, and I would not less willingly be intercessor had his *belle amie* been an abbess."

As he spoke, the Archbishop of Tyre craved audience, for the purpose of requesting Richard's attendance, should his health permit, on a secret conclave of the chiefs of the Crusade, and to explain to him the military and political incidents which had occurred during his illness.

CHAPTER XIX

Must we then sheathe our still victorious sword;
Turn back our forward step, which ever trode
O'er foemen's necks the onward path of glory;
Unclasp the mail, which with a solemn vow,
In God's own house, we hung upon our shoulders;
That vow, as unaccomplish'd as the promise
Which village nurses make to still their children,
And after think no more of?——
—THE CRUSADE, *A Tragedy.*

THE Archbishop of Tyre was an emissary well chosen to communicate to Richard tidings, which from another voice the lion-hearted King would not have brooked to hear, without the most unbounded explosions of resentment. Even this sagacious and reverend prelate found difficulty in inducing him to listen to news, which destroyed all his hopes of gaining back the Holy Sepulchre by force of arms, and acquiring the renown, which the universal all-hail of Christendom was ready to confer upon him, as the Champion of the Cross.

But, by the Archbishop's report, it appeared that Saladin was assembling all the force of his hundred tribes, and that the monarchs of Europe, already disgusted from various motives with the expedition, which had proved so hazardous, and was daily growing more so, had resolved to abandon their purpose. In this they were countenanced by the example of Philip of France, who, with many protestations of regard, and assurances that he would first see his brother of England in safety, declared his intention to return to Europe. His great vassal, the Earl of Champagne, had adopted the same resolution; and it could not excite surprise, that Leopold of Austria, affronted as he had been by Richard, was glad to embrace an opportunity of deserting a cause, in which his haughty opponent was to be considered as chief. Others announced the same purpose; so that it was plain that the King of England was to be left, if he chose to remain, supported only by such volunteers as might, under such depressing circumstances, join themselves to the English army; and by the doubtful aid of Conrade of Montserrat, and the military orders cf the Temple, and of Saint John, who, though they were sworn to wage battle against the Saracens, were at least equally jealous of any European monarch achieving the conquest of Palestine, where, with short-sighted and selfish policy, they proposed to establish independent dominions of their own.

It needed not many arguments to show Richard the truth of his situation; and, indeed, after his first burst of passion, he sat him calmly down, and with gloomy looks, head depressed, and arms folded on his bosom, listened to the Archbishop's reasoning on the impossibility of his carrying on the Crusade when deserted by his companions. Nay, he forebore interruption, even when the prelate ventured, in measured terms, to hint that Richard's own impetuosity had been one main cause of disgusting the princes with the expedition.

"*Confiteor*," answered Richard, with a dejected look, and something of a melancholy smile; "I confess, reverend father, that I ought on some accounts to sing *culpa mea*. But is it not hard that my frailties of temper should be visited with such a penance, that, for a burst or two of natural passion, I should be doomed to see fade before me ungathered such a rich harvest of glory to God, and honour to chivalry?—But it shall *not* fade.—By the soul of the Conqueror, I will plant the Cross on the towers of Jerusalem, or it shall be planted over Richard's grave!"

"Thou may'st do it," said the prelate, "yet not another drop of Christian blood be shed in the quarrel."

"Ah, you speak of compromise, Lord Prelate—but the blood of the infidel hounds must also cease to flow," said Richard.

"There will be glory enough," replied the Archbishop, "in having extorted from Saladin, by force of arms, and by the respect inspired by your fame, such conditions, as at once restore the Holy Sepulchre, open the Holy Land to pilgrims, secure their safety by strong fortresses, and, stronger than all, assure the safety of the Holy City, by conferring on Richard the title of King Guardian of Jerusalem."

"How!" said Richard, his eyes sparkling with unusual light, "I—I—I the King Guardian of the Holy City! Victory itself, but that it *is* victory, could not gain more—scarce so much, when won with unwilling and disunited forces.—But Saladin still proposes to retain his interest in the Holy Land?"

"As a joint sovereign, the sworn ally," replied the Prelate, "of the mighty Richard—his relative—if it may be permitted by marriage."

"By marriage!" said Richard, surprised, yet less so than the Prelate had expected. "Ha!—Ay—Edith Plantagenet. Did I dream this?—or did some one tell me? My head is still weak from this fever, and has been agitated.—Was it the Scot, or the Hakim, or yonder holy hermit, that hinted such a wild bargain?"

"The hermit of Engaddi, most likely," said the Archbishop; "for he hath toiled much in this matter; and since the discontent of the princes has become apparent, and a separation of their forces unavoidable, he hath had many consultations, both with Christian and Pagan, for arranging such a pacification, as may give to Christendom, at least in part, the objects of this holy warfare."

"My kinswoman to an infidel—Ha!" exclaimed Richard, as his eyes began to sparkle.

The Prelate hastened to avert his wrath.

"The Pope's consent must doubtless be first attained, and the holy hermit, who is well known at Rome, will treat with the Holy Father."

"How?—Without our consent first given?" said the King.

"Surely no," said the Bishop, in a quiet and insinuating tone of voice; "only with and under your special sanction."

"My sanction to marry my kinswoman to an infidel?" said Richard; yet he spoke rather in a tone of doubt than as distinctly reprobating the measure proposed. "Could I have dreamed of such a composition when I leaped upon the Syrian shore from the prow of my galley, even as a lion springs on his prey!—And now—But proceed—I will hear with patience."

Equally delighted and surprised to find his task so much easier than he had apprehended, the Archbishop hastened to pour forth before Richard the instances of such alliances in Spain—not without countenance from the Holy See—the incalculable advantages which all Christendom would derive from the union of Richard and Saladin, by a bond so sacred; and, above all, he spoke with great vehemence and unction on the probability that Saladin would, in case of the proposed alliance, exchange his false faith for the true one.

"Hath the Soldan shown any disposition to become Christian?" said Richard; "if so, the king lives not on earth to whom I would grant the hand of a kinswoman, ay, or sister, sooner than to my noble Saladin—ay, though the one came to lay crown and sceptre at her feet, and the other had nothing to offer but his good sword and better heart!"

"Saladin hath heard our Christian teachers," said the Bishop, somewhat evasively,—"my unworthy self—and others—and as he listens with patience, and replies with calmness, it can hardly be but that he be snatched as a brand from the burning. *Magna est veritas, et prævalebit!* Moreover, the hermit of Engaddi, few of whose words have fallen fruitless to the ground, is possessed fully with the belief that there is a calling of the Saracens and the other heathen approaching, to which this marriage shall be matter of induction. He readeth the course of the stars; and dwelling, with maceration of the flesh, in those divine places which the saints have trodden of old, the spirit of Elijah the Tishbite, the founder of his blessed order, hath been with him as it was with the prophet Elisha, the son of Shaphat, when he spread his mantle over him."

King Richard listened to the Prelate's reasoning, with a downcast brow and a troubled look.

"I cannot tell," he said, "how it is with me; but methinks these cold counsels of the Princes of Christendom have infected me too with a lethargy of spirit. The time hath been, that, had a layman proposed such alliance to me, I had struck him to the earth—if a churchman, I had spit at him as a renegade and priest of Baal—yet now this counsel sounds not so strange in mine ear; for why should I not seek for brotherhood and alliance with a Saracen, brave, just, generous—who loves and honours a worthy foe, as if he were a friend,—whilst the Princes of Christendom shrink from the side of their allies, and forsake the cause of Heaven and good knighthood?—But I will possess my patience, and will not think of them. Only one attempt will I make to keep this gallant brotherhood together, if it be possible; and if I fail, Lord Archbishop, we will speak together of thy counsel, which, as now, I neither accept nor altogether reject. Wend we to the Council, my lord—the hour calls us. Thou say'st Richard is hasty and proud—thou shalt see him humble himself like the lowly broom-plant, from which he derives his surname."

With the assistance of those of his privy chamber, the King then hastily robed himself in a doublet and mantle of a dark and uniform colour; and without any mark of regal dignity, excepting a ring of gold upon his head, he hastened with the Archbishop of Tyre to attend the Council, which waited but his presence to commence its sitting.

The pavilion of the Council was an ample tent, having before it the large Banner of the Cross displayed, and another, on which was portrayed a female kneeling, with dishevelled hair and disordered dress, meant to represent the desolate and distressed Church of Jerusalem, and bearing the motto, *Afflictæ sponsæ ne obliviscaris*. Warders, carefully selected, kept every one at a distance from the neighbourhood of this tent, lest the debates, which were sometimes of a loud and stormy character, should reach other ears than those they were designed for.

Here, therefore, the Princes of the Crusade were assembled, awaiting Richard's arrival; and even the brief delay which was thus interposed, was turned to his disadvantage by his enemies; various instances being circulated of his pride, and undue assumption of superiority, of which even the necessity of the present short pause was quoted as an instance. Men strove to fortify each other in their evil opinion of the King of England, and vindicated the offence which each had taken, by putting the most severe construction upon circumstances the most trifling; and all this, perhaps, because they were conscious of an instinctive reverence for the heroic monarch, which it would require more than ordinary efforts to overcome.

They had settled, accordingly, that they should receive him on his entrance with slight notice, and no more respect than was exactly necessary to keep within the bounds of cold ceremonial. But when they beheld that noble form, that princely countenance, somewhat pale from his late illness—the eye which had been called by minstrels the bright star of battle and victory—when his feats, almost surpassing human strength and valour, rushed on their recollection, the Council of Princes simultaneously arose—even the jealous King of France, and the sullen and offended Duke of Austria, arose with one consent, and the assembled princes burst forth with one voice in the acclamation, "God save King Richard of England!—Long life to the valiant Lion's heart!"

With a countenance frank and open as the summer sun when it rises, Richard distributed his thanks around, and congratulated himself on being once more among his royal brethren of the Crusades.

"Some brief words he desired to say," such was his address to the assembly, "though on a subject so unworthy as himself, even at the risk of delaying for a few minutes their consultations for the weal of Christendom, and the advancement of their holy enterprise."

The assembled princes resumed their seats, and there was a profound silence.

"This day," continued the King of England, "is a high festival of the Church; and well becomes it Christian men, at such a tide, to reconcile themselves with their brethren, and confess their faults to each other. Noble princes, and fathers of this holy expedition, Richard is a soldier—his hand is ever readier than his tongue—and his tongue is but too much used to the rough language of his trade. But do not, for Plantagenet's hasty speeches and ill-considered actions, forsake the noble cause of the redemption of Palestine—do not throw away earthly renown and eternal salvation, to be won here if ever they can be won by man, because the act of a soldier may have been hasty, and his speech as hard as the iron which he has worn from childhood. Is Richard in default to any of you, Richard will make compensation both by word and action.—Noble brother of France, have I been so unlucky as to offend you?"

"The Majesty of France has no atonement to seek from that of England," answered Philip with kingly dignity, accepting, at the same time, the offered hand of Richard; "and whatever opinion I may adopt concerning the prosecution of this enterprise, will depend on reasons arising out of the state of my own kingdom, certainly on no jealousy or disgust at my royal and valorous brother."

"Austria," said Richard, walking up to the Archduke, with a mixture of frankness and dignity, while Leopold arose from his seat, as if involuntarily, and with the action of an automaton, whose motions depended upon some external impulse, —"Austria thinks he hath reason to be offended with England; England, that he hath cause to complain of Austria. Let them exchange forgiveness, that the peace of Europe, and the concord of this host, may remain unbroken. We are now joint supporters of a more glorious banner than ever blazed before an earthly prince,—even the Banner of Salvation: let not, therefore, strife be betwixt us, for the symbol of our more worldly dignities; but let Leopold restore the pennon of England, if he has it in his power, and Richard will say, though from no motive save his love for Holy Church, that he repents him of the hasty mood in which he did insult the standard of Austria."

The Archduke stood still, sullen and discontented, with his eyes fixed on the floor, and his countenance lowering with smothered displeasure, which awe, mingled with awkwardness, prevented his giving vent to in words.

The Patriarch of Jerusalem hastened to break the embarrassing silence, and to bear witness for the Archduke of Austria, that he had exculpated himself, by a solemn oath, from all knowledge, direct or indirect, of the aggression done to the Banner of England.

"Then we have done the noble Archduke the greater wrong," said Richard; "and craving his pardon for imputing to him an outrage so cowardly, we extend our hand to him in token of renewed peace and amity.—But how is this? Austria refuses our uncovered hand, as he formerly refused our mailed glove? What! are we neither to be his mate in peace, nor his antagonist in war? Well, let it be so. We will take the slight esteem in which he holds us, as a penance for aught which we may have done against him in heat of blood, and will therefore hold the account between us cleared."

So saying, he turned from the Archduke with an air rather of dignity than scorn, leaving the Austrian apparently as much relieved by the removal of his eye, as is a sullen and truant schoolboy when the glance of his severe pedagogue is withdrawn.

"Noble Earl of Champagne—Princely Marquis of Montserrat—Valiant Grand Master of the Templars—I am here a penitent in the confessional—Do any of you bring a charge, or claim amends from me?"

"I know not on what we could ground any," said the smooth-tongued Conrade, "unless it were that the King of England carries off from his poor brothers of the war all the fame which they might have hoped to gain in the expedition."

"My charge, if I am called to make one," said the Master of the Templars, "is graver and deeper than that of the Marquis of Montserrat. It may be thought ill to beseem a military monk such as I to raise his voice where so many noble princes remain silent; but it concerns our whole host, and not least this noble King of England, that he should hear from some one to his face those charges, which there are enow to bring against him in his absence. We laud and honour the courage and high achievements of the King of England, but we feel aggrieved that he should, on all occasions, seize and maintain a precedence and superiority over us, which it becomes not independent princes to submit to. Much we might yield of our free will to his bravery, his zeal, his wealth, and his power; but he who snatches all, as matter of right, and leaves nothing to grant out of courtesy and favour, degrades us from allies into retainers and vassals, and sullies, in the eyes of our soldiers and subjects, the lustre of our authority, which is no longer independently exercised. Since the royal Richard has asked the truth from us, he must neither be surprised nor angry when he hears one, to whom worldly pomp is prohibited, and secular authority is nothing, saving so far as it advances the prosperity of God's Temple, and the prostration of the lion, which goeth about seeking whom he may devour—when he hears, I say, such a one as I tell him the truth in reply to his question; which truth, even while I speak it, is, I know, confirmed by the heart of every one who hears me, however respect may stifle their voices."

Richard coloured very highly while the Grand Master was making this direct and unvarnished attack upon his conduct, and the murmur of assent which followed it showed plainly, that almost all who were present acquiesced in the justice of the accusation. Incensed, and at the same time mortified, he yet foresaw that to give way to his headlong resentment, would be to give the cold and wary accuser the advantage over him which it was the Templar's principal object to obtain. He, therefore, with a strong effort, remained silent till he had repeated a pater noster, being the course which his confessor had enjoined him to pursue, when anger was likely to obtain dominion over him. The King then spoke with composure, though not without an embittered tone, especially at the outset.

"And is it even so? And are our brethren at such pains to note the infirmities of our natural temper, and the rough precipitance of our zeal, which may sometimes have urged us to issue commands when there was little time to hold council? I could not have thought that offences, casual and unpremeditated like mine, could find such deep root in the hearts of my allies in this most holy cause; that for my sake they should withdraw their hand from the plough when the furrow was near the end; for my sake turn aside from the direct path to Jerusalem, which their swords have opened. I vainly thought that my small services might have outweighed my rash errors—that if it were remembered that I pressed to the van in an assault, it would not be forgotten that I was ever the last in the retreat—that if I elevated my banner upon conquered fields of battle, it was all the advantage that I sought, while others were dividing the spoil. I may have called the conquered city by my name, but it was to others that I yielded the dominion. If I have been headstrong in urging bold counsels, I have not, methinks, spared my own blood or my people's in carrying them into as bold execution—or if I have, in the hurry of march or battle, assumed a command over the soldiers of others, such have been ever treated as my own, when my wealth purchased the provisions and medicines which their own sovereigns could not procure.—But it shames me to remind you of what all but myself seem to have forgotten.—Let us rather look forward to our future measures; and believe me, brethren," he continued, his face kindling with eagerness, "you shall not find the pride, or the wrath, or the ambition of Richard a stumbling-block of offence in the path to which religion and glory summon you, as with the trumpet of an archangel. Oh no, no! never would I survive the thought, that my frailties and infirmities had been the means to sever this goodly fellowship of assembled princes. I would cut off my left hand with my right could my doing so attest my sincerity. I will yield up, voluntarily, all right to command in the host, even mine own liege subjects. They shall be led by such sovereigns as you may nominate, and their King, ever but too apt to exchange the leader's baton for the adventurer's lance, will serve under the banner of Beau-seant among the Templars—ay, or under that of Austria, if Austria will name a brave man to lead his forces. Or, if ye are yourselves a-weary of this war, and feel your armour chafe your tender bodies, leave but with Richard some ten or fifteen thousand of your soldiers to work out the accomplishment of your vow; and when Zion is won," he exclaimed, waving his hand aloft, as if displaying the standard of the Cross over Jerusalem—"when Zion is won, we will write upon her gates, NOT the name of Richard Plantagenet, but of those generous princes who entrusted him with the means of conquest!"

The rough eloquence and determined expression of the military monarch, at once roused the drooping spirits of the Crusaders, reanimated their devotion, and, fixing their attention on the principal object of the expedition, made most of them who were present blush for having been moved by such petty subjects of complaint as had before engrossed them. Eye caught fire from eye, voice lent courage to voice. They resumed, as with one accord, the war-cry with which the sermon of Peter the Hermit was echoed back, and shouted aloud, "Lead us on, gallant Lion's heart—none so worthy to lead where brave men follow. Lead us on—to Jerusalem— to Jerusalem! It is the will of God—it is the will of God! Blessed is he who shall lend an arm to its fulfilment!"

The shout, so suddenly and generally raised, was heard beyond the ring of sentinels who guarded the pavilion of Council, and spread among the soldiers of the host, who, inactive and dispirited by disease and climate, had begun, like their leaders, to droop in resolution; but the reappearance of Richard in renewed vigour, and the well-known shout which echoed from the assembly of the princes, at once rekindled their enthusiasm, and thousands and tens of thousands answered with the same shout of "Zion, Zion!—War, war!—instant battle with the infidels! It is the will of God—it is the will of God!"

The acclamations from without increased in their turn the enthusiasm which prevailed within the pavilion. Those who did not actually catch the flame, were afraid, at least for the time, to seem colder than others. There was no more speech except of a proud advance towards Jerusalem upon the expiry of the truce, and the measures to be taken in the meantime for supplying and recruiting the army. The council broke up, all apparently filled with the same enthusiastic purpose,—which, however, soon faded in the bosom of most, and never had an existence in that of others.

Of the latter class were the Marquis Conrade and the Grand Master of the Templars, who retired together to their quarters ill at ease, and malcontent with the events of the day.

"I ever told it to thee," said the latter, with the cold sardonic expression peculiar to him, "that Richard would burst through the flimsy wiles you spread for him, as would a lion through a spider's web. Thou seest he has but to speak, and his breath agitates these fickle fools as easily as the whirlwind catcheth scattered straws, and sweeps them together, or disperses them at its pleasure."

"When the blast has passed away," said Conrade, "the straws, which it made dance to its pipe, will settle to earth again."

"But know'st thou not besides," said the Templar, "that it seems, if this new purpose of conquest shall be abandoned and pass away, and each mighty prince shall again be left to such guidance as his own scanty brain can supply, Richard may yet probably become King of Jerusalem by compact, and establish those terms of treaty with the Soldan, which thou thyself thought'st him so likely to spurn at?"

"Now, by Mahound and Termagaunt, for Christian oaths are out of fashion," said Conrade, "say'st thou the proud King of England would unite his blood with a heathen Soldan?— My policy threw in that ingredient to make the whole treaty an abomination to him.—As bad for us that he become our master by an agreement, as by victory."

"Thy policy hath ill calculated Richard's digestion," answered the Templar; "I know his mind by a whisper from the Archbishop.—And then thy master-stroke respecting yonder banner, it has passed off with no more respect than two cubits of embroidered silk merited. Marquis Conrade, thy wit begins to halt—I will trust thy fine-spun measures no longer, but will try my own. Know'st thou not the people whom the Saracens call Charegites?"

"Surely," answered the Marquis; "they are desperate and besotted enthusiasts, who devote their lives to the advancement of religion—somewhat like Templars—only they are never known to pause in the race of their calling."

"Jest not," answered the scowling monk; "know, that one of these men has set down, in his bloody vow, the name of the island Emperor yonder, to be hewn down as the chief enemy of the Moslem faith."

M

"A most judicious paynim," said Conrade. "May Mahomet send him his paradise for a reward!"

"He was taken in the camp by one of our squires, and, in private examination, frankly avowed his fixed and determined purpose to me," said the Grand Master.

"Now the heavens pardon them who prevented the purpose of this most judicious Charegite!" answered Conrade.

"He is my prisoner," added the Templar, "and secluded from speech with others, as thou mayst suppose—but prisons have been broken——"

"Chains left unlocked, and captives have escaped," answered the Marquis. "It is an ancient saying,—no sure dungeon but the grave."

"When loose he resumes his quest," continued the military priest; "for it is the nature of this sort of bloodhound never to quit the slot of the prey he has once scented."

"Say no more of it," said the Marquis; "I see thy policy— it is dreadful, but the emergency is imminent."

"I only told thee of it," said the Templar, "that thou mayst keep thyself on thy guard, for the uproar will be dreadful, and there is no knowing on whom the English may vent their rage—Ay, and there is another risk—my page knows the counsels of this Charegite," he continued; "and, moreover, he is a peevish, self-willed fool, whom I would I were rid of, as he thwarts me by presuming to see with his own eyes, not mine. But our holy Order gives me power to put a remedy to such inconvenience. Or stay—the Saracen may find a good dagger in his cell, and I warrant you he uses it as he breaks forth, which will be of a surety so soon as the page enters with his food."

"It will give the affair a colour," said Conrade; "and yet——"

"Yet and but," said the Templar, "are words for fools—wise men neither hesitate nor retract—they resolve and they execute."

CHAPTER XX

When beauty leads the lion in her toils,
Such are her charms, he dare not raise his mane,
Far less expand the terror of his fangs.
So great Alcides made his club a distaff,
And spun to please fair Omphalé.
—ANONYMOUS.

RICHARD, the unsuspicious object of the dark treachery detailed in the closing part of the last chapter, having effected, for the present at least, the triumphant union of the Crusading princes, in a resolution to prosecute the war with vigour, had it next at heart to establish tranquillity in his own family; and, now that he could judge more temperately, to inquire distinctly into the circumstances leading to the loss of his banner, and the nature and the extent of the connection betwixt his kins-woman Edith, and the banished adventurer from Scotland.

Accordingly, the Queen and her household were startled with a visit from Sir Thomas de Vaux, requesting the present attend-ance of the Lady Calista of Montfaucon, the Queen's principal bower-woman, upon King Richard.

"What am I to say, madam?" said the trembling attendant to the Queen. "He will slay us all."

"Nay, fear not, madam," said De Vaux. "His Majesty hath spared the life of the Scottish knight, who was the chief offender, and bestowed him upon the Moorish physician—he will not be severe upon a lady, though faulty."

"Devise some cunning tale, wench," said Berengaria. "My husband hath too little time to make inquiry into the truth."

"Tell the tale as it really happened," said Edith, "lest I tell it for thee."

"With humble permission of her Majesty," said De Vaux, "I would say Lady Edith adviseth well; for although King Richard is pleased to believe what it pleases your Grace to tell him, yet I doubt his having the same deference for the Lady Calista, and in this especial matter."

"The Lord of Gilsland is right," said the Lady Calista, much agitated at the thoughts of the investigation which was to take place: "and, besides, if I had presence of mind enough to forge a plausible story, beshrew me if I think I should have the courage to tell it."

In this candid humour, the Lady Calista was conducted by De Vaux to the King, and made, as she had proposed, a full confession of the decoy by which the unfortunate Knight of the Leopard had been induced to desert his post; exculpating the Lady Edith, who, she was aware, would not fail to exculpate herself, and laying the full burden on the Queen, her mistress, whose share of the frolic, she well knew, would appear the most venial in the eyes of Cœur de Lion. In truth, Richard was a fond—almost an uxorious husband. The first burst of his wrath had long since passed away, and he was not disposed severely to censure what could not now be amended. The wily Lady Calista, accustomed from her earliest childhood to fathom the intrigues of a court and watch the indications of a sove-reign's will, hastened back to the Queen with the speed of a lapwing, charged with the King's commands that she should expect a speedy visit from him; to which the bower-lady added a commentary founded on her own observation, tending to show that Richard meant just to preserve so much severity as might bring his royal consort to repent of her frolic, and then to extend to her and all concerned his gracious pardon.

"Sits the wind in that corner, wench?" said the Queen, much relieved by this intelligence; "believe me that, great commander as he is, Richard will find it hard to circumvent us in this matter; and that, as the Pyrenean shepherds are wont to say in my native Navarre, many a one comes for wool and goes back shorn."

Having possessed herself of all the information which Calista could communicate, the royal Berengaria arrayed herself in her most becoming dress, and awaited with confidence the arrival of the heroic Richard.

He arrived, and found himself in the situation of a prince entering an offending province, in the confidence that his business will only be to inflict rebuke, and receive submission, when he unexpectedly finds it in a state of complete defiance and insurrection. Berengaria well knew the power of her charms, and the extent of Richard's affection, and felt assured that she could make her own terms good, now that the first tremendous explosion of his anger had expended itself without mischief. Far from listening to the King's intended rebuke, as what the levity of her conduct had justly deserved, she extenuated, nay, defended, as a harmless frolic, that which she was accused of. She denied, indeed, with many a pretty form of negation that she had directed Nectabanus absolutely to entice the knight farther than the brink of the Mount on which he kept watch —and indeed this was so far true, that she had not designed Sir Kenneth to be introduced into her tent,—and then, eloquent in urging her own defence, the Queen was far more so in pressing upon Richard the charge of unkindness, in refusing her so poor a boon as the life of an unfortunate knight, who, by her thoughtless prank, had been brought within the danger of martial law. She wept and sobbed while she enlarged on her husband's obduracy on this score, as a rigour which had threatened to make her unhappy for life, whenever she should reflect that she had given, unthinkingly, the remote cause for such a tragedy. The vision of the slaughtered victim would have haunted her dreams—nay, for aught she knew, since such things often happened, his actual spectre might have stood by her waking couch. To all this misery of the mind was she exposed by the severity of one, who, while he pretended to dote upon her slightest glance, would not forego one act of poor revenge, though the issue was to render her miserable.

All this flow of female eloquence was accompanied with the usual arguments of tears and sighs, and uttered with such tone and action, as seemed to show that the Queen's resentment

arose neither from pride nor sullenness, but from feelings hurt
at finding her consequence with her husband less than she had
expected to possess.

The good King Richard was considerably embarrassed. He
tried in vain to reason with one, whose very jealousy of his
affection rendered her incapable of listening to argument, nor
could he bring himself to use the restraint of lawful authority
to a creature so beautiful in the midst of her unreasonable
displeasure. He was, therefore, reduced to the defensive, endeavoured gently to chide her suspicions, and soothe her displeasure, and recalled to her mind that she need not look
back upon the past with recollections either of remorse or
supernatural fear, since Sir Kenneth was alive and well, and
had been bestowed by him upon the great Arabian physician,
who, doubtless, of all men, knew best how to keep him living.
But this seemed the unkindest cut of all, and the Queen's
sorrow was renewed at the idea of a Saracen—a mediciner—
obtaining a boon, for which, with bare head, and on bended
knee, she had petitioned her husband in vain. At this new
charge, Richard's patience began rather to give way, and he
said, in a serious tone of voice, " Berengaria, the physician
saved my life. If it is of value in your eyes, you will not
grudge him a higher recompense than the only one I could
prevail on him to accept."

The Queen was satisfied she had urged her coquettish displeasure to the verge of safety.

" My Richard," she said, " why brought you not that sage
to me, that England's Queen might show how she esteemed
him, who could save from extinction the lamp of chivalry, the
glory of England, and the light of poor Berengaria's life and
hope ? "

In a word, the matrimonial dispute was ended; but, that
some penalty might be paid to justice, both King and Queen
accorded in laying the whole blame on the agent Nectabanus,
who (the Queen being by this time well weary of the poor
dwarf's humour) was, with his royal consort Guenevra, sentenced to be banished from the court; and the unlucky dwarf
only escaped a supplementary whipping, from the Queen's
assurances that he had already sustained personal chastisement.
It was decreed farther, that as an envoy was shortly to be
despatched to Saladin, acquainting him with the resolution of
the Council to resume hostilities so soon as the truce was ended,
and as Richard proposed to send a valuable present to the
Soldan, in acknowledgment of the high benefit he had derived
from the services of El Hakim, the two unhappy creatures
should be added to it as curiosities, which, from their extremely grotesque appearance, and the shattered state of their

intellect, were gifts that might well pass between sovereign and sovereign.

Richard had that day yet another female encounter to sustain; but he advanced to it with comparative indifference, for Edith, though beautiful, and highly esteemed by her royal relative—nay, although she had from his unjust suspicions actually sustained the injury of which Berengaria only affected to complain, still was neither Richard's wife nor mistress, and he feared her reproaches less, although founded in reason, than those of the Queen, though unjust and fantastical. Having requested to speak with her apart, he was ushered into her apartment, adjoining that of the Queen, whose two female Coptish slaves remained on their knees in the most remote corner during the interview. A thin black veil extended its ample folds over the tall and graceful form of the high-born maiden, and she wore not upon her person any female ornament of what kind soever. She arose and made a low reverence when Richard entered, resumed her seat at his command, and, when he sat down beside her, waited, without uttering a syllable, until he should communicate his pleasure.

Richard, whose custom it was to be familiar with Edith, as their relationship authorised, felt this reception chilling, and opened the conversation with some embarrassment.

"Our fair cousin," he at length said, "is angry with us and we own that strong circumstances have induced us, without cause, to suspect her of conduct alien to what we have ever known in her course of life. But while we walk in this misty valley of humanity, men will mistake shadows for substances Can my fair cousin not forgive her somewhat vehement kinsman, Richard?"

"Who can refuse forgiveness to *Richard*," answered Edith "provided Richard can obtain pardon of the *King?*"

"Come, my kinswoman," replied Cœur de Lion, "this is al too solemn. By Our Lady, such a melancholy countenance and this ample sable veil, might make men think thou wert new-made widow, or had lost a betrothed lover, at least. Chee up—thou hast heard doubtless that there is no real cause fo woe—why then keep up the form of mourning?"

"For the departed honour of Plantagenet—for the glory whic hath left my father's house."

Richard frowned. "Departed honour! glory which hath le our house!" he repeated angrily; "but my cousin Edith i privileged. I have judged her too hastily, she has therefore right to deem of me too harshly. But tell me at least in wh I have faulted."

"Plantagenet," said Edith, "should have either pardoned a offence, or punished it. It misbecomes him to assign free me

Christians, and brave knights, to the fetters of the infidels. It becomes him not to compromise and barter, or to grant life under the forfeiture of liberty. To have doomed the unfortunate to death might have been severity, but had a show of justice; to condemn him to slavery and exile, was barefaced tyranny."

"I see, my fair cousin," said Richard, "you are of those pretty ones who think an absent lover as bad as none, or as a dead one. Be patient; half a score of light horsemen may yet follow and redeem the error, if thy gallant have in keeping any secret which might render his death more convenient than his banishment."

"Peace with thy scurril jests!" answered Edith, colouring deeply—"Think rather, that for the indulgence of thy mood thou hast lopped from this great enterprise one goodly limb, deprived the Cross of one of its most brave supporters, and placed a servant of the true God in the hands of the heathen; hast given, too, to minds as suspicious as thou hast shown thine own in this matter, some right to say that Richard Cœur de Lion banished the bravest soldier in his camp, lest his name in battle might match his own."

"I—I!" exclaimed Richard, now indeed greatly moved—"am I one to be jealous of renown?—I would he were here to profess such equality! I would wave my rank and my crown, and meet him, man-like, in the lists, that it might appear whether Richard Plantagenet had room to fear or to envy the prowess of mortal man. Come, Edith, thou think'st not as thou say'st. Let not anger or grief for the absence of thy lover make thee unjust to thy kinsman, who, notwithstanding all thy tetchiness, values thy good report as high as that of any one living."

"The absence of my lover?" said the Lady Edith. "But yes—he may be well termed my lover, who hath paid so dear for the title. Unworthy as I might be of such homage, I was to him like a light, leading him forward in the noble path of chivalry; but that I forgot my rank, or that he presumed beyond his, is false, were a king to speak it."

"My fair cousin," said Richard, "do not put words in my mouth which I have not spoken. I said not you had graced this man beyond the favour which a good knight may earn, even from a princess, whatever be his native condition. But, by Our Lady, I know something of this love-gear—it begins with mute respect and distant reverence; but, when opportunities occur, familiarity increases, and so—But it skills not talking with one who thinks herself wiser than all the world."

"My kinsman's counsels I willingly listen to, when they are such," said Edith, "as convey no insult to my rank and character."

"Kings, my fair cousin, do not counsel, but rather command," said Richard.

"Soldans do indeed command," said Edith, "but it is because they have slaves to govern."

"Come, you might learn to lay aside this scorn of Soldanrie, when you hold so high of a Scot," said the King. "I hold Saladin to be truer to his word than this William of Scotland, who must needs be called a Lion, forsooth—he hath foully faulted towards me, in failing to send the auxiliary aid he promised. Let me tell thee, Edith, thou may'st live to prefer a true Turk to a false Scot."

"No—never!" answered Edith—"not should Richard himself embrace the false religion, which he crossed the seas to expel from Palestine."

"Thou wilt have the last word," said Richard, "and thou shalt have it. Even think of me what thou wilt, pretty Edith. I shall not forget that we are near and dear cousins."

So saying, he took his leave in fair fashion, but very little satisfied with the result of his visit.

It was the fourth day after Sir Kenneth had been dismissed from the camp; and King Richard sat in his pavilion, enjoying an evening breeze from the west, which, with unusual coolness on her wings, seemed breathed from merry England for the refreshment of her adventurous monarch, as he was gradually recovering the full strength which was necessary to carry on his gigantic projects. There was no one with him, De Vaux having been sent to Ascalon to bring up reinforcements and supplies of military munition, and most of his other attendants being occupied in different departments, all preparing for the re-opening of hostilities, and for a grand preparatory review of the army of the Crusaders, which was to take place the next day. The King sat, listening to the busy hum among the soldiery, the clatter from the forges, where horse-shoes were preparing, and from the tents of the armourers, who were repairing harness—the voice of the soldiers, too, as they passed and repassed, was loud and cheerful, carrying with its very tone an assurance of high and excited courage, and an omen of approaching victory. While Richard's ear drank in these sounds with delight, and while he yielded himself to the visions of conquest and of glory which they suggested, an equerry told him that a messenger from Saladin waited without.

"Admit him instantly," said the King, "and with due honour, Josceline."

The English knight accordingly introduced a person, apparently of no higher rank than a Nubian slave, whose appearance was nevertheless highly interesting. He was of superb stature and nobly formed, and his commanding features, although almost jet-black, showed nothing of negro descent. He wore over his coal-black locks a milk-white turban, and over his shoulders a short mantle of the same colour, open in front and at the sleeves, under which appeared a doublet of dressed leopard's skin reaching within a handbreadth of the knee. The rest of his muscular limbs, both legs and arms, were bare, excepting that he had sandals on his feet, and wore a collar and bracelets of silver. A straight broadsword, with a handle of boxwood, and a sheath covered with snake-skin, was suspended from his waist. In his right hand he held a short javelin, with a broad, bright, steel head, of a span in length, and in his left he led, by a leash of twisted silk and gold, a large and noble staghound.

The messenger prostrated himself, at the same time partially uncovering his shoulders, in sign of humiliation, and having touched the earth with his forehead, arose so far as to rest on one knee, while he delivered to the King a silken napkin, enclosing another of cloth of gold, within which was a letter from Saladin in the original Arabic, with a translation into Norman-English, which may be modernised thus:—

"Saladin, King of kings, to Melech Ric, the Lion of England. Whereas, we are informed by thy last message, that thou hast chosen war rather than peace, and our enmity rather than our friendship, we account thee as one blinded in this matter, and trust shortly to convince thee of thine error, by the help of our invincible forces of the thousand tribes, when Mohammed, the Prophet of God, and Allah, the God of the Prophet, shall judge the controversy betwixt us. In what remains, we make noble account of thee, and of the gifts which thou hast sent us, and of the two dwarfs, singular in their deformity as Ysop, and mirthful as the lute of Isaack. And in requital of these tokens from the treasure-house of thy bounty, behold we have sent thee a Nubian slave, named Zohauk, of whom judge not by his complexion, according to the foolish ones of the earth, in respect the dark-rinded fruit hath the most exquisite flavour. Know that he is strong to execute the will of his master, as Rustan of Zablestan; also he is wise to give counsel when thou shalt learn to hold communication with him, for the Lord of Speech hath been stricken with silence betwixt the ivory walls of his palace. We commend him to thy care, hoping the hour may not be distant when he may render thee good service. And herewith we bid thee farewell; trusting that our most holy Prophet may yet call thee to a sight of the truth, failing which illumination, our desire is, for the speedy restoration of thy royal health, that Allah may judge between thee and us in a plain field of battle."

And the missive was sanctioned by the signature and seal of the Soldan.

Richard surveyed the Nubian in silence as he stood before him, his looks bent upon the ground, his arms folded on his bosom, with the appearance of a black marble statue of the most exquisite workmanship, waiting life from the touch of a Prometheus. The King of England, who, as it was emphatically said of his successor Henry the Eighth, loved to look upon A MAN, was well pleased with the thewes, sinews, and symmetry of him whom he now surveyed, and questioned him in the Lingua Franca, "Art thou a pagan?"

The slave shook his head, and raising his finger to his brow, crossed himself in token of his Christianity, then resumed his posture of motionless humility.

"A Nubian Christian, doubtless," said Richard, "and mutilated of the organ of speech by these heathen dogs?"

The mute again slowly shook his head in token of negative, pointed with his forefinger to Heaven, and then laid it upon his own lips.

"I understand thee," said Richard; "thou dost suffer under the infliction of God, not by the cruelty of man. Canst thou clean an armour and belt, and buckle it in time of need?"

The mute nodded, and stepping towards the coat of mail, which hung with the shield and helmet of the chivalrous monarch, upon the pillar of the tent, he handled it with such nicety of address, as sufficiently to show that he fully understood the business of the armour-bearer.

"Thou art an apt, and wilt doubtless be a useful knave—thou shalt wait in my chamber, and on my person," said the King, "to show how much I value the gift of the royal Soldan. If thou hast no tongue, it follows thou canst carry no tales, neither provoke me to be sudden by any unfit reply."

The Nubian again prostrated himself till his brow touched the earth, then stood erect, at some paces distant, as waiting for his new master's commands.

"Nay, thou shalt commence thy office presently," said Richard, "for I see a speck of rust darkening on that shield; and when I shake it in the face of Saladin, it should be bright and unsullied as the Soldan's honour and mine own."

A horn was winded without, and presently Sir Henry Neville entered with a packet of despatches.—"From England, my lord," he said, as he delivered it.

"From England—our own England!" repeated Richard, in a tone of melancholy enthusiasm—"Alas! they little think how hard their Sovereign has been beset by sickness and sorrow—faint friends and forward enemies." Then opening the despatches, he said hastily, "Ha! this comes from no peaceful land—they too have their feuds.—Neville, begone—I must peruse these tidings alone, and at leisure."

Neville withdrew accordingly, and Richard was soon absorbed in the melancholy details which had been conveyed to him from England, concerning the factions that were tearing to pieces his native dominions—the disunion of his brothers, John and Geoffrey, and the quarrels of both with the High Justiciary Longchamp, Bishop of Ely,—the oppressions practised by the nobles upon the peasantry, and rebellion of the latter against their masters, which had produced everywhere scenes of discord, and in some instances the effusion of blood. Details of incidents mortifying to his pride, and derogatory from his authority, were intermingled with the earnest advice of his wisest and most attached counsellors, that he should presently return to England, as his presence offered the only hope of saving the kingdom from all the horrors of civil discord, of which France and Scotland were likely to avail themselves. Filled with the most painful anxiety, Richard read, and again read, the ill-omened letters, compared the intelligence which some of them contained with the same facts as differently stated in others, and soon became totally insensible to whatever was passing around him, although seated, for the sake of coolness, close to the entrance of his tent, and having the curtains withdrawn, so that he could see and be seen by the guards and others who were stationed without.

Deeper in the shadow of the pavilion, and busied with the task his new master had imposed, sat the Nubian slave, with his back rather turned towards the King. He had finished adjusting and cleaning the hauberk and brigandine, and was now busily employed on a broad pavasse, or buckler, of unusual size, and covered with steel-plating, which Richard often used in reconnoitring, or actually storming fortified places, as a more effectual protection against missile weapons, than the narrow triangular shield used on horseback. This pavesse bore neither the royal lions of England, nor any other device, to attract the observation of the defenders of the walls against which it was advanced; the care, therefore, of the armourer was addressed to causing its surface to shine as bright as crystal, in which he seemed to be peculiarly successful. Beyond the Nubian, and scarce visible from without, lay the large dog, which might be termed his brother slave, and which, as if he felt awed by being transferred to a royal owner, was couched close to the side of the mute, with head and ears on the ground, and his limbs and tail drawn close around and under him.

While the Monarch and his new attendant were thus occupied, another actor crept upon the scene, and mingled among the group of English yeomen, about a score of whom, respecting the unusually pensive posture and close occupation of their sovereign, were, contrary to their wont, keeping a silent guard in front of his tent. It was not, however, more vigilant than usual. Some were playing at games of hazard with small pebbles, others spoke together in whispers of the approaching day of battle, and several lay asleep, their bulky limbs folded in their green mantles.

Amid these careless warders glided the puny form of a little old Turk, poorly dressed like a marabout or santon of the desert, a sort of enthusiast, who sometimes ventured into the camp of the Crusaders, though treated always with contumely, and often with violence. Indeed, the luxury and profligate indulgence of the Christian leaders had occasioned a motley concourse in their tents, of musicians, courtesans, Jewish merchants, Copts, Turks, and all the varied refuse of the Eastern nations; so that the caftan and turban, though to drive both from the Holy Land was the professed object of the expedition, were nevertheless neither an uncommon nor an alarming sight in the camp of the Crusaders. When, however, the little insignificant figure we have described approached so nigh as to receive some interruption from the warders, he dashed his dusky green turban from his head, showed that his beard and eyebrows were shaved like those of a professed buffoon, and that the expression of his fantastic and writhen features, as well as of his little black eyes, which glittered like jet, was that of a crazed imagination.

"Dance, marabout," cried the soldiers, acquainted with the manners of these wandering enthusiasts—"dance, or we will scourge thee with our bowstrings, till thou spin as never top did under schoolboy's lash."—Thus shouted the reckless warders, as much delighted at having a subject to tease, as a child when he catches a butterfly, or a schoolboy upon discovering a bird's nest.

The marabout, as if happy to do their behests, bounded from the earth, and spun his giddy round before them with singular agility, which, when contrasted with his slight and wasted figure, and diminutive appearance, made him resemble a withered leaf twirled round and round at the pleasure of the winter's breeze. His single lock of hair streamed upwards from his bald and shaven head, as if some genie upheld him by it; and indeed it seemed as if supernatural art were necessary to the execution of the wild whirling dance, in which scarce the tiptoe of the performer was seen to touch the ground. Amid the vagaries of his performance, he flew here and there, from one spot to another, still approaching, however, though almost imperceptibly, to the entrance of the royal tent; so that, when at length he sunk exhausted on the earth, after two or three bounds still higher than those which he had yet executed, he was not above thirty yards from the King's person.

"Give him water," said one yeoman; "they always crave a drink after their merry-go-round."

"Aha, water, say'st thou, Long Allen?"—exclaimed another archer, with a most scornful emphasis on the despised element; "how wouldst like such beverage thyself, after such a morrice dancing?"

"The devil a water-drop he gets here," said a third. "We will teach the light-footed old infidel to be a good Christian, and drink wine of Cyprus."

"Ay, ay," said a fourth; "and in case he be restive, fetch thou Dick Hunter's horn, that he drenches his mare withal."

A circle was instantly formed around the prostrate and exhausted dervise, and while one tall yeoman raised his feeble form from the ground, another presented to him a huge flagon of wine. Incapable of speech, the old man shook his head, and waved away from him with his hand the liquor forbidden by the Prophet; but his tormentors were not thus to be appeased.

"The horn, the horn!" exclaimed one. "Little difference between a Turk and a Turkish horse, and we will use him conforming."

"By Saint George you will choke him!" said Long Allen; "and, besides, it is a sin to throw away upon a heathen dog as much wine as would serve a good Christian for a treble nightcap."

"Thou know'st not the nature of these Turks and pagans, Long Allen," replied Henry Woodstall; "I tell thee, man, that this flagon of Cyprus will set his brains a-spinning, just in the opposite direction that they went whirling in the dancing, and so bring him, as it were, to himself again.—Choke? he will no more choke on it than Ben's black bitch on the pound of butter."

"And for grudging it," said Tomalin Blacklees, "why shouldst thou grudge the poor paynim devil a drop of drink on earth, since thou know'st he is not to have a drop to cool the tip of his tongue through a long eternity?"

"That were hard laws, look ye," said Long Allen, "only for being a Turk, as his father was before him. Had he been Christian turned heathen, I grant you the hottest corner had been good winter quarters for him."

"Hold thy peace, Long Allen," said Henry Woodstall; "I tell thee that tongue of thine is not the shortest limb about thee, and I prophesy that it will bring thee into disgrace with Father Francis, as once about the black-eyed Syrian wench.— But here comes the horn. Be active a bit, man, wilt thou, and just force open his teeth with the haft of thy dudgeon-dagger."

"Hold, hold—he is conformable," said Tomalin; "see, see he signs for the goblet—give him room, boys. *Oop sey es,* quoth the Dutchman—down it goes like lamb's-wool! Nay, they are true topers when once they begin—your Turk never coughs in his cup, or stints in his liquoring."

In fact, the dervise, or whatever he was, drank, or at least seemed to drink, the large flagon to the very bottom at a single pull; and when he took it from his lips, after the whole contents were exhausted, only uttered, with a deep sigh, the words Allah kerim, or God is merciful. There was a laugh among the yeomen who witnessed this pottle-deep potation, so obstreperous, as to rouse and disturb the King, who, raising his finger, said angrily, "How, knaves, no respect, no observance?"

All were at once hushed into silence, well acquainted with the temper of Richard, which at some times admitted of much military familiarity, and at others exacted the most precise respect, although the latter humour was of much more rare occurrence. Hastening to a more reverent distance from the royal person, they attempted to drag along with them the marabout, who, exhausted apparently by previous fatigue, or over-powered by the potent draught he had just swallowed, resisted being moved from the spot, both with struggles and groans.

"Leave him still, ye fools," whispered Long Allen to his mates; "by Saint Christopher, you will make our Dickon go beside himself, and we shall have his dagger presently fly at our costards. Leave him alone, in less than a minute he will sleep like a dormouse."

At the same moment the Monarch darted another impatient glance to the spot, and all retreated in haste, leaving the dervise on the ground, unable, as it seemed, to stir a single limb or joint of his body. In a moment afterward all was as still and quiet as it had been before the intrusion.

CHAPTER XXI

——and wither'd Murder,
Alarum'd by his sentinel, the wolf,
Whose howl's his watch, thus with his stealthy pace,
With Tarquin's ravishing strides, towards his design
Moves like a ghost.
— MACBETH.

For the space of a quarter of an hour, or longer, after the incident related, all remained perfectly quiet in the front of the royal habitation. The King read, and mused in the entrance of his pavilion—behind, and with his back turned to the same

entrance, the Nubian slave still burnished the ample pavesse—
in front of all, at an hundred paces distant, the yeomen of the
guard stood, sat, or lay extended on the grass, attentive to their
own sports, but pursuing them in silence, while on the esplanade
betwixt them and the front of the tent, lay, scarcely to be
distinguished from a bundle of rags, the senseless form of the
marabout.

But the Nubian had the advantage of a mirror, from the
brilliant reflection which the surface of the highly polished
shield now afforded, by means of which he beheld, to his alarm
and surprise, that the marabout raised his head gently from
the ground, so as to survey all around him, moving with a
well-adjusted precaution, which seemed entirely inconsistent
with a state of ebriety. He couched his head instantly, as if
satisfied he was unobserved, and began, with the slightest
possible appearance of voluntary effort, to drag himself, as if
by chance, ever nearer and nearer to the King, but stopping
and remaining fixed at intervals, like the spider, which, moving
towards her object, collapses into apparent lifelessness, when
she thinks she is the subject of observation. This species of
movement appeared suspicious to the Ethiopian, who, on his
part, prepared himself, as quietly as possible, to interfere, the
instant that interference should seem to be necessary.

The marabout meanwhile glided on gradually and imperceptibly, serpent-like, or rather snail-like, till he was about ten
yards' distance from Richard's person, when, starting on his
feet, he sprung forward with the bound of a tiger, stood at the
King's back in less than an instant, and brandished aloft the
cangiar, or poniard, which he had hidden in his sleeve. Not
the presence of his whole army could have saved their heroic
Monarch—but the motions of the Nubian had been as well
calculated as those of the enthusiast, and ere the latter could
strike, the former caught his uplifted arm. Turning his fanatical wrath upon what thus unexpectedly interposed betwixt
him and his object, the Charegite, for such was the seeming
marabout, dealt the Nubian a blow with the dagger, which,
however, only grazed his arm, while the far superior strength
of the Ethiopian easily dashed him to the ground. Aware of
what had passed, Richard had now arisen, and with little more
of surprise, anger, or interest of any kind in his countenance,
than an ordinary man would show in brushing off and crushing
an intrusive wasp, caught up the stool on which he had been
sitting, and exclaiming only, "Ha, dog!" dashed almost to
pieces the skull of the assassin who uttered twice, once in a
loud, and once in a broken tone, the words "Allah ackbar!"—
God is victorious—and expired at the King's feet.

"Ye are careful warders," said Richard to his archers, in a

tone of scornful reproach, as, aroused by the bustle of what had passed, in terror and tumult they now rushed into his tent;—"watchful sentinels ye are, to leave me to do such hangman's work with my own hand.—Be silent all of you, and cease your senseless clamour! saw ye never a dead Turk before?—Here—cast that carrion out of the camp, strike the head from the trunk, and stick it on a lance, taking care to turn the face to Mecca that he may the easier tell the foul impostor, on whose inspiration he came hither, how he has sped on his errand.—For thee, my swart and silent friend," he added, turning to the Ethiopian—"But how's this?—thou art wounded—and with a poisoned weapon, I warrant me, for by force of stab so weak an animal as that could scarce hope to do more than rase the lion's hide.—Suck the poison from his wound, one of you—the venom is harmless on the lips, though fatal when it mingles with the blood."

The yeomen looked on each other confusedly and with hesitation, the apprehension of so strange a danger prevailing with those who feared no other.

"How now, sirrahs," continued the King, "are you dainty-lipped, or do you fear death that you dally thus?"

"Not the death of a man," said Lord Allen, to whom the King looked as he spoke, "but methinks I would not die like a poisoned rat for the sake of a black chattel there, that is bought and sold in a market like a Martlemas ox."

"His Grace speaks to men of sucking poison," muttered another yeoman, "as if he said, Go to, swallow a gooseberry!"

"Nay," said Richard, "I never bade man do that which I would not do myself."

And, without farther ceremony, and in spite of the general expostulations of those around, and the respectful opposition of the Nubian himself, the King of England applied his lips to the wound of the black slave, treating with ridicule all remonstrances, and overpowering all resistance. He had no sooner intermitted his singular occupation, than the Nubian started from him, and, casting a scarf over his arm, intimated by gestures, as firm in purpose as they were respectful in manner, his determination not to permit the Monarch to renew so degrading an employment. Long Allen also interposed, saying, that if it were necessary to prevent the King engaging again in a treatment of this kind, his own lips, tongue, and teeth, were at the service of the negro (as he called the Ethiopian,) and that he would eat him up bodily, rather than King Richard's mouth should again approach him.

Neville, who entered with other officers, added his remonstrances.

"Nay, nay, make not a needless halloo about a hart that

the hounds have lost, or a danger when it is over," said the King—"the wound will be a trifle, for the blood is scarce drawn—an angry cat had dealt a deeper scratch—and for me, I have but to take a drachm of orvietan by way of precaution, though it is needless."

Thus spoke Richard, a little ashamed, perhaps, of his own condescension, though sanctioned both by humanity and gratitude. But when Neville continued to make remonstrances on the peril to his royal person, the King imposed silence on him."

"Peace, I prithee—make no more of it—I did it but to show these ignorant prejudiced knaves how they might help each other when these cowardly caitiffs come against us with sarbacanes and poisoned shafts.—But," he added, "take thee this Nubian to thy quarters, Neville—I have changed my mind touching him—let him be well cared for—But, hark in thine ear—see that he escapes thee not—there is more in him than seems. Let him have all liberty, so that he leave not the camp. — And you, ye beef-devouring, wine-swilling English mastiffs, get ye to your guard again, and be sure you keep it more warily. Think not you are now in your own land of fair-play, where men speak before they strike, and shake hands ere they cut throats. Danger in our land walks openly, and with his blade drawn, and defies the foe whom he means to assault; but here, he challenges you with a silk glove instead of a steel-gauntlet, cuts your throat with the feather of a turtle-dove, stabs you with the tongue of a priest's brooch, or throttles you with the lace of my lady's bodice. Go to—keep your eyes open and your mouths shut—drink less and look sharper about you; or I will place your huge stomachs on such short allowance, as would pinch that of a patient Scotchman."

The yeomen, abashed and mortified, withdrew to their post, and Neville was beginning to remonstrate with his master upon the risk of passing over thus slightly their negligence upon their duty, and the propriety of an example in a case so peculiarly aggravated as the permitting one so suspicious as the marabout to approach within dagger's length of his person, when Richard interrupted him with "Speak not of it, Neville —wouldst thou have me avenge a petty risk to myself more severely than the loss of England's banner? It has been stolen—stolen by a thief, or delivered up by a traitor, and no blood has been shed for it.—My sable friend, thou art an expounder of mysteries, saith the illustrious Soldan — now would I give thee thine own weight in gold, if, by raising one still blacker than thyself, or by what other means thou wilt, thou couldst show me the thief who did mine honour that wrong. What say'st thou? ha!"

The youth seemed desirous to speak, but uttered only that

N

imperfect sound proper to his melancholy condition, then folded his arms, looked on the King with an eye of intelligence, and nodded in answer to his question.

"How!" said Richard, with joyful impatience. "Wilt thou undertake to make discovery in this matter?"

The Nubian slave repeated the same motion.

"But how shall we understand each other?" said the King. —"Canst thou write, good fellow?"

The slave again nodded in assent.

"Give him writing-tools," said the King. "They were readier in my father's tent than mine—but they be somewhere about, if this scorching climate hath not dried up the ink—Why, this fellow is a jewel — a black diamond, Neville."

"So please you, my liege," said Neville, "if I might speak my poor mind, it were ill dealing in this ware. This man must be a wizard, and wizards deal with the Enemy, who hath most interest to sow tares among the wheat, and bring dissension into our councils, and——"

"Peace, Neville," said Richard. "Hollo to your northern hound when he is close on the haunch of the deer, and hope to recall him, but seek not to stop Plantagenet, when he hath hope to retrieve his honour."

The slave, who during this discussion had been writing, in which art he seemed skilful, now arose, and pressing what he had written to his brow, prostrated himself as usual, ere he delivered it into the King's hands. The scroll was in French, although their intercourse had hitherto been conducted by Richard in the Lingua Franca.

"To Richard, the conquering and invincible King of England, this from the humblest of his slaves. Mysteries are the sealed caskets of Heaven, but wisdom may devise means to open the lock. Were your slaves stationed where the leaders of the Christian host were made to pass before him in order, doubt nothing, that if he who did the injury whereof my King complains shall be among the number, he may be made manifest in his iniquity, though it be hidden under seven veils."

"Now, by Saint George!" said King Richard, "thou hast spoken most opportunely.—Neville, thou know'st, that when we muster our troops to-morrow, the princes have agreed, that to expiate the affront offered to England in the theft of her Banner, the leaders should pass our new standard as it floats on Saint George's Mount, and salute it with formal regard. Believe me, the secret traitor will not dare to absent himself from an expurgation so solemn, lest his very absence should be matter of suspicion. There will we place our sable man o counsel, and, if his art can detect the villain, leave me to deal with him."

"My liege," said Neville, with the frankness of an English baron, "beware what work you begin. Here is the concord of our holy league unexpectedly renewed—will you, upon such suspicion as a negro slave can instil, tear open wounds so lately closed—or will you use the solemn procession, adopted for the reparation of your honour, and establishment of unanimity amongst the discording princes, as the means of again finding out new cause of offence, or reviving ancient quarrels? It were scarce too strong to say, this were a breach of the declaration your Grace made to the assembled Council of the Crusade."

"Neville," said the King, sternly interrupting him, "thy zeal makes thee presumptuous and unmannerly. Never did I promise to abstain from taking whatever means were most promising, to discover the infamous author of the attack on my honour. Ere I had done so, I would have renounced my kingdom—my life. All my declarations were under this necessary and absolute qualification ;—only, if Austria had stepped forth and owned the injury like a man, I proffered, for the sake of Christendom, to have forgiven *him*."

"But," continued the baron anxiously, "what hope that this juggling slave of Saladin will not palter with your Grace ?"

"Peace, Neville," said the King; "thou think'st thyself mighty wise, and art but a fool. Mind thou my charge touching this fellow—there is more in him than thy Westmoreland wit can fathom.—And thou, swart and silent, prepare to perform the feat thou hast promised, and, by the word of a King, thou shalt choose thine own recompense.—Lo, he writes again."

The mute accordingly wrote and delivered to the King, with the same form as before, another slip of paper, containing these words.—"The will of the King is the law to his slave—nor doth it become him to ask guerdon for discharge of his devoir."

"*Guerdon* and *devoir !*" said the King, interrupting himself as he read, and speaking to Neville in the English tongue with some emphasis on the words,—"These Eastern people will profit by the Crusaders—they are acquiring the language of chivalry !—And see, Neville, how discomposed that fellow looks —were it not for his colour, he would blush. I should not think it strange if he understood what I say—they are perilous linguists."

"The poor slave cannot endure your Grace's eye," said Neville ; "it is nothing more."

"Well, but," continued the King, striking the paper with his finger, as he proceeded, "this bold scroll proceeds to say, that our trusty mute is charged with a message from Saladin to the Lady Edith Plantagenet, and craves means and opportunity to deliver it. What think'st thou of a request so modest —ha! Neville?"

"I cannot say," said Neville, "how such freedom may relish with your Grace; but the lease of the messenger's neck would be a short one, who should carry such a request to the Soldan on the part of your Majesty."

"Nay, I thank Heaven that I covet none of his sunburnt beauties," said Richard; "and for punishing this fellow for discharging his master's errand, and that when he has just saved my life—methinks it were something too summary. I'll tell thee, Neville, a secret—for, although our sable and mute minister be present, he cannot, thou know'st, tell it over again, even if he should chance to understand us—I tell thee, that for this fortnight past, I have been under a strange spell, and I would I were disenchanted. There has no sooner any one done me good service, but lo you, he cancels his interest in me by some deep injury; and, on the other hand, he who hath deserved death at my hands for some treachery or some insult, is sure to be the very person, of all others, who confers upon me some obligation that overbalances his demerits, and renders respite of his sentence a debt due from my honour. Thus, thou see'st, I am deprived of the best part of my royal function, since I can neither punish men nor reward them. Until the influence of this disqualifying planet be passed away, I will say nothing concerning the request of this our sable attendant, save that it is an unusually bold one, and that his best chance of finding grace in our eyes will be, to endeavour to make the discovery which he proposes to achieve in our behalf. Meanwhile, Neville, do thou look well to him, and let him be honourably cared for.—And hark thee once more," he said, in a low whisper, "seek out yonder hermit of Engaddi, and bring him to me forthwith, be he saint or savage, madman or sane. Let me see him privately."

Neville retired from the royal tent, signing to the Nubian to follow him, and much surprised at what he had seen and heard, and especially at the unusual demeanour of the King. In general, no task was so easy as to discover Richard's immediate course of sentiment and feeling, though it might, in some cases be difficult to calculate its duration; for no weathercock obeyed the changing wind more readily, than the King his gusts of passion. But, on the present occasion, his manner seemed unusually constrained and mysterious, nor was it easy to guess whether displeasure or kindness predominated in his conduct towards his new dependant, or in the looks with which, from time to time, he regarded him. The ready service which the King had rendered to counteract the bad effects of the Nubian' wound, might seem to balance the obligation conferred on him by the slave, when he intercepted the blow of the assassin ; but it seemed as a much longer account remained to be arranged between them, that the Monarch was doubtful whether the settlement might leave him, upon the whole, debtor or creditor, and that, therefore, he assumed, in the meantime, a neutral demeanour, which might suit with either character. As for the Nubian, by whatever means he had acquired the art of writing the European languages, the King remained convinced that the English tongue at least was unknown to him, since, having watched him closely during the last part of the interview, he conceived it impossible for any one understanding a conversation, of which he was himself the subject, to have so completely avoided the appearance of taking an interest in it.

CHAPTER XXII

Who's there ?—Approach—'tis kindly done—
My learn'd physician and a friend.
—SIR EUSTACE GREY.

OUR narrative retrogrades to a period shortly previous to the incidents last mentioned, when, as the reader must remember, the unfortunate Knight of the Leopard, bestowed upon the Arabian physician by King Richard, rather as a slave than in any other capacity, was exiled from the camp of the Crusaders, in whose ranks he had so often and so brilliantly distinguished himself. He followed his new master, for so we must now term the Hakim, to the Moorish tents which contained his retinue and his property, with the stupid feelings of one who, fallen from the summit of a precipice, and escaping unexpectedly with life, is just able to drag himself from the fatal spot, but without the power of estimating the extent of the damage which he has sustained. Arrived at the tent, he threw himself, without speech of any kind, upon a couch of dressed buffalo's hide, which was pointed out to him by his conductor, and hiding his face betwixt his hands, groaned heavily, as if his heart was on the point of bursting. The physician heard him, as he was giving orders to his numerous domestics to prepare for their departure the next morning before daybreak, and, moved with compassion, interrupted his occupation, to sit down cross-legged, by the side of his couch, and administer comfort according to the Oriental manner.

"My friend," he said, "be of good comfort—for what sayeth the poet—'It is better that a man should be the servant of a

kind master, than be the slave of his own wild passions.' Again,
be of good courage; because, whereas Ysouf Ben Yagoube was
sold to a King by his brethren, even to Pharaoh King of
Egypt, thy King hath, on the other hand, bestowed thee on one
who will be to thee as a brother."

Sir Kenneth made an effort to thank the Hakim, but his
heart was too full, and the indistinct sounds which accompanied
his abortive attempts to reply, induced the kind physician to
desist from his premature endeavours at consolation. He left
his new domestic, or guest, in quiet, to indulge his sorrows, and
having commanded all the necessary preparations for their departure on the morning, sat down upon the carpet of the tent,
and indulged himself in a moderate repast. After he had thus
refreshed himself, similar viands were offered to the Scottish
knight; but though the slaves let him understand that the
next day would be far advanced ere they would halt for the
purpose of refreshment, Sir Kenneth could not overcome the
disgust which he felt against swallowing any nourishment, and
could be prevailed upon to taste nothing, saving a draught of
cold water.

He was awake long after his Arab host had performed his
usual devotions, and betaken himself to his repose, nor had
sleep visited him at the hour of midnight, when a movement
took place among the domestics, which, though attended with
no speech, and very little noise, made him aware they were
loading the camels and preparing for departure. In the course
of these preparations, the last person who was disturbed, excepting the physician himself, was the Knight of Scotland, whom,
about three in the morning, a sort of major-domo, or master
of the household, acquainted that he must arise. He did so,
without farther answer, and followed him into the moonlight,
where stood the camels, most of which were already loaded, and
one only remained kneeling until its burden should be completed.

A little apart from the camels stood a number of horses
ready bridled and saddled, and the Hakim himself, coming
forth, mounted on one of them with as much agility as the
grave decorum or his character permitted, and directed another,
which he pointed out, to be led towards Sir Kenneth. An
English officer was in attendance, to escort them through the
camp of the Causaders, and to ensure their leaving it in safety,
and all was ready for their departure. The pavilion which
they had left was, in the meanwhile, struck with singular
despatch, and the tent-poles and coverings composed the burden
of the last camel—when the physician, pronouncing solemnly
the verse of the Koran, "God be our guide, and Mohammed our
protector in the desert as in the watered field," the whole
cavalcade was instantly in motion.

In traversing the camp, they were challenged by the various sentinels who maintained guard there, and suffered to proceed in silence, or with a muttered curse upon their prophet, as they passed the post of some more zealous Crusader. At length the last barriers were left behind them, and the party formed themselves for the march with military precaution. Two or three horsemen advanced in front as a vanguard; one or two remained a bowshot in the rear; and, wherever the ground admitted, others were detached to keep an outlook on the flanks. In this manner they proceeded onward, while Sir Kenneth, looking back on the moonlight camp, might now indeed seem banished, deprived at once of honour and liberty, from the glimmering banners under which he had hoped to gain additional renown, and the tented dwellings of chivalry, of Christianity, and—of Edith Plantagenet.

The Hakim, who rode by his side, observed, in his usual tone of sententious consolation—"It is unwise to look back when the journey lieth forward;" and as he spoke, the horse of the knight made such a perilous stumble, as threatened to add a practical moral to the tale.

The knight was compelled by this hint to give more attention to the management of his steed, which more than once required the assistance and support of the check-bridle, although, in other respects, nothing could be more easy at once, and active, than the ambling pace at which the animal (which was a mare) proceeded.

"The conditions of that horse," observed the sententious physician, "are like those of human fortune; seeing that amidst his most swift and easy pace, the rider must guard himself against a fall, and that it is when prosperity is at the highest, that our prudence should be awake and vigilant to prevent misfortune."

The overloaded appetite loathes even the honeycomb, and it is scarce a wonder that the knight, mortified and harassed with misfortunes and abasement, became something impatient of hearing his misery made, at every turn, the ground of proverbs and apothegms, however just and apposite.

"Methinks," he said rather peevishly, "I wanted no additional illustration of the instability of fortune—though I would thank thee, Sir Hakim, for thy choice of a steed for me, would the jade but stumble so effectually as at once to break my neck and her own."

"My brother," answered the Arab sage, with imperturbable gravity, "thou speakest as one of the foolish. Thou say'st in thy heart, that the sage should have given you, as his guest, the younger and better horse, and reserved the old one for himself; but know that the defects of the older steed may be compensated by the energies of the young rider, whereas the violence of the young horse requires to be moderated by the cold temper of the older."

So spoke the sage; but neither to this observation did Sir Kenneth return any answer which could lead to a continuance of their conversation, and the physician, wearied, perhaps, of administering comfort to one who would not be comforted, signed to one of his retinue.

"Hassan," he said, "hast thou nothing wherewith to beguile the way?"

Hassan, story-teller and poet by profession, spurred up, upon this summons, to exercise his calling.—"Lord of the palace of life," he said, addressing the physician, "thou, before whom the angel Azrael spreadeth his wings for flight—thou, wiser than Solimaun Ben Daoud, upon whose signet was inscribed the REAL NAME which controls the spirits of the elements— forbid it, Heaven, that while thou travellest upon the track of benevolence, bearing healing and hope wherever thou comest, thine own course should be saddened for lack of the tale and of the song. Behold, while thy servant is at thy side, he will pour forth the treasures of his memory, as the fountain sendeth her stream beside the pathway, for the refreshment of him that walketh thereon."

After this exordium, Hassan uplifted his voice, and began a tale of love and magic, intermixed with feats of warlike achieve- ment, and ornamented with abundant quotations from the Persian poets, with whose compositions the orator seemed familiar. The retinue of the physician, such excepted as were necessarily detained in attendance on the camels, thronged up to the narrator, and pressed as close as deference for their master permitted, to enjoy the delight which the inhabitants of the East have ever derived from this species of exhibition.

At another time, notwithstanding his imperfect knowledge of the language, Sir Kenneth might have been interested in the recitation, which, though dictated by a more extravagant imagination, and expressed in more inflated and metaphorical language, bore yet a strong resemblance to the romances of chivalry, then so fashionable in Europe. But as matters stood with him, he was scarcely even sensible that a man in the centre of the cavalcade recited and sung, in a low tone, for nearly two hours, modulating his voice to the various moods of passion introduced into the tale, and receiving, in return, now low murmurs of applause, now muttered expressions of wonder, now sighs and tears, and sometimes, what it was far more difficult to extract from such an audience, a tribute of smiles, and even laughter.

During the recitation, the attention of the exile, however,

abstracted by his own deep sorrow, was occasionally awakened by the low wail of a dog, secured in a wicker enclosure suspended on one of the camels, which, as an experienced woodsman, he had no hesitation in recognising to be that of his own faithful hound ; and from the plaintive tone of the animal, he had no doubt that he was sensible of his master's vicinity, and, in his way, invoking his assistance for liberty and rescue.

"Alas ! poor Roswal," he said, "thou callest for aid and sympathy upon one in stricter bondage than thou thyself art. I will not seem to heed thee, or return thy affection, since it would serve but to load our parting with yet more bitterness."

Thus passed the hours of night, and the space of dim hazy dawn, which forms the twilight of a Syrian morning. But when the very first line of the sun's disk began to rise above the level horizon, and when the very first level ray shot glimmering in dew along the surface of the desert, which the travellers had now attained, the sonorous voice of El Hakim himself overpowered and cut short the narrative of the tale-teller, while he caused to resound along the sands the solemn summons, which the muezzins thunder at morning from the minaret of every mosque.

"To prayer !—to prayer ! God is the one God.—To prayer—to prayer ! Mohammed is the prophet of God.—To prayer—to prayer ! Time is flying from you.—To prayer—to prayer ! Judgment is drawing nigh to you."

In an instant each Moslem cast himself from his horse, turned his face towards Mecca, and performed with sand an imitation of those ablutions, which were elsewhere required to be made with water, while each individual, in brief but fervent ejaculations, recommended himself to the care, and his sins to the forgiveness, of God and the Prophet. Even Sir Kenneth, whose reason at once and prejudices were offended by seeing his companions in that which he considered as an act of idolatry, could not help respecting the sincerity of their misguided zeal, and being stimulated by their fervour to apply supplications to Heaven in a purer form, wondering, meanwhile, what new-born feelings could teach him to accompany in prayer, though with varied invocation, those very Saracens, whose heathenish worship he had conceived a crime dishonourable to the land in which high miracles had been wrought, and where the day-star of redemption had arisen.

The act of devotion, however, though rendered in such strange society, burst purely from his natural feelings of religious duty, and had its usual effect in composing the spirits, which had been long harassed by so rapid a succession of calamities. The sincere and earnest approach of the Christian to the throne of the Almighty teaches the best lesson of patience under affliction; since wherefore should we mock the Deity with supplications, when we insult Him by murmuring under His decrees? or how, while our prayers have in every word admitted the vanity and nothingness of the things of time in comparison to those of eternity, should we hope to deceive the Searcher of Hearts, by permitting the world and worldly passions to reassume the reins even immediately after a solemn address to Heaven? But Sir Kenneth was not of these. He felt himself comforted and strengthened, and better prepared to execute or submit to whatever his destiny might call upon him to do or to suffer.

Meanwhile, the party of Saracens regained their saddles, and continued their route, and the tale-teller, Hassan, resumed the thread of his narrative; but it was no longer to the same attentive audience. A horseman, who had ascended some high ground on the right hand of the little column, had returned on a speedy gallop to El Hakim, and communicated with him. Four or five more cavaliers had then been despatched, and the little band, which might consist of about twenty or thirty persons, began to follow them with their eyes, as men from whose gestures, and advance or retreat, they were to augur good or evil. Hassan, finding his audience inattentive, or being himself attracted by the dubious appearances on the flank, stinted in his song; and the march became silent, save when a camel-driver called out to his patient charge, or some anxious follower of the Hakim communicated with his next neighbour, in a hurried and low whisper.

This suspense continued until they had rounded a ridge, composed of hillocks of sand, which concealed from their main body the object that had created this alarm among their scouts. Sir Kenneth could now see, at the distance of a mile or more, a dark object moving rapidly on the bosom of the desert, which his experienced eye recognised for a party of cavalry, much superior to their own in numbers, and, from the thick and frequent flashes which flung back the level beams of the rising sun, it was plain that these were Europeans in their complete panoply.

The anxious looks which the horsemen of El Hakim now cast upon their leader, seemed to indicate deep apprehension; while he, with gravity as undisturbed as when he called his followers to prayer, detached two of his best mounted cavaliers, with instructions to approach as closely as prudence permitted to these travellers of the desert, and observe more minutely their numbers, their character, and, if possible, their purpose. The approach of danger, or what was feared as such, was like a stimulating draught to one in apathy, and recalled Sir Kenneth to himself and his situation.

"What fear you from these Christian horsemen, for such they seem?" he said to the Hakim.

"Fear!" said El Hakim, repeating the word disdainfully— "The sage fears nothing but Heaven—but ever expects from wicked men the worst which they can do."

"They are Christians," said Sir Kenneth, "and it is the time of truce—why should you fear a breach of faith?"

"They are the priestly soldiers of the Temple," answered El Hakim, "whose vow limits them to know neither truce nor faith with the worshippers of Islam. May the Prophet blight them, both root, branch, and twig!—Their peace is war, and their faith is falsehood. Other invaders of Palestine have their times and moods of courtesy. The Lion Richard will spare when he has conquered—the eagle Philip will close his wing when he has stricken a prey—even the Austrian bear will sleep when he is gorged; but this horde of ever-hungry wolves know neither pause nor satiety in their rapine.—See'st thou not that they are detaching a party from their main body, and that they take an eastern direction? Yon are their pages and squires, whom they train up in their accursed mysteries, and whom, as lighter mounted, they send to cut us off from our watering-place. But they will be disappointed; I know the war of the desert yet better than they."

He spoke a few words to his principal officer, and his whole demeanour and countenance was at once changed from the solemn repose of an eastern sage, accustomed more to contem-plation than to action, into the prompt and proud expression of a gallant soldier, whose energies are roused by the near approach of a danger, which he at once foresees and despises.

To Sir Kenneth's eyes the approaching crisis had a different aspect, and when Adonbec said to him, "Thou must tarry close by my side," he answered solemnly in the negative.

"Yonder," he said, "are my comrades in arms—the men in whose society I have vowed to fight or fall—on their banner gleams the sign of our most blessed redemption—I cannot fly from the Cross in company with the Crescent."

"Fool!" said the Hakim; "their first action would be to do thee to death, were it only to conceal their breach of the truce."

"Of that I must take my chance," replied Sir Kenneth; "but I wear not the bonds of the infidels an instant longer than I can cast them from me."

"Then will I compel thee to follow me," said El Hakim.

"Compel!" answered Sir Kenneth angrily. "Wert thou not my benefactor, or one who has showed will to be such, and were it not that it is to thy confidence I owe the freedom of these hands, which thou mightest have loaded with fetters, I would show thee that, unarmed as I am, compulsion would be no easy task."

"Enough, enough," replied the Arabian physician, "we lose time even when it is becoming precious."

So saying, he threw his arm aloft, and uttered a loud and shrill cry, as a signal to those of his retinue, who instantly dispersed themselves on the face of the desert, in as many different directions as a chaplet of beads when the string is broken. Sir Kenneth had no time to note what ensued; for, at the same instant, the Hakim seized the rein of his steed, and putting his own to its mettle, both sprung forth at once with the suddenness of light, and at a pitch of velocity which almost deprived the Scottish knight of the power of respiration, and left him absolutely incapable, had he been desirous, to have checked the career of his guide. Practised as Sir Kenneth was in horsemanship from his earliest youth, the speediest horse he had ever mounted was a tortoise in comparison to those of the Arabian sage. They spurned the sand from behind them—they seemed to devour the desert before them—miles flew away with minutes, and yet their strength seemed unabated, and their respiration as free as when they first started upon the wonderful race. The motion, too, as easy as it was swift, seemed more like flying through the air than riding on the earth, and was attended with no unpleasant sensation, save the awe naturally felt by one who is moving at such astonishing speed, and the difficulty of breathing occasioned by their passing through the air so rapidly.

It was not until after an hour of this portentous motion, and when all human pursuit was far, far behind, that the Hakim at length relaxed his speed, and slackening the pace of the horses into a hand gallop, began, in a voice as composed and even as if he had been walking for the last hour, a descant upon the excellence of his coursers to the Scot, who, breathless, half blind, half deaf, and altogether giddy, from the rapidity of this singular ride, hardly comprehended the words which flowed so freely from his companion.

"These horses," he said, "are of the breed called the Winged, equal in speed to aught excepting the Borak of the Prophet. They are fed on the golden barley of Yemen, mixed with spices, and with a small portion of dried sheep's flesh. Kings have given provinces to possess them, and their age is active as their youth. Thou, Nazarene, art the first, save a true believer, that ever had beneath his loins one of this noble race, a gift of the Prophet himself to the blessed Ali, his kinsman and lieutenant, well called the Lion of God. Time lays his touch so lightly on these generous steeds, that the mare on which thou sittest has seen five times five years pass over her, yet retains her pristine speed and vigour, only that in the career the support of a bridle, managed by a hand more experienced than thine, hath now become necessary. May the prophet be blessed, who hath bestowed on the true believers the means of advance and retreat, which causeth their iron-clothed enemies to be worn out with their own ponderous weight! How the horses of yonder dog Templars must have snorted and blown, when they had toiled fetlock-deep in the desert for one-twentieth part of the space which these brave steeds have left behind them, without one thick pant, or a drop of moisture upon their sleek and velvet coats!"

The Scottish knight, who had now begun to recover his breath and powers of attention, could not help acknowledging in his heart the advantage possessed by these Eastern warriors in a race of animals, alike proper for advance or retreat, and so admirably adapted to the level and sandy deserts of Arabia and Syria. But he did not choose to augment the pride of the Moslem by acquiescing in his proud claim of superiority, and therefore suffered the conversation to drop, and looking around him could now, at the more moderate pace at which they moved, distinguish that he was in a country not unknown to him.

The blighted borders and sullen waters of the Dead Sea, the ragged and precipitous chain of mountains arising on the left, the two or three palms clustered together, forming the single green speck on the bosom of the waste wilderness,— objects which, once seen, were scarcely to be forgotten,—showed to Sir Kenneth that they were approaching the fountain called the Diamond of the Desert, which had been the scene of his interview, on a former occasion, with the Saracen Emir Sheer-kohf, or Ilderim. In a few minutes they checked their horses beside the spring, and the Hakim invited Sir Kenneth to descend from horseback, and repose himself as in a place of safety. They unbridled their steeds, El Hakim observing that farther care of them was unnecessary, since they would be speedily joined by some of the best mounted among his slaves, who would do what farther was needful.

"Meantime," he said, spreading some food on the grass, "eat and drink, and be not discouraged. Fortune may raise up or abase the ordinary mortal, but the sage and the soldier should have minds beyond her control."

The Scottish knight endeavoured to testify his thanks by showing himself docile; but though he strove to eat out of complaisance, the singular contrast between his present situation, and that which he had occupied on the same spot, when the envoy of princes, and the victor in combat, came like a cloud over his mind, and fasting, lassitude, and fatigue, oppressed his bodily powers. El Hakim examined his hurried pulse, his red and inflamed eye, his heated hand, and his shortened respiration.

"The mind," he said, "grows wise by watching, but her sister, the body, of coarser materials, needs the support of repose. Thou must sleep; and that thou mayst do so to refreshment, thou must take a draught mingled with this elixir."

He drew from his bosom a small crystal vial, cased in silver filigree-work, and dropped into a little golden drinking cup a small portion of a dark-coloured fluid.

"This," he said, "is one of those productions which Allah hath sent on earth for a blessing, though man's weakness and wickedness have sometimes converted it into a curse. It is powerful as the wine-cup of the Nazarene to drop the curtain on the sleepless eye, and to relieve the burden of the overloaded bosom; but when applied to the purposes of indulgence and debauchery, it rends the nerves, destroys the strength, weakens the intellect, and undermines life. But fear not thou to use its virtues in the time of need, for the wise man warns him by the same firebrand with which the madman burneth the tent." *

"I have seen too much of thy skill, sage Hakim," said Sir Kenneth, "to debate thine hest;" and swallowed the narcotic, mingled as it was with some water from the spring, then wrapped him in the haik, or Arab cloak, which had been fastened to his saddle-pommel, and, according to the directions of the physician, stretched himself at ease in the shade to await the promised repose. Sleep came not at first, but in her stead a train of pleasing yet not rousing or awaking sensations. A state ensued, in which, still conscious of his own identity and his own condition, the knight felt enabled to consider them not only without alarm and sorrow, but as composedly as he might have viewed the story of his misfortunes acted upon a stage, or rather as a disembodied spirit might regard the transactions of its past existence. From this state of repose, amounting almost to apathy respecting the past, his thoughts were carried forward to the future, which, in spite of all that existed to overcloud the prospect, glittered with such hues, as under much happier auspices his unstimulated imagination had not been able to produce, even in its most exalted state. Liberty, fame, successful love, appeared to be the certain and not very distant prospect, of the enslaved exile, the dishonoured knight, even of the dispairing lover, who had placed his hopes of happiness so far beyond the prospect of chance, in her wildest possibilities, serving to countenance his wishes. Gradu-

---

* Some preparation of opium seems to be intimated.

ally as the intellectual sight became overclouded, these gay visions became obscure, like the dying hues of sunset, until they were at last lost in total oblivion; and Sir Kenneth lay extended at the feet of El Hakim, to all appearance, but for his deep respiration, as inanimate a corpse, as if life had actually departed.

CHAPTER XXIII

'Mid these wild scenes Enchantment waves her hand,
To change the face of the mysterious land ;
Till the bewildering scenes around us seem
The vain productions of a feverish dream.
—ASTOLPHO, A ROMANCE.

WHEN the Knight of the Leopard awoke from his long and profound repose, he found himself in circumstances so different from those in which he had lain down to sleep, that he doubted whether he was not still dreaming, or whether the scene had not been changed by magic. Instead of the damp grass, he lay on a couch of more than Oriental luxury, and some kind hands had, during his repose, stripped him of the cassock of chamois which he wore under his armour, and substituted a night dress of the finest linen, and a loose gown of silk. He had been canopied only by the palm trees of the desert, but now he lay beneath a silken pavilion, which blazed with the richest colours of the Chinese loom, while a slight curtain of gauze, displayed around his couch, was calculated to protect his repose from the insects, to which he had, ever since his arrival in these climates, been a constant and passive prey. He looked around, as if to convince himself that he was actually awake, and all that fell beneath his eye partook of the splendour of his dormitory. A portable bath of cedar, lined with silver, was ready for use, and steamed with the odours which had been used in preparing it. On a small stand of ebony beside the couch stood a silver vase, containing sherbet of the most exquisite quality, cold as snow, and which the thirst that followed the use of the strong narcotic rendered peculiarly delicious. Still farther to dispel the dregs of intoxication which it had left behind, the knight resolved to use the bath, and experienced in doing so a delightful refreshment. Having dried himself with napkins of the Indian wool, he would willingly have resumed his own coarse garments, that he might go forth to see whether the world was as much changed without as within the place of his repose. These, however, were nowhere to be seen, but in their place he found a Saracen dress of rich materials, with sabre and poniard.

and all befitting an emir of distinction. He was able to suggest no motive to himself for this exuberance of care, expecting a suspicion that these attentions were intended to shake him in his religious profession; as indeed it was well known that the high esteem of the European knowledge and courage, made the Soldan unbounded in his gifts to those who, having become his prisoners, had been induced to take the turban. Sir Kenneth, therefore, crossing himself devoutly, resolved to set all such snares at defiance; and that he might do so the more firmly, conscientiously determined to avail himself as moderately as possible of the attentions and luxuries thus liberally heaped upon him. Still, however, he felt his head oppressed and sleepy, and aware, too, that his undress was not fit for appearing abroad, he reclined upon the couch, and was again locked in the arms of slumber.

But this time his rest was not unbroken; for he was awakened by the voice of the physician at the door of the tent, inquiring after his health, and whether he had rested sufficiently.—"May I enter your tent?" he concluded, "for the curtain is drawn before the entrance."

"The master," replied Sir Kenneth, determined to show that he was not surprised into forgetfulness of his own condition, "need demand no permission to enter the tent of the slave."

"But if I come not as a master?" said El Hakim, still without entering.

"The physician," answered the knight, "hath free access to the bedside of his patient."

"Neither come I now as a physician," replied El Hakim; "and therefore I still request permission, ere I come under the covering of thy tent."

"Whoever comes as a friend," said Sir Kenneth, "and such thou hast hitherto shown thyself to me, the habitation of the friend is ever open to him."

"Yet once again," said the Eastern sage, after the periphrastical manner of his countrymen, "supposing that I come not as a friend?"

"Come as thou wilt," said the Scottish knight, somewhat impatient of this circumlocution,—"be what thou wilt—thou knowest well it is neither in my power nor my inclination to refuse thee entrance."

"I come then," said El Hakim, "as your ancient foe; but a fair and a generous one."

He entered as he spoke; and when he stood before the bedside of Sir Kenneth, the voice continued to be that of Adonbec the Arabian physician, but the form, dress, and features were those of Ilderim of Kurdistan, called Sheerkohf. Sir Kenneth

gazed upon him, as if he expected the vision to depart, like
something created by his imagination.

"Doth it so surprise thee," said Ilderim, "and thou an
approved warrior, to see that a soldier knows somewhat of the
art of healing?—I say to thee, Nazarene, that an accomplished
cavalier should know how to dress his steed as well as how to
ride him; how to forge his sword upon the stithy, as well as
how to use it in battle; how to burnish his arms, as well as
how to wear them; and, above all, how to cure wounds as well
as how to inflict them."

As he spoke, the Christian knight repeatedly shut his eyes,
and while they remained closed, the idea of the Hakim, with
his long flowing dark robes, high Tartar cap, and grave gestures,
was present to his imagination; but so soon as he opened them,
the graceful and richly-gemmed turban, the light hauberk of
steel rings entwisted with silver, which glanced brilliantly as it
obeyed every inflection of the body, the features freed from
their formal expression, less swarthy, and no longer shadowed
by the mass of hair (now limited to a well-trimmed beard),
announced the soldier and not the sage.

"Art thou still so much surprised," said the Emir, "and hast
thou walked in the world with such little observance, as to
wonder that men are not always what they seem?—Thou thyself
—art thou what thou seemest?"

"No, by St. Andrew!" exclaimed the knight; "for to the
whole Christian camp I seem a traitor, and I know myself to be
a true though an erring man."

"Even so I judged thee," said Ilderim, "and as we had eaten
salt together, I deemed myself bound to rescue thee from death
and contumely.—But wherefore lie you still on your couch,
since the sun is high in the heavens? or are the vestments
which my sumpter-camels have afforded unworthy of your
wearing?"

"Not unworthy, surely, but unfitting for it," replied the
Scot; "give me the dress of a slave, noble Ilderim, and I will
don it with pleasure; but I cannot brook to wear the habit of
the free Eastern warrior, with the turban of the Moslem."

"Nazarene," answered the Emir, "thy nation so easily entertains suspicion, that it may well render themselves suspected.
Have I not told thee that Saladin desires no converts saving
those whom the holy prophet shall dispose to submit themselves
to his law; violence and bribery are alike alien to his plan for
extending the true faith. Hearken to me, my brother. When
the blind man was miraculously restored to sight, the scales
dropped from his eyes at the Divine pleasure—think'st thou
that any earthly leech could have removed them? No. Such
mediciner might have tormented the patient with his instru-

o

ments, or perhaps soothed him with his balsams and cordials, but dark as he was must the darkened man have remained; and it is even so with the blindness of the understanding. If there be those among the Franks, who, for the sake of worldly lucre, have assumed the turban of the Prophet, and followed the laws of Islam, with their own consciences be the blame. Themselves sought out the bait—it was not flung to them by the Soldan. And when they shall hereafter be sentenced, as hypocrites, to the lowest gulf of hell, below Christian and Jew, magician and idolater, and condemned to eat the fruit of the tree Yacoun, which is the heads of demons—to themselves, not to the Soldan, shall their guilt and their punishment be attributed. Wherefore wear, without doubt or scruple, the vesture prepared for you, since if you proceed to the camp of Saladin, your own native dress will expose you to troublesome observation, and perhaps to insult."

"*If* I go to the camp of Saladin?" said Sir Kenneth, repeating the words of the Emir. "Alas! am I a free agent, and rather must I *not* go wherever your pleasure carries me?"

"Thine own will may guide thine own motions," said the Emir, "as freely as the wind which moveth the dust of the desert in what direction it chooseth. The noble enemy who met, and well-nigh mastered my sword, cannot become my slave like him who has crouched beneath it. If wealth and power would tempt thee to join our people, I could ensure thy possessing them; but the man who refused the favours of the Soldan when the axe was at his head, will not, I fear, now accept them, when I tell him he has his free choice."

"Complete your generosity, noble Emir," said Sir Kenneth, "by forbearing to show me a mode of requital, which conscience forbids me to comply with. Permit me rather to express, as bound in courtesy, my gratitude for this most chivalrous bounty, this undeserved generosity."

"Say not underserved," replied the Emir Ilderim; "was it not through thy conversation, and thy account of the beauties which grace the court of the Melech Ric, that I ventured me thither in disguise, and thereby procured a sight the most blessed that I have ever enjoyed—that I ever shall enjoy, until the glories of Paradise beam on my eyes?"

"I understand you not," said Sir Kenneth, colouring alternately, and turning pale, as one who felt that the conversation was taking a tone of the most painful delicacy.

"Not understand me!" exclaimed the Emir. "If the sight I saw in the tent of King Richard escaped thine observation, I will account it duller than the edge of a buffoon's wooden falchion. True, thou wert under sentence of death at the time; but, in my case, had my head been dropping from the trunk, the last strained glances of my eyeballs had distinguished with delight such a vision of loveliness, and the head would have rolled itself towards the incomparable houris, to kiss with its quivering lips the hem of their vestments.—Yonder royalty of England, who for her superior loveliness deserves to be Queen of the universe—what tenderness in her blue eye!—what lustre in her tresses of dishevelled gold!—By the tomb of the prophet, I scarce think that the houri who shall present to me the diamond cup of immortality, will deserve so warm a caress!"

"Saracen," said Sir Kenneth sternly, "thou speakest of the wife of Richard of England, of whom men think not and speak not as a woman to be won, but as a Queen to be revered."

"I cry you mercy," said the Saracen. "I had forgotten your superstitious veneration for the sex, which you consider rather fit to be wondered at and worshipped, than wooed and possessed. I warrant, since thou exactest such profound respect to yonder tender piece of frailty, whose every motion, step, and look, bespeaks her very woman, less than absolute adoration must not be yielded to her of the dark tresses, and nobly speaking eye. *She*, indeed, I will allow, hath in her noble port and majestic mien something at once pure and firm—yet even she, when pressed by opportunity and a forward lover, would, I warrant thee, thank him in her heart, rather for treating her as a mortal than as a goddess."

"Respect the kinswoman of Cœur de Lion!" said Sir Kenneth, in a tone of unrepressed anger.

"Respect her!" answered the Emir in scorn—"by the Caaba, and if I do, it shall be rather as the bride of Saladin."

"The Infidel Soldan is unworthy to salute even a spot that has been pressed by the foot of Edith Plantagenet!" exclaimed the Christian, springing from his couch.

"Ha! what said the Giaour?" exclaimed the Emir, laying his hand on his poniard hilt, while his forehead glowed like glancing copper, and the muscles of his lips and cheeks wrought till each curl of his beard seemed to twist and screw itself, as if alive with instinctive wrath. But the Scottish knight, who had stood the lion anger of Richard, was unappalled at the tiger-like mood of the chafed Saracen.

"What I have said," continued Sir Kenneth, with folded arms and dauntless look, "I would, were my hands loose, maintain on foot or horseback against all mortals; and would hold it not the most memorable deed of my life to support it with my good broadsword against a score of these sickles and bodkins," pointing at the curved sabre and small poniard of the Emir.

The Saracen recovered his composure as the Christian spoke,

so far as to withdraw his hand from his weapon, as if the motion had been without meaning; but still continued in deep ire.

"By the sword of the prophet," he said, "which is the key both of Heaven and Hell, he little values his own life, brother, who uses the language thou dost! Believe me, that were thine hands loose, as thou term'st it, one single true believer would find them so much to do, that thou wouldst soon wish them fettered again in manacles of iron."

"Sooner would I wish them hewn off by the shoulder-blades!" replied Sir Kenneth.

"Well. Thy hands are bound at present," said the Saracen, in a more amicable tone, "bound by thine own gentle sense of courtesy, nor have I any present purpose of setting them at liberty. We have proved each other's strength and courage ere now, and we may again meet in a fair field;—and shame befall him who shall be the first to part from his foeman! But now we are friends, and I look for aid from thee, rather than hard terms or defiances."

"We *are* friends," repeated the knight; and there was a pause, during which the fiery Saracen paced the tent, like the lion, who, after violent irritation, is said to take that method of cooling the distemperature of his blood, ere he stretches himself to repose in his den. The colder European remained unaltered in posture and aspect; yet he, doubtless, was also engaged in subduing the angry feelings which had been so unexpectedly awakened.

"Let us reason of this calmly," said the Saracen; "I am a physician, as thou knowest, and it is written, that he who would have his wound cured, must not shrink when the leech probes and tents it. Seest thou, I am about to lay my finger on the sore. Thou lovest this kinswoman of the Melech Ric—Unfold the veil that shrouds thy thoughts—or unfold it not if thou wilt, for mine eyes see through its coverings."

"I *loved* her," answered Sir Kenneth, after a pause, "as a man loves Heaven's grace, and sued for her favour like a sinner for Heaven's pardon."

"And you love her no longer?" said the Saracen.

"Alas!" answered Sir Kenneth, "I am no longer worthy to love her.—I prithee cease this discourse—thy words are poniards to me."

"Pardon me but a moment," continued Ilderim. "When thou, a poor and obscure soldier, didst so boldly and so highly fix thine affection, tell me, hadst thou good hope of its issue?"

"Love exists not without hope," replied the knight; "but mine was as nearly allied to despair, as that of the sailor swimming for his life, who, as he surmounts billow after billow, catches by intervals some gleam of the distant beacon, which shows him there is land in sight, though his sinking heart and wearied limbs assure him that he shall never reach it."

"And now," said Ilderim, "these hopes are sunk—that solitary light is quenched for ever?"

"For ever," answered Sir Kenneth, in the tone of an echo from the bosom of a ruined sepulchre.

"Methinks," said the Saracen, "if all thou lackest were some such distant meteoric glimpse of happiness as thou hadst formerly, thy beacon-light might be rekindled, thy hope fished up from the ocean in which it has sunk, and thou thyself, good knight, restored to the exercise and amusement of nourishing thy fantastic passion upon a diet as unsubstantial as moon-light; for, if thou stoodst to-morrow fair in reputation as ever thou wert, she whom thou lovest will not be less the daughter of princes, and the elected bride of Saladin."

"I would it so stood," said the Scott, "and if I did not——"

He stopt short, like a man who is afraid of boasting, under circumstances which did not permit his being put to the test. The Saracen smiled as he concluded the sentence.

"Thou wouldst challenge the Soldan to single combat?" said he.

"And if I did," said Sir Kenneth haughtily, "Saladin's would neither be the first nor the best turban that I have couched lance at."

"Ay, but methinks the Soldan might regard it as too un-equal a mode of periling the chance of a royal bride, and the event of a great war," said the Emir.

"He may be met with in the front of battle," said the knight, his eyes gleaming with the ideas which such a thought inspired.

"He has been ever found there," said Ilderim; "nor is it his wont to turn his horse's head from any brave encounter.—But it was not of the Soldan that I meant to speak. In a word, if it will content thee to be placed in such reputation as may be attained by detection of the thief who stole the Banner of England, I can put thee in a fair way of achieving this task—that is, if thou wilt be governed; for what says Lokman, 'If the child would walk, the nurse must lead him—if the ignorant would understand, the wise must instruct.'"

"And thou art wise, Ilderim," said the Scot, "wise though a Saracen, and generous though an infidel. I have witnessed that thou are both. Take, then, the guidance of this matter; and so thou ask nothing of me contrary to my loyalty and my Christian faith, I will obey thee punctually. Do what thou hast said, and take my life when it is accomplished."

"Listen thou to me, then," said the Saracen. "Thy noble hound is now recovered, by the blessing of that divine medicine which healeth man and beast, and by his sagacity shall those who assailed him be discovered."

"Ha!" said the knight,—"methinks I comprehend thee—I was dull not to think of this!"

"But tell me," added the Emir, "hast thou any followers or retainers in the camp, by whom the animal may be known?"

"I dismissed," said Sir Kenneth, "my old attendant, thy patient, with a varlet that waited on him, at the time when I expected to suffer death, giving him letters for my friends in Scotland—there are none other to whom the dog is familiar. But then my own person is well known—my very speech will betray me, in a camp where I have played no mean part for many months."

"Both he and thou shalt be disguised, so as to escape even close examination.—I tell thee," said the Saracen, "that not thy brother in arms—not thy brother in blood—shall discover thee, if thou be guided by my counsels. Thou hast seen me do matters more difficult—he that can call the dying from the darkness of the shadow of death, can easily cast a mist before the eyes of the living. But mark me—there is still the condition annexed to this service, that thou deliver a letter of Saladin to the niece of the Melech Ric, whose name is as difficult to our Eastern tongue and lips, as her beauty is delightful to our eyes."

Sir Kenneth paused before he answered, and the Saracen observing his hesitation, demanded of him, "if he feared to undertake this message?"

"Not if there were death in the execution," said Sir Kenneth; "I do but pause to consider whether it consists with my honour to bear the letter of the Soldan, or with that of the Lady Edith to receive it from a heathen prince."

"By the head of Mohammed, and by the honour of a soldier—by the tomb at Mecca, and by the soul of my father," said the Emir, "I swear to thee that the letter is written in all honour and respect. The song of the nightingale will sooner blight the rose-bower she loves, than will the words of the Soldan offend the ears of the lovely kinswoman of England."

"Then," said the knight, "I will bear the Soldan's letter faithfully, as if I were his born vassal,—understanding, that beyond this simple act of service which I will render with fidelity, from me of all men he can least expect mediation or advice in this his strange love-suit."

"Saladin is noble," answered the Emir, "and will not spur a generous horse to a leap which he cannot achieve.—Come with me to my tent," he added, "and thou shalt be presently equipped with a disguise as unsearchable as midnight; so thou mayst walk the camp of the Nazarenes as if thou hadst on thy finger the signet of the Giaougi." *

* Perhaps the same with Gyges.

CHAPTER XXIV

——A grain of dust
Soiling our cup, will make our sense reject
Fastidiously the draught which we did thirst for ;
A rusted nail, placed near the faithful compass,
Will sway it from the truth, and wreck the argosy.
Even this small cause of anger and disgust
Will break the bonds of amity 'mongst princes,
And wreck their noblest purposes.

—THE CRUSADE.

THE reader can now have little doubt who the Ethiopian slave really was, with what purpose he had sought Richard's camp, and wherefore and with what hope he now stood close to the person of that monarch, as, surrounded by his valiant peers of England and Normandy, Cœur de Lion stood on the summit of Saint George's Mount, with the Banner of England by his side, borne by the most goodly person in the army, being his own natural brother, William with the Long Sword, Earl of Salisbury, the offspring of Henry the Second's amour with the celebrated Rosamond of Woodstock.

From several expressions in the King's conversation with Neville on the preceding day, the Nubian was left in anxious doubt whether his disguise had not been penetrated, especially as that the King seemed to be aware in what manner the agency of the dog was expected to discover the thief who stole the banner, although the circumstance of such an amimal's having been wounded on the occasion, had been scarce mentioned in Richard's presence. Nevertheless, as the King continued to treat him in no other manner than his exterior required, the Nubian remained uncertain whether he was or was not discovered, and determined not to throw his disguise aside voluntarily.

Meanwhile, the powers of the various Crusading princes, arrayed under their royal and princely leaders, swept in long order around the base of the little mound ; and as those of each different country passed by, their commanders advanced a step or two up the hill, and made a signal of courtesy to Richard and to the Standard of England, "in sign of regard and amity," as the protocol of the ceremony heedfully expressed it, " not of subjection or vassalage." The spiritual dignitaries, who in those days veiled not their bonnets to created being, bestowed on the King and his symbol of command their blessing instead of rendering obeisance.

Thus the long files marched on, and, diminished as they were by so many causes, appeared still an iron host to whom the conquest of Palestine might seem an easy task. The soldiers, inspired by the consciousness of united strength, sat erect in their steel saddles, while it seemed that the trumpets sounded more cheerfully shrill, and the steeds, refreshed by rest and provender, chafed on the bit, and trod the ground more proudly. On they passed, troop after troop, banners waving, spears glancing, plumes dancing, in long perspective —a host composed of different nations, complexions, languages, arms, and appearances, but all fired, for the time, with the holy yet romantic purpose of rescuing the distressed daughter of Zion from her thraldom, and redeeming the sacred earth, which more than mortal had trodden, from the yoke of the unbelieving Pagan. And it must be owned, that if, in other circumstances, the species of courtesy rendered to the King of England by so many warriors, from whom he claimed no natural allegiance, had in it something that might have been thought humilating, yet the nature and cause of the war was so fitted to his pre-eminently chivalrous character, and renowned feats in arms, that claims, which might elsewhere have been urged, were there forgotten ; and the brave did willing homage to the bravest, in an expedition where the most undaunted and energetic courage was necessary to success.

The good King was seated on horseback about half-way up the Mount, a morion on his head, surmounted by a crown, which left his manly features exposed to public view, as, with cool and considerate eye, he perused each rank as it passed him, and returned the salutation of the leaders. His tunic was of sky-coloured velvet, covered with plates of silver, and his hose of crimson silk, slashed with cloth of gold. By his side stood the seeming Ethiopian slave, holding the noble dog in a leash, such as was used in woodcraft. It was a circumstance which attracted no notice, for many of the princes of the Crusade had introduced black slaves into their household, in imitation of the barbarous splendour of the Saracens. Over the King's head streamed the large folds of the banner, and, as he looked to it from time to time, he seemed to regard a ceremony, indifferent to himself personally, as important, when considered as atoning an indignity offered to the kingdom which he ruled. In the background, and on the very summit of the Mount, a wooden turret, erected for the occasion, held the Queen Berengaria and the principal ladies of the court. To this the King looked from time to time, and then ever and anon his eyes were turned on the Nubian and the dog, but only when such leaders approached, as, from circumstances of previous ill-will, he suspected of being accessory to the theft of the standard, or whom he judged capable of a crime so mean.

Thus, he did not look in that direction when Philip Augustus

THE NUBIAN'S HOUND ATTACKS CONRADE

PAINTING BY JOHANNOT

of France approached at the head of his splendid troops of Gallic chivalry—nay, he anticipated the motions of the French King, by descending the Mount as the latter came up the ascent, so that they met in the middle space, and blended their greetings so gracefully, that it appeared they met in fraternal equality. The sight of the two greatest princes in Europe, in rank at once and power, thus publicly avowing their concord, called forth bursts of thundering acclaim from the Crusading host at many miles' distance, and made the roving Arab scouts of the desert alarm the camp of Saladin with intelligence, that the army of the Christians was in motion. Yet who but the King of kings can read the hearts of monarchs? Under this smooth show of courtesy, Richard nourished displeasure and suspicion against Philip, and Philip meditated withdrawing himself and his host from the army of the Cross, and leaving Richard to accomplish or fail in the enterprise with his own unassisted forces.

Richard's demeanour was different when the dark-armed knights and squires of the Temple chivalry approached—men with countenances bronzed to Asiatic blackness by the suns of Palestine, and the admirable state of whose horses and appointments far surpassed even that of the choicest troops of France and England. The King cast a hasty glance aside, but the Nubian stood quiet, and his trusty dog sat at his feet, watching, with a sagacious yet pleased look, the ranks which now passed before them. The King's look turned again on the chivalrous Templars, as the Grand Master, availing himself of his mingled character, bestowed his benediction on Richard as a priest, instead of doing him reverence as a military leader.

"The misproud and amphibious caitiff puts the monk upon me," said Richard to the Earl of Salisbury. "But, Long-Sword, we will let it pass. A punctilio must not lose Christendom the services of these experienced lances, because their victories have rendered them overweening.—Lo you, here comes our valiant adversary, the Duke of Austria—mark his manner and bearing, Long-Sword—and thou, Nubian, let the hound have full view of him. By Heaven, he brings his buffoons along with him!"

In fact, whether from habit, or, which is more likely, to intimate contempt of the ceremonial he was about to comply with, Leopold was attended by his *spruch-sprecher* and his jester, and as he advanced towards Richard, he whistled in what he wished to be considered as an indifferent manner, though his heavy features evinced the sullenness, mixed with the fear, with which a truant schoolboy may be seen to approach his master.

As the reluctant dignitary made, with discomposed and sulky

look, the obeisance required, the *spruch-sprecher* shook his baton, and proclaimed, like a herald, that, in what he was now doing, the Archduke of Austria was not to be held derogating from the rank and privileges of a sovereign prince; to which the jester answered with a sonorous *amen*, which provoked much laughter among the bystanders.

King Richard looked more than once at the Nubian and his dog; but the former moved not, nor did the latter strain at the leash, so that Richard said to the slave with some scorn, "Thy success in this enterprise, my sable friend, even though thou hast brought thy hound's sagacity to back thine own, will not, I fear, place thee high in the rank of wizards, or much augment thy merits towards our person."

The Nubian answered, as usual, only by a low obeisance.

Meantime the troops of the Marquis of Montserrat next passed in order before the King of England. That powerful and wily baron, to make the greater display of his forces, had divided them into two bodies. At the head of the first, consisting of his vassals and followers, and levied from his Syrian possessions, came his brother Enguerrand, and he himself followed, leading on a gallant band of twelve hundred Stradiots, a kind of light cavalry raised by the Venetians in their Dalmatian possessions, and of which they had entrusted the command to the Marquis, with whom the republic had many bonds of connection. These Stradiots were clothed in a fashion partly European, but partaking chiefly of the Eastern fashion. They wore, indeed, short hauberks, but had over them parti-coloured tunics of rich stuffs, with large wide pantaloons and half-boots. On their heads were straight upright caps, similar to those of the Greeks, and they carried small round targets, bows and arrows, scimitars, and poniards. They were mounted on horses, carefully selected, and well maintained at the expense of the State of Venice; their saddles and appointments resembled those of the Turks, and they rode in the same manner, with short stirrups and upon a high seat. These troops were of great use in skirmishing with the Arabs, though unable to engage in close combat, like the iron-sheathed men-at-arms of Western and Northern Europe.

Before this goodly band came Conrade, in the same garb with the Stradiots, but of such rich stuff that he seemed to blaze with gold and silver, and the milk-white plume, fastened in his cap by a clasp of diamonds, seemed tall enough to sweep the clouds. The noble steed which he reined bounded and caracoled, and displayed his spirit and agility in a manner which might have troubled a less admirable horseman than the Marquis, who gracefully ruled him with the one hand, while the other displayed the baton, whose predominancy over the ranks which he led seemed equally absolute. Yet his authority over the Stradiots was more in show than in substance; for there paced beside him, on an ambling palfrey of soberest mood, a little old man, dressed entirely in black, without beard or moustache, and having an appearance altogether mean and insignificant, when compared with the blaze of splendour around him. But this mean-looking old man was one of those deputies whom the Venetian government sent into camps to overlook the conduct of the generals to whom the leading was consigned, and to maintain that jealous system of espial and control which had long distinguished the policy of the republic.

Conrade, who, by cultivating Richard's humour, had attained a certain degree of favour with him, no sooner was come within his ken than the King of England descended a step or two to meet him, exclaiming, at the same time, "Ha, Lord Marquis, thou at the head of the fleet Stradoits, and thy black shadow attending thee as usual, whether the sun shines or not!—May not one ask thee whether the rule of the troops remains with the shadow or the substance?"

Conrade was commencing his reply with a smile, when Roswal, the noble hound, uttering a furious and savage yell, sprung forward. The Nubian, at the same time, slipped the leash, and the hound, rushing on, leaped upon Conrade's noble charger, and seizing the Marquis by the throat, pulled him down from the saddle. The plumed rider lay rolling on the sand, and the frightened horse fled in wild career through the camp.

"Thy hound hath pulled down the right quarry, I warrant him," said the King to the Nubian, "and I vow to Saint George he is a stag of ten tynes!—Pluck the dog off, lest he throttle him."

The Ethiopian, accordingly, though not without difficulty, disengaged the dog from Conrade, and fastened him up, still highly excited, and struggling in the leash. Meanwhile many crowded to the spot, especially followers of Conrade and officers of the Stradiots, who, as they saw their leader lie gazing wildly on the sky, raised him up amid a tumultuary cry of—"Cut the slave and his hound to pieces!"

But the voice of Richard, loud and sonorous, was heard clear above all other exclamations—"He dies the death who injures the hound! He hath but done his duty, after the sagacity with which God and nature have endowed the brave animal.— Stand forward for a false traitor, thou Conrade, Marquis of Montserrat! I impeach thee of treason."

Several of the Syrian leaders had now come up, and Conrade, vexation, and shame, and confusion struggling with passion in his manner and voice, exclaimed, "What means this?—With what am I charged?—Why this base usage, and these reproachful terms?—Is this the league of concord which England renewed but so lately?"

"Are the Princes of the Crusade turned hares or deers in the eyes of King Richard, that he should slip hounds on them?" said the sepulchral voice of the Grand Master of the Templars.

"It must be some singular accident—some fatal mistake," said Philip of France, who rode up at the same moment.

"Some deceit of the Enemy," said the Archbishop of Tyre.

"A stratagem of the Saracens," cried Henry of Champagne—"It were well to hang up the dog, and put the slave to the torture."

"Let no man lay hand upon them," said Richard, "as he loves his own life!—Conrade, stand forth, if thou darest, and deny the accusation which this mute animal hath in his noble instinct brought against thee, of injury done to him, and foul scorn to England!"

"I never touched the banner," said Conrade hastily.

"Thy words betray thee, Conrade!" said Richard; "for how didst thou know, save from conscious guilt, that the question is concerning the banner?"

"Hast thou then not kept the camp in turmoil on that and no other score?" answered Conrade; "and dost thou impute to a prince and an ally a crime, which, after all, was probably committed by some paltry felon for the sake of the gold thread? Or wouldst thou now impeach a confederate on the credit of a dog?"

By this time the alarm was becoming general, so that Philip of France interposed.

"Princes and nobles," he said, "you speak in presence of those whose swords will soon be at the throats of each other, if they hear their leaders at such terms together. In the name of Heaven, let us draw off, each his own troops, into their separate quarters, and ourselves meet an hour hence in the Pavilion of Council, to take some order in this new state of confusion."

"Content," said King Richard, "though I should have liked to have interrogated that caitiff while his gay doublet was yet besmirched with sand—But the pleasure of France shall be ours in this matter."

The leaders separated as was proposed, each prince placing himself at the head of his own forces; and then was heard on all sides the crying of war-cries, and the sounding of gathering-notes upon bugles and trumpets, by which the different stragglers were summoned to their prince's banner; and the troops were shortly seen in motion, each taking different routes through the camp to their own quarters. But although any immediate act of violence was thus prevented, yet the accident which had taken place dwelt on every mind; and those foreigners, who had that morning hailed Richard as the worthiest to lead their army, now resumed their prejudices against his pride and intolerance, while the English, conceiving the honour of their country connected with the quarrel, of which various reports had gone about, considered the natives of other countries jealous of the fame of England and her King, and disposed to undermine it by the meanest arts of intrigue. Many and various were the rumours spread upon the occasion, and there was one which averred that the Queen and her ladies had been much alarmed by the tumult, and that one of them had swooned.

The Council assembled at the appointed hour. Conrade had in the meanwhile laid aside his dishonoured dress, and with it the shame and confusion which, in spite of his talents and promptitude, had at first overwhelmed him, owing to the strangeness of the accident, and suddenness of the accusation. He was now robed like a prince, and entered the council-chamber attended by the Archduke of Austria, the Grand Masters both of the Temple and of the Order of Saint John, and several other potentates, who made a show of supporting him and defending his cause, chiefly perhaps from political motives, or because they themselves nourished a personal enmity against Richard.

This appearance of union in favour of Conrade was far from influencing the King of England. He entered the Council with his usual indifference of manner, and in the same dress in which he had just alighted from horseback. He cast a careless and somewhat scornful glance on the leaders, who had with studied affectation arranged themselves around Conrade as if owning his cause, and in the most direct terms charged Conrade of Montserrat with having stolen the Banner of England, and wounded the faithful animal who stood in its defence.

Conrade arose boldly to answer, and in despite, as he expressed himself, of man and brute, king or dog, avouched his innocence of the crime charged.

"Brother of England," said Philip, who willingly assumed the character of moderator of the assembly, "this is an unusual impeachment. We do not hear you avouch your own knowledge of this matter, farther than your belief resting upon the demeanour of this hound towards the Marquis of Montserrat. Surely the word of a knight and a prince should bear him out against the barking of a cur?"

"Royal brother," returned Richard, "recollect that the Almighty, who gave the dog to be companion of our pleasures and our toils, hath invested him with a nature noble and incapable of deceit. He forgets neither friend nor foe—

remembers, and with accuracy, both benefit and injury. He
hath a share of man's intelligence, but no share of man's falsehood. You may bribe a soldier to slay a man with his sword,
or a witness to take life by false accusation; but you cannot
make a hound tear his benefactor—he is the friend of man,
save when man justly incurs his enmity. Dress yonder Marquis in what peacock-robes you will—disguise his appearance—
alter his complexion with drugs and washes—hide him amidst
an hundred men—I will yet pawn my sceptre that the hound
detects him, and expresses his resentment, as you have this
day beheld. This is no new incident, although a strange one.
Murderers and robbers have been, ere now, convicted, and
suffered death under such evidence, and men have said that
the finger of God was in it. In thine own land, royal brother,
and upon such an occasion, the matter was tried by a solemn
duel betwixt the man and the dog, as appellant and defendant
in a challenge of murder. The dog was victorious, the man
was punished, and the crime was confessed. Credit me, royal
brother, that hidden crimes have often been brought to light
by the testimony even of inanimate substances, not to mention
animals far inferior in instinctive sagacity to the dog, who is
the friend and companion of our race."

"Such a duel there hath indeed been, royal brother," answered Philip, "and that in the reign of one of our predecessors, to whom God be gracious. But it was in the olden time,
nor can we hold it a precedent fitting for this occasion. The
defendant in that case was a private gentleman, of small rank
or respect; his offensive weapons were only a club, his defensive a leathern jerkin. But we cannot degrade a prince to the
disgrace of using such rude arms, or to the ignominy of such a
combat."

"I never meant that you should," said King Richard; "it
were foul play to hazard the good hound's life against that of
such a double-faced traitor as this Conrade hath proved himself. But there lies our own glove—we appeal him to the
combat in respect of the evidence we brought forth against
him—a king, at least, is more than the mate of a marquis."

Conrade made no hasty effort to seize on the pledge which
Richard cast into the middle of the assembly, and King Philip
had time to reply, ere the Marquis made a motion to lift the
glove.

"A king," said he of France, "is as much more than a
match for the Marquis Conrade, as a dog would be less. Roya
Richard, this cannot be permitted. You are the leader of our
expedition—the sword and buckler of Christendom."

"I protest against such a combat," said the Venetian prove-
ditore, "until the King of England shall have repaid the fifty

thousand bezants which he is indebted to the republic. It is enough to be threatened with the loss of our debt, should our debtor fall by the hands of the pagans, without the additional risk of his being slain in brawls amongst Christians, concerning dogs and banners."

"And I," said William with the Long Sword, Earl of Salisbury, "protest in my turn against my royal brother perilling his life, which is the property of the people of England, in such a cause.—Here, noble brother, receive back your glove, and think only as if the wind had blown it from your hand. Mine shall lie in its stead. A king's son, though with the bar sinister on his shield, is at least a match for this marmozet of a Marquis."

"Princes and nobles," said Conrade, "I will not accept of King Richard's defiance. He hath been chosen our leader against the Saracens, and if *his* conscience can answer the accusation of provoking an ally to the field on a quarrel so frivolous, *mine*, at least, cannot endure the reproach of accepting it. But touching his bastard brother, William of Woodstock, or against any other who shall adopt, or shall dare to stand godfather to this most false charge, I will defend my honours in the lists, and prove whosoever impeaches it a false liar."

"The Marquis of Montserrat," said the Archbishop of Tyre, "hath spoken like a wise and moderate gentleman; and methinks this controversy might, without dishonour to any party, end at this point."

"Methinks it might so terminate," said the King of France, "provided King Richard will recall his accusation, as made upon over slight grounds."

"Philip of France," answered Cœur de Lion, "my words shall never do my thoughts so much injury. I have charged yonder Conrade as a thief, who, under cloud of night, stole from its place the emblem of England's dignity. I still believe and charge him to be such; and when a day is appointed for the combat, doubt not that, since Conrade declines to meet us in person, I will find a champion to appear in support of my challenge; for thou, William, must not thrust thy long sword into this quarrel without our special licence."

"Since my rank makes me arbiter in this most unhappy matter," said Philip of France, "I appoint the fifth day from hence for the decision thereof, by way of combat, according to knightly usage—Richard, King of England, to appear by his champion as appellant, and Conrade, Marquis of Montserrat, in his own person as defendant. Yet I own, I know not where to find neutral ground where such a quarrel may be fought out; for it must not be in the neighbourhood of this camp, where the soldiers would make faction on the different sides."

"It were well," said Richard, "to apply to the generosity of the royal Saladin, since, heathen as he is, I have never known knight more fulfilled of nobleness, or to whose good faith we may so peremptorily entrust ourselves. I speak thus for those who may be doubtful of mishap—for myself, wherever I see my foe, I make that spot my battle-ground."

"Be it so," said Philip; "we will make this matter known to Saladin, although it be showing to an enemy the unhappy spirit of discord which we would willingly hide from ourselves, were it possible. Meanwhile, I dismiss this assembly, and charge you all, as Christian men and noble knights, that ye let this unhappy feud breed no farther brawling in the camp, but regard it as a thing solemnly referred to the judgment of God, to whom each of you should pray that He will dispose of victory in the combat according to the truth of the quarrel; and therewith may His will be done!"

"Amen, Amen!" was answered on all sides; while the Templar whispered the Marquis, "Conrade, wilt thou not add a petition to be delivered from the power of the dog, as the Psalmist hath it?"

"Peace, thou——!" replied the Marquis; "there is a revealing demon abroad, which may report, amongst other tidings how far thou dost carry the motto of the order—*Feriatur Leo.*"

"Thou wilt stand the brunt of challenge?" said the Templar

"Doubt me not," said Conrade. "I would not, indeed have willingly met the iron arm of Richard himself, and I shame not to confess that I rejoice to be free of his encounter But, from his bastard brother downward, the man breathes not in his ranks whom I fear to meet."

"It is well you are so confident," continued the Templar "and in that case, the fangs of yonder hound have done more to dissolve this league of princes, than either thy devices, or the dagger of the Charegite. Seest thou how, under a brow studiously overclouded, Philip cannot conceal the satisfaction which he feels at the prospect of release from the alliance which sat so heavy on him? Mark how Henry of Champagne smiles to himself, like a sparkling goblet of his own wine—and see the chuckling delight of Austria, who thinks his quarrel is about to be avenged, without risk or trouble of his own. Hush, he approaches—A most grievous chance, most royal Austria, that these breaches in the walls of our Zion——'

"If thou meanest this Crusade," replied the Duke, "I would it were crumbled to pieces, and each were safe at home!—speak this in confidence."

"But," said the Marquis of Montserrat, "to think this dis

union should be made by the hands of King Richard, for whose pleasure we have been contented to endure so much, and to whom we have been as submissive as slaves to a master, in hopes that he would use his valour against our enemies, instead of exercising it upon our friends!"

"I see not that he is so much more valorous than others," said the Archduke. "I believe, had the noble Marquis met him in the lists he would have had the better; for though the islander deals heavy blows with the pole-axe, he is not so very dexterous with the lance. I should have cared little to have met him myself on our old quarrel, had the weal of Christendom permitted to sovereign princes to breathe themselves in the lists——And if thou desirest it, noble Marquis, I will myself be your godfather in this combat."

"And I also," said the Grand Master.

"Come, then, and take your nooning in our tent, noble sirs," said the Duke, "and we'll speak of this business, over some right *nierenstein*."

They entered together accordingly.

"What said our patron and these great folks together?" said Jonas Schwanker to his companion, the *spruch-sprecher*, who had used the freedom to press nigh to his master when the counsel was dismissed, while the jester waited at a more respectful distance.

"Servant of Folly," said the *spruch-sprecher*, "moderate thy curiosity—it beseems not that I should tell to thee the counsels of our master."

"Man of Wisdom, you mistake," answered Jonas; "we are both the constant attendants on our patron, and it concerns us alike to know whether thou or I—Wisdom or Folly, have the deeper interest in him."

"He told to the Marquis," answered the *spruch-sprecher*, "and to the Grand Master, that he was aweary of these wars, and would be glad he was safe at home."

"That is a drawn cast, and counts for nothing in the game," said the jester; "it was most wise to think thus, but great folly to tell it to others—proceed."

"Ha, hem!" said the *spruch-sprecher*; "he next said to them, that Richard was not more valorous than others, or over dexterous in the tilt-yard."

"Woodcock of my side," said Schwanker; "this was egregious folly. What next?"

"Nay, I am something oblivious," replied the man of wisdom, "he invited them to a goblet of *nierenstein*."

"That hath a show of wisdom in it," said Jonas, "thou may'st mark it to thy credit in the meantime; but an he drink too much, as is most likely, I will have it pass to mine. Anything more?"

"Nothing worth memory," answered the orator, "only he wished he had taken the occasion to meet Richard in the lists."

"Out upon it—out upon it!" said Jonas—"this is such dotage of folly, that I am well-nigh ashamed of winning the game by it—Ne'ertheless, fool as he is, we will follow him, most sage *spruch-sprecher*, and have our share of the wine of *nierenstein*."

CHAPTER XXV

> Yet this inconsistency is such,
> As thou, too, shalt adore ;
> I could not love thee, love, so much,
> Loved I not honour more.
> —MONTROSE'S LINES.

WHEN King Richard returned to his tent, he commanded the Nubian to be brought before him. He entered with his usual ceremonial reverence, and having prostrated himself, remained standing before the King, in the attitude of a slave awaiting the orders of his master. It was perhaps well for him, that the preservation of his character required his eyes to be fixed on the ground, since the keen glance with which Richard for some time surveyed him in silence, would, if fully encountered, have been difficult to sustain.

"Thou canst well of woodcraft," said the King, after a pause "and hast started thy game and brought him to bay, as abl as if Tristrem himself had taught thee.* But this is not all— he must be brought down at force, I myself would have liked to have levelled my hunting-spear at him. There are, it seems respects which prevent this. Thou art about to return to th camp of the Soldan, bearing a letter, requiring of his courtes to appoint neutral ground for the deed of chivalry, and, shoul it consist with his pleasure, to concur with us in witnessing i Now, speaking conjecturally, we think thou might'st find in tha camp some cavalier, who, for the love of truth, and his ow augmentation of honour, will do battle with this same traito of Montserrat."

The Nubian raised his eyes and fixed them on the King wit a look of eager ardour ; then raised them to Heaven with suc solemn gratitude, that the water soon glistened in them—the

---

* A universal tradition, ascribed to Sir Tristrem, famous for his love the fair Queen Yseult—the laws concerning the practice of woodcraft, *venerie*, as it was called, being those that related to the rules of the chas were deemed of much consequence during the middle ages.

bent his head, as affirming what Richard desired, and resumed his usual posture of submissive attention.

"It is well," said the King; "and I see thy desire to oblige me in this matter. And herein, I must needs say, lies the excellence of such a servant as thou, who hast not speech either to debate our purpose, or to require explanation of what we have determined. An English serving-man, in thy place, had given me his dogged advice to trust the combat with some good lance of my household, who, from my brother Long-Sword downwards, are all on fire to do battle in my cause; and a chattering Frenchman had made a thousand attempts to discover wherefore I look for a champion from the camp of the infidels. But thou, my silent agent, canst do mine errand without questioning or comprehending it; with thee, to hear is to obey."

A bend of the body, and a genuflection, were the appropriate answer of the Ethiopian to these observations.

"And now to another point," said the King, and speaking suddenly and rapidly.—"Have you yet seen Edith Plantagenet?"

The mute looked up as in the act of being about to speak,—nay, his lips had begun to utter a distinct negative,—when the abortive attempt died away in the imperfect murmurs of the dumb.

"Why, lo you there!" said the King. "The very sound of the name of a royal maiden, of beauty so surpassing as that of our lovely cousin, seems to have power enough well-nigh to make the dumb speak. What miracles then might her eye work upon such a subject! I will make the experiment, friend slave. Thou shalt see this choice beauty of our court, and do the errand of the princely Soldan."

Again a joyful glance—again a genuflection—but, as he rose, the King laid his hand heavily on his shoulder, and proceeded with stern gravity thus.—"Let me in one thing warn you, my sable envoy. Even if thou shouldst feel that the kindly influence of her, whom thou art soon to behold, should loosen the bonds of thy tongue, presently imprisoned, as the good Soldan expresses it, within the ivory walls of its castle, beware how thou changest thy taciturn character, or speakest a word in her presence, even if thy powers of utterance were to be miraculously restored. Believe me, that I should have thy tongue extracted by the roots, and its ivory palace, that is, I presume, its range of teeth, drawn out one by one. Wherefore be wise and silent still."

The Nubian, so soon as the King had removed his heavy grasp from his shoulder, bent his head, and laid his hand on his lips, in token of silent obedience.

But Richard again laid his hand on him more gently, and added, "This behest we lay on thee as on a slave. Wert thou knight and gentleman, we would require thine honour in pledge of thy silence, which is one especial condition of our present trust."

The Ethiopian raised his body proudly, looked full at the King, and laid his right hand on his heart.

Richard then summoned his chamberlain.

"Go, Neville," he said, "with this slave, to the tent of our royal consort, and say it is our pleasure that he have an audience—a private audience—of our cousin Edith. He is charged with a commission to her. Thou canst show him the way also, in case he requires thy guidance, though thou may'st have observed it is wonderful how familiar he already seems to be with the purlieus of our camp.—And thou, too, friend Ethiop," the King continued, "what thou dost, do quickly, and return hither within the half-hour."

"I stand discovered," thought the seeming Nubian, as, with downcast looks and folded arms, he followed the hasty stride of Neville towards the tent of Queen Berengaria.—"I stand undoubtedly discovered and unfolded to King Richard; yet I cannot perceive that his resentment is hot against me. If I understood his words, and surely it is impossible to misinterpret them, he gives me a noble chance of redeeming my honour upon the crest of this false Marquis, whose guilt I read in his craven eye and quivering lip, when the charge was made against him.—Roswal, faithfully hast thou served thy master, and most dearly shall thy wrong be avenged!—But what is the meaning of my present permission to look upon her, whom I had despaired ever to see again?—And why, or how, can the royal Plantagenet consent that I should see his divine kinswoman either as the messenger of the heathen Saladin, or as the guilty exile whom he so lately expelled from his camp—his audacious avowal of the affection which is his pride, being the greatest enhancement of his guilt? That Richard should consent to her receiving a letter from an infidel lover, by the hands of one of such disproportioned rank, are either of them circumstances equally incredible, and, at the same time, inconsistent with each other. But Richard, when unmoved by his heady passions, is liberal, generous, and truly noble, and as such, I will deal with him, and act according to his instructions, direct or implied, seeking to know no more than may gradually unfold itself without my officious inquiry. To him who has given me so brave an opportunity to vindicate my tarnished honour, I owe acquiescence and obedience, and, painful as it may be, the debt shall be paid. And yet," thus the proud swelling of his heart farther suggested,—"Cœur de Lion, as he is called, might have measured the feelings of others by his own. *I* urge an address to his kinswoman! *I*, who never spoke word to her when I took a royal prize from her hand—when I was accounted not the lowest in feats of chivalry among the defenders of the Cross! *I* approach her when in a base disguise, and in a servile habit—and, alas! when my actual condition is that of a slave, with a spot of dishonour on that which was once my shield! *I* do this! He little knows me. Yet I thank him for the opportunity which may make us all better acquainted with each other."

As he arrived at this conclusion, they paused before the entrance of the Queen's pavilion.

They were of course admitted by the guards, and Neville, leaving the Nubian in a small apartment, or antechamber, which was but too well remembered by him, passed into that which was used as the Queen's presence-chamber. He communicated his royal master's pleasure in a low and respectful tone of voice, very different from the bluntness of Thomas de Vaux, to whom Richard was everything, and the rest of the court, including Berengaria herself, was nothing. A burst of laughter followed the communication of his errand.

"And what like is the Nubian slave, who comes ambassador on such an errand from the Soldan?—a Negro, De Neville, is he not?" said a female voice easily recognised for that of Berengaria. "A Negro, is he not, De Neville, with black skin, a head curled like a ram's, a flat nose, and blubber lips—ha, worthy Sir Henry?"

"Let not your Grace forget the shin-bones," said another voice, "bent outwards like the edge of a Saracen scimitar."

"Rather like the bow of a Cupid, since he comes upon a lover's errand," said the Queen. "Gentle Neville, thou art ever prompt to pleasure us poor women, who have so little to pass away our idle moments. We must see this messenger of love. Turks and Moors have I seen many, but Negro never."

"I am created to obey your Grace's commands, so you will bear me out with my sovereign for doing so," answered the debonair knight. "Yet, let me assure your Grace, you will see somewhat different from what you expect."

"So much the better—uglier yet than our imaginations can fancy, yet the chosen love-messenger of this gallant Soldan!"

"Gracious madam," said the Lady Calista, "may I implore you would permit the good knight to carry this messenger straight to the Lady Edith, to whom his credentials are addressed? We have already escaped hardly for such a frolic."

"Escaped?"—repeated the Queen scornfully. "Yet thou mayst be right, Calista, in thy caution—let this Nubian, as thou callest him, first do his errand to our cousin—Besides, he is mute too—is he not?"

" He is, gracious madam," answered the knight.

"Royal sport have these Eastern ladies," said Berengaria, "attended by those before whom they may say anything, yet who can report nothing. Whereas, in our camp, as the Prelate of St. Jude's is wont to say, a bird of the air will carry the matter."

"Because," said De Neville, "your Grace forgets· that you speak within canvas walls."

The voices sunk on this observation, and after a little whispering, the English knight again returned to the Ethiopian, and made him a sign to follow. He did so, and Neville conducted him to a pavilion, pitched somewhat apart from that of the Queen, for the accommodation, it seemed, of the Lady Edith and her attendants. One of her Coptic maidens received the message communicated by Sir Henry Neville, and, in the space of a very few minutes, the Nubian was ushered into Edith's presence, while Neville was left on the outside of the tent. The slave who introduced him withdrew on a signal from her mistress, and it was with humiliation, not of the posture only but of the very inmost soul, that the unfortunate knight, thus strangely disguised, threw himself on one knee, with looks bent on the ground, and arms folded on his bosom, like a criminal who expects his doom. Edith was clad in the same manner as when she received King Richard, her long transparent dark veil hanging around her like the shade of a summer night on a beautiful landscape, disguising and rendering obscure the beauties which it could not hide. She held in her hand a silver lamp, fed with some aromatic spirit, which burned with unusual brightness.

When Edith came within a step of the kneeling and motionless slave, she held the light towards his face, as if to peruse his features more attentively, then turned from him, and placed her lamp so as to throw the shadow of his face in profile upon the curtain which hung beside. She at length spoke in a voice composed, yet deeply sorrowful.

"Is it you?—Is it indeed you, brave Knight of the Leopard—gallant Sir Kenneth of Scotland—is it indeed you?—thus servilely disguised—thus surrounded by an hundred dangers?"

At hearing the tones of his lady's voice thus unexpectedly addressed to him, and in a tone of compassion approaching to tenderness, a corresponding reply rushed to the knight's lips, and scarce could Richard's commands and his own promised silence, prevent his answering, that the sight he saw, the sounds he just heard, were sufficient to recompense the slavery of a life, and dangers which threatened that life every hour. He *did* recollect himself, however, and a deep and impassioned sigh was his only reply to the high-born Edith's question.

"I see—I know I have guessed right," continued Edith. "I marked you from your first appearance near the platform on which I stood with the Queen. I knew, too, your valiant hound. She is no true lady, and is unworthy of the service of such a knight as thou art, from whom disguises of dress or hue could conceal a faithful servant. Speak, then, without fear to Edith Plantagenet. She knows how to grace in adversity the good knight who served, honoured, and did deeds of arms in her name, when fortune befriended him.—Still silent! Is it fear or shame that keeps thee so? Fear should be unknown to thee; and for shame, let it remain with those who have wronged thee."

The knight, in despair at being obliged to pay the mute in an interview so interesting, could only express his mortification by sighing deeply, and laying his finger upon his lips. Edith stepped back, as if somewhat displeased.

"What!" she said, "the Asiatic mute in very deed, as well as in attire? This I looked not for—Or thou mayst scorn me, perhaps, for thus boldly acknowledging that I have heedfully observed the homage thou hast paid me? Hold no unworthy thoughts of Edith on that account. She knows well the bounds which reserve and modesty prescribe to high-born maidens. and she knows when and how far they should give place to gratitude—to a sincere desire that it were in her power to repay services and repair injuries, arising from the devotion which a good knight bore towards her.—Why fold thy hands together, and wring them with so much passion?—Can it be," she added, shrinking back at the idea—"that their cruelty has actually deprived thee of speech? Thou shakest thy head. Be it a spell—be it obstinacy, I question thee no farther, but leave thee to do thine errand after thine own fashion. I also can be mute."

The disguised knight made an action as if at once lamenting his own condition, and deprecating her displeasure, while at the same time he presented to her, wrapped, as usual, in fine silk and cloth of gold, the letter of the Soldan. She took it, surveyed it carelessly, then laid it aside, and bending her eyes once more on the knight, she said in a low tone—"Not even a word to do thine errand to me?"

He pressed both his hands to his brow, as if to intimate the pain which he felt at being unable to obey her; but she turned from him in anger.

"Begone!" she said. "I have spoken enough—too much— to one who will not waste on me a word in reply. Begone!— and say if I have wronged thee, I have done penance; for if I have been the unhappy means of dragging thee down from a station of honour, I have, in this interview, forgotten my own worth, and lowered myself in thy eyes and in my own."

She covered her eyes with her hand, and seemed deeply agitated. Sir Kenneth would have approached, but she waved him back.

' Stand off! thou whose soul Heaven hath suited to its new station! Aught less dull and fearful than a slavish mute had spoken a word of gratitude, were it but to reconcile me to my own degradation. Why pause you?—begone!"

The disguised knight almost involuntarily looked towards the letter as an apology for protracting his stay. She snatched it up, saying in a tone of irony and contempt, "I had forgotten —the dutiful slave waits an answer to his message.—How's this—from the Soldan!"

She hastily ran over the contents, which were expressed both in Arabic and French, and when she had done, she laughed in bitter anger.

"Now this passes imagination!" she said; "no jongleur can show so deft a transmutation! His legerdemain can transform zechins and bezants into doits and maravedies; but can his art convert a Christian knight, ever esteemed among the bravest of the Holy Crusade, into the dust-kissing slave of a heathen Soldan — the bearer of a Paynim's insolent proposals to a Christian maiden — nay, forgetting the laws of honourable chivalry, as well as of religion? But it avails not talking to the willing slave of a heathen hound. Tell your master, when his scourge shall have found thee a tongue, that which thou hast seen me do."—So saying, she threw the Soldan's letter on the ground, and placed her foot upon it—"And say to him, that Edith Plantagenet scorns the homage of an unchristened Pagan."

With these words she was about to shoot from the knight, when, kneeling at her feet in bitter agony, he ventured to lay his hand upon her robe, and oppose her departure.

"Heardst thou not what I said, dull slave?" she said, turning short round on him, and speaking with emphasis; "tell the heathen Soldan, thy master, that I scorn his suit as much as I despise the prostration of a worthless renegade to religion and chivalry—to God and to his lady!"

So saying, she burst from him, tore her garment from his grasp, and left the tent.

The voice of Neville, at the same time, summoned him from without. Exhausted and stupefied by the distress he had undergone during this interview from which he could only have extricated himself by breach of the engagement which he had formed with King Richard, the unfortunate knight staggered rather than walked after the English baron, till they reached the royal pavilion, before which a party of horsemen had just dismounted. There was light and motion within the tent, and when Neville entered with his disguised attendant, they found the king, with several of his nobility, engaged in welcoming those who were newly arrived.

CHAPTER XXVI

" The tears I shed must ever fall!
    I weep not for an absent swain,
For time may happier hours recall,
    And parted lovers meet again.

I weep not for the silent dead,
    Their pains are past, their sorrows o'er,
And those that loved their steps must tread,
    When death shall join to part no more."

But worse than absence, worse than death,
    She wept her lover's sullied fame,
And, fired with all the pride of birth,
    She wept a soldier's injured name. '
                     —BALLAD.

THE frank and bold voice of Richard was heard in joyous gratulation.

"Thomas de Vaux! stout Tom of the Gills! by the head of King Henry, thou art welcome to me as ever was flask of wine to a jolly toper! I should scarce have known how to order my battle array, unless I had thy bulky form in my eye as a landmark to form my ranks upon. We shall have blows anon, Thomas, if the saints be gracious to us; and had we fought in thine absence, I would have looked to hear of thy being found hanging upon an elder tree."

"I should have borne my disappointment with more Christian patience, I trust," said Thomas de Vaux, "than to have died the death of an apostate. But I thank your Grace for my welcome, which is the more generous, as it respects a banquet of blows, of which, saving your pleasure, you are ever too apt to engross the larger share; but here have I brought one, to whom your Grace will, I know, give a yet warmer welcome."

The person who now stepped forward to make obeisance to Richard, was a young man of low stature and slight form. His dress was as modest as his figure was unimpressive, but he bore on his bonnet a gold buckle, with a gem, the lustre of which could only be rivalled by the brilliancy of the eye which the bonnet shaded. It was the only striking feature in his countenance; but when once noticed, it uniformly made a strong impression on the spectator. About his neck there hung in a scarf of sky-blue silk a *wrest,* as it was called,— that is, the key with which a harp is tuned, and which was of solid gold.

This personage would have kneeled reverently to Richard, but the monarch raised him in joyful haste, pressed him to his bosom warmly, and kissed him on either side of the face.

"Blondel de Nesle!" he exclaimed joyfully—"welcome from Cyprus, my king of minstrels!—welcome to the King of England, who rates not his own dignity more highly than he does thine. I have been sick, man, and, by my soul, I believe it was for lack of thee; for, were I halfway to the gate of Heaven, methinks thy strains could call me back.—And what news, my gentle master, from the land of the lyre? Anything fresh from the *trouveurs* of Provence?—anything from the minstrels of merry Normandy!—above all, hast thou thyself been busy?— But I need not ask thee—thou canst not be idle, if thou wouldst —thy noble qualities are like a fire burning within, and compel thee to pour thyself out in music and song."

"Something I have learned, and something I have done, noble King," answered the celebrated Blondel, with a retiring modesty, which all Richard's enthusiastic admiration of his skill had been unable to banish.

"We will hear thee, man—we will hear thee instantly," said the King;—then touching Blondel's shoulder kindly, he added, "that is, if thou art not fatigued with thy journey; for I would sooner ride my best horse to death than injure a note of thy voice."

"My voice is, as ever, at the service of my royal patron," said Blondel; "but your Majesty," he added, looking at some papers on the table, "seems more importantly engaged, and the hour waxes late."

"Not a whit, man, not a whit, my dearest Blondel. I did but sketch an array of battle against the Saracens, a thing of a moment—almost as soon done as the routing of them."

"Methinks, however," said Thomas de Vaux, "it were not unfit to inquire what soldiers your Grace hath to array. I bring reports on that subject from Ascalon."

"Thou art a mule, Thomas," said the King—"a very mule for dulness and obstinacy!—Come, nobles—a hall—a hall!— range ye around him—Give Blondel the tabouret—Where is his harp-bearer?—or, soft—lend him my harp, his own may be damaged by the journey."

"I would your Grace would take my report," said Thomas de Vaux. "I have ridden far, and have more list to my bed than to have my ears tickled."

"*Thy* ears tickled!" said the King; "that must be with a woodcock's feather, and not with sweet sounds. Hark thee, Thomas, do thine ears know the singing of Blondel from the braying of an ass?"

"In faith, my liege," replied Thomas, "I cannot well say; but setting Blondel out of the question, who is a born gentleman, and doubtless of high acquirements, I shall never, for the sake of your Grace's question, look on a minstrel, but I shall think upon an ass."

"And might not your manners," said Richard, "have excepted me, who am a gentleman born as well as Blondel, and, like him, a guild-brother of the Joyeuse science?"

"Your Grace should remember," said De Vaux, smiling, "that 'tis useless asking for manners from a mule."

"Most truly spoken," said the King; "and an ill-conditioned animal thou art—But come hither, master mule, and be unloaded that thou may'st get thee to thy litter, without any music being wasted on thee.—Meantime, do thou, good brother of Salisbury, go to our consort's tent, and tell her that Blondel has arrived, with his budget fraught with the newest minstrelsy—Bid her come hither instantly, and do thou escort her, and see that our cousin, Edith Plantagenet, remain not behind."

His eye then rested for a moment on the Nubian, with that expression of doubtful meaning, which his countenance usually displayed when he looked at him.

"Has our silent and secret messenger returned?—Stand up, slave, behind the back of De Neville, and thou shalt hear presently sounds which will make thee bless God that He afflicted thee rather with dumbness than deafness."

So saying, he turned from the rest of the company towards De Vaux, and plunged immediately into the military details which that baron laid before him.

About the time that the Lord of Gilsland had finished his audience, a messenger announced that the Queen and her attendants were approaching the royal tent.—"A flask of wine, ho!" said the King; "of old King Isaac's long-saved Cyprus, which we won when we stormed Famagosta—fill to the stout Lord of Gilsland, gentles—a more careful and faithful servant never had any prince."

"I am glad," said Thomas de Vaux, "that your Grace finds the mule a useful slave, though his voice be less musical than horse-hair or wire."

"What, thou canst not yet digest that quip of the mule?" said Richard. "Wash it down with a brimming flagon, man, or thou wilt choke upon it.—Why, so—well pulled!—and now I will tell thee, thou art a soldier as well as I, and we must brook each other's jests in the hall, as each other's blows in the tourney, and love each other the harder we hit. By my faith, if thou didst not hit me as hard as I did thee in our late encounter, thou givest all thy wit to the thrust. But here lies the difference betwixt thee and Blondel. Thou art but my comrade—I might say my pupil—in the art of war; Blondel is my master in the science of minstrelsy and music. To thee I permit the freedom of intimacy—to him I must do reverence, as to my superior in his art. Come, man, be not peevish, but remain and hear our glee."

"To see your Majesty in such cheerful mood," said the Lord of Gilsland, "by my faith, I could remain till Blondel had achieved the great Romance of King Arthur, which lasts for three days."

"We will not tax your patience so deeply," said the King. "But see yonder glare of torches without shows that our consort approaches—Away to receive her, man, and win thyself grace in the brightest eyes of Christendom.—Nay, never stop to adjust thy cloak. See, thou hast let Neville come between the wind and the sails of thy galley.

"He was never before me in the field of battle," said De Vaux, not greatly pleased to see himself anticipated by the more active service of the chamberlain.

"No, neither he nor any one went before thee there, my good Tom of the Gills," said the King, "unless it was ourself now and then."

"Ay, my liege," said De Vaux, "and let us do justice to the unfortunate;—the unhappy Knight of the Leopard hath been before me too, at a season; for, look you, he weighs less on horseback, and so——"

"Hush!" said the King, interrupting him in a peremptory tone—"not a word of him,"—and instantly stepped forward to greet his royal consort; and when he had done so, he presented to her Blondel, as king of minstrelsy, and his master in the gay science. Berengaria, who well knew that her royal husband's passion for poetry and music almost equalled his appetite for warlike fame, and that Blondel was his special favourite, took anxious care to receive him with all the flattering distinctions due to one whom the King delighted to honour. Yet it was evident that, though Blondel made suitable returns to the compliments showered on him something too abundantly by the royal beauty, he owned with deeper reverence and more humble gratitude the simple and graceful welcome of Edith, whose kindly greeting appeared to him, perhaps, sincere in proportion to its brevity and simplicity.

Both the Queen and her royal husband were aware of this distinction, and Richard, seeing his consort somewhat piqued at the preference assigned to his cousin, by which perhaps he himself did not feel much gratified, said in the hearing of both, —"We minstrels, Berengaria, as thou may'st see by the bearing of our master Blondel, pay more reverence to a severe judge, like our kinswoman, than to a kindly partial friend, like thyself, who is willing to take our worth upon trust."

Edith was moved by this sarcasm of her royal kinsman, and hesitated not to reply, that, "to be a harsh and severe judge, was not an attribute proper to her alone of all the Plantagenets."

She had perhaps said more, having some touch of the temper of that house, which, deriving their name and cognisance from the lowly broom (*Planta Genista*), assumed as an emblem of humility, were perhaps one of the proudest families that ever ruled in England; but her eye, when kindling in her reply, suddenly caught those of the Nubian, although he endeavoured to conceal himself behind the nobles who were present, and she sunk upon a seat, turning so pale, that the Queen Berengaria deemed herself obliged to call for water and essences, and to go through the other ceremonies appropriate to a lady's swoon. Richard, who better estimated Edith's strength of mind, called to Blondel to assume his seat and commence his lay, declaring that minstrelsy was worth every other recipe to recall a Plantagenet to life.—"Sing us," he said, "that song of the Bloody Vest, of which thou didst formerly give me the argument, ere I left Cyprus; thou must be perfect in it by this time, or, as our yeomen say, thy bow is broken."

The anxious eye of the minstrel, however, dwelt on Edith, and it was not till he observed her returning colour that he obeyed the repeated commands of the King. Then, accompanying his voice with the harp, so as to grace, but yet not drown, the sense of what he sung, he chanted in a sort of recitative, one of those ancient adventures of love and knighthood, which were wont of yore to win the public attention. So soon as he began to prelude, the insignificance of his personal appearance seemed to disappear, and his countenance glowed with energy and inspiration. His full, manly, mellow voice, so absolutely under command of the purest taste, thrilled on every ear, and to every heart. Richard, rejoiced as after victory, called out the appropriate summons for silence,

"Listen, lords, in bower and hall;"

while with the zeal of a patron at once and a pupil, he arranged the circle around, and hushed them into silence; and he himself sat down with an air of expectation and interest, not altogether unmixed with the gravity of the professed critic. The courtiers turned their eyes on the King, that they might be ready to trace and imitate the emotions his features should express, and Thomas de Vaux yawned tremendously, as one who submitted unwillingly to a wearisome penance. The song of Blondel was of course in the Norman language; but the verses which follow express its meaning and its manner :—

THE BLOODY VEST.

'Twas near the fair city of Benevent,
When the sun was setting on bough and bent,
And knights were preparing in bower and tent,
On the eve of the Baptist's tournament ;
When in Lincoln green a stripling gent,
Well seeming a page by a princess sent,
Wander'd the camp, and, still as he went,
Inquired for the Englishman, Thomas à Kent.

Far hath he fared, and farther must fare,
Till he finds his pavilion nor stately nor rare,—
Little save iron and steel was there :
And, as lacking the coin to pay armourer's care,
With his sinewy arms to the shoulders bare,
The good knight with hammer and file did repair
The mail that to-morrow must see him wear,
For the honour of Saint John and his lady fair.

" Thus speaks my lady," the page said he,
And the knight bent lowly both head and knee,
" She is Benevent's Princess so high in degree,
And thou art as lowly as knight may well be—
He that would climb so lofty a tree,
Or spring such a gulf as divides her from thee,
Must dare some high deed, by which all men may see
His ambition is back'd by his hie chivalrie.

"Therefore thus speaks my lady," the fair page he said,
And the knight lowly louted with hand and with head,
" Fling aside the good armour in which thou art clad,
And don thou this weed of her night-gear instead,
For a hauberk of steel, a kirtle of thread :
And charge thus attired, in the tournament dread,
And fight as thy wont is where most blood is shed,
And bring honour away, or remain with the dead."

Untroubled in his look, and untroubled in his breast,
The knight the weed hath taken, and reverently hath kiss'd :
'Now blessed be the moment, the messenger be blest !
Much honour'd do I hold me in my lady's high behest ;
And say unto my lady, in this dear night-weed dress'd.
To the best armed champion I will not veil my crest ;
But if I live and bear me well 'tis her turn to take the test."
Here, gentles, ends the foremost fytte of the Lay of the Bloody Vest.

THE TALISMAN

Blondel resumed the lay; but, as extemporaneous composition was familiar to him, he failed not to comply with the King's hints, and was perhaps not displeased to show with how much ease he could new-model a poem, even while in the act of recitation.

THE BLOODY VEST.

FYTTE SECOND.

The Baptist's fair morrow beheld gallant feats—
There was winning of honour, and losing of seats—
There was hewing with falchions, and splintering of staves,
The victors won glory, the vanquish'd won graves.
Oh, many a knight there fought bravely and well,
Yet one was accounted his peers to excel,
And 'twas he whose sole armour on body and breast,
Seem'd the weed of a damsel when bound for her rest.

There were some dealt him wounds, that were bloody and sore,
But others respected his plight, and forebore.
"It is some oath of honour," they said, "and I trow,
'Twere unknightly to slay him achieving his vow."
Then the Prince, for his sake, bade the tournament cease,
He flung down his warder, the trumpets sung peace ;
And the judges declare, and competitors yield,
That the Knight of the Night-gear was first in the field.

The feast it was nigh, and the mass it was nigher,
When before the fair Princess low louted a squire,
And deliver'd a garment unseemly to view,
With sword-cut and spear-thrust, all hack'd and pierced through :
All rent and all tatter'd, all clotted with blood,
With foam of the horses, with dust, and with mud,
Not the point of that lady's small finger, I ween,
Could have rested on spot was unsullied and clean.

"This token my master, Sir Thomas à Kent,
Restores to the Princess of fair Benevent :
He that climbs the tall tree has won right to the fruit,
He that leaps the wide gulf should prevail in his suit ;
Through life's utmost peril the prize I have won,
And now must the faith of my mistress be shown ;
For she who prompts knights on such danger to run,
Must avouch his true service in front of the sun.

"I restore," says my master, "the garment I've worn,
And I claim of the Princess to don it in turn ;
For its stains and its rents she should prize it the more,
Since by shame 'tis unsullied, though crimson'd with gore."
Then deep blush'd the Princess—yet kiss'd she and press'd
The blood-spotted robes to her lips and her breast.
"Go tell my true knight, church and chamber shall show,
If I value the blood on this garment or no."

THE DEAD SEA

FROM THE PAINTING BY D. ROBERTS, R.A.

And when it was time for the nobles to pass,
In solemn procession to minster and mass,
The first walk'd the Princess in purple and pall,
But the blood-besmear'd night-robe she wore over all ;
And eke, in the hall, where they all sat at dine,
When she knelt to her father and proffer'd the wine,
Over all her rich robes and state jewels she wore
That wimple unseemly bedabbled with gore.

Then lords whisper'd ladies, as well you may think,
And ladies replied, with nod, titter, and wink ;
And the Prince, who in anger and shame had look'd down,
Turn'd at length to his daughter, and spoke with a frown :
"Now since thou hast publish'd thy folly and guilt,
E'en atone with thy hand for the blood thou hast spilt ;
Yet sore for your boldness you both will repent,
When you wander as exiles from fair Benevent."

Then out spoke stout Thomas, in hall where he stood,
Exhausted and feeble, but dauntless of mood :
"The blood that I lost for this daughter of thine,
I pour'd forth as freely as flask gives its wine ;
And if for my sake she brooks penance and blame,
Do not doubt I will save her from suffering and shame ;
And light will she reck of thy princedom and rent,
When I hail her, in England, the Countess of Kent."

A murmur of applause ran through the assembly, following
the example of Richard himself, who loaded with praises his
favourite minstrel, and ended by presenting him with a ring of
considerable value. The Queen hastened to distinguish the
favourite by a rich bracelet, and many of the nobles who were
present followed the royal example.

"Is our cousin Edith," said the King, "become insensible to
the sound of the harp she once loved ?"

"She thanks Blondel for his lay," replied Edith, "but doubly
the kindness of the kinsman who suggested it."

"Thou art angry, cousin," said the King; "angry because
thou hast heard of a woman more wayward than thyself. But
you escape me not—I will walk a space homeward with you
towards the Queen's pavilion—we must have conference together
ere the night has waned into morning."

The Queen and her attendants were now on foot, and the
other guests withdrew from the royal tent. A train with
blazing torches, and an escort of archers, awaited Berengaria
without the pavilion, and she was soon on her way homeward.
Richard, as he had proposed, walked beside his kinswoman,
and compelled her to accept of his arm as her support, so that
they could speak to each other without being overheard.

Q

"What answer, then, am I to return to the noble Soldan?" said Richard. "The Kings and Princes are falling from me, Edith—this new quarrel hath alienated them once more. I would do something for the Holy Sepulchre by composition, if not by victory; and the chance of my doing this depends, alas! on the caprice of a woman. I would lay my single spear in the rest against ten of the best lances in Christendom, rather than argue with a wilful wench, who knows not what is for her own good.—What answer, coz, am I to return to the Soldan? It must be decisive."

"Tell him," said Edith, "that the poorest of the Plantagenets will rather wed with misery than with misbelief."

"Shall I say with *slavery*, Edith?" said the King—"Methinks that is nearer thy thoughts."

"There is no room," said Edith, "for the suspicion you so grossly insinuate. Slavery of the body might have been pitied, but that of the soul is only to be despised. Shame to thee, King of merry England. Thou hast enthralled both the limbs and the spirit of a knight, one scarce less famed than thyself."

"Should I not prevent my kinswoman from drinking poison, by sullying the vessel which contained it, if I saw no other means of disgusting her with the fatal liquor?" replied the King.

"It is thyself," answered Edith, "that would press me to drink poison, because it is proffered in a golden chalice."

"Edith," said Richard, "I cannot force thy resolution; but beware you shut not the door which Heaven opens. The hermit of Engaddi, he whom Popes and Councils have regarded as a prophet, hath read in the stars that thy marriage shall reconcile me with a powerful enemy, and that thy husband shall be Christian, leaving thus the fairest ground to hope, that the conversion of the Soldan, and the bringing in of the sons of Ishmael to the pale of the Church, will be the consequence of thy wedding with Saladin. Come, thou must make some sacrifice rather than mar such happy prospects."

"Men may sacrifice rams and goats," said Edith, "but not honour and conscience. I have heard that it was the dishonour of a Christian maiden, which brought the Saracens into Spain —the shame of another is no likely mode of expelling them from Palestine."

"Dost thou call it shame to become an Empress?" said the King.

"I call it shame and dishonour to profane a Christian sacrament, by entering into it with an infidel whom it cannot bind; and I call it foul dishonour, that I, the descendant of a Christian princess, should become of free will the head of a harem of heathen concubines."

"Well, kinswoman," said the King, after a pause, "I must not quarrel with thee, though I think thy dependent condition might have dictated more compliance."

"My liege," replied Edith, "your Grace hath worthily succeeded to all the wealth, dignity, and dominion of the House of Plantaganet,—do not, therefore, begrudge your poor kinswoman some small share of their pride."

"By my faith, wench," said the King, "thou hast unhorsed me with that very word; so we will kiss and be friends. I will presently despatch thy answer to Saladin. But after all, coz, were it not better to suspend your answer till you have seen him? Men say he is pre-eminently handsome."

"There is no chance of our meeting, my lord," said Edith.

"By Saint George, but there is next to a certainty of it," said the King; "for Saladin will doubtless afford us a free field for the doing of this new battle of the Standard, and will witness it himself. Berengaria is wild to behold it also, and I dare be sworn not a feather of you, her companions and attendants, will remain behind—least of all thou thyself, fair coz. But come, we have reached the pavilion, and must part—not in unkindness, though—nay, thou must seal it with thy lip as well as thy hand, sweet Edith—it is my right as a sovereign to kiss my pretty vassals."

He embraced her respectfully and affectionately, and returned through the moonlight camp, humming to himself such snatches of Blondel's lay as he could recollect.

On his arrival he lost no time in making up his despatches for Saladin, and delivered them to the Nubian, with a charge to set out by peep of day on his return to the Soldan.

CHAPTER XXVII

We heard the Tecbir,—so these Arabs call
Their shout of onset, when, with loud acclaim,
They challenge Heaven to give them victory.
—SIEGE OF DAMASCUS.

ON the subsequent morning, Richard was invited to a conference by Philip of France, in which the latter, with many expressions of high esteem for his brother of England, communicated to him, in terms extremely courteous, but too explicit to be misunderstood, his positive intention to return to Europe, and to the cares of his kingdom, as entirely despairing of future success in their undertaking, with their diminished forces and civil discords. Richard remonstrated, but in vain; and when the conference ended, he received without surprise a manifesto from the Duke of Austria, and several other princes, announcing a resolution similar to that of Philip, and in no modified terms, assigning, for their defection from the cause of the Cross, the inordinate ambition and arbitrary domination of Richard of England. All hopes of continuing the war with any prospect of ultimate success were now abandoned, and Richard, while he shed bitter tears over his disappointed hopes of glory, was little consoled by the recollection, that the failure was in some degree to be imputed to the advantages which he had given his enemies by his own hasty and imprudent temper.

"They had not dared to have deserted my father thus," he said to De Vaux, in the bitterness of his resentment.—"No slanders they could have uttered against so wise a king would have been believed in Christendom; whereas,—fool that I am! —I have not only afforded them a pretext for deserting me, but even a colour for casting all the blame of the rupture upon my unhappy foibles."

These thoughts were so deeply galling to the King, that De Vaux was rejoiced when the arrival of an ambassador from Saladin turned his reflections into a different channel.

This new envoy was an Emir much respected by the Soldan, whose name was Abdallah el Hadgi. He derived his descent from the family of the Prophet, and the race or tribe of Hashem, in witness of which genealogy he wore a green turban of large dimensions. He had also three times performed the journey to Mecca, from which he derived his epithet of El Hadgi, or the Pilgrim. Notwithstanding these various pretensions to sanctity, Abdallah was (for an Arab) a boon companion, who enjoyed a merry tale, and laid aside his gravity so far as to quaff a blithe flagon, when secrecy ensured him against scandal. He was likewise a statesman, whose abilities had been used by Saladin in various negotiations with the Christian princes, and particularly with Richard, to whom El Hadgi was personally known and acceptable. Animated by the cheerful acquiescence with which the envoy of Saladin afforded a fair field for the combat, a safe conduct for all who might choose to witness it, and offered his own person as a guarantee of his fidelity, Richard soon forgot his disappointed hopes, and the approaching dissolution of the Christian league, in the interesting discussions preceding a combat in the lists.

The station, called the Diamond of the Desert, was assigned for the place of conflict, as being nearly at an equal distance betwixt the Christian and Saracen camps. It was agreed that Conrade of Montserrat, the defendant, with his godfathers, the Archduke of Austria and the Grand Master of the Templars, should appear there on the day fixed for the combat, with an

hundred armed followers, and no more ; that Richard of England, and his brother Salisbury, who supported the accusation,
should attend with the same number, to protect his champion ;
and that the Soldan should bring with him a guard of five
hundred chosen followers, a band considered as not more than
equal to the two hundred Christian lances. Such persons of
consideration as either party chose to invite to witness the
contest, were to wear no other weapons than their swords, and
to come without defensive armour. The Soldan undertook the
preparations of the lists, and to provide accommodations and
refreshments of every kind for all who were to assist at the
solemnity ; and his letters expressed, with much courtesy, the
pleasure which he anticipated in the prospect of a personal and
peaceful meeting with the Melech Ric, and his anxious desire
to render his reception as agreeable as possible.

All preliminaries being arranged, and communicated to the
defendant and his godfathers, Abdallah the Hadgi was admitted to a more private interview, where he heard with delight
the strains of Blondel. Having first carefully put his green
turban out of sight, and assumed a Greek cap in its stead, he
requited the Norman minstrel's music with a drinking song
from the Persian, and quaffed a hearty flagon of Cyprus wine,
to show that his practice matched his principles. On the next
day, grave and sober as the water-drinker Mirglip, he bent his
brow to the ground before Saladin's footstool, and rendered to
the Soldan an account of his embassy.

On the day before that appointed for the combat, Conrade
and his friends set off by daybreak to repair to the place assigned, and Richard left the camp at the same hour, and for
the same purpose ; but, as had been agreed upon, he took his
journey by a different route, a precaution which had been
judged necessary, to prevent the possibility of a quarrel betwixt
their armed attendants.

The good King himself was in no humour for quarrelling
with any one. Nothing could have added to his pleasurable
anticipations of a desperate and bloody combat in the lists,
except his being in his own royal person one of the combatants ; and he was half in charity again even with Conrade
of Montserrat. Lightly armed, richly dressed, and gay as a
bridegroom on the eve of his nuptials, Richard caracoled along
by the side of Queen Berengaria's litter, pointing out to her the
various scenes through which they passed, and cheering with
tale and song the bosom of the inhospitable wilderness. The
former route of the Queen's pilgrimage to Engaddi had been on
the other side of the chain of mountains, so that the ladies were
strangers to the scenery of the desert ; and though Berengaria
knew her husband's disposition too well not to endeavour to

seem interested in what he was pleased either to say or to sing, she could not help indulging some female fears when she found herself in the howling wilderness with so small an escort, which seemed almost like a moving speck on the bosom of the plain, and knew, at the same time, they were not so distant from the camp of Saladin but what they might be in a moment surprised and swept off by an overpowering host of his fiery-footed cavalry, should the Pagan be faithless enough to embrace an opportunity thus tempting. But when she hinted these suspicions to Richard, he repelled them with displeasure and disdain. "It were worse than ingratitude," he said, "to doubt the good faith of the generous Soldan."

Yet the same doubts and fears recurred more than once, not to the timid mind of the Queen alone, but to the firmer and more candid soul of Edith Plantagenet, who had no such confidence in the faith of the Moslem as to render her perfectly at ease when so much in their power; and her surprise had been far less than her terror, if the desert around had suddenly resounded with the shout of Alla hu! and a band of Arab cavalry had pounced on them like vultures on their prey. Nor were these suspicions lessened, when, as evening approached, they were aware of a single Arab horseman, distinguished by his turban and long lance, hovering on the edge of a small eminence like a hawk poised in the air, and who instantly, on the appearance of the royal retinue, darted off with the speed of the same bird, when it shoots down the wind and disappears from the horizon.

"We must be near the station," said King Richard; "and yonder cavalier is one of Saladin's outposts—methinks I hear the noise of the Moorish horns and cymbals. Get you into order, my hearts, and form yourselves around the ladies soldier-like and firmly."

As he spoke, each knight, squire, and archer hastily closed in upon his appointed ground, and they proceeded in the most compact order, which made their numbers appear still smaller; and to say the truth, though there might be no fear, there was anxiety as well as curiosity in the attention with which they listened to the wild bursts of Moorish music, which came ever and anon more distinctly from the quarter in which the Arab horseman had been seen to disappear.

De Vaux spoke in a whisper to the King—"Were it not well, my liege, to send a page to the top of that sand-bank? Or would it stand with your pleasure that I prick forward? Methinks, by all yonder clash and clang, if there be no more than five hundred men beyond the sand-hills, half of the Soldan's retinue must be drummers and cymbal tossers.— Shall I spur on?"

The Baron had checked his horse with the bit, and was just about to strike him with the spurs, when the King exclaimed— "Not for the world. Such a caution would express suspicion, and could do little to prevent surprise, which, however, I apprehend not."

They advanced accordingly in close and firm order till they surmounted the line of low sand-hills, and came in sight of the appointed station, when a splendid, but at the same time a startling, spectacle awaited them.

The Diamond of the Desert, so lately a solitary fountain, distinguished only amid the waste by solitary groups of palm-trees, was now the centre of an encampment, the embroidered flags and gilded ornaments of which glittered far and wide, and reflected a thousand rich tints against the setting sun. The coverings of the large pavilions were of the gayest colours, scarlet, bright yellow, pale blue, and other gaudy and gleaming hues, and the tops of their pillars, or tent-poles, were decorated with golden pomegranates and small silken flags. But, besides these distinguished pavilions, there were, what Thomas de Vaux considered as a portentous number of the ordinary black tents of the Arabs, being sufficient, as he conceived, to accommodate, according to the Eastern fashion, a host of five thousand men. A number of Arabs and Curds, fully corresponding to the extent of the encampment, were hastily assembling, each leading his horse in his hand, and their muster was accompanied by an astonishing clamour of their noisy instruments of martial music, by which, in all ages, the warfare of the Arabs has been animated.

They soon formed a deep and confused mass of dismounted cavalry in front of their encampment, when, at the signal of a shrill cry, which arose high over the clangour of the music, each cavalier sprung to his saddle. A cloud of dust arising at the moment of this manœuvre, hid from Richard and his attendants the camp, the palm-trees, and the distant ridge of mountains, as well as the troops whose sudden movement had raised the cloud, and ascending high over their heads, formed itself into the fantastic forms of writhed pillars, domes, and minarets. Another shrill yell was heard from the bosom of this cloudy tabernacle. It was the signal for the cavalry to advance, which they did at full gallop, disposing themselves as they came forward, so as to come in at once on the front, flanks, and rear of Richard's little bodyguard, who were thus surrounded and almost choked by the dense clouds of dust enveloping them on each side, through which were seen alternately, and lost, the grim forms and wild faces of the Saracens, brandishing and tossing their lances in every possible direction, with the wildest cries and halloos, and frequently only reining up their horses when within a spear's length of the Christians, while those in the rear discharged over the heads of both parties thick volleys of arrows. One of these struck the litter in which the Queen was seated, who loudly screamed, and the red spot was on Richard's brow in an instant.

"Ha! Saint George," he exclaimed, "we must take some order with this infidel scum!"

But Edith, whose litter was near, thrust her head out, and with her hand holding one of the shafts, exclaimed, "Royal Richard, beware what you do! see, these arrows are headless!"

"Noble, sensible wench!" exclaimed Richard; "by Heaven, thou shamest us all by thy readiness of thought and eye.—Be not moved, my English hearts," he exclaimed to his followers—"their arrows have no heads—and their spears, too, lack the steel-points. It is but a wild welcome, after their savage fashion, though doubtless they would rejoice to see us daunted or disturbed. Move onward, slow and steady."

The little phalanx moved forward accordingly, accompanied on all sides by the Arabs, with the shrillest and most piercing cries, the bowmen, meanwhile, displaying their agility by shooting as near the crests of the Christians as was possible, without actually hitting them, while the lancers charged each other with such rude blows of their blunt weapons, that more than one of them lost his saddle, and well-nigh his life, in this rough sport. All this, though designed to express welcome, had rather a doubtful appearance in the eyes of the Europeans.

As they had advanced nearly half-way towards the camp, King Richard and his suite forming, as it were, the nucleus round which this tumultuary body of horsemen howled, whooped, skirmished, and galloped, creating a scene of indescribable confusion, another shrill cry was heard, on which all these irregulars, who were on the front and upon the flanks of the little body of Europeans, wheeled off, and forming themselves into a long and deep column, followed with comparative order and silence in the rear of Richard's troop. The dust began now to dissipate in their front, when there advanced to meet them, through that cloudy veil, a body of cavalry of a different and more regular description, completely armed with offensive and defensive weapons, and who might well have served as a bodyguard to the proudest of Eastern monarchs. This splendid troop consisted of five hundred men, and each horse which it contained was worth an earl's ransom. The riders were Georgian and Circassian slaves in the very prime of life; their helmets and hauberks were formed of steel-rings, so bright that they shone like silver; their vestures were of the gayest colours, and some of cloth of gold or silver; the sashes were twisted with silk and gold, their rich turbans were plumed and jewelled, and their sabres and poniards, of Damascene steel, were adorned with gold and gems on hilt and scabbard.

This splendid array advanced to the sound of military music, and when they met the Christian body, they opened their files to the right and left, and let them enter between their ranks. Richard now assumed the foremost place in his troop, aware that Saladin himself was approaching. Nor was it long when, in the centre of his bodyguard, surrounded by his domestic officers, and those hideous negroes who guard the Eastern harem, and whose misshapen forms were rendered yet more frightful by the richness of their attire, came the Soldan, with the look and manners of one on whose brow Nature had written, This is a King! In his snow-white turban, vest, and wide Eastern trousers, wearing a sash of scarlet silk, without any other ornament, Saladin might have seemed the plainest dressed man in his own guard. But closer inspection discerned in his turban that inestimable gem, which was called by the poets, the Sea of Light; the diamond on which his signet was engraved, and which he wore in a ring, was probably worth all the jewels of the English crown, and a sapphire, which termi- nated the hilt of his canjiar, was of not much inferior value. It should be added, that to protect him from the dust, which, in the vicinity of the Dead Sea, resembles the finest ashes, or, perhaps, out of Oriental pride, the Soldan wore a sort of veil attached to his turban, which partly obscured the view of his noble features. He rode a milk-white Arabian, which bore him as if conscious and proud of his noble burden.

There was no need of farther introduction. The two heroic monarchs, for such they both were, threw themselves at once from horseback, and the troops halting and the music suddenly ceasing, they advanced to meet each other in profound silence, and, after a courteous inclination on either side, they embraced as brethren and equals. The pomp and display upon both sides attracted no farther notice—no one saw aught save Richard and Saladin, and they too beheld nothing but each other. The looks with which Richard surveyed Saladin were, however, more intently curious than those which the Soldan fixed upon him; and the Soldan also was the first to break silence.

"The Melech Ric is welcome to Saladin as water to this desert. I trust he hath no distrust of this numerous array. Excepting the armed slaves of my household, those who sur- round you with eyes of wonder and of welcome, are, even the humblest of them, the privileged nobles of my thousand tribes; for who that could claim a title to be present would remain at home when such a Prince was to be seen as Richard, with the terrors of whose name, even on the sands of Yemen, the nurse stills her child, and the free Arab subdues his restive steed!"

"And these are all nobles of Araby?" said Richard, looking around on wild forms with their persons covered with haicks, their countenances swart with the sunbeams, their teeth as white as ivory, their black eyes glancing with fierce and preternatural lustre from under the shade of their turbans, and their dress being in general simple, even to meanness.

"They claim such rank," said Saladin; "but though numerous, they are within the conditions of the treaty, and bear no arms but the sabre—even the iron of their lances is left behind."

"I fear," muttered De Vaux in English, "they have left them where they can be soon found.—A most flourishing House of Peers, I confess, and would find Westminster Hall something too narrow for them."

"Hush, De Vaux," said Richard, "I command thee.—Noble Saladin," he said, "suspicion and thou cannot exist on the same ground—See'st thou," pointing to the litters—"I too have brought some champions with me, though armed, perhaps, in breach of agreement, for bright eyes and fair features are weapons which cannot be left behind."

The Soldan, turning to the litters, made an obeisance as lowly as if looking towards Mecca, and kissed the sand in token of respect.

"Nay," said Richard,—"they will not fear a closer encounter, brother; wilt thou not ride towards their litters, and the curtains will be presently withdrawn?"

"That may Allah prohibit!" said Saladin, "since not an Arab looks on who would not think it shame to the noble ladies to be seen with their faces uncovered."

"Thou shalt see them, then, in private, brother," answered Richard.

"To what purpose?" answered Saladin mournfully. "Thy last letter was, to the hopes which I had entertained, like water to fire; and wherefore should I again light a flame, which may indeed consume, but cannot cheer me?—But will not my brother pass to the tent which his servant hath prepared for him? My principal black slave hath taken order for the reception of the Princesses—the officers of my household will attend your followers, and ourself will be the chamberlain of the royal Richard."

He led the way accordingly to a splendid pavilion, where was everything that royal luxury could devise. De Vaux, who was in attendance, then removed the chappe (*capa*), or long riding-cloak which Richard wore, and he stood before Saladin in the close dress which showed to advantage the strength and symmetry of his person, while it bore a strong contrast to the flowing robes which disguised the thin frame of the Eastern monarch. It was Richard's two-handed sword that chiefly attracted the attention of the Saracen, a broad straight blade, the seemingly unwieldy length of which extended well-nigh from the shoulder to the heel of the wearer.

"Had I not," said Saladin, "seen this brand flaming in the front of battle, like that of Azrael, I had scarce believed that human arm could wield it. Might I request to see the Melech Ric strike one blow with it in peace, and in pure trial of strength?"

"Willingly, noble Saladin," answered Richard; and looking around for something whereon to exercise his strength, he saw a steel mace, held by one of the attendants, the handle being of the same metal, and about an inch and a half in diameter— this he placed on a block of wood.

The anxiety of De Vaux for his master's honour led him to whisper in English—"For the blessed Virgin's sake, beware what you attempt, my liege! Your full strength is not as yet returned—give no triumph to the infidel."

"Peace, fool!" said Richard, standing firm on his ground, and casting a fierce glance around—"thinkest thou that I can fail in *his* presence?"

The glittering broadsword, wielded by both his hands, rose aloft to the King's left shoulder, circled round his head, descended with the sway of some terrific engine, and the bar of iron rolled on the ground in two pieces, as a woodsman would sever a sapling with a hedging-bill.

"By the head of the Prophet, a most wonderful blow!" said the Soldan, critically and accurately examining the iron bar which had been cut asunder; and the blade of the sword was so well tempered as to exhibit not the least token of having suffered by the feat it had performed. He then took the King's hand, and looking on the size and muscular strength which it exhibited, laughed as he placed it beside his own, so lank and thin, so inferior in brawn and sinew.

"Ay, look well," said De Vaux, in English, "it will be long ere your long jackanapes's fingers do such a feat with your fine gilded reaping-hook there."

"Silence, De Vaux," said Richard; "by Our Lady, he understands or guesses thy meaning,—be not so broad, I pray thee."

The Soldan, indeed, presently said—"Something I would fain attempt—though, wherefore should the weak show their inferiority in presence of the strong? Yet, each land hath its own exercises, and this may be new to the Melech Ric."—So saying, he took from the floor a cushion of silk and down, and placed it upright on one end.—"Can thy weapon, my brother, sever that cushion?" he said to King Richard.

"No, surely," replied the King; "no sword on earth, were it the Excalibar of King Arthur, can cut that which opposes no steady resistance to the blow."

"Mark, then," said Saladin; and tucking up the sleeve of his gown, showed his arm, thin indeed and spare, but which constant exercise had hardened into a mass consisting of nought but bone, brawn, and sinew. He unsheathed his scimitar, a curved and narrow blade, which glittered not like the swords of the Franks, but was, on the contrary, of a dull blue colour, marked with ten millions of meandering lines, which showed how anxiously the metal had been welded by the armourer. Wielding this weapon, apparently so inefficient when compared to that of Richard, the Soldan stood resting his weight upon his left foot, which was slightly advanced; he balanced himself a little as if to steady his aim, then stepping at once forward, drew the scimitar across the cushion, applying the edge so dexterously, and with so little apparent effort, that the cushion seemed rather to fall asunder than to be divided by violence.

"It is a juggler's trick," said De Vaux, darting forward and snatching up the portion of the cushion which had been cut off, as if to assure himself of the reality of the feat,—"there is gramarye in this."

The Soldan seemed to comprehend him, for he undid the sort of veil which he had hitherto worn, laid it double along the edge of his sabre, extended the weapon edgeways in the air, and drawing it suddenly through the veil, although it hung on the blade entirely loose, severed that also into two parts, which floated to different sides of the tent, equally displaying the extreme temper and sharpness of the weapon, and the exquisite dexterity of him who used it.

"Now, in good faith, my brother," said Richard, "thou art even matchless at the trick of the sword, and right perilous were it to meet thee! Still, however, I put some faith in a downright English blow, and what we cannot do by sleight we eke out by strength. Nevertheless, in truth thou art as expert in inflicting wounds, as my sage Hakim in curing them. I trust I shall see the learned leech—I have much to thank him for, and had brought some small present."

As he spoke, Saladin exchanged his turban for a Tartar cap. He had no sooner done so, than De Vaux opened at once his extended mouth and his large round eyes, and Richard gazed with scarce less astonishment, while the Soldan spoke in a grave and altered voice:—"The sick man, sayeth the poet, while he is yet infirm, knoweth the physician by his step; but when he is recovered, he knoweth not even his face when he looks upon him."

" A miracle !—a miracle ! " exclaimed Richard.

" Of Mahound's working, doubtless," said Thomas de Vaux.

" That I should lose my learned Hakim," said Richard, " merely by absence of his cap and robe, and that I should find him again in my royal brother Saladin ! "

" Such is oft the fashion of the world," answered the Soldan ; " the tattered robe makes not always the dervisch."

" And it was through thy intercession," said Richard, " that yonder Knight of the Leopard was saved from death—and by thy artifice that he revisited my camp in disguise ? "

" Even so," replied Saladin ; " I was physician enough to know, that unless the wounds of his bleeding honour were stanched, the days of his life must be few. His disguise was more easily penetrated than I had expected from the success of my own."

" An accident," said King Richard (probably alluding to the circumstance of his applying his lips to the wound of the supposed Nubian), " let me first know that his skin was artificially discoloured ; and that hint once taken, detection became easy, for his form and person are not to be forgotten. I confidently expect that he will do battle on the morrow."

" He is full in preparation, and high in hope," said the Soldan. " I have furnished him with weapons and horse, thinking nobly of him from what I have seen under various disguises."

" Knows he now," said Richard, " to whom he lies under obligation ? "

" He doth," replied the Saracen—" I was obliged to confess my person when I unfolded my purpose."

" And confessed he aught to you ? " said the King of England.

" Nothing explicit," replied the Soldan ; " but from much that passed between us, I conceive his love is too highly placed to be happy in its issue."

" And thou knowest, that his daring and insolent passion crossed thine own wishes ? " said Richard.

" I might guess so much," said Saladin ; " but his passion had existed ere my wishes had been formed—and, I must now add, is likely to survive them. I cannot, in honour, revenge me for my disappointment on him who had no hand in it. Or, if this high-born dame loved him better than myself, who can say that she did not justice to a knight of her own religion, who is full of nobleness ? "

" Yet of too mean lineage to mix with the blood of Plantagenet," said Richard haughtily.

" Such may be your maxims in Frangistan," replied the Soldan. " Our poets of the Eastern countries say, that a valiant camel-driver is worthy to kiss the lip of a fair Queen, when a cowardly prince is not worthy to salute the hem of her garment. But with your permission, noble brother, I must take leave of thee for the present, to receive the Duke of Austria and yonder Nazarene knight, much less worthy of hospitality, but who must yet be suitably entreated, not for their sakes, but for mine own honour—for what saith the sage Lokman? 'Say not that the food is lost unto thee which is given to the stranger—for if his body be strengthened and fattened therewithal, not less is thine own worship and good name cherished and augmented.'"

The Saracen Monarch departed from King Richard's tent, and having indicated to him, rather with signs than with speech, where the pavilion of the Queen and her attendants was pitched, he went to receive the Marquis of Montserrat and his attendants, for whom, with less goodwill, but with equal splendour, the magnificent Soldan had provided accommodations. The most ample refreshments, both in the Oriental, and after the European fashion, were spread before the royal and princely guests of Saladin, each in their own separate pavilion; and so attentive was the Soldan to the habits and taste of his visitors, that Grecian slaves were stationed to present them with the goblet, which is the abomination of the sect of Mohammed. Ere Richard had finished his meal, the ancient Omrah, who had brought the Soldan's letter to the Christian camp, entered with a plan of the ceremonial to be observed on the succeeding day of combat. Richard, who knew the taste of his old acquaintance, invited him to pledge him in a flagon of wine of Schiraz; but Abdallah gave him to understand, with a rueful aspect, that self-denial, in the present circumstances, was a matter in which his life was concerned; for that Saladin, tolerant in many respects, both observed, and enforced by high penalties, the laws of the Prophet.

"Nay, then," said Richard, "if he loves not wine, that lightener of the human heart, his conversion is not to be hoped for, and the prediction of the mad priest of Engaddi goes like chaff down the wind."

The King then addressed himself to settle the articles of combat, which cost a considerable time, as it was necessary on some points to consult with the opposite parties, as well as with the Soldan.

They were at length finally agreed upon, and adjusted by a protocol in French and in Arabian, which was subscribed by Saladin, as umpire of the field, and by Richard and Leopold as guarantees for the two combatants. As the Omrah took his final leave of King Richard for the evening, De Vaux entered.

"The good knight," he said, "who is to do battle to-morrow, requests to know, whether he may not to-night pay duty to his royal godfather?"

"Hast thou seen him, De Vaux?" said the King, smiling; "and didst thou know an ancient acquaintance?"

"But our Lady of Lanercost," answered De Vaux, "there are so many surprises and changes in this land, that my poor brain turns. I scarce knew Sir Kenneth of Scotland, till his good hound, that had been for a short while under my care, came and fawned on me; and even then I only knew the tyke by the depth of his chest, the roundness of his foot, and his manner of baying; for the poor gaze-hound was painted like any Venetian courtesan."

"Thou art better skilled in brutes than men, De Vaux," said the King.

"I will not deny," said De Vaux, "I have found them oft-times the honester animals. Also, your Grace is pleased to term me sometimes a brute myself; besides that I serve the Lion, whom all men acknowledge the king of brutes."

"By Saint George, there thou brokest thy lance fairly on my brow," said the King. "I have ever said thou hast a sort of wit, De Vaux—marry, one must strike thee with a sledge-hammer ere it can be made to sparkle. But to the present gear—is the good knight well armed and equipped?"

"Fully, my liege, and nobly," answered De Vaux; "I know the armour well—it is that which the Venetian commissary offered your Highness, just ere you became ill, for five hundred bezants."

"And he hath sold it to the infidel Soldan, I warrant me, for a few ducats more, and present payment. These Venetians would sell the sepulchre itself!"

"The armour will never be borne in a nobler cause," said De Vaux.

"Thanks to the nobleness of the Saracen," said the King, "not to the avarice of the Venetians."

"I would to God your Grace would be more cautious," said the anxious De Vaux.—"Here are we deserted by all our allies, for points of offence given to one or another; we cannot hope to prosper upon the land, and we have only to quarrel with the amphibious republic, to lose the means of retreat by sea!"

"I will take care," said Richard impatiently, "but school me no more. Tell me rather, for it is of interest, hath the knight a confessor?"

"He hath," answered De Vaux; "the hermit of Engaddi, who erst did him that office when preparing for death, attends him on the present occasion; the fame of the duel having brought him hither."

"'Tis well," said Richard; "and now for the knight's request. Say to him, Richard will receive him when the discharge of his devoir beside the Diamond of the Desert shall have atoned for his fault beside the Mount of Saint George; and as thou passest through the camp, let the Queen know I will visit her pavilion—and tell Blondel to meet me there."

De Vaux departed, and in about an hour afterwards, Richard, wrapping his mantle around him, and taking his ghittern in his hand, walked in the direction of the Queen's pavilion. Several Arabs passed him, but always with averted heads, and looks fixed upon the earth, though he could observe that all gazed earnestly after him when he was past. This led him justly to conjecture that his person was known to them; but that either the Soldan's commands, or their own Oriental politeness, forbade them to seem to notice a sovereign who desired to remain incognito.

When the King reached the pavilion of his Queen, he found it guarded by those unhappy officials whom Eastern jealousy places around the zenana. Blondel was walking before the door, and touched his rote from time to time, in a manner which made the Africans show their ivory teeth, and bear burden with their strange gestures and shrill unnatural voices.

"What art thou after with this herd of black cattle, Blondel?" said the King; "wherefore goest thou not into the tent?"

"Because my trade can neither spare the head nor the fingers," said Blondel; "and these honest blackamoors threatened to cut me joint from joint if I pressed forward."

"Well, enter with me," said the King, "and I will be thy safeguard."

The blacks accordingly lowered pikes and swords to King Richard, and bent their eyes on the ground, as if unworthy to look upon him. In the interior of the pavilion, they found Thomas de Vaux in attendance on the Queen. While Berengaria welcomed Blondel, King Richard spoke for some time secretly and apart with his fair kinswoman.

At length, "Are we still foes, my fair Edith?" he said, in a whisper.

"No, my liege," said Edith, in a voice just so low as not to interrupt the music—"none can bear enmity against King Richard, when he deigns to show himself, as he really is, generous and noble, as well as valiant and honourable."

So saying, she extended her hand to him. The King kissed it in token of reconciliation, and then proceeded.

"You think, my sweet cousin, that my anger in this matter was feigned; but you are deceived. The punishment I inflicted upon this knight was just; for he had betrayed—no matter for how tempting a bribe, fair cousin—the trust committed to him. But I rejoice, perchance as much as you, that to-morrow gives him a chance to win the field, and throw back the stain

which for a time clung to him, upon the actual thief and
traitor. No!—future times may blame Richard for impetuous
folly; but they shall say, that in rendering judgment, he was
just when he should, and merciful when he could."

"Laud not thyself, cousin King," said Edith. "They may
call thy justice cruelty—thy mercy caprice."

"And do not thou pride thyself," said the King, "as if thy
knight, who hath not yet buckled on his armour, were unbelting
it in triumph—Conrade of Montserrat is held a good lance.
What if the Scot should lose the day?"

"It is impossible!" said Edith firmly—"My own eyes saw
yonder Conrade tremble and change colour, like a base thief.
He is guilty—and the trial by combat is an appeal to the
justice of God—I myself, in such a cause, would encounter him
without fear."

"By the mass, I think thou wouldst, wench," said the King,
"and beat him to boot; for there never breathed a truer
Plantagenet than thou."

He paused, and added in a very serious tone,—"See that thou
continue to remember what is due to thy birth."

"What means that advice, so seriously given at this moment?"
said Edith. "Am I of such light nature as to forget my name
—my condition?"

"I will speak plainly, Edith," answered the King, "and as
to a friend,—What will this knight be to you, should he come
off victor from yonder lists?"

"To *me*?" said Edith, blushing deep with shame and displeasure,—"What *can* he be to me more than an honoured
knight, worthy of such grace as Queen Berengaria might confer
on him, had he selected her for his lady, instead of a more unworthy choice? The meanest knight may devote himself to
the service of an empress, but the glory of his choice," she said
proudly, "must be his reward."

"Yet he hath served and suffered much for you," said the
King.

"I have paid his services with honour and applause, and his
sufferings with tears," answered Edith. "Had he desired other
reward, he would have done wisely to have bestowed his affections within his own degree."

"You would not then wear the bloody night-gear for his
sake?" said King Richard.

"No more," answered Edith, "than I would have required
him to expose his life by an action, in which there was more
madness than honour."

"Maidens talk ever thus," said the King; "but when the
favoured lover presses his suit, she says, with a sigh, her stars
had decreed otherwise."

R

"Your Grace has now, for the second time, threatened me with the influence of my horoscope," Edith replied with dignity. "Trust me, my liege, whatever be the power of the stars, your poor kinswoman will never wed either infidel or obscure adventurer.—Permit me, that I listen to the music of Blondel, for the tone of your royal admonitions is scarce so grateful to the ear."

The conclusion of the evening offered nothing worthy of notice.

CHAPTER XXVIII

Heard ye the din of battle bray,
Lance to lance, and horse to horse?
—GRAY.

It had been agreed, on account of the heat of the climate, that the judicial combat, which was the cause of the present assemblage of various nations at the Diamond of the Desert, should take place at one hour after sunrise. The wide lists, which had been constructed under the inspection of the Knight of the Leopard, enclosed a space of hard sand, which was one hundred and twenty yards long by forty in width. They extended in length from north to south, so as to give both parties the equal advantage of the rising sun. Saladin's royal seat was erected on the western side of the enclosure, just in the centre, where the combatants were expected to meet in mid encounter. Opposed to this was a gallery with closed casements, so contrived, that the ladies, for whose accommodation it was erected, might see the fight without being themselves exposed to view. At either extremity of the lists was a barrier, which could be opened or shut at pleasure. Thrones had been also erected, but the Archduke, perceiving that his was lower than King Richard's, refused to occupy it; and Cœur de Lion, who would have submitted to much ere any formality should have interfered with the combat, readily agreed that the sponsors, as they were called, should remain on horseback during the fight. At one extremity of the lists were placed the followers of Richard, and opposed to them were those who accompanied the defender, Conrade. Around the throne destined for the Soldan, were ranged his splendid Georgian Guards, and the rest of the enclosure was occupied by Christian and Mohammedan spectators.

Long before daybreak, the lists were surrounded by even a larger number of Saracens than Richard had seen on the preceding evening. When the first ray of the sun's glorious orb

arose above the desert, the sonorous call, " To prayer, to prayer ! "
was poured forth by the Soldan himself, and answered by others,
whose rank and zeal entitled them to act as muezzins. It was
a striking spectacle to see them all sink to earth, for the
purpose of repeating their devotions, with their faces turned to
Mecca. But when they arose from the ground, the sun's rays,
now strengthening fast, seemed to confirm the Lord of Gilsland's conjecture of the night before. They were flashed back
from many a spear-head, for the pointless lances of the preceding day were certainly no longer such. De Vaux pointed it
out to his master, who answered with impatience, that he had
perfect confidence in the good faith of the Soldan ; but if
De Vaux was afraid of his bulky body, he might retire.

Soon after this the noise of timbrels was heard, at the sound
of which the whole Saracen cavaliers threw themselves from
their horses, and prostrated themselves, as if for a second morning prayer. This was to give an opportunity to the Queen
with Edith and her attendants, to pass from the pavilion to
the gallery intended for them. Fifty guards of Saladin's
seraglio escorted them, with naked sabres, whose orders were,
to cut to pieces whomsoever, were he prince or peasant, should
venture to gaze on the ladies as they passed, or even presume
to raise his head until the cessation of the music should make
all men aware that they were lodged in their gallery, not to be
gazed on by the curious eye.

This superstitious observance of Oriental reverence to the
fair sex, called forth from Queen Berengaria some criticisms very
unfavourable to Saladin and his country. But their den, as the
royal fair called it, being securely closed and guarded by their
able attendants, she was under the necessity of contenting
herself with seeing, and laying aside for the present the still
more exquisite pleasure of being seen.

Meantime the sponsors of both champions went, as was their
duty, to see that they were duly armed, and prepared for combat. The Archduke of Austria was in no hurry to perform this
part of the ceremony, having had rather an unusually severe
debauch upon wine of Schiraz the preceding evening. But the
Grand Master of the Temple, more deeply concerned in the
event of the combat, was early before the tent of Conrade
of Montserrat. To his great surprise, the attendants refused
him admittance.

" Do you not know me, ye knaves ? " said the Grand Master,
in great anger.

" We do, most valiant and reverend," answered Conrade's
squire ; " but even *you* may not at present enter—the Marquis
is about to confess himself."

" Confess himself ! " exclaimed the Templar, in a tone where alarm mingled with surprise and scorn—"and to whom, I pray thee?"

"My master bid me be secret," said the squire; on which the Grand Master pushed past him, and entered the tent almost by force.

The Marquis of Montserrat was kneeling at the feet of the Hermit of Engaddi, and in the act of beginning his confession.

"What means this, Marquis?" said the Grand Master, "up, for shame—or, if you must needs confess, am not I here?"

"I have confessed to you too often already," replied Conrade, with a pale cheek and a faltering voice. "For God's sake, Grand Master, begone, and let me unfold my conscience to this holy man."

"In what is he holier than I am?" said the Grand Master. —"Hermit, prophet, madman—say, if thou darest, in what thou excellest me?"

"Bold and bad man," replied the Hermit, "know that I am like the latticed window, and the divine light passes through to avail others, though, alas! it helpeth not me. Thou art like the iron stanchions, which neither receive light themselves, nor communicate it to any one."

"Prate not to me, but depart from this tent," said the Grand Master; "the Marquis shall not confess this morning, unless it be to me, for I part not from his side."

"Is this *your* pleasure?" said the Hermit to Conrade; "for think not I will obey that proud man, if you continue to desire my assistance."

"Alas!" said Conrade irresolutely, "what would you have me say?—Farewell for a while—we will speak anon."

"Oh, procrastination!" exclaimed the Hermit, "thou art a soul-murderer!—Unhappy man, farewell—not for a while, but until we both shall meet—no matter where.—And for thee," he added, turning to the Grand Master, "TREMBLE!"

"Tremble!" replied the Templar contemptuously, "I cannot if I would."

The Hermit heard not his answer, having left the tent.

"Come! to this gear hastily," said the Grand Master, "since thou wilt needs go through the foolery.—Hark thee—I think I know most of thy frailties by heart, so we may omit the detail, which may be somewhat a long one, and begin with the absolution. What signifies counting the spots of dirt that we are about to wash from our hands?"

"Knowing what thou art thyself," said Conrade, "it is blasphemous to speak of pardoning another."

"That is not according to the canon, Lord Marquis," said the Templar,—"thou art more scrupulous than orthodox. Th absolution of the wicked priest is as effectual as if he were himself a saint,—otherwise God help the poor penitent! What wounded man inquires whether the surgeon that tents his gashes have clean hands or no!—Come, shall we to this toy?"

"No," said Conrade, "I will rather die unconfessed than mock the sacrament."

"Come, noble Marquis," said the Templar, "rouse up your courage, and speak not thus. In an hour's time thou shalt stand victorious in the lists, or confess thee in thy helmet, like a valiant knight."

"Alas, Grand Master!" answered Conrade, "all augurs ill for this affair. The strange discovery by the instinct of a dog —the revival of this Scottish knight, who comes into the lists like a spectre—all betokens evil."

"Pshaw!" said the Templar, "I have seen thee bend thy lance boldly against him in sport, and with equal chance of success—think thou art but in a tournament, and who bears him better in the tilt-yard than thou?—Come, squires and armourers, your master must be accoutred for the field."

The attendants entered accordingly, and began to arm the Marquis.

"What morning is without?" said Conrade.

"The sun rises dimly," answered a squire.

"Thou seest, Grand Master," said Conrade, "nought smiles on us."

"Thou wilt fight the more coolly, my son," answered the Templar; "thank Heaven, that hath tempered the sun of Palestine to suit thy occasion."

Thus jested the Grand Master; but his jests had lost their influence on the harassed mind of the Marquis, and, notwithstanding his attempts to seem gay, his gloom communicated itself to the Templar.

"This craven," he thought, "will lose the day in pure faintness and cowardice of heart, which he calls tender conscience. I, whom visions and auguries shake not—who am firm in my purpose as the living rock—I should have fought the combat myself.—Would to God the Scot may strike him dead on the spot—it were next best to his winning the victory. But come what will, he must have no other confessor than myself—our sins are too much in common, and he might confess my share with his own."

While these thoughts passed through his mind, he continued to assist the Marquis in arming, but it was in silence.

The hour at length arrived, the trumpets sounded, the knights rode into the lists armed at all points, and mounted like men who were to do battle for a kingdom's honour. They wore their visors up, and riding around the lists three times,

showed themselves to the spectators. Both were goodly persons,
and both had noble countenances. But there was an air of
manly confidence on the brow of the Scot—a radiancy of
hope, which amounted even to cheerfulness, while, although
pride and effort had recalled much of Conrade's natural courage,
there lowered still on his brow a cloud of ominous despondence.
Even his steed seemed to tread less lightly and blithely to the
trumpet-sound than the noble Arab which was bestrode by
Sir Kenneth; and the *spruch-sprecher* shook his head while he
observed, that while the challenger rode around the lists in the
course of the sun, that is, from right to left, the defender made
the same circuit *widdersins*, that is, from left to right, which is
in most countries held ominous.

A temporary altar was erected just beneath the gallery
occupied by the Queen, and beside it stood the Hermit in the
dress of his order, as a Carmelite friar. Other churchmen were
also present. To this altar the challenger and defender were
successively brought forward, conducted by their respective
sponsors. Dismounting before it, each knight avouched the
justice of his cause by a solemn oath on the Evangelists, and
prayed that his success might be according to the truth or
falsehood of what he then swore. They also made oath, that
they came to do battle in knightly guise, and with the usual
weapons, disclaiming the use of spells, charms, or magical
devices, to incline victory to their side. The challenger pronounced his vow with a firm and manly voice, and a bold and
cheerful countenance. When the ceremony was finished, the
Scottish knight looked at the gallery, and bent his head to
the earth, as if in honour of those invisible beauties which
were enclosed within; then, loaded with armour as he was,
sprung to the saddle without the use of the stirrup, and made
his courser carry him in a succession of caracoles to his station
at the eastern extremity of the lists. Conrade also presented
himself before the altar with boldness enough; but his voice,
as he took the oath, sounded hollow, as if drowned in his
helmet. The lips with which he appealed to Heaven to
adjudge victory to the just quarrel, grew white as they uttered
the impious mockery. As he turned to remount his horse, the
Grand Master approached him closer, as if to rectify something about the sitting of his gorget, and whispered,—"Coward
and fool!—recall thy senses, and do me this battle bravely, else,
by Heaven, shouldst thou escape him, thou escapest not *me!*"

The savage tone in which this was whispered perhaps
completed the confusion of the Marquis's nerves, for he
stumbled as he made to horse; and though he recovered his
feet, sprung to the saddle with his usual agility, and displayed
his address in horsemanship as he assumed his position opposite

to the challenger's, yet the accident did not escape those who were on the watch for omens, which might predict the fate of the day.

The priests, after a solemn prayer, that God would show the rightful quarrel, departed from the lists. The trumpets of the challenger then rung a flourish, and a herald-at-arms proclaimed at the eastern end of the lists,—"Here stands a good knight, Sir Kenneth of Scotland, champion for the royal King Richard of England, who accuseth Conrade, Marquis of Montserrat, of foul treason and dishonour done to the said King."

When the words Kenneth of Scotland announced the name and character of the champion, hitherto scarce generally known, a loud and cheerful acclaim burst from the followers of King Richard, and hardly, notwithstanding repeated commands of silence, suffered the reply of the defendant to be heard. He, of course, avouched his innocence, and offered his body for battle. The esquires of the combatants now approached, and delivered to each his shield and lance, assisting to hang the former around his neck, that his two hands might remain free, one for the management of the bridle, the other to direct the lance.

The shield of the Scot displayed his old bearing, the leopard, but with the addition of a collar and broken chain, in allusion to his late captivity. The shield of the Marquis bore, in reference to his title, a serrated and rocky mountain. Each shook his lance aloft, as if to ascertain the weight and toughness of the unwieldy weapon, and then laid it in the rest. The sponsors, heralds, and squires now retired to the barriers, and the combatants sat opposite to each other, face to face, with couched lance and closed visor, the human form so completely enclosed, that they looked more like statues of molten iron, than beings of flesh and blood. The silence of suspense was now general — men breathed thicker, and their very souls seemed seated in their eyes, while not a sound was to be heard save the snorting and pawing of the good steeds, who, sensible of what was about to happen, were impatient to dash into career. They stood thus for perhaps three minutes, when, at a signal given by the Soldan, an hundred instruments rent the air with their brazen clamours, and each champion striking his horse with the spurs, and slacking the rein, the horses started into full gallop, and the knights met in mid space with a shock like a thunderbolt. The victory was not in doubt— no, not one moment. Conrade, indeed, showed himself a prac- tised warrior; for he struck his antagonist knightly in the midst of his shield, bearing his lance so straight and true, that it shivered into splinters from the steel spear-head up to the very gauntlet. The horse of Sir Kenneth recoiled two or three yards and fell on his haunches, but the rider easily raised him with hand and rein. But for Conrade, there was no recovery. Sir Kenneth's lance had pierced through the shield, through a plated corselet of Milan steel, through a *secret*, or coat of linked mail, worn beneath the corselet, had wounded him deep in the bosom, and borne him from his saddle, leaving the truncheon of the lance fixed in his wound. The sponsors, heralds, and Saladin himself, descending from his throne, crowded around the wounded man; while Sir Kenneth, who had drawn his sword ere yet he discovered his antagonist was totally helpless, now commanded him to avow his guilt. The helmet was hastily unclosed, and the wounded man, gazing wildly on the skies, replied—"What would you more?—God hath decided justly—I am guilty—but there are worse traitors in the camp than I.—In pity to my soul, let me have a confessor!"

He revived as he uttered these words.

"The talisman—the powerful remedy, royal brother," said King Richard to Saladin.

"The traitor," answered the Soldan, "is more fit to be dragged from the lists to the gallows by the heels, than to profit by its virtues:—and some such fate is in his look," he added, after gazing fixedly upon the wounded man; "for though his wound may be cured, yet Azrael's seal is on the wretch's brow."

"Nevertheless," said Richard, "I pray you do for him what you may, that he may at least have time for confession—Slay not soul and body! To him one half-hour of time may be worth more, by ten thousandfold, than the life of the oldest patriarch."

"My royal brother's wish shall be obeyed," said Saladin.—"Slaves, bear this wounded man to our tent."

"Do not so," said the Templar, who had hitherto stood gloomily looking on in silence.—"The royal Duke of Austria and myself will not permit this unhappy Christian Prince to be delivered over to the Saracens, that they may try their spells upon him. We are his sponsors, and demand that he be assigned to our care."

"That is, you refuse the certain means offered to recover him?" said Richard.

"Not so," said the Grand Master, recollecting himself.—"If the Soldan useth lawful medicines, he may attend the patient in my tent."

"Do so, I pray thee, good brother," said Richard to Saladin, "though the permission be ungraciously yielded. But now to a more glorious work.—Sound, trumpets—shout England—in honour of England's champion!"

Drum, clarion, trumpet, and cymbal rung forth at once, and the deep and regular shout, which for ages has been the English acclamation, sounded amidst the shrill and irregular yells of the Arabs, like the diapason of the organ amid the howling of a storm. There was silence at length.

"Brave Knight of the Leopard," resumed Cœur de Lion, "thou hast shown that the Ethiopian *may* change his skin and the Leopard his spots, though clerks quote Scripture for the impossibility. Yet I have more to say to you when I have conducted you to the presence of the ladies, the best judges, and best rewarders of deeds of chivalry."

The Knight of the Leopard bowed assent.

"And thou, princely Saladin, wilt also attend them. I promise thee our Queen will not think herself welcome, if she lacks the opportunity to thank her royal host for her most princely reception."

Saladin bent his head gracefully, but declined the invitation.

"I must attend the wounded man," he said. "The leech leaves not his patient more than the champion the lists, even if he be summoned to a bower like those of Paradise. And farther, royal Richard, know that the blood of the East flows not so temperately in the presence of beauty, as that of your land. What saith the Book itself?—Her eye is as the edge of the sword of the Prophet, who shall look upon it? He that would not be burnt avoideth to tread on hot embers—wise men spread not the flax before a bickering torch—He, saith the sage, who hath forfeited a treasure, doth not wisely to turn back his head to gaze at it."

Richard, it may be believed, respected the motives of delicacy which flowed from manners so different from his own, and urged his request no farther.

"At noon," said the Soldan, as he departed, "I trust ye will all accept a collation under the black camel-skin tent of a chief of Curdistan."

The same invitation was circulated among the Christians, comprehending all those of sufficient importance to be admitted to sit at a feast made for princes.

"Hark!" said Richard, "the timbrels announce that our Queen and her attendants are leaving their gallery—and see, the turbans sink on the ground, as if struck down by a destroying angel. All lie prostrate, as if the glance of an Arab's eye could sully the lustre of a lady's cheek! Come, we will to the pavilion, and lead our conqueror thither in triumph.—How I pity that noble Soldan, who knows but of love as it is known to those of inferior nature!"

Blondel tuned his harp to its boldest measure, to welcome the introduction of the victor into the pavilion of Queen

Berengaria. He entered, supported on either side by his sponsors, Richard and William Longsword, and knelt gracefully down before the Queen, though more than half the homage was silently rendered to Edith, who sat on her right hand.

"Unarm him, my mistresses," said the King, whose delight was in the execution of such chivalrous usages—"Let Beauty honour Chivalry! Undo his spurs, Berengaria; Queen though thou be, thou owest him what marks of favour thou canst give. —Unlace his helmet, Edith—by this hand, thou shalt, wert thou the proudest Plantagenet of the line, and he the poorest knight on earth!"

Both ladies obeyed the royal commands,—Berengaria with bustling assiduity, as anxious to gratify her husband's humour, and Edith blushing and growing pale alternately, as slowly and awkwardly she undid, with Longsword's assistance, the fastenings, which secured the helmet to the gorget.

"And what expect you from beneath this iron shell?" said Richard, as the removal of the casque gave to view the noble countenance of Sir Kenneth, his face glowing with recent exertion, and not less so with present emotion. "What think ye of him, gallants and beauties?" said Richard. "Doth he resemble an Ethiopian slave, or doth he present the face of an obscure and nameless adventurer? No, by my good sword!— Here terminate his various disguises. He hath knelt down before you, unknown save by his worth—he arises, equally distinguished by birth and fortune. The adventurous knight, Kenneth, arises David, Earl of Huntingdon, Prince Royal of Scotland!"

There was a general exclamation of surprise, and Edith dropped from her hand the helmet which she had just received.

"Yes, my masters," said the King, "it is even so. Ye know how Scotland deceived us when she proposed to send this valiant Earl, with a bold company of her best and noblest, to aid our arms in this conquest of Palestine, but failed to comply with her engagements. This noble youth, under whom the Scottish Crusaders were to have been arrayed, thought foul scorn that his arm should be withheld from the holy warfare, and joined us at Sicily with a small train of devoted and faithful attendants, which was augmented by many of his countrymen to whom the rank of their leader was unknown. The confidants of the Royal Prince had all, saving one old follower, fallen by death, when his secret, but too well kept, had nearly occasioned my cutting off, in a Scottish adventurer, one of the noblest hopes of Europe.—Why did you not mention your rank, noble Huntingdon, when endangered by my hasty and passionate sentence?—Was it that you thought Richard capable of abusing the advantage I possessed over the heir of a King whom I have so often found hostile?"

"I did you not that injustice, royal Richard," answered the Earl of Huntingdon; "but my pride brooked not that I should avow myself Prince of Scotland in order to save my life, endangered for default of loyalty. And, moreover, I had made my vow to preserve my rank unknown till the Crusade should be accomplished; nor did I mention it save *in articulo mortis*, and under the seal of confession, to yonder reverend hermit."

"It was the knowledge of that secret, then, which made the good man so urgent with me to recall my severe sentence?" said Richard. "Well did he say, that, had this good knight fallen by my mandate, I should have wished the deed undone though it had cost me a limb—A limb!—I should have wished it undone had it cost me my life—since the world would have said that Richard had abused the condition in which the heir of Scotland had placed himself, by his confidence in his generosity."

"Yet may we know of your grace by what strange and happy chance this riddle was at length read?" said the Queen Berengaria.

"Letters were brought to us from England," said the King, "in which we learnt, among other unpleasant news, that the King of Scotland had seized upon three of our nobles, when on a pilgrimage to Saint Ninian, and alleged as a cause, that his heir, being supposed to be fighting in the ranks of the Teutonic Knights, against the heathen of Borussia, was, in fact, in our camp and in our power; and, therefore, William proposed to hold these nobles as hostages for his safety. This gave me the first light on the real rank of the Knight of the Leopard, and my suspicions were confirmed by De Vaux, who, on his return from Ascalon, brought back with him the Earl of Huntingdon's sole attendant, a thick-skulled slave, who had gone thirty miles to unfold to De Vaux a secret he should have told to me."

"Old Strauchan must be excused," said the Lord of Gilsland. "He knew from experience that my heart is somewhat softer than if I wrote myself Plantagenet."

"Thy heart soft? thou commodity of old iron—and Cumberland flint that thou art!" exclaimed the King.—"It is we Plantagenets who boast soft and feeling hearts, Edith," turning to his cousin, with an expression which called the blood into her cheek—"Give me thy hand, my fair cousin, and, Prince of Scotland, thine."

"Forbear, my lord," said Edith, hanging back, and endeavouring to hide her confusion, under an attempt to rally her royal kinsman's credulity. "Remember you not that my hand was to be the signal of converting to the Christian faith the Saracen and Arab, Saladin and all his turbaned host?"

"Ay, but the wind of prophecy hath chopped about, and sits now in another corner," replied Richard.

"Mock not, lest your bonds be made strong," said the Hermit, stepping forward. "The heavenly host write nothing but truth in their brilliant records—it is man's eyes which are too weak to read their characters aright. Know, that when Saladin and Kenneth of Scotland slept in my grotto, I read in the stars, that there rested under my roof a prince, the natural foe of Richard, with whom the fate of Edith Plantagenet was to be united. Could I doubt that this must be the Soldan, whose rank was well known to me, as he often visited my cell to converse on the revolutions of the heavenly bodies?—Again the lights of the firmament proclaimed that this Prince, the husband of Edith Plantagenet, should be a Christian; and I—weak and wild interpreter!—argued thence the conversion of the noble Saladin, whose good qualities seemed often to incline him towards the better faith. The sense of my weakness hath humbled me to the dust, but in the dust I have found comfort! I have not read aright the fate of others—who can assure me but that I may h ve miscalculated mine own? God will not have us break into His council-house or spy out His hidden mysteries. We must wait His time with watching and prayer—with fear and with hope. I came hither the stern seer—the proud prophet—skilled, as I thought, to instruct princes, and gifted even with supernatural powers, but burdened with a weight which I deemed no shoulders but mine could have borne. But my bands have been broken! I go hence humble in mine ignorance, penitent—and not hopeless."

With these words he withdrew from the assembly; and it is recorded, that, from that period, his frenzy fits seldom occurred, and his penances were of a milder character, and accompanied with better hopes of the future. So much is there of self-opinion, even in insanity, that the conviction of his having entertained and expressed an unfounded prediction with so much vehemence, seemed to operate like loss of blood on the human frame, to modify and lower the fever of the brain.

It is needless to follow into farther particulars the conferences at the royal tent, or to inquire whether David, Earl of Huntingdon, was as mute in the presence of Edith Plantagenet, as when he was bound to act under the character of an obscure and nameless adventurer. It may be well believed that he there expressed, with suitable earnestness, the passion to which he had so often before found it difficult to give words.

The hour of noon now approached, and Saladin waited to receive the Princes of Christendom in a tent, which, but for its large size, differed little from that of the ordinary shelter of the common Curdman, or Arab; yet, beneath its ample and sable covering, was prepared a banquet after the most gorgeous fashion of the East, extended upon carpets of the richest stuffs, with cushions laid for the guests. But we cannot stop to describe the cloth of gold and silver—the superb embroidery in Arabesque—the shawls of Cashmere—and the muslins of India, which were here unfolded in all their splendour; far less to tell the different sweetmeats, ragouts edged with rice coloured in various manners, with all the other niceties of Eastern cookery. Lambs roasted whole, and game and poultry dressed in pilaus, were piled in vessels of gold, and silver, and porcelain, and intermixed with large mazers of sherbert, cooled in snow and ice from the caverns of Mount Lebanon. A magnificent pile of cushions at the head of the banquet, seemed prepared for the master of the feast, and such dignitaries as he might call to share that place of distinction, while from the roof of the tent in all quarters, but over this seat of eminence in particular, waved many a banner and pennon, the trophies of battles won, and kingdoms overthrown. But amongst and above them all, a long lance displayed a shroud, the banner of Death, with this impressive inscription—"Saladin, King of Kings—Saladin, Victor of Victors—Saladin must die." Amid these preparations, the slaves who had arranged the refreshments stood with drooped heads and folded arms, mute and motionless as monumental statuary, or as automata, which waited the touch of the artist to put them in motion.

Expecting the approach of his princely guests, the Soldan, imbued, as most were, with the superstitions of his time, paused over a horoscope and corresponding scroll, which had been sent to him by the Hermit of Engaddi when he departed from the camp.

"Strange and mysterious science," he muttered to himself, "which, pretending to draw the curtain of futurity, misleads those whom it seems to guide, and darkens the scene which it pretends to illuminate! Who would not have said that I was that enemy most dangerous to Richard, whose enmity was to be ended by marriage with his kinswoman? Yet it now appears that a union betwixt this gallant Earl and the lady will bring about friendship betwixt Richard and Scotland, an enemy more dangerous than I, as a wild-cat in a chamber is more to be dreaded than a lion in a distant desert.—But then," he continued to mutter to himself, "the combination intimates, that this husband was to be Christian.—Christian?" he repeated after a pause,—"That gave the insane fanatic star-gazer hopes that I might renounce my faith! but me, the faithful follower of our Prophet—me it should have undeceived. Lie there, mysterious scroll," he added, thrusting it under the pile of cushions; "strange are thy bodements and fatal, since, even when true in themselves, they work upon those who attempt to decipher their meaning, all the effects of falsehood.—How now, what means this intrusion?"

He spoke to the dwarf Nectabanus, who rushed into the tent fearfully agitated, with each strange and disproportioned feature wrenched by horror into still more extravagant ugliness,—his mouth open, his eyes staring, his hands, with their shrivelled and deformed fingers, widely expanded.

"What now?" said the Soldan sternly.

"*Accipe hoc!*" groaned out the dwarf.

"Ha! say'st thou?" answered Saladin.

"*Accipe hoc!*" replied the panic-struck creature, unconscious, perhaps, that he repeated the same words as before.

"Hence! I am in no vein for foolery," said the Emperor.

"Nor am I farther fool," said the dwarf, "than to make my folly help out my wits to earn my bread, poor helpless wretch! —Hear, hear me, great Soldan!"

"Nay, if thou hast actual wrong to complain of," said Saladin, "fool or wise, thou art entitled to the ear of a King.— Retire hither with me;" and he led him into the inner tent.

Whatever their conference related to, it was soon broken off by the fanfare of the trumpets, announcing the arrival of the various Christian princes, whom Saladin welcomed to his tent with a royal courtesy well becoming their rank and his own; but chiefly he saluted the young Earl of Huntingdon, and generously congratulated him upon prospects, which seemed to have interfered with and overclouded those which he had himself entertained.

"But think not," said the Soldan, "thou noble youth, that the Prince of Scotland is more welcome to Saladin, than was Kenneth to the solitary Ilderim when they met in the desert! or the distressed Ethiop to the Hakim Adonbec. A brave and generous disposition like thine hath a value independent of condition and birth, as the cool draught which I here proffer thee, is as delicious from an earthen vessel as from a goblet of gold."

The Earl of Huntingdon made a suitable reply, gratefully acknowledging the various important services he had received from the generous Soldan; but when he had pledged Saladin in the bowl of sherbet, which the Soldan had proffered to him, he could not help remarking with a smile, "The brave cavalier, Ilderim, knew not of the formation of ice, but the munificent Soldan cools his sherbet with snow."

"Wouldst thou have an Arab or a Curdman as wise as a Hakim?" said the Soldan. "He who does on a disguise must make the sentiments of his heart and the learning of his head accord with the dress which he assumes. I desired to see how a brave and single-hearted cavalier of Frangistan would conduct himself in debate with such a chief as I then seemed; and *I* questioned the truth of a well-known fact, to know by what arguments thou wouldst support thy assertion."

While they were speaking, the Archduke of Austria, who stood a little apart, was struck with the mention of iced sherbet, and took with pleasure and some bluntness the deep goblet, as the Earl of Huntingdon was about to replace it.

"Most delicious!" he exclaimed, after a deep draught, which the heat of the weather, and the feverishness following the debauch of the preceding day, had rendered doubly acceptable. He sighed as he handed the cup to the Grand Master of the Templars. Saladin made a sign to the dwarf, who advanced and pronounced, with a harsh voice, the words, *Accipe hoc!* The Templar started, like a steed who sees a lion under a bush, beside the pathway; yet instantly recovered, and to hide, perhaps, his confusion, raised the goblet to his lips—but those lips never touched that goblet's rim. The sabre of Saladin left its sheath as lightning leaves the cloud. It was waved in the air, —and the head of the Grand Master rolled to the extremity of the tent, while the trunk remained for a second standing, with the goblet still clenched in its grasp, then fell, the liquor mingling with the blood that spurted from the veins.

There was a general exclamation of treason, and Austria, nearest to whom Saladin stood with the bloody sabre in his hand, started back as if apprehensive that his turn was to come next. Richard and others laid hand on their swords.

"Fear nothing, noble Austria," said Saladin, as composedly as if nothing had happened, "nor you, royal England, be wroth at what you have seen. Not for his manifold treasons;—not for the attempt which, as may be vouched by his own squire, he instigated against King Richard's life;—not that he pursued the Prince of Scotland and myself in the desert, reducing us to save our lives by the speed of our horses;—not that he had stirred up the Maronites to attack us upon this very occasion, had I not brought up unexpectedly so many Arabs as rendered the scheme abortive;—not for any or all of these crimes does he now lie there, although each were deserving such a doom;— but because, scarce half-an-hour ere he polluted our presence, as the simoom empoisons the atmosphere, he poniarded his comrade and accomplice, Conrade of Montserrat, lest he should confess the infamous plots in which they had both been engaged."

"How! Conrade murdered?—And by the Grand Master, his sponsor and most intimate friend!" exclaimed Richard. "Noble

Soldan, I would not doubt thee—yet this must be proved—otherwise——"

"There stands the evidence," said Saladin, pointing to the terrified dwarf. "Allah, who sends the fire-fly to illuminate the night-season, can discover secret crimes by the most contemptible means."

The Soldan proceeded to tell the dwarf's story, which amounted to this.—In his foolish curiosity, or, as he partly confessed, with some thoughts of pilfering, Nectabanus had strayed into the tent of Conrade, which had been deserted by his attendants, some of whom had left the encampment to carry the news of his defeat to his brother, and others were availing themselves of the means which Saladin had supplied for revelling. The wounded man slept under the influence of Saladin's wonderful talisman, so that the dwarf had opportunity to pry about at pleasure, until he was frightened into concealment by the sound of a heavy step. He skulked behind a curtain, yet could see the motions, and hear the words of the Grand Master, who entered, and carefully secured the covering of the pavilion behind him. His victim started from sleep, and it would appear that he instantly suspected the purpose of his old associate, for it was in a tone of alarm that he demanded wherefore he disturbed him?

"I come to confess and absolve thee," answered the Grand Master.

Of their farther speech the terrified dwarf remembered little, save that Conrade implored the Grand Master not to break a wounded reed, and that the Templar struck him to the heart with a Turkish dagger, with the words *Accipe hoc*—words which long afterwards haunted the terrified imagination of the concealed witness.

"I verified the tale," said Saladin, "by causing the body to be examined; and I made this unhappy being, whom Allah hath made the discoverer of the crime, repeat in your own presence the words which the murderer spoke, and you yourselves saw the effect which they produced upon his conscience!"

The Soldan paused, and the King of England broke silence :—

"If this be true, as I doubt not, we have witnessed a great act of justice, though it bore a different aspect. But wherefore in this presence? wherefore with thine own hand?"

"I had designed otherwise," said Saladin; "but had I not hastened his doom, it had been altogether averted, since, if I had permitted him to taste of my cup, as he was about to do, how could I, without incurring the brand of inhospitality, have done him to death as he deserved? Had he murdered my father, and afterwards partaken of my food and my bowl, not a hair of his head could have been injured by me. But

DEATH OF THE TEMPLAR

PAINTING BY JOHANNOT

cnough of him—let his carcass and his memory be removed from amongst us."

The body was carried away, and the marks of the slaughter obliterated or concealed with such ready dexterity, as showed that the case was not altogether so uncommon as to paralyse the assistants and officers of Saladin's household.

But the Christian princes felt that the scene which they had beheld weighed heavily on their spirits, and although, at the courteous invitation of the Soldan, they assumed their seats at the banquet, yet it was with the silence of doubt and amazement. The spirits of Richard alone surmounted all cause for suspicion or embarrassment. Yet he, too, seemed to ruminate on some proposition, as if he were desirous of making it in the most insinuating and acceptable manner which was possible. At length he drank off a large bowl of wine, and addressing the Soldan, desired to know whether it was not true that he had honoured the Earl of Huntingdon with a personal encounter.

Saladin answered, with a smile, that he had proved his horse and his weapons with the heir of Scotland, as cavaliers are wont to do with each other when they meet in the desert—and modestly added, that though the combat was not entirely decisive, he had not, on his part, much reason to pride himself on the event. The Scot, on the other hand, disclaimed the attributed superiority, and wished to assign it to the Soldan.

"Enough of honour thou hast had in the encounter," said Richard, "and I envy thee more for that, than for the smiles of Edith Plantagenet, though one of them might reward a bloody day's work.—But what say you, noble princes; is it fitting that such a royal ring of chivalry should break up without something being done for future times to speak of? What is the overthrow and death of a traitor, to such a fair garland of honour as is here assembled, and which ought not to part without witnessing something more worthy of their regard? How say you, princely Soldan—What if we two should now, and before this fair company, decide the long-contended question for this land of Palestine, and end at once these tedious wars? Yonder are the lists ready, nor can Paynimrie ever hope a better champion than thou. I, unless worthier offers, will lay down my gauntlet in behalf of Chris-endom, and, in all love and honour, we will do mortal battle for the possession of Jerusalem."

There was a deep pause for the Soldan's answer. His cheek and brow coloured highly, and it was the opinion of many present, that he hesitated whether he should accept the challenge. At length he said, "Fighting for the Holy City against those whom we regard as idolaters, and worshippers of

S

stocks and stones, and graven images, I might confide that Allah would strengthen my arm ; or if I fell beneath the sword of the Melech Ric, I could not pass to Paradise by a more glorious death. But Allah has already given Jerusalem to the true believers, and it were a tempting the God of the Prophet to peril, upon my own personal strength and skill, that which I hold securely by the superiority of my forces.

"If not for Jerusalem, then," said Richard, in the tone of one who would entreat a favour of an intimate friend, "yet, for the love of honour, let us run at least three courses with grinded lances ? "

"Even this," said Saladin, half smiling at Cœur de Lion's affectionate earnestness for the combat, "even this may I not lawfully do. The master places the shepherd over the flock, not for the shepherd's own sake, but for the sake of the sheep. Had I a son to hold the sceptre when I fell, I might have had the liberty, as I have the will, to brave this bold encounter ; but your own Scripture sayeth, that when the herdsman is smitten, the sheep are scattered."

"Thou hast had all the fortune," said Richard, turning to the Earl of Huntingdon with a sigh. "I would have given the best year in my life for that one half-hour beside the Diamond of the Desert ! "

The chivalrous extravagance of Richard awakened the spirits of the assembly, and when at length they arose to depart, Saladin advanced and took Cœur de Lion by the hand.

"Noble King of England," he said, "we now part, never to meet again. That your league is dissolved, no more to be reunited, and that your native forces are far too few to enable you to prosecute your enterprise, is as well known to me as to yourself. I may not yield you up that Jerusalem which you so much desire to hold. It is to us, as to you, a Holy City. But whatever other terms Richard demands of Saladin, shall be as willingly yielded as yonder fountain yields its waters ; Ay, and the same shall be as frankly afforded by Saladin if Richard stood in the desert with but two archers in his train ! "

The next day saw Richard's return to his own camp, and in a short space afterwards, the young Earl of Huntingdon was espoused by Edith Plantagenet. The Soldan sent, as a nuptial present on this occasion, the celebrated TALISMAN ; but though many cures were wrought by means of it in Europe, none equalled in success and celebrity those which the Soldan achieved. It is still in existence, having been bequeathed by the Earl of Huntingdon to a brave knight of Scotland, Sir

Simon of the Lee, in whose ancient and highly honoured family it is still preserved; and although charmed stones have been dismissed from the modern Pharmacopœia, its virtues are still applied to for stopping blood, and in cases of canine madness.

Our story closes here, as the terms on which Richard relinquished his conquests are to be found in every history of the period.

END OF THE TALISMAN

CHRONICLES OF THE CANONGATE

CHRONICLES OF THE CANONGATE

SIC ITUR AD ASTRA

MR. CROFTANGRY INTRODUCES ANOTHER TALE

> Together both on the high lawns appear'd.
> Under the opening eyelids of the morn
> They drove afield.   —ELEGY ON LYCIDAS.

I HAVE sometimes wondered why all the favourite occupations and pastimes of mankind go to the disturbance of that happy state of tranquillity, that *Otium*, as Horace terms it, which he says is the object of all men's prayers, whether preferred from sea or land; and that the undisturbed repose, of which we are so tenacious, when duty or necessity compels us to abandon it, is precisely what we long to exchange for a state of excitation, as soon as we may prolong it at our own pleasure. Briefly, you have only to say to a man, "remain at rest," and you instantly inspire the love of labour. The sportsman toils like his gamekeeper, the master of the pack takes as severe exercise as his whipper-in, the statesman or politician drudges more than the professional lawyer; and to come to my own case, the volunteer author subjects himself to the risk of painful criticism, and the assured certainty of mental and manual labour, just as completely as his needy brother, whose necessities compel him to assume the pen.

These reflections have been suggested by an annunciation on the part of Janet, "that the little Gillie-whitefoot was come from the printing-office."

"Gillie-blackfoot you should call him, Janet," was my response, "for he is neither more nor less than an imp of the devil, come to torment me for *copy*, for so the printers call a supply of manuscript for the press."

"Now, Cot forgie your honour," said Janet; "for it is no like your ainsell to give such names to a faitherless bairn."

"I have got nothing else to give him, Janet—he must wait a little."

"Then I have got some breakfast to give the bit gillie," said Janet; "and he can wait by the fireside in the kitchen, till

279

your honour's ready; and cood enough for the like of him, if he was to wait your honour's pleasure all day."

"But, Janet," said I to my little active superintendent, on her return to the parlour, after having made her hospitable arrangements, "I begin to find this writing our Chronicles is rather more tiresome than I expected, for here comes this little fellow to ask for manuscript—that is, for something to print—and I have got none to give him."

"Your honour can be at nae loss; I have seen you write fast and fast enough; and for subjects, you have the whole High-lands to write about, and I am sure you know a hundred tales better than that about Hamish MacTavish, for it was but about a young cateran and an auld carline, when all's done; and if they had burned the rudas queen for a witch, I am thinking, maybe, they would not have tyned their coals—and her to gar her neer-do-weel son shoot a gentleman Cameron! I am third cousin to the Camerons mysell—my blood warms to them— And if you want to write about deserters, I am sure there were deserters enough on the top of Arthur's Seat, when the Mac-Raas broke out, and on that woeful day beside Leith Pier— Ohonari?"——

Here Janet began to weep, and to wipe her eyes with her apron. For my part, the idea I wanted was supplied, but I hesitated to make use of it. Topics, like times, are apt to become common by frequent use. It is only an ass like Justice Shallow, who would pitch upon the over-scutched tunes, which the carmen whistled, and try to pass them off as his *fancies* and his *good-nights*. Now, the Highlands, though formerly a rich mine for original matter, are, as my friend Mrs. Bethune Baliol warned me, in some degree worn out by the incessant labour of modern romancers and novelists, who, ending in those remote regions primitive habits and manners, have vainly imagined that the public can never tire of them; and so kilted High-landers are to be found as frequently, and nearly of as genuine descent, on the shelves of a circulating library, as at a Caledonian ball. Much might have been made at an earlier time out of the history of a Highland regiment, and the singular revolu-tion of ideas which must have taken place in the minds of those who composed it, when exchanging their native hills for the battle-fields of the Continent, and their simple, and some-times indolent domestic habits, for the regular exertions de-manded by modern discipline. But the market is forestalled. There is Mrs. Grant of Laggan, has drawn the manners, customs, and superstitions of the mountains in their natural unsophisticated state;* and my friend, General Stewart of

* Letters from the Mountains, 3 vols.—Essays on the Superstitions of the Highlanders—The Highlanders, and other Poems, &c.

Garth,* in giving the real history of the Highland regiments, has rendered any attempt to fill up the sketch with fancy colouring extremely rash and precarious. Yet I, too, have still a lingering fancy to add a stone to the cairn; and, without calling in imagination to aid the impressions of juvenile recollection, I may just attempt to embody one or two scenes illustrative of the Highland character, and which belong peculiarly to the Chronicles of the Canongate, to the grey-headed eld of whom they are as familiar as to Chrystal Croftangry. Yet I will not go back to the days of clanship and claymores. Have at you, gentle reader, with a tale of Two Drovers. An oyster may be crossed in love, says the gentle Tilburina—and a drover may be touched on a point of honour, says the Chronicler of the Canongate.

* The gallant and amiable author of the History of the Highland Regiments, in whose glorious services his own share had been great, went out Governor of St. Lucia in 1828, and died in that island on the 18th of December 1829,—no man more regretted, or perhaps by a wider circle of friends and acquaintance.

THE TWO DROVERS

CHAPTER I

IT was the day after Doune Fair when my story commences.
It had been a brisk market; several dealers had attended from
the northern and midland counties in England, and English
money had flown so merrily about as to gladden the hearts of
the Highland farmers. Many large droves were about to set
off for England, under the protection of their owners, or of the
topsmen whom they employed in the tedious, laborious, and
responsible office of driving the cattle for many hundred miles,
from the market where they had been purchased, to the fields or
farmyards where they were to be fattened for the shambles.

The Highlanders, in particular, are masters of this difficult
trade of driving, which seems to suit them as well as the trade
of war. It affords exercise for all their habits of patient endurance and active exertion. They are required to know perfectly
the drove-roads, which lie over the wildest tracks of the country,
and to avoid as much as possible the highways, which distress
the feet of the bullocks, and the turnpikes, which annoy the
spirit of the drover; whereas on the broad green or grey track,
which leads across the pathless moor, the herd not only move
at ease and without taxation, but, if they mind their business,
may pick up a mouthful of food by the way. At night, the
drovers usually sleep along with their cattle, let the weather be
what it will; and many of these hardy men do not once rest
under a roof during a journey on foot from Lochaber to Lin-
colnshire. They are paid very highly, for the trust reposed is
of the last importance, as it depends on their prudence, vigilance, and honesty, whether the cattle reach the final market
in good order, and afford a profit to the grazier. But as they
maintain themselves at their own expense, they are especially
economical in that particular. At the period we speak of, a
Highland drover was victualled for his long and toilsome journey with a few handfuls of oatmeal, and two or three onions,
renewed from time to time, and a ram's horn filled with whisky,
which he used regularly, but sparingly, every night and morning. His dirk, or *skene-dhu* (*i.e.*, black-knife), so worn as to

be concealed beneath the arm, or by the folds of the plaid, was his only weapon, excepting the cudgel with which he directed the movements of the cattle. A Highlander was never so happy as on these occasions. There was a variety in the whole journey, which exercised the Celt's natural curiosity and love of motion; there were the constant change of place and scene, the petty adventures incidental to the traffic, and the intercourse with the various farmers, graziers, and traders, intermingled with occasional merry-makings, not the less acceptable to Donald that they were void of expense;—and there was the consciousness of superior skill; for the Highlander, a child amongst flocks, is a prince amongst herds, and his natural habits induce him to disdain the shepherd's slothful life, so that he feels himself nowhere more at home than when following a gallant drove of his country cattle in the character of their guardian.

Of the number who left Doune in the morning, and with the purpose we described, not a *Glunamie* of them all cocked his bonnet more briskly, or gartered his tartan hose under knee over a pair of more promising *spiogs* (legs), than did Robin Oig M'Combich, called familiarly Robin Oig, that is, Young, or the Lesser, Robin. Though small of stature, as the epithet Oig implies, and not very strongly limbed, he was as light and alert as one of the deer of his mountains. He had an elasticity of step, which, in the course of a long march, made many a stout fellow envy him; and the manner in which he busked his plaid and adjusted his bonnet, argued a consciousness that so smart a John Highlandman as himself would not pass unnoticed among the Lowland lasses. The ruddy cheek, red lips, and white teeth, set off a countenance which had gained by exposure to the weather a healthful and hardy rather than a rugged hue. If Robin Oig did not laugh, or even smile frequently, as indeed is not the practice among his countrymen, his bright eyes usually gleamed from under his bonnet with an expression of cheerfulness ready to be turned into mirth.

The departure of Robin Oig was an incident in the little town, in and near which he had many friends, male and female. He was a topping person in his way, transacted considerable business on his own behalf, and was entrusted by the best farmers in the Highlands, in preference to any other drover in that district. He might have increased his business to any extent had he condescended to manage it by deputy; but except a lad or two, sister's sons of his own, Robin rejected the idea of assistance, conscious, perhaps, how much his reputation depended upon his attending in person to the practical discharge of his duty in every instance. He remained, therefore, contented with the highest premium given to persons of his description, and comforted himself with the hopes that a few journeys to

England might enable him to conduct business on his own account, in a manner becoming his birth. For Robin Oig's father, Lachlan M'Combich (or *son of my friend,* his actual clan-surname being M'Gregor), had been so called by the celebrated Rob Roy, because of the particular friendship which had subsisted between the grandsire of Robin and that renowned cateran. Some people even say, that Robin Oig derived his Christian name from one as renowned in the wilds of Loch-lomond as ever was his namesake, Robin Hood, in the precincts of merry Sherwood. "Of such ancestry," as James Boswell says, "who would not be proud?" Robin Oig was proud accordingly; but his frequent visits to England and to the Lowlands had given him tact enough to know that pretensions, which still gave him a little right to distinction in his own lonely glen, might be both obnoxious and ridiculous if preferred elsewhere. The pride of birth, therefore, was like the miser's treasure, the secret subject of his contemplation, but never exhibited to strangers as a subject of boasting.

Many were the words of gratulation and good luck which were bestowed on Robin Oig. The judges commended his drove, especially Robin's own property, which were the best of them. Some thrust out their snuff-mulls for the parting pinch —others tendered the *doch-an-dorrach,* or parting cup. All cried—"Good-luck travel out with you and come home with you.—Give you luck in the Saxon market—brave notes in the *leabhar-dhu*" (black pocket-book), "and plenty of English gold in the *sporran*" (pouch of goat-skin).

The bonny lasses made their adieus more modestly, and more than one, it was said, would have given her best brooch to be certain that it was upon her that his eye last rested as he turned towards the road.

Robin Oig had just given the preliminary "*Hoo-hoo!*" to urge forward the loiterers of the drove, when there was a cry behind him.

"Stay, Robin—bide a blink. Here is Janet of Tomahourich —auld Janet, your father's sister."

"Plague on her, for an auld Highland witch and spaewife," said a farmer from the Carse of Stirling; "she'll cast some of her cantrips on the cattle."

"She canna do that," said another sapient of the same profession—"Robin Oig is no the lad to leave any of them without tying Saint Mungo's knot on their tails, and that will put to her speed the best witch that ever flew over Dimayet upon a broomstick."

It may not be indifferent to the reader to know, that the Highland cattle are peculiarly liable to be *taken,* or infected, by spells and witchcraft; which judicious people guard against, by knitting knots of peculiar complexity on the tuft of hair which terminates the animal's tail.

But the old woman who was the object of the farmer's suspicion, seemed only busied about the drover, without paying any attention to the drove. Robin, on the contrary, appeared rather impatient of her presence.

"What auld-world fancy," he said, "has brought you so early from the ingle-side this morning, Muhme? I am sure I bid you good-even, and had your God-speed, last night."

"And left me more siller than the useless old woman will use till you come back again, bird of my bosom," said the sibyl. "But it is little I would care for the food that nourishes me, or the fire that warms me, or for God's blessed sun itself, if aught but weel should happen to the grandson of my father. So let me walk the *deasil* round you, that you may go safe out into the foreign land, and come safe home."

Robin Oig stopped, half embarrassed, half laughing, and signing to those near that he only complied with the old woman to soothe her humour. In the meantime, she traced around him, with wavering steps, the propitiation, which some have thought has been derived from the Druidical mythology. It consists, as is well known, in the person who makes the *deasil* walking three times round the person who is the object of the ceremony, taking care to move according to the course of the sun. At once, however, she stopped short, and exclaimed, in a voice of alarm and horror, "Grandson of my father, there is blood on your hand."

"Hush, for God's sake, aunt," said Robin Oig; "you will bring more trouble on yourself with this Taishataragh" (second sight) "than you will be able to get out of for many a day."

The old woman only repeated, with a ghastly look, "There is blood on your hand, and it is English blood. The blood of the Gael is richer and redder. Let us see—let us——"

Ere Robin Oig could prevent her, which, indeed, could only have been done by positive violence, so hasty and peremptory were her proceedings, she had drawn from his side the dirk which lodged in the folds of his plaid, and held it up, exclaiming, although the weapon gleamed clear and bright in the sun, "Blood, blood—Saxon blood again. Robin Oig M'Combich, go not this day to England!"

"Prutt trutt," answered Robin Oig, "that will never do neither—it would be next thing to running the country. For shame, Muhme—give me the dirk. You cannot tell by the colour the difference betwixt the blood of a black bullock and a white one, and you speak of knowing Saxon from Gaelic blood. All men have their blood from Adam, Muhme. Give me my skene-dhu, and let me go on my road. I should have been half way to Stirling Brig by this time.—Give me my dirk, and let me go."

"Never will I give it to you," said the old woman—"Never will I quit my hold on your plaid, unless you promise me not to wear that unhappy weapon."

The women around him urged him also, saying few of his aunt's words fell to the ground; and as the Lowland farmers continued to look moodily on the scene, Robin Oig determined to close it at any sacrifice.

"Well, then," said the young drover, giving the scabbard of the weapon to Hugh Morrison, "you Lowlanders care nothing for these freats. Keep my dirk for me. I cannot give it to you, because it was my father's; but your drove follows ours, and I am content it should be in your keeping, not in mine.—Will this do, Muhme?"

"It must," said the old woman—"that is, if the Lowlander is mad enough to carry the knife."

The strong westlandman laughed aloud.

"Goodwife," said he, "I am Hugh Morrison from Glenae, come of the Manly Morrisons of auld langsyne, that never took short weapon against a man in their lives. And neither needed they. They had their broadswords, and I have this bit supple," showing a formidable cudgel; "for dirking ower the board, I leave that to John Highlandman—Ye needna snort, none of you Highlanders, and you in especial, Robin. I'll keep the bit knife, if you are feared for the auld spaewife's tale, and give it back to you whenever you want it."

Robin was not particularly pleased with some part of Hugh Morrison's speech; but he had learned in his travels more patience than belonged to his Highland constitution originally, and he accepted the service of the descendant of the Manly Morrisons without finding fault with the rather depreciating manner in which it was offered.

"If he had not had his morning in his head, and been but a Dumfries-shire hog into the boot, he would have spoken more like a gentleman. But you cannot have more of a sow than a grumph. It's shame my father's knife should ever slash a haggis for the like of him."

Thus saying (but saying it in Gaelic), Robin drove on his cattle, and waved farewell to all behind him. He was in the greater haste, because he expected to join at Falkirk a comrade and brother in profession, with whom he proposed to travel in company.

Robin Oig's chosen friend was a young Englishman, Harry Wakefield by name, well known at every northern market, and in his way as much famed and honoured as our Highland driver of bullocks. He was nearly six feet high, gallantly formed to keep the rounds at Smithfield, or maintain the ring at a wrestling match; and although he might have been over-matched, perhaps, among the regular professors of the Fancy, yet, as a yokel, or rustic, or a chance customer, he was able to give a bellyful to any amateur of the pugilistic art. Doncaster races saw him in his glory, betting his guinea, and generally successfully; nor was there a main fought in Yorkshire, the feeders being persons of celebrity, at which he was not to be seen, if business permitted. But though a *sprack* lad, and fond of pleasure and its haunts, Harry Wakefield was steady, and not the cautious Robin Oig M'Combich himself was more attentive to the main chance. His holidays were holidays indeed; but his days of work were dedicated to steady and persevering labour. In countenance and temper, Wakefield was the model of old England's merry yeomen, whose clothyard shafts, in so many hundred battles, asserted her superiority over the nations, and whose good sabres, in our own time, are her cheapest and most assured defence. His mirth was readily excited; for, strong in limb and constitution, and fortunate in circumstances, he was disposed to be pleased with everything about him; and such difficulties as he might occasionally encounter, were, to a man of his energy, rather matter of amusement than serious annoyance. With all the merits of a sanguine temper, our young English drover was not without his defects. He was irascible, sometimes to the verge of being quarrelsome; and perhaps not the less inclined to bring his disputes to a pugilistic decision, because he found few antagonists able to stand up to him in the boxing ring.

It is difficult to say how Harry Wakefield and Robin Oig first became intimates; but it is certain a close acquaintance had taken place betwixt them, although they had apparently few common subjects of conversation or of interest, so soon as their talk ceased to be of bullocks. Robin Oig, indeed, spoke the English language rather imperfectly upon any other topics but stots and kyloes, and Harry Wakefield could never bring his broad Yorkshire tongue to utter a single word of Gaelic. It was in vain Robin spent a whole morning, during a walk over Minch Moor, in attempting to teach his companion to utter, with true precision, the shibboleth *Llhu*, which is the Gaelic for a calf. From Traquair to Murder Cairn, the hill rung with the discordant attempts of the Saxon upon the unmanageable monosyllable, and the heartfelt laugh which followed every failure. They had, however, better modes of awakening the echoes; for Wakefield could sing many a ditty to the praise of Moll, Susan, and Cicely, and Robin Oig had a particular gift at whistling interminable pibrochs through all their in-volutions, and, what was more agreeable to his companion's southern ear, knew many of the northern airs, both lively and pathetic, to which Wakefield learned to pipe a bass. Thus, though Robin could hardly have comprehended his companion's stories about horse-racing, and cock-fighting, or fox-hunting, and although his own legends of clan-fights and *creaghs*, varied with talk of Highland goblins and fairy folk, would have been caviare to his companion, they contrived nevertheless to find a degree of pleasure in each other's company, which had for three years back induced them to join company and travel together, when the direction of their journey permitted. Each, indeed, found his advantage in this companionship; for where could the Englishman have found a guide through the Western Highlands like Robin Oig M'Combich? and when they were on what Harry called the *right* side of the border, his patronage, which was extensive, and his purse, which was heavy, were at all times at the service of his Highland friend, and on many occasions his liberality did him genuine yeoman's service.

CHAPTER II

Were ever two such loving friends !—
How could they disagree?
Oh thus it was, he loved them dear,
And thought how to requite him,
And having no friend left but he,
He did resolve to fight him.
—DUKE UPON DUKE.

THE pair of friends had traversed with their usual cordiality the grassy wilds of Liddesdale, and crossed the opposite part of Cumberland, emphatically called The Waste. In these solitary regions, the cattle under the charge of our drovers derived their subsistence chiefly by picking their food as they went along the drove-road, or sometimes by the tempting opportunity of a *start and overloup*, or invasion of the neighbouring pasture, where an occasion presented itself. But now the scene changed before them ; they were descending towards a fertile and enclosed country, where no such liberties could be taken with impunity, or without a previous arrangement and bargain with the possessors of the ground. This was more especially the case, as a great northern fair was upon the eve of taking place, where both the Scotch and English drover expected to dispose of a part of their cattle, which it was desirable to produce in the market, rested and in good order. Fields were therefore difficult to be obtained, and only upon high terms. This necessity occasioned a temporary separation betwixt the two friends, who went to bargain, each as he could, for the separate accommodation of his herd. Unhappily it chanced that both of them, unknown to each other, thought of bargaining for the ground they wanted on the property of a country gentleman of some fortune, whose estate lay in the neighbourhood. The English drover applied to the bailiff on the property, who was known to him. It chanced that the Cumbrian Squire, who had entertained some suspicions of his manager's honesty, was taking occasional measures to ascertain how far they were well founded, and had desired that any inquiries about his enclosures, with a view to occupy them for a temporary purpose, should be referred to himself. As, however, Mr. Ireby had gone the day before upon a journey of some miles' distance to the northward, the bailiff chose to consider the check upon his full powers as for the time removed, and concluded that he should best consult his master's interest, and perhaps his own, in making an agreement with Harry Wakefield. Meanwhile, ignorant of what his comrade was doing, Robin Oig, on his side, chanced to be overtaken by a good-looking smart little man upon a pony, most knowingly hogged and cropped, as was then the fashion, the rider wearing tight leather breeches, and long-necked bright spurs. This cavalier asked one or two pertinent questions about markets and the price of stock. So Robin, seeing him a well-judging civil gentleman, took the freedom to ask him whether he could let him know if there was any grass-land to be let in that neighbourhood, for the temporary accommodation of his drove. He could not have put the question to more willing ears. The gentleman of the buckskin was the proprietor, with whose bailiff Harry Wakefield had dealt, or was in the act of dealing.

"Thou art in good luck, my canny Scot," said Mr. Ireby, "to have spoken to me, for I see thy cattle have done their day's work, and I have at my disposal the only field within three miles that is to be let in these parts."

"The drove can pe gang two, three, four miles very pratty weel indeed," said the cautious Highlander; "put what would his honour be axing for the peasts pe the head, if she was to tak the park for twa or three days?"

"We won't differ, Sawney, if you let me have six stots for winterers, in the way of reason."

"And which peasts wad your honour pe for having?"

"Why—let me see—the two black — the dun one — yon doddy—him with the twisted horn—the brocket—How much by the head?"

"Ah," said Robin, "your honour is a shudge—a real shudge

T

—I couldna have set off the pest six peasts petter mysell, me that ken them as if they were my pairns, puir things."

"Well, how much per head, Sawney?" continued Mr. Ireby.

"It was high markets at Doune and Falkirk," answered Robin.

And thus the conversation proceeded, until they had agreed on the *prix juste* for the bullocks, the Squire throwing in the temporary accommodation of the enclosure for the cattle into the boot, and Robin making, as he thought, a very good bargain, provided the grass was but tolerable. The Squire walked his pony alongside of the drove, partly to show him the way, and see him put into possession of the field, and partly to learn the latest news of the northern markets.

They arrived at the field, and the pasture seemed excellent. But what was their surprise when they saw the bailiff quietly inducting the cattle of Harry Wakefield into the grassy Goshen which had just been assigned to those of Robin Oig M'Combich by the proprietor himself!—Squire Ireby set spurs to his horse, dashed up to his servant, and learning what had passed between the parties, briefly informed the English drover that his bailiff had let the ground without his authority, and that he might seek grass for his cattle wherever he would, since he was to get none there. At the same time he rebuked his servant severely for having transgressed his commands, and ordered him instantly to assist in ejecting the hungry and weary cattle of Harry Wakefield, which were just beginning to enjoy a meal of unusual plenty, and to introduce those of his comrade, whom the English drover now began to consider as a rival.

The feelings which arose in Wakefield's mind would have induced him to resist Mr. Ireby's decision; but every Englishman has a tolerably accurate sense of law and justice, and John Fleecebumpkin, the bailiff, having acknowledged that he had exceeded his commission, Wakefield saw nothing else for it than to collect his hungry and disappointed charge, and drive them on to seek quarters elsewhere. Robin Oig saw what had happened with regret, and hastened to offer to his English friend to share with him the disputed possession. But Wakefield's pride was severely hurt, and he answered disdainfully, "Take it all, man—take it all—never make two bites of a cherry — thou canst talk over the gentry, and blear a plain man's eye—Out upon you, man—I would not kiss any man's dirty latchets for leave to bake in his oven."

Robin Oig, sorry but not surprised at his comrade's displeasure, hastened to entreat his friend to wait but an hour till he had gone to the Squire's house to receive payment for the cattle he had sold, and he would come back and help him to drive the cattle into some convenient place of rest, and explain to him the whole mistake they had both of them fallen into. But the Englishman continued indignant: " Thou hast been selling, hast thou? Ay, ay—thou is a cunning lad for kenning the hours of bargaining. Go to the devil with thyself, for I will ne'er see thy fause loon's visage again—thou should be ashamed to look me in the face."

" I am ashamed to look no man in the face," said Robin Oig, something moved; "and, moreover, I will look you in the face this blessed day, if you will bide at the clachan down yonder."

" Mayhap you had as well keep away," said his comrade; and turning his back on his former friend, he collected his unwilling associates, assisted by the bailiff, who took some real and some affected interest in seeing Wakefield accommodated.

After spending some time in negotiating with more than one of the neighbouring farmers, who could not, or would not, afford the accommodation desired, Henry Wakefield at last, and in his necessity, accomplished his point by means of the landlord of the ale-house at which Robin Oig and he had agreed to pass the night, when they first separated from each other. Mine host was content to let him turn his cattle on a piece of barren moor, at a price little less than the bailiff had asked for the disputed enclosure; and the wretchedness of the pasture, as well as the price paid for it, were set down as exaggerations of the breach of faith and friendship of his Scottish crony. This turn of Wakefield's passions was encouraged by the bailiff (who had his own reasons for being offended against poor Robin, as having been the unwitting cause of his falling into disgrace with his master), as well as by the innkeeper, and two or three chance guests, who stimulated the drover in his resentment against his quondam associate,—some from the ancient grudge against the Scots, which, when it exists anywhere, is to be found lurking in the Border counties, and some from the general love of mischief, which characterises mankind in all ranks of life, to the honour of Adam's children be it spoken. Good John Barleycorn also, who always heightens and exaggerates the prevailing passions, be they angry or kindly, was not wanting in his offices on this occasion; and confusion to false friends and hard masters was pledged in more than one tankard.

In the meanwhile Mr. Ireby found some amusement in detaining the northern drover at his ancient hall. He caused a cold round of beef to be placed before the Scot in the butler's pantry, together with a foaming tankard of home-brewed, and took pleasure in seeing the hearty appetite with which these unwonted edibles were discussed by Robin Oig M'Combich. The Squire himself lighting his pipe, compounded between his patrician dignity and his love of agricultural gossip, by walking up and down while he conversed with his guest.

"I passed another drove," said the Squire, "with one of your countrymen behind them — they were something less beasts than your drove, doddies most of them—a big man was with them—none of your kilts though, but a decent pair of breeches —D'ye know who he may be?"

"Hout ay—that might, could, and would be Hughie Morrison —I didna think he could hae peen sae weel up. He has made a day on us; but his Argyleshires will have wearied shanks. How far was he pehind?"

"I think about six or seven miles," answered the Squire, "for I passed them at the Christenbury Crag, and I overtook you at the Hollan Bush. If his beasts be leg-weary, he will be may be selling bargains."

"Na, na, Hughie Morrison is no the man for pargains—ye maun come to some Highland body like Robin Oig hersell for the like of these—put I maun pe wishing you goot night, and twenty of them let alane ane, and I maun down to the Clachan to see if the lad Harry Waakfelt is out of his humdudgeons yet."

The party at the alehouse were still in full talk, and the treachery of Robin Oig still the theme of conversation, when the supposed culprit entered the apartment. His arrival, as usually happens in such a case, put an instant stop to the discussion of which he had furnished the subject, and he was received by the company assembled with that chilling silence, which, more than a thousand exclamations, tells an intruder that he is unwelcome. Surprised and offended, but not appalled by the reception which he experienced, Robin entered with an undaunted and even a haughty air, attempted no greeting, as he saw he was received with none, and placed himself by the side of the fire, a little apart from a table at which Harry Wakefield, the bailiff, and two or three other persons, were seated. The ample Cumbrian kitchen would have afforded plenty of room, even for a larger separation.

Robin, thus seated, proceeded to light his pipe, and call for a pint of twopenny.

"We have no twopence ale," answered Ralph Heskett, the landlord; "but as thou find'st thy own tobacco, it's like thou mayst find thy own liquor too—it's the wont of thy country, I wot."

"Shame, goodman," said the landlady, a blithe bustling housewife, hastening herself to supply the guest with liquor—"Thou knowest well enow what the strange man wants, and it's thy trade to be civil, man. Thou shouldst know, that if the Scot likes a small pot, he pays a sure penny."

Without taking any notice of this nuptial dialogue, the Highlander took the flagon in his hand, and addressing the company generally, drank the interesting toast of "Good Markets," to the party assembled.

"The better that the wind blew fewer dealers from the north," said one of the farmers, "and fewer Highland runts to eat up the English meadows."

"Saul of my pody, put you are wrang there, my friend," answered Robin, with composure; "it is your fat Englishmen that eat up our Scots cattle, puir things."

"I wish there was a summat to eat up their drovers," said another; "a plain Englishman canna make bread within a kenning of them."

"Or an honest servant keep his master's favour, but they will come sliding in between him and the sunshine," said the bailiff.

"If these pe jokes," said Robin Oig, with the same composure, "there is ower mony jokes upon one man."

"It is no joke, but downright earnest," said the bailiff. "Harkye, Mr. Robin Ogg, or whatever is your name, it's right we should tell you that we are all of one opinion, and that is, that you, Mr. Robin Ogg, have behaved to our friend, Mr. Harry Wakefield here, like a raff and a blackguard."

"Nae doubt, nae doubt," answered Robin, with great composure; "and you are a set of very pretty judges, for whose prains or pehaviour I wad not gie a pinch of sneeshing. If Mr. Harry Waakfelt kens where he is wranged, he kens where he may be righted."

"He speaks truth," said Wakefield, who had listened to what passed, divided between the offence which he had taken at Robin's late behaviour, and the revival of his habitual feelings of regard.

He now arose, and went towards Robin, who got up from his seat as he approached, and held out his hand.

"That's right, Harry—go it—serve him out," resounded on all sides—"tip him the nailer—show him the mill."

"Hold your peace all of you, and be——," said Wakefield; and then addressing his comrade, he took him by the extended hand, with something alike of respect and defiance. "Robin," he said, "thou hast used me ill enough this day; but if you mean, like a frank fellow, to shake hands, and make a tussle for love on the sod, why I'll forgie thee, man, and we shall be better friends than ever."

"And would it not pe petter to pe cood friends without more of the matter?" said Robin; "we will be much petter friendships with our panes hale than proken."

Harry Wakefield dropped the hand of his friend, or rather threw it from him.

"I did not think I had been keeping company for three years with a coward."

"Coward pelongs to none of my name," said Robin, whose eyes began to kindle, but keeping the command of his temper. "It was no coward's legs or hands, Harry Waakfelt, that drew you out of the fords of Frew, when you was drifting ower the plack rock, and every eel in the river expected his share of you."

"And that is true enough, too," said the Englishman, struck by the appeal.

"Adzooks!" exclaimed the bailiff—"sure Harry Wakefield, the nattiest lad at Whitson Tryste, Wooler Fair, Carlisle Sands, or Stagshaw Bank, is not going to show white feather? Ah, this comes of living so long with kilts and bonnets—men forget the use of their daddles."

"I may teach you, Master Fleecebumpkin, that I have not lost the use of mine," said Wakefield, and then went on. "This will never do, Robin. We must have a turn-up, or we shall be the talk of the country-side. I'll be d——d if I hurt thee—I'll put on the gloves gin thou like. Come, stand forward like a man."

"To pe peaten like a dog," said Robin; "is there any reason in that? If you think I have done you wrong, I'll go before your shudge, though I neither know his law nor his language."

A general cry of "No, no—no law, no lawyer! a bellyful and be friends," was echoed by the bystanders.

"But," continued Robin, "if I am to fight, I've no skill to fight like a jackanapes, with hands and nails."

"How would you fight then?" said his antagonist; "though I am thinking it would be hard to bring you to the scratch anyhow."

"I would fight with proadswords, and sink point on the first plood drawn——like a gentlemans."

A loud shout of laughter followed the proposal, which indeed had rather escaped from poor Robin's swelling heart, than been the dictate of his sober judgment.

"Gentleman, quotha!" was echoed on all sides, with a shout of unextinguishable laughter; "a very pretty gentleman, God wot—Canst get two swords for the gentlemen to fight with, Ralph Heskett?"

"No, but I can send to the armory at Carlisle, and lend them two forks, to be making shift with in the meantime."

"Tush, man," said another, "the bonny Scots come into the world with the blue bonnet on their heads, and dirk and pistol at their belt."

"Best send post," said Mr. Fleecebumpkin, "to the Squire of Corby Castle, to come and stand second to the *gentleman*."

In the midst of this torrent of general ridicule, the Highlander instinctively griped beneath the folds of his plaid.

"But it's better not," he said in his own language. "A hundred curses on the swine-eaters, who know neither decency nor civility!"

"Make room, the pack of you," he said, advancing to the door.

But his former friend interposed his sturdy bulk, and opposed his leaving the house; and when Robin Oig attempted to make his way by force, he hit him down on the floor, with as much ease as a boy bowls down a nine-pin.

"A ring, a ring!" was now shouted, until the dark rafters, and the hams that hung on them, trembled again, and the very platters on the *bink* clattered against each other. "Well done, Harry,"—"Give it him home, Harry,"—"Take care of him now,—he sees his own blood!"

Such were the exclamations, while the Highlander, starting from the ground, all his coldness and caution lost in frantic rage, sprung at his antagonist with the fury, the activity, and the vindictive purpose, of an incensed tiger-cat. But when could rage encounter science and temper? Robin Oig again went down in the unequal contest; and as the blow was necessarily a severe one, he lay motionless on the floor of the kitchen. The landlady ran to offer some aid, but Mr. Fleecebumpkin would not permit her to approach.

"Let him alone," he said, "he will come to within time, and come up to the scratch again. He has not got half his broth yet."

"He has got all I mean to give him, though," said his antagonist, whose heart began to relent towards his old associate; "and I would rather by half give the rest to yourself, Mr. Fleecebumpkin, for you pretend to know a thing or two, and Robin had not art enough even to peel before setting to, but fought with his plaid dangling about him.—Stand up, Robin, my man! all friends now; and let me hear the man that will speak a word against you, or your country, for your sake."

Robin Oig was still under the dominion of his passion, and eager to renew the onset; but being withheld on the one side by the peace-making Dame Heskett, and on the other, aware that Wakefield no longer meant to renew the combat, his fury sunk into gloomy sullenness.

"Come, come, never grudge so much at it, man," said the brave-spirited Englishman, with the placability of his country, "shake hands, and we will be better friends than ever."

"Friends!" exclaimed Robin Oig, with strong emphasis— "friends!—Never. Look to yourself, Harry Waakfelt."

"Then the curse of Cromwell on your proud Scots stomach, as the man says in the play, and you may do your worst, and be d——d ! for one man can say nothing more to another after a tussle, than that he is sorry for it."

On these terms the friends parted ; Robin Oig drew out, in silence, a piece of money, threw it on the table, and then left the alehouse. But turning at the door, he shook his hand at Wakefield, pointing with his forefinger upwards, in a manner which might imply either a threat or a caution. He then disappeared in the moonlight.

Some words passed after his departure, between the bailiff, who piqued himself on being a little of a bully, and Harry Wakefield, who, with generous inconsistency, was now not indisposed to begin a new combat in defence of Robin Oig's reputation, "although he could not use his daddles like an Englishman, as it did not come natural to him." But Dame Heskett prevented this second quarrel from coming to a head by her peremptory interference. "There should be no more fighting in her house," she said ; "there had been too much already.—And you, Mr. Wakefield, may live to learn," she added, "what it is to make a deadly enemy out of a good friend."

"Pshaw, dame ! Robin Oig is an honest fellow, and will never keep malice."

"Do not trust to that—you do not know the dour temper of the Scots, though you have dealt with them so often. I have a right to know them, my mother being a Scot."

"And so is well seen on her daughter," said Ralph Heskett.

This nuptial sarcasm gave the discourse another turn ; fresh customers entered the tap-room or kitchen, and others left it. The conversation turned on the expected markets, and the report of prices from different parts both of Scotland and England — treaties were commenced, and Harry Wakefield was lucky enough to find a chap for a part of his drove, and at a very considerable profit ; an event of consequence more than sufficient to blot out all remembrances of the unpleasant scuffle in the earlier part of the day. But there remained one party from whose mind that recollection could not have been wiped away by the possession of every head of cattle betwixt Esk and Eden.

This was Robin Oig M'Combich.—"That I should have had no weapon," he said, "and for the first time in my life !— Blighted be the tongue that bids the Highlander part with the dirk—the dirk—ha ! the English blood !—My Muhme's word —when did her word fall to the ground ?"

The recollection of the fatal prophecy confirmed the deadly intention which instantly sprang up in his mind.

"Ha ! Morrison cannot be many miles behind ; and if it were a hundred, what then ?"

His impetuous spirit had now a fixed purpose and motive of action, and he turned the light foot of his country towards the wilds, through which he knew, by Mr. Ireby's report, that Morrison was advancing. His mind was wholly engrossed by the sense of injury—injury sustained from a friend; and by the desire of vengeance on one whom he now accounted his most bitter enemy. The treasured ideas of self-importance and self-opinion—of ideal birth and quality, had become more precious to him, like the hoard to the miser, because he could only enjoy them in secret. But that hoard was pillaged, the idols which he had secretly worshipped had been desecrated and profaned. Insulted, abused, and beaten, he was no longer worthy, in his own opinion, of the name he bore, or the lineage which he belonged to—nothing was left to him—nothing but revenge; and, as the reflection added a galling spur to every step, he determined it should be as sudden and signal as the offence.

When Robin Oig left the door of the alehouse, seven or eight English miles at least lay betwixt Morrison and him. The advance of the former was slow, limited by the sluggish pace of his cattle; the last left behind him stubble-field and hedge-row, crag and dark heath, all glittering with frost-rime in the broad November moonlight, at the rate of six miles an hour. And now the distant lowing of Morrison's cattle is heard; and now they are seen creeping like moles in size and slowness of motion on the broad face of the moor; and now he meets them —passes them, and stops their conductor.

"May good betide us," said the Southlander—"Is this you, Robin M'Combich, or your wraith?"

"It is Robin Oig M'Combich," answered the Highlander, "and it is not.—But never mind that, put pe giving me the skene-dhu."

"What! you are for back to the Highlands—The devil!— Have you selt all off before the fair? This beats all for quick markets!"

"I have not sold—I am not going north—May pe I will never go north again.—Give me pack my dirk, Hugh Morrison, or there will pe words petween us."

"Indeed, Robin, I'll be better advised before I gie it back to you—it is a wanchancy weapon in a Highlandman's hand, and I am thinking you will be about some barns-breaking."

"Prutt, trutt! let me have my weapon," said Robin Oig impatiently.

"Hooly and fairly," said his well-meaning friend. "I'll tell you what will do better than these dirking doings—Ye ken Highlander, and Lowlander, and Border-men, are a' ae man's bairns when you are over the Scots dyke. See, the Eskdale callants, and fighting Charlie of Liddesdale, and the Lockerby lads, and the four dandies of Lustruther, and a wheen mair grey plaids, are coming up behind, and if you are wranged, there is the hand of a Manly Morrison, we'll see you righted, if Carlisle and Stanwix baith took up the feud."

"To tell you the truth," said Robin Oig, desirous of eluding the suspicions of his friend, "I have inlisted with a party of the Black Watch, and must march off to-morrow morning."

"Inlisted! Were you mad or drunk?—You must buy yourself off—I can lend you twenty notes, and twenty to that, if the drove sell."

"I thank you—thank ye, Hughie; but I go with goodwill the gate that I am going,—so the dirk—the dirk!"

"There it is for you then, since less wunna serve. But think on what I was saying.—Waes me, it will be sair news in the braes of Balquidder, that Robin Oig M'Combich should have run an ill gate, and ta'en on."

"Ill news in Balquidder, indeed!" echoed poor Robin. "But Cot speed you, Hughie, and send you good marcats. Ye winna meet with Robin Oig again, either at tryste or fair."

So saying, he shook hastily the hand of his acquaintance, and set out in the direction from which he had advanced, with the spirit of his former pace.

"There is something wrang with the lad," muttered the Morrison to himself; "but we'll maybe see better into it the morn's morning."

But long ere the morning dawned, the catastrophe of our tale had taken place. It was two hours after the affray had happened, and it was totally forgotten by almost every one, when Robin Oig returned to Heskett's inn. The place was filled at once by various sorts of men, and with noises corresponding to their character. There were the grave low sounds of men engaged in busy traffic, with the laugh, the song, and the riotous jest of those who had nothing to do but to enjoy themselves. Among the last was Harry Wakefield, who, amidst a grinning group of smock-frocks, hobnailed shoes, and jolly English physiognomies, was trolling forth the old ditty,

> "What though my name be Roger,
> Who drives the plough and cart"—

when he was interrupted by a well-known voice saying in a high and stern tone, marked by the sharp Highland accent, "Harry Waakfelt—if you be a man, stand up!"

"What is the matter?—what is it?" the guests demanded of each other.

"It is only a d——d Scotsman," said Fleecebumpkin, who was by this time very drunk, "whom Harry Wakefield helped to his broth the day, who is now come to have *his cauld kail* het again."

"Harry Waakfelt," repeated the same ominous summons, "stand up, if you be a man!"

There is something in the tone of deep and concentrated passion, which attracts attention and imposes awe, even by the very sound. The guests shrunk back on every side, and gazed at the Highlander as he stood in the middle of them, his brows bent, and his features rigid with resolution.

"I will stand up with all my heart, Robin, my boy, but it shall be to shake hands with you, and drink down all unkindness. It is not the fault of your heart, man, that you don't know how to clench your hands."

By this time he stood opposite to his antagonist; his open and unsuspecting look strangely contrasted with the stern purpose, which gleamed wild, dark, and vindictive in the eyes of the Highlander.

"'Tis not thy fault, man, that, not having the luck to be an Englishman, thou canst not fight more than a school-girl."

"I *can* fight," answered Robin Oig sternly, but calmly, "and you shall know it. You, Harry Waakfelt, showed me to-day how the Saxon churls fight—I show you now how the Highland Dunnié-wassel fights."

He seconded the word with the action, and plunged the dagger, which he suddenly displayed, into the broad breast of the English yeoman, with such fatal certainty and force, that the hilt made a hollow sound against the breast-bone, and the double-edged point split the very heart of his victim. Harry Wakefield fell and expired with a single groan. His assassin next seized the bailiff by the collar, and offered the bloody poniard to his throat, whilst dread and surprise rendered the man incapable of defence.

"It were very just to lay you beside him," he said, "but the blood of a base pick-thank shall never mix on my father's dirk, with that of a brave man."

As he spoke, he cast the man from him with so much force that he fell on the floor, while Robin, with his other hand, threw the fatal weapon into the blazing turf-fire.

"There," he said, "take me who likes—and let fire cleanse blood if it can."

The pause of astonishment still continuing, Robin Oig asked for a peace-officer, and a constable having stepped out, he surrendered himself to his custody.

"A bloody night's work you have made of it," said the constable.

"Your own fault," said the Highlander. "Had you kept his hands off me twa hours since, he would have been now as well and merry as he was twa minutes since."

"It must be sorely answered," said the peace-officer.

"Never you mind that—death pays all debts; it will pay that too."

The horror of the bystanders began now to give way to indignation; and the sight of a favourite companion murdered in the midst of them, the provocation being, in their opinion, so utterly inadequate to the excess of vengeance, might have induced them to kill the perpetrator of the deed even upon the very spot. The constable, however, did his duty on this occasion, and with the assistance of some of the more reasonable persons present, procured horses to guard the prisoner to Carlisle, to abide his doom at the next assizes. While the escort was preparing, the prisoner neither expressed the least interest nor attempted the slightest reply. Only before he was carried from the fatal apartment, he desired to look at the dead body, which, raised from the floor, had been deposited upon the large table (at the head of which Harry Wakefield had presided but a few minutes before, full of life, vigour, and animation), until the surgeons should examine the mortal wound. The face of the corpse was decently covered with a napkin. To the surprise and horror of the bystanders, which displayed itself in a general *Ah !* drawn through clenched teeth and half-shut lips, Robin Oig removed the cloth, and gazed with a mournful but steady eye on the lifeless visage, which had been so lately animated, that the smile of good-humoured confidence in his own strength, of conciliation at once, and contempt towards his enemy, still curled his lip. While those present expected that the wound, which had so lately flooded the apartment with gore, would send forth fresh streams at the touch of the homicide, Robin Oig replaced the covering, with the brief exclamation—"He was a pretty man !"

My story is nearly ended. The unfortunate Highlander stood his trial at Carlisle. I was myself present, and as a young Scottish lawyer, or barrister at least, and reputed a man of some quality, the politeness of the Sheriff of Cumberland offered me a place on the bench. The facts of the case were proved in the manner I have related them; and whatever might be at first the prejudice of the audience against a crime so un-English as that of assassination from revenge, yet when the rooted national prejudices of the prisoner had been explained, which made him consider himself as stained with indelible dishonour, when subjected to personal violence; when his previous patience, moderation, and endurance, were considered, the generosity of the English audience was inclined to regard his crime as the wayward aberration of a false idea of honour rather than as flowing from a heart naturally savage, or perverted by habitual vice. I shall never forget the charge of the venerable Judge to the jury, although not at that time liable to be much affected either by that which was eloquent or pathetic.

"We have had," he said, "in the previous part of our duty" (alluding to some former trials), "to discuss crimes which infer disgust and abhorrence, while they call down the well-merited vengeance of the law. It is now our still more melancholy task to apply its salutary though severe enactments to a case of a very singular character, in which the crime (for a crime it is, and a deep one) arose less out of the malevolence of the heart, than the error of the understanding—less from any idea of committing wrong, than from an unhappily perverted notion of that which is right. Here we have two men, highly esteemed, it has been stated, in their rank of life, and attached, it seems, to each other as friends, one of whose lives has been already sacrificed to a punctilio, and the other is about to prove the vengeance of the offended laws; and yet both may claim our commiseration at least, as men acting in ignorance of each other's national prejudices, and unhappily misguided rather than voluntarily erring from the path of right conduct.

"In the original cause of the misunderstanding, we must in justice give the right to the prisoner at the bar. He had acquired possession of the enclosure, which was the object of competition, by a legal contract with the proprietor, Mr. Ireby; and yet, when accosted with reproaches undeserved in themselves, and galling doubtless to a temper at least sufficiently susceptible of passion, he offered notwithstanding to yield up half his acquisition, for the sake of peace and good neighbourhood, and his amicable proposal was rejected with scorn. Then follows the scene at Mr. Heskett the publican's, and you will observe how the stranger was treated by the deceased, and, I am sorry to observe, by those around, who seem to have urged him in a manner which was aggravating in the highest degree. While he asked for peace and for composition, and offered submission to a magistrate, or to a mutual arbiter, the prisoner was insulted by a whole company, who seem on this occasion to have forgotten the national maxim of 'fair play'; and while attempting to escape from the place in peace, he was intercepted, struck down, and beaten to the effusion of his blood.

"Gentlemen of the jury, it was with some impatience that I heard my learned brother, who opened the case for the crown, give an unfavourable turn to the prisoner's conduct on this occasion. He said the prisoner was afraid to encounter his antagonist in fair fight, or to submit to the laws of the ring; and that, therefore, like a cowardly Italian, he had recourse to his fatal stiletto, to murder the man whom he dared not meet in manly encounter. I observed the prisoner shrink from this part of the accusation with the abhorrence natural to a brave man; and as I would wish to make my words impressive, when I point his real crime, I must secure his opinion of my impartiality, by rebutting everything that seems to me a false accusation. There can be no doubt that the prisoner is a man of resolution—too much resolution—I wish to Heaven that he had less, or rather that he had had a better education to regulate it.

"Gentlemen, as to the laws my brother talks of, they may be known in the Bull-ring, or the Bear-garden, or the Cockpit, but they are not known here. Or, if they should be so far admitted as furnishing a species of proof that no malice was intended in this sort of combat, from which fatal accidents do sometimes arise, it can only be so admitted when both parties are *in pari casu*, equally acquainted with, and equally willing to refer themselves to, that species of arbitrament. But will it be contended that a man of superior rank and education is to be subjected, or is obliged to subject himself, to this coarse and brutal strife, perhaps in opposition to a younger, stronger, or more skilful opponent? Certainly even the pugilistic code, if founded upon the fair play of Merry Old England, as my brother alleges it to be, can contain nothing so preposterous. And, gentlemen of the jury, if the laws would support an English gentleman, wearing, we will suppose, his sword, in defending himself by force against a violent personal aggression of the nature offered to this prisoner, they will not less protect a foreigner and a stranger, involved in the same unpleasing circumstances. If, therefore, gentlemen of the jury, when thus pressed by a *vis major*, the object of obloquy to a whole company, and of direct violence from one at least, and, as he might reasonably apprehend, from more, the panel had produced the weapon which his countrymen, as we are informed, generally carry about their persons, and the same unhappy circumstance had ensued which you have heard detailed in evidence, I could not in my conscience have asked from you a verdict of murder. The prisoner's personal defence might, indeed, even in that case, have gone more or less beyond the *Moderamen inculpatæ tutelæ*, spoken of by lawyers, but the punishment incurred would have been that of manslaughter, not of murder. I beg leave to add, that I should have thought this milder species of charge was demanded in the case supposed, notwithstanding the statute of James I. cap. 8, which takes the case of slaughter by stabbing with a short weapon, even without malice prepense, out of the benefit of clergy. For this statute of stabbing, as it is termed, arose out of a temporary cause; and as the real guilt is the same, whether the slaughter be committed by the dagger, or by sword or pistol, the benignity of the modern law places them all on the same, or nearly the same footing.

"But, gentlemen of the jury, the pinch of the case lies in the interval of two hours interposed betwixt the reception of the injury and the fatal retaliation. In the heat of affray and *chaude mêlée*, law, compassionating the infirmities of humanity, makes allowance for the passions which rule such a stormy moment—for the sense of present pain, for the apprehension of farther injury, for the difficulty of ascertaining with due accuracy the precise degree of violence which is necessary to protect the person of the individual, without annoying or injuring the assailant more than is absolutely requisite. But the time necessary to walk twelve miles, however speedily performed, was an interval sufficient for the prisoner to have recollected himself; and the violence with which he carried his purpose into effect, with so many circumstances of deliberate determination, could neither be induced by the passion of anger, nor that of fear. It was the purpose and the act of predetermined revenge, for which law neither can, will, nor ought to have sympathy or allowance.

"It is true, we may repeat to ourselves, in alleviation of this poor man's unhappy action, that his case is a very peculiar one. The country which he inhabits was, in the days of many now alive, inaccessible to the laws, not only of England, which have not even yet penetrated thither, but to those to which our neighbours of Scotland are subjected, and which must be supposed to be, and no doubt actually are, founded upon the general principles of justice and equity which pervade every civilised country. Amongst their mountains, as among the North American Indians, the various tribes were wont to make war upon each other, so that each man was obliged to go armed for his own protection. These men, from the ideas which they entertained of their own descent and of their own consequence, regarded themselves as so many cavaliers or men-at-arms, rather than as the peasantry of a peaceful country. Those laws of the ring, as my brother terms them, were unknown to the race of warlike mountaineers; that decision of quarrels by no other weapons than those which nature has given every man, must to them have seemed as vulgar and as preposterous as to the Noblesse of France. Revenge, on the other hand, must have been as familiar to their habits of society as to those of the Cherokees or Mohawks. It is indeed, as described by Bacon, at bottom, a kind of wild untutored justice ; for the fear of retaliation must withhold the hands of the oppressor where there is no regular law to check daring violence. But though all this may be granted, and though we may allow that, such having been the case of the Highlands in the days of the prisoner's fathers, many of the opinions and sentiments must still continue to influence the present generation, it cannot, and ought not, even in this most painful case, to alter the administration of the law, either in your hands, gentlemen of the jury, or in mine. The first object of civilisation is to place the general protection of the law, equally administered, in the room of that wild justice, which every man cut and carved for himself, according to the length of his sword and the strength of his arm. The law says to the subjects, with a voice only nferior to that of the Deity, 'Vengeance is mine.' The instant that there is time for passion to cool, and reason to interpose, an injured party must become aware, that the law assumes the exclusive cognisance of the right and wrong betwixt the parties, and opposes her inviolable buckler to every attempt of the private party to right himself. I repeat, that this unhappy man ought personally to be the object rather of our pity than our abhorrence, for he failed in his ignorance, and from mistaken notions of honour. But his crime is not the less that of murder, gentlemen, and in your high and important office, it is your duty so to find. Englishmen have their angry passions as well as Scots; and should this man's action remain unpunished, you may unsheath, under various pretences, a thousand daggers betwixt the Land's-end and the Orkneys."

The venerable Judge thus ended what, to judge by his apparent emotion, and by the tears which filled his eyes, was really a painful task. The jury, according to his instructions, brought in a verdict of Guilty; and Robin Oig M'Combich, *alias* M'Gregor, was sentenced to death, and left for execution, which took place accordingly. He met his fate with great firmness, and acknowledged the justice of his sentence. But he repelled indignantly the observations of those who accused him of attacking an unarmed man. "I give a life for the life I took," he said, "and what can I do more?"

MY AUNT MARGARET'S MIRROR

"There are times,
When Fancy plays her gambols, in despite
Even of our watchful senses, when in sooth
Substance seems shadow, shadow substance seems,
When the broad, palpable, and mark'd partition,
'Twixt that which is and is not, seems dissolved,
As if the mental eye gain'd power to gaze
Beyond the limits of the existing world.
Such hours of shadowy dreams I better love
Than all the gross realities of life."
                                        —ANONYMOUS.

MY AUNT MARGARET was one of that respected sisterhood, upon whom devolve all the trouble and solicitude incidental to the possession of children, excepting only that which attends their entrance into the world. We were a large family, of very different dispositions and constitutions. Some were dull and peevish—they were sent to Aunt Margaret to be amused ; some were rude, romping, and boisterous—they were sent to Aunt Margaret to be kept quiet, or rather that their noise might be removed out of hearing : those who were indisposed were sent with the prospect of being nursed—those who were stubborn, with the hope of their being subdued by the kindness of Aunt Margaret's discipline ; in short, she had all the various duties of a mother, without the credit and dignity of the maternal character. The busy scene of her various cares is now over—of the invalids and the robust, the kind and the rough, the peevish and pleased children, who thronged her little parlour from morning to night, not one now remains alive but myself ; who, afflicted by early infirmity, was one of the most delicate of her nurslings, yet, nevertheless, have outlived them all.

It is still my custom, and shall be so while I have the use of my limbs, to visit my respected relation at least three times a-week. Her abode is about half a mile from the suburbs of the town in which I reside ; and is accessible not only by the high-road, from which it stands at some distance, but by means of a greensward footpath, leading through some pretty meadows. I have so little left to torment me in life, that it is one of my greatest vexations to know that several of these sequestered fields have been devoted as sites for building. In that which is nearest the town, wheelbarrows have been at work for several weeks in such numbers, that, I verily believe, its whole surface, to the depth of at least eighteen inches, was mounted in these monotrochs at the same moment, and in the act of being transported from one place to another. Huge triangular piles of planks are also reared in different parts of the devoted messuage; and a little group of trees, that still grace the eastern end, which rises in a gentle ascent, have just received warning to quit, expressed by a daub of white paint, and are to give place to a curious grove of chimneys.

It would, perhaps, hurt others in my situation to reflect that this little range of pasturage once belonged to my father (whose family was of some consideration in the world), and was sold by patches to remedy distresses in which he involved himself in an attempt by commercial adventure to redeem his diminished fortune. While the building scheme was in full operation, this circumstance was often pointed out to me by the class of friends who are anxious that no part of your misfortunes should escape your observation. "Such pasture-ground!— lying at the very town's end—in turnips and potatoes, the parks would bring £20 per acre, and if leased for building—Oh, it was a gold mine!—And all sold for an old song out of the ancient possessor's hands!" My comforters cannot bring me to repine much on this subject. If I could be allowed to look back on the past without interruption, I could willingly give up the enjoyment of present income, and the hope of future profit, to those who have purchased what my father sold. I regret the alteration of the ground only because it destroys associations, and I would more willingly (I think) see the Earl's Closes in the hands of strangers, retaining their silvan appearance, than know them for my own, if torn up by agriculture, or covered with buildings. Mine are the sensations of poor Logan:

> " The horrid plough has rased the green
> Where yet a child I stray'd;
> The axe has felled the hawthorn screen,
> The schoolboy's summer shade."

I hope, however, the threatened devastation will not be consummated in my day. Although the adventurous spirit of times short while since passed gave rise to the undertaking, I have been encouraged to think, that the subsequent changes have so far damped the spirit of speculation, that the rest of the woodland footpath leading to Aunt Margaret's retreat will be left undisturbed for her time and mine. I am interested in this, for every step of the way, after I have passed through the green already mentioned, has for me something of early remembrance:—There is the stile at which I can recollect a cross

child's-maid upbraiding me with my infirmity, as she lifted me
coarsely and carelessly over the flinty steps, which my brothers
traversed with shout and bound. I remember the suppressed
bitterness of the moment, and, conscious of my own inferiority,
the feeling of envy with which I regarded the easy movements
and elastic steps of my more happily formed brethren. Alas!
these goodly barks have all perished on life's wide ocean, and
only that which seemed so little seaworthy, as the naval phrase
goes, has reached the port when the tempest is over. Then
there is the pool, where, manœuvring our little navy, constructed out of the broad water flags, my elder brother fell in,
and was scarce saved from the watery element to die under
Nelson's banner. There is the hazel copse also, in which my
brother Henry used to gather nuts, thinking little that he was
to die in an Indian jungle in quest of rupees.

There is so much more of remembrance about the little walk,
that—as I stop, rest on my crutch-headed cane, and look round
with that species of comparison between the thing I was and
that which I now am—it almost induces me to doubt my
own identity; until I find myself in face of the honeysuckle
porch of Aunt Margaret's dwelling, with its irregularity of front,
and its odd projecting latticed windows; where the workmen
seem to have made a study that no one of them should resemble
another, in form, size, or in the old-fashioned stone entablature
and labels which adorn them. This tenement, once the manor-
house of Earl's Closes, we still retain a slight hold upon; for,
in some family arrangements, it had been settled upon Aunt
Margaret during the term of her life. Upon this frail tenure
depends, in a great measure, the last shadow of the family of
Bothwell of Earl's Closes, and their last slight connection with
their paternal inheritance. The only representative will then
be an infirm old man, moving not unwillingly to the grave, which
has devoured all that were dear to his affections.

When I have indulged such thoughts for a minute or two, I
enter the mansion, which is said to have been the gatehouse
only of the original building, and find one being on whom
time seems to have made little impression; for the Aunt
Margaret of to-day bears the same proportional age to the Aunt
Margaret of my early youth, that the boy of ten years old does
to the man of (by'r Lady!) some fifty-six years. The old
lady's invariable costume has doubtless some share in confirm-
ing one in the opinion, that time has stood still with Aunt
Margaret.

The brown or chocolate-coloured silk gown, with ruffles of
the same stuff at the elbow, within which are others of Mechlin
lace—the black silk gloves, or mitts, the white hair combed
back upon a roll, and the cap of spotless cambric, which closes

around the venerable countenance, as they were not the costume
of 1780, so neither were they that of 1826; they are altogether
a style peculiar to the individual Aunt Margaret. There she
still sits, as she sat thirty years since, with her wheel or the
stocking, which she works by the fire in winter, and by the
window in summer; or, perhaps, venturing as far as the porch
in an unusually fine summer evening. Her frame, like some
well-constructed piece of mechanics, still performs the opera-
tions for which it had seemed destined; going its round with
an activity which is gradually diminished, yet indicating no
probability that it will soon come to a period.

The solicitude and affection which had made Aunt Margaret
the willing slave to the inflictions of a whole nursery, have
now for their object the health and comfort of one old and
infirm man, the last remaining relative of her family, and the
only one who can still find interest in the traditional stores
which she hoards, as some miser hides the gold which he desires
that no one should enjoy after his death.

My conversation with Aunt Margaret generally relates little
either to the present or to the future: for the passing day we
possess as much as we require, and we neither of us wish for
more; and for that which is to follow we have on this side of
the grave neither hopes, nor fears, nor anxiety. We therefore
naturally look back to the past; and forget the present fallen
fortunes and declined importance of our family, in recalling the
hours when it was wealthy and prosperous.

With this slight introduction, the reader will know as much
of Aunt Margaret and her nephew as is necessary to comprehend the following conversation and narrative.

Last week, when, late in a summer evening, I went to call
on the old lady to whom my reader is now introduced, I was
received by her with all her usual affection and benignity;
while, at the same time, she seemed abstracted and disposed to
silence. I asked her the reason. "They have been clearing
out the old chapel," she said; "John Clayhudgeons having, it
seems, discovered that the stuff within—being, I suppose, the
remains of our ancestors—was excellent for top-dressing the
meadows."

Here I started up with more alacrity than I have displayed
for some years; but sat down while my aunt added, laying her
hand upon my sleeve, "The chapel has been long considered
as common ground, my dear, and used for a penfold, and what
objection can we have to the man for employing what is his
own, to his own profit? Besides, I did speak to him, and he
very readily and civilly promised, that, if he found bones or
monuments, they should be carefully respected and reinstated;
and what more could I ask? So, the first stone they found

bore the name of Margaret Bothwell, 1585, and I have caused it to be laid carefully aside, as I think it betokens death; and having served my namesake two hundred years, it has just been cast up in time to do me the same good turn. My house has been long put in order, as far as the small earthly concerns require it, but who shall say that their account with Heaven is sufficiently revised?"

"After what you have said, aunt," I replied, "perhaps I ought to take my hat and go away, and so I should, but that there is on this occasion a little alloy mingled with our devotion. To think of death at all times is a duty—to suppose it nearer, from the finding of an old gravestone, is superstition; and you, with your strong useful common sense, which was so long the prop of a fallen family, are the last person whom I should have suspected of such weakness."

"Neither would I have deserved your suspicions, kinsman," answered Aunt Margaret, "if we were speaking of any incident occurring in the actual business of human life. But for all this I have a sense of superstition about me, which I do not wish to part with. It is a feeling which separates me from this age, and links me with that to which I am hastening; and even when it seems, as now, to lead me to the brink of the grave, and bids me gaze on it, I do not love that it should be dispelled. It soothes my imagination, without influencing my reason or conduct."

"I profess, my good lady," replied I, "that had any one but you made such a declaration, I should have thought it as capricious as that of the clergyman, who, without vindicating his false reading, preferred, from habit's sake, his old Mumpsimus to the modern Sumpsimus."

"Well," answered my aunt, "I must explain my inconsistency in this particular, by comparing it to another. I am, as you know, a piece of that old-fashioned thing called a Jacobite; but I am so in sentiment and feeling only; for a more loyal subject never joined in prayers for the health and wealth of George the Fourth, whom God long preserve! But I dare say that kind-hearted sovereign would not deem that an old woman did him much injury if she leaned back in her arm-chair, just in such a twilight as this, and thought of the high-mettled men, whose sense of duty called them to arms against his grandfather; and how, in a cause which they deemed that of their rightful prince and country,

'They fought till their hands to the broadsword were glued,
They fought against fortune with hearts unsubdued.'

Do not come at such a moment, when my head is full of plaids, pibrochs, and claymores, and ask my reason to admit what, I am afraid, it cannot deny—I mean, that the public advantage

peremptorily demanded that these things should cease to exist.
I cannot, indeed, refuse to allow the justice of your reasoning ;
but yet, being convinced against my will, you will gain little by
your motion. You might as well read to an infatuated lover the
catalogue of his mistress's imperfections ; for, when he has been
compelled to listen to the summary, you will only get for answer,
that, ' he lo'es her a' the better.' "

I was not sorry to have changed the gloomy train of Aunt
Margaret's thoughts, and replied in the same tone, " Well, I
can't help being persuaded that our good king is the more sure
of Mrs. Bothwell's loyal affection, that he has the Stuart right of
birth, as well as the Act of Succession in his favour."

" Perhaps my attachment, were its source of consequence,
might be found warmer for the union of the rights you mention,"
said Aunt Margaret ; " but, upon my word, it would be as
sincere if the king's right were founded only on the will of
the nation, as declared at the Revolution. I am none of your
jure divino folk."

" And a Jacobite notwithstanding."

" And a Jacobite notwithstanding ; or rather, I will give
you leave to call me one of the party which, in Queen Anne's
time, were called *Whimsicals* ; because they were sometimes
operated upon by feelings, sometimes by principle. After all,
it is very hard that you will not allow an old woman to be as
inconsistent in her political sentiments, as mankind in general
show themselves in all the various courses of life ; since you
cannot point out one of them, in which the passions and prejudices of those who pursue it are not perpetually carrying us
away from the path which our reason points out."

" True, aunt ; but you are a wilful wanderer, who should be
forced back into the right path."

" Spare me, I entreat you," replied Aunt Margaret. " You
remember the Gaelic song, though I dare say I mispronounce
the words—

' Hatil mohatil, na dowski mi.'
' I am asleep, do not waken me.'

I tell you, kinsman, that the sort of waking dreams which my
imagination spins out, in what your favourite Wordsworth calls
' moods of my own mind,' are worth all the rest of my more
active days. Then, instead of looking forwards as I did in
youth, and forming for myself fairy palaces, upon the verge of
the grave, I turn my eyes backward upon the days and manners
of my better time ; and the sad, yet soothing recollections come
so close and interesting, that I almost think it sacrilege to be
wiser, or more rational, or less prejudiced, than those to whom I
looked up in my younger years."

" I think I now understand what you mean," I answered, " and can comprehend why you should occasionally prefer the twilight of illusion to the steady light of reason."

" Where there is no task," she rejoined, " to be performed, we may sit in the dark if we like it—if we go to work, we must ring for candles."

" And amidst such shadowy and doubtful light," continued I, " imagination frames her enchanted and enchanting visions, and sometimes passes them upon the senses for reality."

" Yes," said Aunt Margaret, who is a well-read woman, " to those who resemble the translator of Tasso,

> ' Prevailing poet, whose undoubting mind
> Believed the magic wonders which he sung.'

It is not required for this purpose, that you should be sensible of the painful horrors which an actual belief in such prodigies inflicts—such a belief, nowadays, belongs only to fools and children. It is not necessary that your ears should tingle, and your complexion change, like that of Theodore, at the approach of the spectral huntsman. All that is indispensable for the enjoyment of the milder feeling of supernatural awe is, that you should be susceptible of the slight shuddering which creeps over you when you hear a tale of terror—that well-vouched tale which the narrator, having first expressed his general disbelief of all such legendary lore, selects and produces, as having something in it which he has been always obliged to give up as inexplicable. Another symptom is, a momentary hesitation to look round you, when the interest of the narrative is at the highest; and the third, a desire to avoid looking into a mirror, when you are alone, in your chamber, for the evening. I mean such are signs which indicate the crisis, when a female imagination is in due temperature to enjoy a ghost story. I do not pretend to describe those which express the same disposition in a gentleman."

" This last symptom, dear aunt, of shunning the mirror, seems likely to be a rare occurrence amongst the fair sex."

" You are a novice in toilet fashions, my dear kinsman. All women consult the looking-glass with anxiety before they go into company; but when they return home, the mirror has not the same charm. The die has been cast—the party has been successful or unsuccessful, in the impression which she desired to make. But, without going deeper into the mysteries of the dressing-table, I will tell you that I myself, like many other honest folk, do not like to see the blank black front of a large mirror in a room dimly lighted, and where the reflection of the candle seems rather to lose itself in the deep obscurity of the glass, than to be reflected back again into the apartment. That

space of inky darkness seems to be a field for Fancy to play her
revels in. She may call up other features to meet us, instead
of the reflection of our own; or, as in the spells of Hallowe'en,
which we learned in childhood, some unknown form may be
seen peeping over our shoulder. In short, when I am in a
ghost-seeing humour, I make my handmaiden draw the green
curtains over the mirror before I go into the room, so that she
may have the first shock of the apparition, if there be any to
be seen. But, to tell you the truth, this dislike to look into a
mirror in particular times and places, has, I believe, its original
foundation in a story which came to me by tradition from my
grandmother, who was a party concerned in the scene of which
I will now tell you."

THE MIRROR

CHAPTER I

You are fond (said my aunt) of sketches of the society which has passed away. I wish I could describe to you Sir Philip Forester, the "chartered libertine" of Scottish good company, about the end of the last century. I never saw him indeed; but my mother's traditions were full of his wit, gallantry, and dissipation. This gay knight flourished about the end of the 17th and beginning of the 18th century. He was the Sir Charles Easy and the Lovelace of his day and country: renowned for the number of duels he had fought, and the successful intrigues which he had carried on. The supremacy which he had attained in the fashionable world was absolute; and when we combine it with one or two anecdotes, for which, "if laws were made for every degree," he ought certainly to have been hanged, the popularity of such a person really serves to show, either that the present times are much more decent, if not more virtuous, than they formerly were; or, that high breeding then was 'of more difficult attainment than that which is now so called; and, consequently, entitled the successful professor to a proportionable degree of plenary indulgences and privileges. No beau of this day could have borne out so ugly a story as that of Pretty Peggy Grindstone, the miller's daughter at Sillermills — it had well-nigh made work for the Lord Advocate. But it hurt Sir Philip Forester no more than the hail hurts the hearthstone. He was as well received in society as ever, and dined with the Duke of A—— the day the poor girl was buried. She died of heart-break. But that has nothing to do with my story.

Now, you must listen to a single word upon kith, kin, and ally; I promise you I will not be prolix. But it is necessary to the authenticity of my legend, that you should know that Sir Philip Forester, with his handsome person, elegant accomplishments, and fashionable manners, married the younger Miss Falconer of King's-Copland. The elder sister of this lady had previously become the wife of my grandfather, Sir Geoffrey Bothwell, and brought into our family a good fortune. Miss

Jemima, or Miss Jemmie Falconer, as she was usually called, had also about ten thousand pounds sterling—then thought a very handsome portion indeed.

The two sisters were extremely different, though each had their admirers while they remained single. Lady Bothwell had some touch of the old King's-Copland blood about her. She was bold, though not to the degree of audacity; ambitious, and desirous to raise her house and family; and was, as has been said, a considerable spur to my grandfather, who was otherwise an indolent man; but whom, unless he has been slandered, his lady's influence involved in some political matters which had been more wisely let alone. She was a woman of high principle, however, and masculine good sense, as some of her letters testify, which are still in my wainscot cabinet.

Jemmie Falconer was the reverse of her sister in every respect. Her understanding did not reach above the ordinary pitch, if, indeed, she could be said to have attained it. Her beauty, while it lasted, consisted, in a great measure, of delicacy of complexion and regularity of features, without any peculiar force of expression. Even these charms faded under the sufferings attendant on an ill-sorted match. She was passionately attached to her husband, by whom she was treated with a callous, yet polite indifference, which, to one whose heart was as tender as her judgment was weak, was more painful perhaps than absolute ill-usage. Sir Philip was a voluptuary, that is, a completely selfish egotist, whose disposition and character resembled the rapier he wore, polished, keen, and brilliant, but inflexible and unpitying. As he observed carefully all the usual forms towards his lady, he had the art to deprive her even of the compassion of the world; and useless and unavailing as that may be while actually possessed by the sufferer, it is, to a mind like Lady Forester's, most painful to know she has it not.

The tattle of society did its best to place the peccant husband above the suffering wife. Some called her a poor spiritless thing, and declared that, with a little of her sister's spirit, she might have brought to reason any Sir Philip whatsoever, were it the termagant Falconbridge himself. But the greater part of their acquaintance affected candour, and saw faults on both sides; though, in fact, there only existed the oppressor and the oppressed. The tone of such critics was—"To be sure, no one will justify Sir Philip Forester, but then we all know Sir Philip, and Jemmie Falconer might have known what she had to expect from the beginning.—What made her set her cap at Sir Philip?—He would never have looked at her if she had not thrown herself at his head, with her poor ten thousand pounds. I am sure, if it is money he wanted, she spoiled his market. I know where Sir Philip could have done much better.— And then, if she *would* have the man, could not she try to make him more comfortable at home, and have his friends oftener, and not plague him with the squalling children, and take care all was handsome and in good style about the house? I declare I think Sir Philip would have made a very domestic man, with a woman who knew how to manage him."

Now these fair critics, in raising their profound edifice of domestic felicity, did not recollect that the corner-stone was wanting; and that to receive good company with good cheer, the means of the banquet ought to have been furnished by Sir Philip; whose income (dilapidated as it was) was not equal to the display of hospitality required, and, at the same time, to the supply of the good knight's *menus plaisirs.* So, in spite of all that was so sagely suggested by female friends, Sir Philip carried his good-humour everywhere abroad, and left at home a solitary mansion and a pining spouse.

At length, inconvenienced in his money affairs, and tired even of the short time which he spent in his own dull house, Sir Philip Forester determined to take a trip to the Continent, in the capacity of a volunteer. It was then common for men of fashion to do so; and our knight perhaps was of opinion that a touch of the military character, just enough to exalt, but not render pedantic, his qualities as a *beau garçon,* was necessary to maintain possession of the elevated situation which he held in the ranks of fashion.

Sir Philip's resolution threw his wife into agonies of terror, by which the worthy baronet was so much annoyed, that, contrary to his wont, he took some trouble to soothe her apprehensions; and once more brought her to shed tears, in which sorrow was not altogether unmingled with pleasure. Lady Bothwell asked, as a favour, Sir Philip's permission to receive her sister and her family into her own house during his absence on the Continent. Sir Philip readily assented to a proposition which saved expense, silenced the foolish people who might have talked of a deserted wife and family, and gratified Lady Bothwell, for whom he felt some respect, as for one who often spoke to him, always with freedom, and sometimes with severity, without being deterred either by his raillery, or the *prestige* of his reputation.

A day or two before Sir Philip's departure, Lady Bothwell took the liberty of asking him, in her sister's presence, the direct question, which his timid wife had often desired, but never ventured, to put to him.

"Pray, Sir Philip, what route do you take when you reach the Continent?"

"I go from Leith to Helvoet by a packet with advices."

"That I comprehend perfectly," said Lady Bothwell dryly; "but you do not mean to remain long at Helvoet, I presume, and I should like to know what is your next object?"

"You ask me, my dear lady," answered Sir Philip, "a question which I have not dared to ask myself. The answer depends on the fate of war. I shall, of course, go to head-quarters, wherever they may happen to be for the time; deliver my letters of introduction; learn as much of the noble art of war as may suffice a poor interloping amateur; and then take a glance at the sort of thing of which we read so much in the Gazette."

"And I trust, Sir Philip," said Lady Bothwell, "that you will remember that you are a husband and a father; and that though you think fit to indulge this military fancy, you will not let it hurry you into dangers which it is certainly unnecessary for any save professional persons to encounter?"

"Lady Bothwell does me too much honour," replied the adventurous knight, "in regarding such a circumstance with the slightest interest. But to soothe your flattering anxiety, I trust your ladyship will recollect, that I cannot expose to hazard the venerable and paternal character which you so obligingly recommend to my protection, without putting in some peril an honest fellow, called Philip Forester, with whom I have kept company for thirty years, and with whom, though some folk consider him a coxcomb, I have not the least desire to part."

"Well, Sir Philip, you are the best judge of your own affairs; I have little right to interfere—you are not my husband."

"God forbid!" said Sir Philip hastily; instantly adding, however, "God forbid that I should deprive my friend Sir Geoffrey of so inestimable a treasure."

"But you are my sister's husband," replied the lady; "and I suppose you are aware of her present distress of mind"——

"If hearing of nothing else from morning to night can make me aware of it," said Sir Philip, "I should know something of the matter."

"I do not pretend to reply to your wit, Sir Philip," answered Lady Bothwell; "but you must be sensible that all this distress is on account of apprehensions for your personal safety."

"In that case, I am surprised that Lady Bothwell, at least, should give herself so much trouble upon so insignificant a subject."

"My sister's interest may account for my being anxious to learn something of Sir Philip Forester's motions; about which otherwise, I know, he would not wish me to concern myself. I have a brother's safety, too, to be anxious for."

"You mean Major Falconer, your brother by the mother's

side :—What can he possibly have to do with our present
agreeable conversation ?"

"You have had words together, Sir Philip," said Lady
Bothwell.

"Naturally ; we are connections," replied Sir Philip, "and
as such have always had the usual intercourse."

"That is an evasion of the subject," answered the lady.
"By words, I mean angry words, on the subject of your usage
of your wife."

"If," replied Sir Philip Forester, "you suppose Major Falconer simple enough to intrude his advice upon me, Lady
Bothwell, in my domestic matters, you are indeed warranted
in believing that I might possibly be so far displeased with
the interference, as to request him to reserve his advice till it
was asked."

"And, being on these terms, you are going to join the very
army in which my brother Falconer is now serving ?"

"No man knows the path of honour better than Major
Falconer," said Sir Philip. "An aspirant after fame, like me,
cannot choose a better guide than his footsteps."

Lady Bothwell rose and went to the window, the tears gush-
ing from her eyes.

"And this heartless raillery," she said, "is all the consideration that is to be given to our apprehensions of a quarrel which
may bring on the most terrible consequences ? Good God ! of
what can men's hearts be made, who can thus dally with the
agony of others ?"

Sir Philip Forester was moved ; he laid aside the mocking
tone in which he had hitherto spoken.

"Dear Lady Bothwell," he said, taking her reluctant hand,
"we are both wrong :—you are too deeply serious ; I, perhaps,
too little so. The dispute I had with Major Falconer was of
no earthly consequence. Had anything occurred betwixt us
that ought to have been settled *par voie du fait*, as we say in
France, neither of us are persons that are likely to postpone
such a meeting. Permit me to say, that were it generally
known that you or my Lady Forester are apprehensive of such
a catastrophe, it might be the very means of bringing about
what would not otherwise be likely to happen. I know your
good sense, Lady Bothwell, and that you will understand me
when I say, that really my affairs require my absence for some
months ;—this Jemima cannot understand ; it is a perpetual
recurrence of questions, why can you not do this, or that, or
the third thing ; and, when you have proved to her that her
expedients are totally ineffectual, you have just to begin the
whole round again. Now, do you tell her, dear Lady Bothwell, that *you* are satisfied. She is, you must confess, one of

those persons with whom authority goes farther than reasoning. Do but repose a little confidence in me, and you shall see how amply I will repay it."

Lady Bothwell shook her head, as one but half satisfied. "How difficult it is to extend confidence, when the basis on which it ought to rest has been so much shaken! But I will do my best to make Jemima easy; and farther, I can only say, that for keeping your present purpose, I hold you responsible both to God and man."

"Do not fear that I will deceive you," said Sir Philip; "the safest conveyance to me will be through the general post-office Helvoetsluys, where I will take care to leave orders for forwarding my letters. As for Falconer, our only encounter will be over a bottle of Burgundy! so make yourself perfectly easy on his score."

Lady Bothwell could *not* make herself easy; yet she was sensible that her sister hurt her own cause by *taking on*, as the maid-servants call it, too vehemently; and by showing before every stranger, by manner, and sometimes by words also, a dissatisfaction with her husband's journey, that was sure to come to his ears, and equally certain to displease him. But there was no help for this domestic dissension, which ended only with the day of separation.

I am sorry I cannot tell, with precision, the year in which Sir Philip Forester went over to Flanders; but it was one of those in which the campaign opened with extraordinary fury; and many bloody, though indecisive, skirmishes were fought between the French on the one side, and the Allies on the other. In all our modern improvements, there are none, perhaps, greater than in the accuracy and speed with which intelligence is transmitted from any scene of action to those in this country whom it may concern. During Marlborough's campaigns, the sufferings of the many who had relations in, or along with, the army, were greatly augmented by the suspense in which they were detained for weeks, after they had heard of bloody battles, in which, in all probability, those for whom their bosoms throbbed with anxiety had been personally engaged. Amongst those who were most agonised by this state of uncertainty, was the—I had almost said deserted— wife of the gay Sir Philip Forester. A single letter had informed her of his arrival on the Continent—no others were received. One notice occurred in the newspapers, in which Volunteer Sir Philip Forester was mentioned as having been entrusted with a dangerous reconnoissance, which he had executed with the greatest courage, dexterity, and intelligence, and received the thanks of the commanding officer. The sense of his having acquired distinction brought a momentary glow into the lady's pale cheek; but it was instantly lost in ashen whiteness at the recollection of his danger. After this, they had no news whatever, neither from Sir Philip, nor even from their brother Falconer. The case of Lady Forester was not indeed different from that of hundreds in the same situation; but a feeble mind is necessarily an irritable one, and the suspense which some bear with constitutional indifference or philosophical resignation, and some with a disposition to believe and hope the best, was intolerable to Lady Forester, at once solitary and sensitive, low-spirited, and devoid of strength of mind, whether natural or acquired.

CHAPTER II

As she received no farther news of Sir Philip, whether directly or indirectly, his unfortunate lady began now to feel a sort of consolation, even in those careless habits which had so often given her pain. "He is so thoughtless," she repeated a hundred times a day to her sister, "he never writes when things are going on smoothly; it is his way: had anything happened he would have informed us."

Lady Bothwell listened to her sister without attempting to console her. Probably she might be of opinion, that even the worst intelligence which could be received from Flanders might not be without some touch of consolation; and that the Dowager Lady Forester, if so she was doomed to be called, might have a source of happiness unknown to the wife of the gayest and finest gentleman in Scotland. This conviction became stronger as they learned from inquiries made at head-quarters, that Sir Philip was no longer with the army; though whether he had been taken or slain in some of those skirmishes which were perpetually occurring, and in which he loved to distinguish himself, or whether he had, for some unknown reason or capricious change of mind, voluntarily left the service, none of his countrymen in the camp of the Allies could form even a conjecture. Meantime his creditors at home became clamorous, entered into possession of his property, and threatened his person, should he be rash enough to return to Scotland. These additional disadvantages aggravated Lady Bothwell's displeasure against the fugitive husband; while her sister saw nothing in any of them, save what tended to increase her grief for the absence of him whom her imagination now represented, —as it had before marriage,—gallant, gay, and affectionate.

About this period there appeared in Edinburgh a man of

singular appearance and pretensions. He was commonly called
the Paduan Doctor, from having received his education at
that famous university. He was supposed to possess some rare
receipts in medicine, with which, it was affirmed, he had
wrought remarkable cures. But though, on the one hand, the
physicians of Edinburgh termed him an empiric, there were
many persons, and among them some of the clergy, who, while
they admitted the truth of the cures and the force of his
remedies, alleged that Doctor Baptisti Damiotti made use of
charms and unlawful arts in order to obtain success in his
practice. The resorting to him was even solemnly preached
against, as a seeking of health from idols, and a trusting to the
help which was to come from Egypt. But the protection which
the Paduan Doctor received from some friends of interest and
consequence, enabled him to set these imputations at defiance,
and to assume, even in the city of Edinburgh, famed as it was
for abhorrence of witches and necromancers, the dangerous
character of an expounder of futurity. It was at length
rumoured, that for a certain gratification, which, of course, was
not an inconsiderable one, Doctor Baptisti Damiotti could tell
the fate of the absent, and even show his visitors the personal
form of their absent friends, and the action in which they were
engaged at the moment. This rumour came to the ears of
Lady Forester, who had reached that pitch of mental agony in
which the sufferer will do anything, or endure anything, that
suspense may be converted into certainty.

Gentle and timid in most cases, her state of mind made her
equally obstinate and reckless, and it was with no small surprise
and alarm that her sister, Lady Bothwell, heard her express a
resolution to visit this man of art, and learn from him the fate
of her husband. Lady Bothwell remonstrated on the improba-
bility that such pretentions as those of this foreigner could be
founded in anything but imposture.

" I care not," said the deserted wife, " what degree of ridicule
I may incur ; if there be any one chance out of a hundred that
I may obtain some certainty of my husband's fate, I would not
miss that chance for whatever else the world can offer me."

Lady Bothwell next urged the unlawfulness of resorting to
such sources of forbidden knowledge.

"Sister," replied the sufferer, "he who is dying of thirst
cannot refrain from drinking even poisoned water. She who
suffers under suspense must seek information, even were the
powers which offer it unhallowed and infernal. I go to learn
my fate alone ; and this very evening will I know it : the sun
that rises to-morrow shall find me, if not more happy, at least
more resigned."

"Sister," said Lady Bothwell, "if you are determined upon

this wild step, you shall not go alone. If this man be an impostor, you may be too much agitated by your feelings to detect his villainy. If, which I cannot believe, there be any truth in what he pretends, you shall not be exposed alone to a communication of so extraordinary a nature. I will go with you, if indeed you determine to go. But yet reconsider your project, and renounce inquiries which cannot be prosecuted without guilt, and perhaps without danger.

Lady Forester threw herself into her sister's arms, and, clasping her to her bosom, thanked her a hundred times for the offer of her company; while she declined with a melancholy gesture the friendly advice with which it was accompanied.

When the hour of twilight arrived,—which was the period when the Paduan Doctor was understood to receive the visits of those who came to consult with him,—the two ladies left their apartments in the Canongate of Edinburgh, having their dress arranged like that of women of an inferior description, and their plaids disposed around their faces as they were worn by the same class; for, in those days of aristocracy, the quality of the wearer was generally indicated by the manner in which her plaid was disposed, as well as by the fineness of its texture. It was Lady Bothwell who had suggested this species of disguise, partly to avoid observation as they should go to the conjurer's house, and partly in order to make trial of his penetration, by appearing before him in a feigned character. Lady Forester's servant, of tried fidelity, had been employed by her to propitiate the Doctor by a suitable fee, and a story intimating that a soldier's wife desired to know the fate of her husband; a subject upon which, in all probability, the sage was very frequently consulted.

To the last moment, when the palace clock struck eight, Lady Bothwell earnestly watched her sister, in hopes that she might retreat from her rash undertaking; but as mildness, and even timidity, is capable at times of vehement and fixed purposes, she found Lady Forester resolutely unmoved and determined when the moment of departure arrived. Ill satisfied with the expedition, but determined not to leave her sister at such a crisis, Lady Bothwell accompanied Lady Forester through more than one obscure street and lane, the servant walking before and acting as their guide. At length he suddenly turned into a narrow court, and knocked at an arched door, which seemed to belong to a building of some antiquity. It opened, though no one appeared to act as porter; and the servant stepping aside from the entrance, motioned the ladies to enter. They had no sooner done so than it shut, and excluded their guide. The two ladies found themselves in a small vestibule, illuminated by a dim lamp, and having, when the door was closed, no communication with the external light or air. The door of an inner apartment, partly open, was at the farther side of the vestibule.

"We must not hesitate now, Jemima," said Lady Bothwell, and walked forwards into the inner room, where, surrounded by books, maps, philosophical utensils, and other implements of peculiar shape and appearance, they found the man of art.

There was nothing very peculiar in the Italian's appearance. He had the dark complexion and marked features of his country, seemed about fifty years old, and was handsomely, but plainly, dressed in a full suit of black clothes, which was then the universal costume of the medical profession. Large wax-lights, in silver sconces, illuminated the apartment, which was reasonably furnished. He rose as the ladies entered; and, notwithstanding the inferiority of their dress, received them with the marked respect due to their quality, and which foreigners are usually punctilious in rendering to those to whom such honours are due.

Lady Bothwell endeavoured to maintain her proposed incognito; and, as the Doctor ushered them to the upper end of the room, made a motion declining his courtesy as unfitted for their condition. "We are poor people, sir," she said; "only my sister's distress has brought us to consult your worship whether"——

He smiled as he interrupted her—"I am aware, madam, of your sister's distress, and its cause; I am aware, also, that I am honoured with a visit from two ladies of the highest consideration—Lady Bothwell and Lady Forester. If I could not distinguish them from the class of society which their present dress would indicate, there would be small possibility of my being able to gratify them by giving the information which they come to seek."

"I can easily understand," said Lady Bothwell——

"Pardon my boldness to interrupt you, milady," cried the Italian; "your ladyship was about to say, that you could easily understand that I had got possession of your names by means of your domestic. But in thinking so, you do injustice to the fidelity of your servant, and, I may add, to the skill of one who is also not less your humble servant — Baptista Damiotti."

"I have no intention to do either, sir," said Lady Bothwell, maintaining a tone of composure, though somewhat surprised, "but the situation is something new to me. If you know who we are, you also know, sir, what brought us here."

"Curiosity to know the fate of a Scottish gentleman of rank, now, or lately, upon the Continent," answered the seer; "his name is Il Cavaliero Philippo Forester; a gentleman who has the honour to be husband to this lady, and, with your lady-ship's permission, for using plain language, the misfortune not to value as it deserves that inestimable advantage."

Lady Forester sighed deeply, and Lady Bothwell replied—

"Since you know our object without our telling it, the only question that remains is, whether you have the power to relieve my sister's anxiety?"

"I have, madam," answered the Paduan scholar; "but there is still a previous inquiry. Have you the courage to behold with your own eyes what the Cavaliero Philippo Forester is now doing? or will you take it on my report?"

"That question my sister must answer for herself," said Lady Bothwell.

"With my own eyes will I endure to see whatever you have power to show me," said Lady Forester, with the same deter-mined spirit which had stimulated her since her resolution was taken upon this subject.

"There may be danger in it."

"If gold can compensate the risk," said Lady Forester, taking out her purse.

"I do not such things for the purpose of gain," answered the foreigner. "I dare not turn my art to such a purpose. If I take the gold of the wealthy, it is but to bestow it on the poor; nor do I ever accept more than the sum I have already received from your servant. Put up your purse, madam; an adept needs not your gold."

Lady Bothwell considering this rejection of her sister's offer as a mere trick of an empiric, to induce her to press a larger sum upon him, and willing that the scene should be commenced and ended, offered some gold in turn, observing that it was only to enlarge the sphere of his charity.

"Let Lady Bothwell enlarge the sphere of her own charity," said the Paduan, "not merely in giving of alms, in which I know she is not deficient, but in judging the character of others; and let her oblige Baptista Damiotti by believing him honest, till she shall discover him to be a knave. Do not be surprised, madam, if I speak in answer to your thoughts rather than your expressions, and tell me once more whether you have courage to look on what I am prepared to show?"

"I own, sir," said Lady Bothwell, "that your words strike me with some sense of fear; but whatever my sister desires to witness, I will not shrink from witnessing along with her."

"Nay, the danger only consists in the risk of your resolution failing you. The sight can only last for the space of seven minutes; and should you interrupt the vision by speaking a single word, not only would the charm be broken, but some danger might result to the spectators. But if you can remain steadily silent for the seven minutes, your curiosity will be gratified without the slightest risk; and for this I will engage my honour."

Internally Lady Bothwell thought the security was but an indifferent one; but she suppressed the suspicion, as if she had believed that the adept, whose dark features wore a half-formed smile, could in reality read even her most secret reflections. A solemn pause then ensued, until Lady Forester gathered courage enough to reply to the physician, as he termed himself, that she would abide with firmness and silence the sight which he had promised to exhibit to them. Upon this, he made them a low obeisance, and, saying he went to prepare matters to meet their wish, left the apartment. The two sisters, hand in hand, as if seeking by that close union to divert any danger which might threaten them, sat down on two seats in immediate contact with each other: Jemima seeking support in the manly and habitual courage of Lady Bothwell; and she, on the other hand, more agitated than she had expected, endeavouring to fortify herself by the desperate resolution which circumstances had forced her sister to assume. The one perhaps said to herself, that her sister never feared anything; and the other might reflect, that what so feeble a minded woman as Jemima did not fear, could not properly be a subject of apprehension to a person of firmness and resolution like herself.

In a few moments the thoughts of both were diverted from their own situation, by a strain of music so singularly sweet and solemn, that, while it seemed calculated to avert or dispel any feeling unconnected with its harmony, increased, at the same time, the solemn excitation which the preceding interview was calculated to produce. The music was that of some instrument with which they were unacquainted; but circumstances afterwards led my ancestress to believe that it was that of the harmonica, which she heard at a much later period in life.

When these heaven-born sounds had ceased, a door opened in the upper end of the apartment, and they saw Damiotti, standing at the head of two or three steps, sign to them to advance. His dress was so different from that which he had worn a few minutes before, that they could hardly recognise him; and the deadly paleness of his countenance, and a certain stern rigidity of muscles, like that of one whose mind is made up to some strange and daring action, had totally changed the somewhat sarcastic expression with which he had previously regarded them both, and particularly Lady Bothwell. He was barefooted, excepting a species of sandals in the antique fashion; his legs were naked beneath the knees; above them he wore hose, and a doublet of dark crimson silk close to his body; and over that a flowing loose robe, something resembling a surplice, of snow-white linen; his throat and neck were uncovered, and his long, straight, black hair was carefully combed down at full length.

As the ladies approached at his bidding, he showed no gesture of that ceremonious courtesy of which he had been formerly lavish. On the contrary, he made the signal of advance with an air of command; and when, arm in arm, and with insecure steps, the sisters approached the spot where he stood, it was with a warning frown that he pressed his finger to his lips, as if reiterating his condition of absolute silence, while, stalking before them, he led the way into the next apartment.

This was a large room, hung with black, as if for a funeral. At the upper end was a table, or rather a species of altar, covered with the same lugubrious colour, on which lay divers objects resembling the usual implements of sorcery. These objects were not indeed visible as they advanced into the apartment; for the light which displayed them, being only that of two expiring lamps, was extremely faint. The master—to use the Italian phrase for persons of this description—approached the upper end of the room with a genuflection like that of a Catholic to the crucifix, and at the same time crossed himself. The ladies followed in silence, and arm in arm. Two or three low broad steps led to a platform in front of the altar, or what resembled such. Here the sage took his stand, and placed the ladies beside him, once more earnestly repeating by signs his injunctions of silence. The Italian then, extending his bare arm from under his linen vestment, pointed with his forefinger to five large flambeaux, or torches, placed on each side of the altar. They took fire successively at the approach of his hand, or rather of his finger, and spread a strong light through the room. By this the visitors could discern that, on the seeming altar, were disposed two naked swords laid crosswise; a large open book, which they conceived to be a copy of the Holy Scriptures, but in a language to them unknown; and beside this mysterious volume was placed a human skull. But what struck the sisters most was a very tall and broad mirror, which occupied all the space behind the altar, and, illumined by the lighted torches, reflected the mysterious articles which were laid upon it.

The master then placed himself between the two ladies, and, pointing to the mirror, took each by the hand, but without speaking a syllable. They gazed intently on the polished and sable space to which he had directed their attention. Suddenly the surface assumed a new and singular appearance. It no longer simply reflected the objects placed before it, but, as if it had self-contained scenery of its own, objects began to appear within it, at first in a disorderly, indistinct, and miscellaneous manner, like form arranging itself out of chaos; at length, in distinct and defined shape and symmetry. It was thus that, after some shifting of light and darkness over the face of the wonderful glass, a long perspective of arches and columns began to arrange itself on its sides, and a vaulted roof on the upper part of it; till, after many oscillations, the whole vision gained a fixed and stationary appearance, representing the interior or a foreign church. The pillars were stately, and hung with scutcheons; the arches were lofty and magnificent; the floor was lettered with funeral inscriptions. But there were no separate shrines, no images, no display of chalice or crucifix on the altar. It was, therefore, a Protestant church upon the Continent. A clergyman, dressed in the Geneva gown and band, stood by the communion-table, and, with the Bible opened before him, and his clerk awaiting in the background, seemed prepared to perform some service of the church to which he belonged.

At length there entered the middle aisle of the building a numerous party, which appeared to be a bridal one, as a lady and gentleman walked first, hand in hand, followed by a large concourse of persons of both sexes, gaily, nay richly, attired. The bride, whose features they could distinctly see, seemed not more than sixteen years old, and extremely beautiful. The bridegroom, for some seconds, moved rather with his shoulder towards them, and his face averted; but his elegance of form and step struck the sisters at once with the same apprehension. As he turned his face suddenly, it was frightfully realised, and they saw, in the gay bridegroom before them, Sir Philip Forester. His wife uttered an imperfect exclamation, at the sound of which the whole scene stirred and seemed to separate.

"I could compare it to nothing," said Lady Bothwell, while recounting the wonderful tale, "but to the dispersion of the reflection offered by a deep and calm pool, when a stone is suddenly cast into it, and the shadows become dissipated and broken." The master pressed both the ladies' hands severely, as if to remind them of their promise, and of the danger which they incurred. The exclamation died away on Lady Forester's tongue, without attaining perfect utterance, and the scene in the glass, after the fluctuation of a minute, again resumed to the eye its former appearance of a real scene, existing within the mirror, as if represented in a picture, save that the figures were movable instead of being stationary.

The representation of Sir Philip Forester, now distinctly visible in form and feature, was seen to lead on towards the clergyman that beautiful girl, who advanced at once with diffidence, and with a species of affectionate pride. In the meantime, and just as the clergyman had arranged the bridal company before him, and seemed about to commence the service, another group of persons, of whom two or three were officers, entered the church. They moved, at first, forward, as though they came to witness the bridal ceremony, but suddenly one of the officers, whose back was towards the spectators, detached himself from his companions, and rushed hastily towards the marriage party, when the whole of them turned towards him, as if attracted by some exclamation which had accompanied his advance. Suddenly the intruder drew his sword; the bridegroom unsheathed his own, and made towards him; swords were also drawn by other individuals, both of the marriage party, and of those who had last entered. They fell into a sort of confusion, the clergyman, and some elder and graver persons, labouring apparently to keep the peace, while the hotter spirits on both sides brandished their weapons. But now the period of brief space during which the soothsayer, as he pretended, was permitted to exhibit his art, was arrived. The fumes again mixed together, and dissolved gradually from observation; the vaults and columns of the church rolled asunder, and disappeared; and the front of the mirror reflected nothing save the blazing torches, and the melancholy apparatus placed on the altar or table before it.

The doctor led the ladies, who greatly required his support, into the apartment from whence they came; where wine, essences, and other means of restoring suspended animation, had been provided during his absence. He motioned them to chairs, which they occupied in silence; Lady Forester, in particular, wringing her hands, and casting her eyes up to heaven, but without speaking a word, as if the spell had been still before her eyes.

"And what we have seen is even now acting?" said Lady Bothwell, collecting herself with difficulty.

"That," answered Baptista Damiotti, "I cannot justly, or with certainty, say. But it is either now acting, or has been acted, during a short space before this. It is the last remarkable transaction in which the Cavalier Forester has been engaged."

Lady Bothwell then expressed anxiety concerning her sister, whose altered countenance, and apparent unconsciousness of what passed around her, excited her apprehensions how it might be possible to convey her home.

"I have prepared for that," answered the adept; "I have directed the servant to bring your equipage as near to this place as the narrowness of the street will permit. Fear not for your sister; but give her, when you return home, this composing draught, and she will be better to-morrow morning. Few," he added, in a melancholy tone, "leave this house as well in health as they entered it. Such being the consequence of seeking knowledge by mysterious means, I leave you to judge the condition of those who have the power of gratifying such irregular curiosity. Farewell, and forget not the potion."

"I will give her nothing that comes from you," said Lady Bothwell; "I have seen enough of your art already. Perhaps you would poison us both to conceal your own necromancy. But we are persons who want neither the means of making our wrongs known, nor the assistance of friends to right them."

"You have had no wrongs from me, madam," said the adept. "You sought one who is little grateful for such honour. He seeks no one, and only gives responses to those who invite and call upon him. After all, you have but learned a little sooner the evil which you must still be doomed to endure. I hear your servant's step at the door, and will detain your ladyship and Lady Forester no longer. The next packet from the Continent will explain what you have already partly witnessed. Let it not, if I may advise, pass too suddenly into your sister's hands."

So saying, he bid Lady Bothwell good-night. She went, lighted by the adept, to the vestibule, where he hastily threw a black cloak over his singular dress, and opening the door, entrusted his visitors to the care of the servant. It was with difficulty that Lady Bothwell sustained her sister to the carriage, though it was only twenty steps distant. When they arrived at home, Lady Forester required medical assistance. The physician of the family attended, and shook his head on feeling her pulse.

"Here has been," he said, "a violent and sudden shock on the nerves. I must know how it has happened."

Lady Bothwell admitted they had visited the conjurer, and that Lady Forester had received some bad news respecting her husband, Sir Philip.

"That rascally quack would make my fortune were he to stay in Edinburgh," said the graduate; "this is the seventh nervous case I have heard of his making for me, and all by effect of terror." He next examined the composing draught which Lady Bothwell had unconsciously brought in her hand, tasted it, and pronounced it very germane to the matter, and what would save an application to the apothecary. He then paused, and looking at Lady Bothwell very significantly, at length added, "I suppose I must not ask your ladyship anything about this Italian warlock's proceedings?"

"Indeed, Doctor," answered Lady Bothwell, "I consider what passed as confidential; and though the man may be a rogue, yet, as we were fools enough to consult him, we should, I think, be honest enough to keep his counsel."

"*May* be a knave—come," said the Doctor, "I am glad to hear your ladyship allows such a possibility in anything that comes from Italy."

"What comes from Italy may be as good as what comes from Hanover, Doctor. But you and I will remain good friends, and that it may be so, we will say nothing of Whig and Tory."

"Not I," said the Doctor, receiving his fee, and taking his hat; "a Carolus serves my purpose as well as a Willielmus. But I should like to know why old Lady Saint Ringan's, and all that set, go about wasting their decayed lungs in puffing this foreign fellow."

"Ay—you had best set him down a Jesuit, as Scrub says." On these terms they parted.

The poor patient—whose nerves, from an extraordinary state of tension, had at length become relaxed in as extraordinary a degree—continued to struggle with a sort of imbecility, the growth of superstitious terror, when the shocking tidings were brought from Holland, which fulfilled even her worst expectations.

They were sent by the celebrated Earl of Stair, and contained the melancholy event of a duel betwixt Sir Philip Forester and his wife's half-brother, Captain Falconer, of the Scotch-Dutch, as they were then called, in which the latter had been killed. The cause of quarrel rendered the incident still more shocking. It seemed that Sir Philip had left the army suddenly, in consequence of being unable to pay a very considerable sum, which he had lost to another volunteer at play. He had changed his name, and taken up his residence at Rotterdam, where he had insinuated himself into the good graces of an ancient and rich burgomaster, and, by his handsome person and graceful manners, captivated the affections of his only child, a very young person of great beauty, and the heiress of much wealth. Delighted with the specious attractions of his proposed son-in-law, the wealthy merchant—whose idea of the British character was too high to admit of his taking any precaution to acquire evidence of his condition and circumstances—gave his consent to the marriage. It was about to be celebrated in the principal church of the city, when it was interrupted by a singular occurrence.

Captain Falconer having being detached to Rotterdam to bring up a part of the brigade of Scottish auxiliaries, who were in quarters there, a person of consideration in the town, to whom he had been formerly known, proposed to him for amusement to go to the high church, to see a countryman of his own married to the daughter of a wealthy burgomaster. Captain Falconer went accordingly, accompanied by his Dutch acquaintance with a party of his friends, and two or three officers of the Scotch brigade. His astonishment may be conceived when he saw his own brother-in-law, a married man, on the point of leading to the altar the innocent and beautiful creature, upon whom he was about to practise a base and unmanly deceit. He proclaimed his villainy on the spot, and the marriage was interrupted of course. But against the opinion of more thinking men, who considered Sir Philip Forester as having thrown himself out of the rank of men of honour, Captain Falconer admitted him to the privilege of such, accepted a challenge from him, and in the rencounter received a mortal wound. Such are the ways of Heaven, mysterious in our eyes. Lady Forester never recovered the shock of this dismal intelligence.

"And did this tragedy," said I, "take place exactly at the time when the scene in the mirror was exhibited?"

"It is hard to be obliged to maim one's story," answered my aunt; "but, to speak the truth, it happened some days sooner than the apparition was exhibited."

"And so there remained a possibility," said I, "that by some secret and speedy communication the artist might have received early intelligence of that incident."

"The incredulous pretended so," replied my aunt.

"What became of the adept?" demanded I.

"Why, a warrant came down shortly afterwards to arrest him for high treason, as an agent of the Chevalier St. George; and Lady Bothwell, recollecting the hints which had escaped the Doctor, an ardent friend of the Protestant succession, did then call to remembrance, that this man was chiefly *prôné* among the ancient matrons of her own political persuasion. It certainly seemed probable that intelligence from the Continent, which could easily have been transmitted by an active and powerful agent, might have enabled him to prepare such a scene of phantasmagoria as she had herself witnessed. Yet there were so many difficulties in assigning a natural explanation, that, to the day of her death, she remained in great doubt on the subject, and much disposed to cut the Gordian knot, by admitting the existence of supernatural agency."

"But, my dear aunt," said I, "what became of the man of skill?"

"Oh, he was too good a fortune-teller not to be able to foresee that his own destiny would be tragical if he waited the arrival of the man with the silver greyhound upon his sleeve. He made, as we say, a moonlight flitting, and was nowhere to be seen or heard of. Some noise there was about papers or letters found in the house, but it died away, and Doctor Baptista Damiotti was soon as little talked of as Galen or Hippocrates."

"And Sir Philip Forester," said I, "did he too vanish for ever from the public scene?"

"No," replied my kind informer. "He was heard of once more, and it was upon a remarkable occasion. It is said that we Scots, when there was such a nation in existence, have, among our full peck of virtues, one or two little barleycorns of vice. In particular, it is alleged that we rarely forgive, and never forget, any injuries received; that we used to make an idol of our resentment, as poor Lady Constance did of her grief; and are addicted, as Burns says, to 'nursing our wrath to keep it warm.' Lady Bothwell was not without this feeling; and, I believe, nothing whatever, scarce the restoration of the Stuart line, could have happened so delicious to her feelings as an opportunity of being revenged on Sir Philip Forester, for the deep and double injury which had deprived her of a sister and of a brother. But nothing of him was heard or known till many a year had passed away."

At length—it was on a Fastern's E'en (Shrovetide) assembly, at which the whole fashion of Edinburgh attended, full and frequent, and when Lady Bothwell had a seat amongst the lady patronesses, that one of the attendants on the company whispered into her ear, that a gentleman wished to speak with her in private.

"In private? and in an assembly-room?—he must be mad— Tell him to call upon me to-morrow morning."

"I said so, my lady," answered the man; "but he desired me to give you this paper."

She undid the billet, which was curiously folded and sealed. It only bore the words, *On business of life and death*," written in a hand which she had never seen before. Suddenly it occurred to her, that it might concern the safety of some of her political friends; she therefore followed the messenger to a small apartment where the refreshments were prepared, and from which the general company was excluded. She found an old man, who, at her approach, rose up and bowed profoundly. His appearance indicated a broken constitution; and his dress, though sedulously rendered conforming to the etiquette of a ball-room, was worn and tarnished, and hung in folds about his emaciated person. Lady Bothwell was about to feel for her purse, expecting to get rid of the supplicant at the expense of a little money, but some fear of a mistake arrested her purpose. She therefore gave the man leisure to explain himself.

"I have the honour to speak with the Lady Bothwell?"

"I am Lady Bothwell; allow me to say, that this is no time or place for long explanations.—What are your commands with me?"

"Your ladyship," said the old man, "had once a sister."

"True ; whom I loved as my own soul."

"And a brother."

"The bravest, the kindest, the most affectionate!" said Lady Bothwell.

"Both these beloved relatives you lost by the fault of an unfortunate man," continued the stranger.

"By the crime of an unnatural, bloody-minded murderer," said the lady.

"I am answered," replied the old man, bowing, as if to withdraw.

"Stop, sir, I command you," said Lady Bothwell.—"Who are you, that, at such a place and time, come to recall these horrible recollections? I insist upon knowing."

"I am one who intends Lady Bothwell no injury ; but, on the contrary, to offer her the means of doing a deed of Christian charity, which the world would wonder at, and which Heaven would reward ; but I find her in no temper for such a sacrifice as I was prepared to ask."

"Speak out, sir ; what is your meaning?" said Lady Bothwell.

"The wretch that has wronged you so deeply," rejoined the stranger, "is now on his death-bed. His days have been days of misery, his nights have been sleepless hours of anguish—yet he cannot die without your forgiveness. His life has been an unremitting penance—yet he dares not part from his burden while your curses load his soul."

"Tell him," said Lady Bothwell sternly, "to ask pardon of that Being whom he has so greatly offended ; not of an erring mortal like himself. What could my forgiveness avail him?"

"Much," answered the old man. "It will be an earnest of that which he may then venture to ask from his Creator, lady, and from yours. Remember, Lady Bothwell, you too have a death-bed to look forward to ; your soul may, all human souls must, feel the awe of facing the judgment-seat, with the wounds of an untented conscience, raw, and rankling—what thought would it be then that should whisper, ' I have given no mercy, how then shall I ask it?'"

"Man, whosoever thou mayst be," replied Lady Bothwell, "urge me not so cruelly. It would be but blasphemous hypocrisy to utter with my lips the words which every throb of my heart protests against. They would open the earth and give to light the wasted form of my sister—the bloody form of my murdered brother—forgive him?—Never, never!"

"Great God!" cried the old man, holding up his hands, "is it thus the worms which thou hast called out of dust obey the commands of their Maker? Farewell, proud and unforgiving woman. Exult that thou hast added to a death in want and pain the agonies of religious despair; but never again mock Heaven by petitioning for the pardon which thou hast refused to grant."

He was turning from her.

"Stop," she exclaimed; "I will try; yes, I will try to pardon him."

"Gracious lady," said the old man, "you will relieve the over-burdened soul, which dare not sever itself from its sinful companion of earth without being at peace with you. What do I know—your forgiveness may perhaps preserve for penitence the dregs of a wretched life."

"Ha!" said the lady, as a sudden light broke on her, "it is the villain himself!" And grasping Sir Philip Forester—for it was he, and no other—by the collar, she raised a cry of "Murder, murder! Seize the murderer!"

At an exclamation so singular, in such a place, the company thronged into the apartment, but Sir Philip Forester was no longer there. He had forcibly extricated himself from Lady Bothwell's hold, and had run out of the apartment which opened on the landing-place of the stair. There seemed no escape in that direction, for there were several persons coming up the steps, and others descending. But the unfortunate man was desperate. He threw himself over the balustrade, and alighted safely in the lobby, though a leap of fifteen feet at least, then dashed into the street and was lost in darkness. Some of the Bothwell family made pursuit, and, had they come up with the fugitive, they might have perhaps slain him; for in those days men's blood ran warm in their veins. But the police did not interfere; the matter most criminal having happened long since, and in a foreign land. Indeed, it was always thought, that this extraordinary scene originated in a hypocritical experiment, by which Sir Philip desired to ascertain whether he might return to his native country in safety from the resentment of a family which he had injured so deeply. As the result fell out so contrary to his wishes, he is believed to have returned to the Continent, and there died in exile.

So closed the tale of the MYSTERIOUS MIRROR.

THE TAPESTRIED CHAMBER;

OR,

THE LADY IN THE SACQUE

THE following narrative is given from the pen, so far as memory permits, in the same character in which it was presented to the author's ear; nor has he claim to farther praise, or to be more deeply censured, than in proportion to the good or bad judgment which he has employed in selecting his materials, as he has studiously avoided any attempt at ornament, which might interfere with the simplicity of the tale.

At the same time, it must be admitted, that the particular class of stories which turns on the marvellous, possesses a stronger influence when told than when committed to print. The volume taken up at noonday, though rehearsing the same incidents, conveys a much more feeble impression than is achieved by the voice of the speaker on a circle of fireside auditors, who hang upon the narrative as the narrator details the minute incidents which serve to give it authenticity, and lowers his voice with an affectation of mystery while he approaches the fearful and wonderful part. It was with such advantages that the present writer heard the following events related, more than twenty years since, by the celebrated Miss Seaward, of Litchfield, who, to her numerous accomplishments, added, in a remarkable degree, the power of narrative in private conversation. In its present form, the tale must necessarily lose all the interest which was attached to it, by the flexible voice and intelligent features of the gifted narrator. Yet still, read aloud, to an undoubting audience by the doubtful light of the closing evening, or in silence, by a decaying taper, and amidst the solitude of a half-lighted apartment, it may redeem its character as a good ghost story. Miss Seaward always affirmed that she had derived her information from an authentic source, although she suppressed the names of the two persons chiefly concerned. I will not avail myself of any particulars I may have since received concerning the localities of the detail, but suffer them to rest

under the same general description in which they were first
related to me; and, for the same reason, I will not add to,
or diminish the narrative, by any circumstances, whether more
or less material, but simply rehearse, as I heard it, a story of
supernatural terror.

About the end of the American war, when the officers of
Lord Cornwallis's army, which surrendered at York-town, and
others, who had been made prisoners during the impolitic and
ill-fated controversy, were returning to their own country, to
relate their adventures, and repose themselves after their
fatigues; there was amongst them a general officer, to whom
Miss S. gave the name of Browne, but merely, as I understood,
to save the inconvenience of introducing a nameless agent in
the narrative. He was an officer of merit, as well as a gentleman
of high consideration for family and attainments.

Some business had carried General Browne upon a tour
through the western counties, when, in the conclusion of a
morning stage, he found himself in the vicinity of a small country
town, which presented a scene of uncommon beauty, and of a
character peculiarly English.

The little town, with its stately old church, whose tower bore
testimony to the devotion of ages long past, lay amidst pasture
and corn-fields of small extent, but bounded and divided with
hedge-row timber of great age and size. There were few marks
of modern improvement. The environs of the place intimated
neither the solitude of decay, nor the bustle of novelty; the
houses were old, but in good repair; and the beautiful little
river murmured freely on its way to the left of the town, neither
restrained by a dam, nor bordered by a towing-path.

Upon a gentle eminence, nearly a mile to the southward of
the town, were seen, amongst many venerable oaks and tangled
thickets, the turrets of a castle, as old as the wars of York and
Lancaster, but which seemed to have received important altera-
tions during the age of Elizabeth and her successors. It had
not been a place of great size; but whatever accommodation it
formerly afforded, was, it must be supposed, still to be obtained
within its walls; at least, such was the inference which General
Browne drew from observing the smoke arise merrily from
several of the ancient wreathed and carved chimney-stalks.
The wall of the park ran alongside of the highway for two or
three hundred yards; and through the different points by which
the eye found glimpses into the woodland scenery, it seemed to
be well stocked. Other points of view opened in succession;
now a full one, of the front of the old castle, and now a side
glimpse at its particular towers; the former rich in all the
bizarrerie of the Elizabethan school, while the simple and solid

strength of other parts of the building seemed to show that they had been raised more for defence than ostentation.

Delighted with the partial glimpses which he obtained of the castle through the woods and glades by which this ancient feudal fortress was surrounded, our military traveller was determined to inquire whether it might not deserve a nearer view, and whether it contained family pictures or other objects of curiosity worthy of a stranger's visit; when, leaving the vicinity of the park, he rolled through a clean and well-paved street, and stopped at the door of a well-frequented inn.

Before ordering horses to proceed on his journey, General Browne made inquiries concerning the proprietor of the château which had so attracted his admiration, and was equally surprised and pleased at hearing in reply a nobleman named whom we shall call Lord Woodville. How fortunate! Much of Browne's early recollections, both at school and at college, had been connected with young Woodville, whom, by a few questions, he now ascertained to be the same with the owner of this fair domain. He had been raised to the peerage by the decease of his father a few months before, and, as the General learned from the landlord, the term of mourning being ended, was now taking possession of his paternal estate, in the jovial season of merry autumn, accompanied by a select party of friends to enjoy the sports of a country famous for game.

This was delightful news to our traveller. Frank Woodville had been Richard Browne's fag at Eton, and his chosen intimate at Christ Church; their pleasures and their tasks had been the same; and the honest soldier's heart warmed to find his early friend in possession of so delightful a residence, and of an estate, as the landlord assured him with a nod and a wink, fully adequate to maintain and add to his dignity. Nothing was more natural than that the traveller should suspend a journey, which there was nothing to render hurried, to pay a visit to an old friend under such agreeable circumstances.

The fresh horses, therefore, had only the brief task of conveying the General's travelling carriage to Woodville Castle. A porter admitted them at a modern Gothic Lodge, built in that style to correspond with the Castle itself, and at the same time rang a bell to give warning of the approach of visitors. Apparently the sound of the bell had suspended the separation of the company, bent on the various amusements of the morning; for, on entering the court of the château, several young men were lounging about in their sporting dresses, looking at, and criticising, the dogs which the keepers held in readiness to attend their pastime. As General Browne alighted, the young lord came to the gate of the hall, and for an instant gazed, as at a stranger, upon the countenance of his friend on which war, with its fatigues and its wounds, had made a great alteration. But the uncertainty lasted no longer than till the visitor had spoken, and the hearty greeting which followed was such as can only be exchanged betwixt those who have passed together the merry days of careless boyhood or early youth.

"If I could have formed a wish, my dear Browne," said Lord Woodville, "it would have been to have you here, of all men, upon this occasion, which my friends are good enough to hold as a sort of holiday. Do not think you have been unwatched during the years you have been absent from us. I have traced you through your dangers, your triumphs, your misfortunes, and was delighted to see that, whether in victory or defeat, the name of my old friend was always distinguished with applause."

The General made a suitable reply, and congratulated his friend on his new dignities, and the possession of a place and domain so beautiful.

"Nay, you have seen nothing of it as yet," said Lord Woodville, "and I trust you do not mean to leave us till you are better acquainted with it. It is true, I confess, that my present party is pretty large, and the old house, like other places of the kind, does not possess so much accommodation as the extent of the outward walls appears to promise. But we can give you a comfortable old-fashioned room ; and I venture to suppose that your campaigns have taught you to be glad of worse quarters."

The General shrugged his shoulders, and laughed. "I presume," he said, "the worst apartment in your château is considerably superior to the old tobacco-cask, in which I was fain to take up my night's lodging when I was in the Bush, as the Virginians call it, with the light corps. There I lay, like Diogenes himself, so delighted with my covering from the elements, that I made a vain attempt to have it rolled on to my next quarters ; but my commander for the time would give way to no such luxurious provision, and I took farewell of my beloved cask with tears in my eyes."

"Well, then, since you do not fear your quarters," said Lord Woodville, "you will stay with me a week at least. Of guns, dogs, fishing-rods, flies, and means of sport by sea and land, we have enough and to spare : you cannot pitch on an amusement, but we will pitch on the means of pursuing it. But if you prefer the gun and pointers, I will go with you myself, and see whether you have mended your shooting since you have been amongst the Indians of the back settlements."

The General gladly accepted his friendly host's proposal in all its points. After a morning of manly exercise, the company met at dinner, where it was the delight of Lord Woodville

Y

to conduce to the display of the high properties of his recovered friend, so as to recommend him to his guests, most of whom were persons of distinction. He led General Browne to speak of the scenes he had witnessed; and as every word marked alike the brave officer and the sensible man, who retained possession of his cool judgment under the most imminent dangers, the company looked upon the soldier with general respect, as on one who had proved himself possessed of an uncommon portion of personal courage—that attribute, of all others, of which everybody desires to be thought possessed.

The day at Woodville Castle ended as usual in such mansions. The hospitality stopped within the limits of good order; music, in which the young lord was a proficient, succeeded to the circulation of the bottle: cards and billiards, for those who preferred such amusements, were in readiness: but the exercise of the morning required early hours, and not long after eleven o'clock the guests began to retire to their several apartments.

The young lord himself conducted his friend, General Browne, to the chamber destined for him, which answered the description he had given of it, being comfortable, but old-fashioned. The bed was of the massive form used in the end of the seventeenth century, and the curtains of faded silk, heavily trimmed with tarnished gold. But then the sheets, pillows, and blankets looked delightful to the campaigner, when he thought of his mansion, the cask. There was an air of gloom in the tapestry hangings, which, with their worn-out graces, curtained the walls of the little chamber, and gently undulated as the autumnal breeze found its way through the ancient lattice-window, which pattered and whistled as the air gained entrance. The toilet, too, with its mirror, turbaned, after the manner of the beginning of the century, with a coiffure of murrey-coloured silk, and its hundred strange-shaped boxes, providing for arrangements which had been obsolete for more than fifty years, had an antique, and in so far a melancholy, aspect. But nothing could blaze more brightly and cheerfully than the two large wax candles; or if aught could rival them, it was the flaming bickering fagots in the chimney, that sent at once their gleam and their warmth through the snug apartment; which, notwithstanding the general antiquity of its appearance, was not wanting in the least convenience that modern habits rendered either necessary or desirable.

"This is an old-fashioned sleeping apartment, General," said the young lord; "but I hope you will find nothing that makes you envy your old tobacco-cask."

"I am not particular respecting my lodgings," replied the General; "yet were I to make any choice, I would prefer this chamber by many degrees, to the gayer and more modern rooms of your family mansion. Believe me, that when I unite its modern air of comfort with its venerable antiquity, and recollect that it is your lordship's property, I shall feel in better quarters here, than if I were in the best hotel London could afford."

"I trust—I have no doubt—that you will find yourself as comfortable as I wish you, my dear General," said the young nobleman; and once more bidding his guest good-night, he shook him by the hand and withdrew.

The General again looked round him, and internally congratulating himself on his return to peaceful life, the comforts of which were endeared by the recollection of the hardships and dangers he had lately sustained, undressed himself, and prepared himself for a luxurious night's rest.

Here, contrary to the custom of this species of tale, we leave the General in possession of his apartment until the next morning.

The company assembled for breakfast at an early hour, but without the appearance of General Browne, who seemed the guest that Lord Woodville was desirous of honouring above all whom his hospitality had assembled around him. He more than once expressed surprise at the General's absence, and at length sent a servant to make inquiry after him. The man brought back information that General Browne had been walking abroad since an early hour of the morning, in defiance of the weather, which was misty and ungenial.

"The custom of a soldier," said the young nobleman to his friends; "many of them acquire habitual vigilance, and cannot sleep after the early hour at which their duty usually commands them to be alert."

Yet the explanation which Lord Woodville thus offered to the company seemed hardly satisfactory to his own mind, and it was in a fit of silence and abstraction that he awaited the return of the General. It took place near an hour after the breakfast bell had rung. He looked fatigued and feverish. His hair, the powdering and arrangement of which was at this time one of the most important occupations of a man's whole day, and marked his fashion as much as, in the present time, the tying of a cravat, or the want of one, was dishevelled, uncurled, void of powder, and dank with dew. His clothes were huddled on with a careless negligence, remarkable in a military man, whose real or supposed duties are usually held to include some attention to the toilet; and his looks were haggard and ghastly in a peculiar degree.

"So you have stolen a march upon us this morning, my dear General," said Lord Woodville; "or you have not found your bed so much to your mind as I had hoped and you seemed to expect. How did you rest last night?"

"Oh, excellently well! remarkably well! never better in my life," said General Browne rapidly, and yet with an air of embarrassment which was obvious to his friend. He then hastily swallowed a cup of tea, and neglecting or refusing whatever else was offered, seemed to fall into a fit of abstraction.

"You will take the gun to-day, General?" said his friend and host, but had to repeat the question twice ere he received the abrupt answer, "No, my lord; I am sorry I cannot have the honour of spending another day with your lordship; my post horses are ordered, and will be here directly."

All who were present showed surprise, and Lord Woodville immediately replied, "Post horses, my good friend! what can you possibly want with them, when you promised to stay with me quietly for at least a week?"

"I believe," said the General, obviously much embarrassed, "that I might, in the pleasure of my first meeting with your lordship, have said something about stopping here a few days; but I have since found it altogether impossible."

"That is very extraordinary," answered the young nobleman. "You seemed quite disengaged yesterday, and you cannot have had a summons to-day; for our post has not come up from the town, and therefore you cannot have received any letters."

General Browne, without giving any farther explanation, muttered something of indispensable business, and insisted on the absolute necessity of his departure in a manner which silenced all opposition on the part of his host, who saw that his resolution was taken, and forbore farther importunity.

"At least, however," he said, "permit me, my dear Browne, since go you will or must, to show you the view from the terrace, which the mist, that is now rising, will soon display."

He threw open a sash window, and stepped down upon the terrace as he spoke. The General followed him mechanically, but seemed little to attend to what his host was saying, as, looking across an extended and rich prospect, he pointed out the different objects worthy of observation. Thus they moved on till Lord Woodville had attained his purpose of drawing his guest entirely apart from the rest of the company, when, turning round upon him with an air of great solemnity, he addressed him thus :—

"Richard Browne, my old and very dear friend, we are now alone. Let me conjure you to answer me upon the word of a friend, and the honour of a soldier. How did you in reality rest during last night?"

"Most wretchedly indeed, my lord," answered the General, in the same tone of solemnity; "so miserably, that I would not run the risk of such a second night, not only for all the lands belonging to this castle, but for all the country which I see from this elevated point of view."

"This is most extraordinary," said the young lord, as if speaking to himself; "then there must be something in the reports concerning that apartment." Again turning to the General, he said, "For God's sake, my dear friend, be candid with me, and let me know the disagreeable particulars, which have befallen you under a roof, where, with consent of the owner, you should have met nothing save comfort."

The General seemed distressed by this appeal, and paused a moment before he replied. "My dear lord," he at length said, "what happened to me last night is of a nature so peculiar and so unpleasant, that I could hardly bring myself to detail it even to your lordship, were it not that, independent of my wish to gratify any request of yours, I think that sincerity on my part may lead to some explanation about a circumstance equally painful and mysterious. To others, the communication I am about to make, might place me in the light of a weak-minded, superstitious fool, who suffered his own imagination to delude and bewilder him; but you have known me in childhood and youth, and will not suspect me of having adopted in manhood the feelings and frailties from which my early years were free." Here he paused, and his friend replied :—

"Do not doubt my perfect confidence in the truth of your communication, however strange it may be," replied Lord Woodville; "I know your firmness of disposition too well, to suspect you could be made the object of imposition, and am aware that your honour and your friendship will equally deter you from exaggerating whatever you may have witnessed."

"Well then," said the General, "I will proceed with my story as well as I can, relying upon your candour; and yet distinctly feeling that I would rather face a battery than recall to my mind the odious recollections of last night."

He paused a second time, and then perceiving that Lord Woodville remained silent and in an attitude of attention, he commenced, though not without obvious reluctance, the history of his night's adventures in the Tapestried Chamber.

"I undressed and went to bed, so soon as your lordship left me yesterday evening; but the wood in the chimney, which nearly fronted my bed, blazed brightly and cheerfully, and, aided by a hundred exciting recollections of my childhood and youth, which had been recalled by the unexpected pleasure of meeting your lordship, prevented me from falling immediately asleep. I ought, however, to say, that these reflections were all of a pleasant and agreeable kind, grounded on a sense of having for a time exchanged the labour, fatigues, and dangers of my profession, for the enjoyments of a peaceful life, and the reunion of those friendly and affectionate ties, which I had torn asunder at the rude summons of war.

"While such pleasing reflections were stealing over my mind, and gradually lulling me to slumber, I was suddenly aroused by a sound like that of the rustling of a silken gown, and the tapping of a pair of high-heeled shoes, as if a woman were walking in the apartment. Ere I could draw the curtain to see what the matter was, the figure of a little woman passed between the bed and the fire. The back of this form was turned to me, and I could observe, from the shoulders and neck, it was that of an old woman, whose dress was an old-fashioned gown, which, I think, ladies call a sacque; that is, a sort of robe, completely loose in the body, but gathered into broad plaits upon the neck and shoulders, which fall down to the ground, and terminate in a species of train.

"I thought the intrusion singular enough, but never harboured for a moment the idea that what I saw was anything more than the mortal form of some old woman about the establishment, who had a fancy to dress like her grandmother, and who, having perhaps (as your lordship mentioned that you were rather straitened for room) been dislodged from her chamber for my accommodation, had forgotten the circumstance, and returned by twelve to her old haunt. Under this persuasion I moved myself in bed and coughed a little, to make the intruder sensible of my being in possession of the premises.—She turned slowly round, but, gracious heaven! my lord, what a countenance did she display to me! There was no longer any question what she was, or any thought of her being a living being. Upon a face which wore the fixed features of a corpse, were imprinted the traces of the vilest and most hideous passions which had animated her while she lived. The body of some atrocious criminal seemed to have been given up from the grave, and the soul restored from the penal fire, in order to form, for a space, a union with the ancient accomplice of its guilt. I started up in bed, and sat upright, supporting myself on my palms, as I gazed on this horrible spectre. The hag made, as it seemed, a single and swift stride to the bed where I lay, and squatted herself down upon it, in precisely the same attitude which I had assumed in the extremity of horror, advancing her diabolical countenance within half a yard of mine, with a grin which seemed to intimate the malice and the derision of an incarnate fiend."

Here General Browne stopped, and wiped from his brow the cold perspiration with which the recollection of his horrible vision had covered it.

"My lord," he said, "I am no coward. I have been in all the mortal dangers incidental to my profession, and I may truly boast, that no man ever knew Richard Browne dishonour the sword he wears; but in these horrible circumstances, under the eyes, and as it seemed, almost in the grasp of an incarnation of an evil spirit, all firmness forsook me, all manhood melted from me like wax in the furnace, and I felt my hair individually bristle. The current of my life-blood ceased to flow, and I sank back in a swoon, as very a victim to panic terror as ever was a village girl, or a child of ten years old. How long I lay in this condition I cannot pretend to guess.

"But I was roused by the castle clock striking one, so loud that it seemed as if it were in the very room. It was some time before I dared open my eyes, lest they should again encounter the horrible spectacle. When, however, I summoned courage to look up, she was no longer visible. My first idea was to pull my bell, wake the servants, and remove to a garret or a hay-loft, to be ensured against a second visitation. Nay, I will confess the truth, that my resolution was altered, not by the shame of exposing myself, but by the fear that, as the bell-cord hung by the chimney, I might, in making my way to it, be again crossed by the fiendish hag, who, I figured to myself, might be still lurking about some corner of the apartment.

"I will not pretend to describe what hot and cold fever-fits tormented me for the rest of the night, through broken sleep, weary vigils, and that dubious state which forms the neutral ground between them. A hundred terrible objects appeared to haunt me; but there was the great difference betwixt the vision which I have described, and those which followed, that I knew the last to be deceptions of my own fancy and over-excited nerves.

"Day at last appeared, and I rose from my bed ill in health, and humiliated in mind. I was ashamed of myself as a man and a soldier, and still more so, at feeling my own extreme desire to escape from the haunted apartment, which, however, conquered all other considerations; so that, huddling on my clothes with the most careless haste, I made my escape from your lordship's mansion, to seek in the open air some relief to my nervous system, shaken as it was by this horrible rencounter with a visitant, for such I must believe her, from the other world. Your lordship has now heard the cause of my discomposure, and of my sudden desire to leave your hospitable castle. In other places I trust we may often meet; but God protect me from ever spending a second night under that roof!"

Strange as the General's tale was, he spoke with such a deep air of conviction, that it cut short all the usual commentaries which are made on such stories. Lord Woodville never once asked him if he was sure he did not dream of the apparition, or suggested any of the possibilities by which it is fashionable to explain supernatural appearances, as wild vagaries of the fancy, or deceptions of the optic nerves. On the contrary, he seemed deeply impressed with the truth and reality of what he had heard; and, after a considerable pause, regretted, with much appearance of sincerity, that his early friend should in his house have suffered so severely.

"I am the more sorry for your pain, my dear Browne," he continued, "that it is the unhappy, though most unexpected result of an experiment of my own! You must know, that for my father and grandfather's time, at least, the apartment which was assigned to you last night, had been shut on account of reports that it was disturbed by supernatural sights and noises. When I came, a few weeks since, into possession of the estate, I thought the accommodation, which the castle afforded for my friends, was not extensive enough to permit the inhabitants of the invisible world to retain possession of a comfortable sleeping apartment. I therefore caused the Tapestried Chamber, as we call it, to be opened; and without destroying its air of antiquity, I had such new articles of furniture placed in it as became the modern times. Yet as the opinion that the room was haunted very strongly prevailed among the domestics, and was also known in the neighbourhood and to many of my friends, I feared some prejudice might be entertained by the first occupant of the Tapestried Chamber, which might tend to revive the evil report which it had laboured under, and so disappoint my purpose of rendering it a useful part of the house. I must confess, my dear Browne, that your arrival yesterday, agreeable to me for a thousand reasons besides, seemed the most favourable opportunity of removing the unpleasant rumours which attached to the room, since your courage was indubitable, and your mind free of any pre-occupation on the subject. I could not, therefore, have chosen a more fitting subject for my experiment."

"Upon my life," said General Browne, somewhat hastily, "I am infinitely obliged to your lordship—very particularly indebted indeed. I am likely to remember for some time the consequences of the experiment, as your lordship is pleased to call it."

"Nay, now you are unjust, my dear friend," said Lord Woodville. "You have only to reflect for a single moment, in order to be convinced that I could not augur the possibility of the pain to which you have been so unhappily exposed. I was yesterday morning a complete sceptic on the subject of supernatural appearances. Nay, I am sure that had I told you what was said about that room, those very reports would have induced you, by your own choice, to select it for your accommodation.

It was my misfortune, perhaps my error, but really cannot be termed my fault, that you have been afflicted so strangely."

"Strangely indeed!" said the General, resuming his good temper; "and I acknowledge that I have no right to be offended with your lordship for treating me like what I used to think myself—a man of some firmness and courage. But I see my post horses are arrived, and I must not detain your lordship from your amusement."

"Nay, my old friend," said Lord Woodville, "since you cannot stay with us another day, which, indeed, I can no longer urge, give me at least half-an-hour more. You used to love pictures, and I have a gallery of portraits, some of them by Vandyke, representing ancestry to whom this property and castle formerly belonged. I think that several of them will strike you as possessing merit."

General Browne accepted the invitation, though somewhat unwillingly. It was evident he was not to breathe freely or at ease till he left Woodville Castle far behind him. He could not refuse his friend's invitation, however; and the less so, that he was a little ashamed of the peevishness which he had displayed towards his well-meaning entertainer.

The General, therefore, followed Lord Woodville through several rooms, into a long gallery hung with pictures, which the latter pointed out to his guest, telling the names, and giving some account of the personages whose portraits presented themselves in progression. General Browne was but little interested in the details which these accounts conveyed to him. They were, indeed, of the kind which are usually found in an old family gallery. Here was a cavalier who had ruined the estate in the royal cause; there a fine lady who had reinstated it by contracting a match with a wealthy Roundhead. There hung a gallant who had been in danger for corresponding with the exiled Court at Saint Germains; here one who had taken arms for William at the Revolution; and there a third that had thrown his weight alternately into the scale of Whig and Tory.

While Lord Woodville was cramming these words into his guest's ear, "against the stomach of his sense," they gained the middle of the gallery, when he beheld General Browne suddenly start, and assume an attitude of the utmost surprise, not un-mixed with fear, as his eyes were caught and suddenly riveted by a portrait of an old lady in a sacque, the fashionable dress of the end of the seventeenth century.

"There she is!" he exclaimed; "there she is, in form and features, though inferior in demoniac expression to the accursed hag who visited me last night!"

"If that be the case," said the young nobleman, "there can remain no longer any doubt of the horrible reality of your apparition. That is the picture of a wretched ancestress of mine, of whose crimes a black and fearful catalogue is recorded in a family history in my charter-chest. The recital of them would be too horrible; it is enough to say, that in yon fatal apartment incest and unnatural murder were committed. I will restore it to the solitude to which the better judgment of those who preceded me had consigned it; and never shall any one, so long as I can prevent it, be exposed to a repetition of the supernatural horrors which could shake such courage as yours."

Thus the friends, who had met with such glee, parted in a very different mood; Lord Woodville to command the Tapestried Chamber to be unmantled, and the door built up; and General Browne to seek in some less beautiful country, and with some less dignified friend, forgetfulness of the painful night which he had passed in Woodville Castle.

348   DEATH OF THE LAIRD'S JOCK

DEATH OF THE LAIRD'S JOCK

To the Editor of the " Keepsake"

YOU have asked me, sir, to point out a subject for the pencil, and I feel the difficulty of complying with your request; although I am not certainly unaccustomed to literary composition, or a total stranger to the stores of history and tradition, which afford the best copies for the painter's art. But although *sicut pictura poesis* is an ancient and undisputed axiom—although poetry and painting both address themselves to the same object of exciting the human imagination, by presenting to it pleasing or sublime images of ideal scenes; yet the one conveying itself through the ears to the understanding, and the other applying itself only to the eyes, the subjects which are best suited to the bard or tale-teller are often totally unfit for painting, where the artist must present in a single glance all that his art has power to tell us. The artist can neither recapitulate the past nor intimate the future. The single *now* is all which he can present; and hence, unquestionably, many subjects which delight us in poetry, or in narrative, whether real or fictitious, cannot with advantage be transferred to the canvass.

Being in some degree aware of these difficulties, though doubtless unacquainted both with their extent, and the means by which they may be modified or surmounted, I have, nevertheless, ventured to draw up the following traditional narrative as a story in which, when the general details are known, the interest is so much concentrated in one strong moment of agonising passion, that it can be understood, and sympathised with, at a single glance. I therefore presume that it may be acceptable as a hint to some one among the numerous artists, who have of late years distinguished themselves as rearing up and supporting the British school.

Enough has been said and sung about

The well-contested ground,
The warlike border-land—

to render the habits of the tribes who inhabited them before

347

the union of England and Scotland familiar to most of your readers. The rougher and sterner features of their character were softened by their attachment to the fine arts, from which has arisen the saying that, on the frontiers, every dale had its battle, and every river its song. A rude species of chivalry was in constant use, and single combats were practised as the amusement of the few intervals of truce which suspended the exercise of war. The inveteracy of this custom may be inferred from the following incident :—

Bernard Gilpin, the apostle of the North, the first who undertook to preach the Protestant doctrines to the Border dalesmen, was surprised, on entering one of their churches, to see a gauntlet, or mail-glove, hanging above the altar. Upon inquiring the meaning of a symbol so indecorous being displayed in that sacred place, he was informed by the clerk, that the glove was that of a famous swordsman, who hung it there as an emblem of a general challenge and gage of battle, to any who should dare to take the fatal token down. "Reach it to me," said the reverend churchman. The clerk and sexton equally declined the perilous office; and the good Bernard Gilpin was obliged to remove the glove with his own hands, desiring those who were present to inform the champion, that he, and no other, had possessed himself of the gage of defiance. But the champion was as much ashamed to face Bernard Gilpin as the officials of the church had been to displace his pledge of combat.

The date of the following story is about the latter years of Queen Elizabeth's reign; and the events took place in Liddesdale, a hilly and pastoral district of Roxburghshire, which, on a part of its boundary, is divided from England only by a small river.

During the good old times of *rugging and riving* (that is, tugging and tearing), under which term the disorderly doings of the warlike age are affectionately remembered, this valley was principally cultivated by the sept or clan of the Armstrongs. The chief of this warlike race was the Laird of Mangertown. At the period of which I speak, the estate of Mangertown, with the power and dignity of chief, was possessed by John Armstrong, a man of great size, strength, and courage. While his father was alive, he was distinguished from others of his clan who bore the same name, by the epithet of the *Laird's Jock*, that is to say, the Laird's son Jock, or Jack. This name he distinguished by so many bold and desperate achievements, that he retained it even after his father's death, and is mentioned under it both in authentic records and in tradition. Some of his feats are recorded in the Minstrelsy of the Scottish Border, and others mentioned in contemporary chronicles.

At the species of singular combat which we have described,

the Laird's Jock was unrivalled; and no champion of Cumberland, Westmoreland, or Northumberland, could endure the sway of the huge two-handed sword which he wielded, and which few others could even lift. This "awful sword," as the common people term it, was as dear to him as Durindana or Fushberta to their respective masters, and was nearly as formidable to his enemies as those renowned falchions proved to the foes of Christendom. The weapon had been bequeathed to him by a celebrated English outlaw named Hobbie Noble, who, having committed some deed for which he was in danger from justice, fled to Liddesdale, and became a follower, or rather a brother-in-arms, to the renowned Laird's Jock; till, venturing into England with a small escort, a faithless guide, and with a light single-handed sword instead of his ponderous brand, Hobbie Noble, attacked by superior numbers, was made prisoner and executed.

With this weapon, and by means of his own strength and address, the Laird's Jock maintained the reputation of the best swordsman on the Border side, and defeated or slew many who ventured to dispute with him the formidable title.

But years pass on with the strong and the brave as with the feeble and the timid. In process of time, the Laird's Jock grew incapable of wielding his weapons, and finally of all active exertion even of the most ordinary kind. The disabled champion became at length totally bed-ridden, and entirely dependent for his comfort on the pious duties of an only daughter, his perpetual attendant and companion.

Besides this dutiful child, the Laird's Jock had an only son, upon whom devolved the perilous task of leading the clan to battle, and maintaining the warlike renown of his native country, which was now disputed by the English upon many occasions. The young Armstrong was active, brave, and strong, and brought home from dangerous adventures many tokens of decided success. Still the ancient chief conceived, as it would seem, that his son was scarce yet entitled by age and experience to be entrusted with the two-handed sword, by the use of which he had himself been so dreadfully distinguished.

At length, an English champion, one of the name of Foster (if I rightly recollect), had the audacity to send a challenge to the best swordsman in Liddesdale; and young Armstrong, burning for chivalrous distinction, accepted the challenge.

The heart of the disabled old man swelled with joy when he heard that the challenge was passed and accepted, and the meeting fixed at a neutral spot, used as the place of rencontre upon such occasions, and which he himself had distinguished by numerous victories. He exulted so much in the conquest which he anticipated, that, to nerve his son to still bolder exertions, he conferred upon him, as champion of his clan and province, the celebrated weapon which he had hitherto retained in his own custody.

This was not all. When the day of combat arrived, the Laird's Jock, in spite of his daughter's affectionate remonstrances, determined, though he had not left his bed for two years, to be a personal witness of the duel. His will was still a law to his people, who bore him on their shoulders, wrapped in plaids and blankets, to the spot where the combat was to take place, and seated him on a fragment of rock, which is still called the Laird's Jock's stone. There he remained with eyes fixed on the lists or barrier, within which the champions were about to meet. His daughter, having done all she could for his accommodation, stood motionless beside him, divided between anxiety for his health, and for the event of the combat to her beloved brother. Ere yet the fight began, the old men gazed on their chief, now seen for the first time after several years, and sadly compared his altered features and wasted frame, with the paragon of strength and manly beauty which they once remembered. The young men gazed on his large form and powerful make, as upon some antediluvian giant who had survived the destruction of the Flood.

But the sound of the trumpets on both sides recalled the attention of every one to the lists, surrounded as they were by numbers of both nations eager to witness the event of the day. The combatants met. It is needless to describe the struggle : the Scottish champion fell. Foster, placing his foot on his antagonist, seized on the redoubted sword, so precious in the eyes of its aged owner, and brandished it over his head as a trophy of his conquest. The English shouted in triumph. But the despairing cry of the aged champion, who saw his country dishonoured, and his sword, long the terror of their race, in possession of an Englishman, was heard high above the acclamations of victory. He seemed, for an instant, animated by all his wonted power ; for he started from the rock on which he sat, and while the garments with which he had been invested fell from his wasted frame, and showed the ruins of his strength, he tossed his arms wildly to heaven, and uttered a cry of indignation, horror, and despair, which, tradition says, was heard to a preternatural distance, and resembled the cry of a dying lion more than a human sound.

His friends received him in their arms as he sank utterly exhausted by the effort, and bore him back to his castle in mute sorrow ; while his daughter at once wept for her brother, and endeavoured to mitigate and soothe the despair of her father. But this was impossible ; the old man's only tie to life was rent rudely asunder, and his heart had broken with it. The death of his son had no part in his sorrow. If he thought of him at all, it was as the degenerate boy, through whom the honour of his country and clan had been lost; and he died in the course of three days, never even mentioning his name, but pouring out unintermitted lamentations for the loss of his sword.

I conceive, that the instant when the disabled chief was roused into a last exertion by the agony of the moment is favourable to the object of a painter. He might obtain the full advantage of contrasting the form of the rugged old man, in the extremity of furious despair, with the softness and beauty of the female form. The fatal field might be thrown into perspective, so as to give full effect to these two principal figures, and with the single explanation that the piece represented a soldier beholding his son slain, and the honour of his country lost, the picture would be sufficiently intelligible at the first glance. If it was thought necessary to show more clearly the nature of the conflict, it might be indicated by the pennon of Saint George being displayed at one end of the lists, and that of Saint Andrew at the other.

I remain, Sir,

Your obedient servant,

THE AUTHOR OF WAVERLEY.

Printed by BALLANTYNE, HANSON & CO.
Edinburgh & London